Very Valentine

Very Valentine

Adriana Trigiani

W F HOWES LTD

This large print edition published in 2009 by
W F Howes Ltd
Unit 4, Rearsby Business Park, Gaddesby Lane,
Rearsby, Leicester LE7 4YH

1 3 5 7 9 10 8 6 4 2

First published in the United Kingdom in 2009
by Simon & Schuster

A CIP catalogue record for this book is available
from the British Library

ISBN 978 1 40744 159 7

Typeset by Palimpsest Book Production Limited,
Grangemouth, Stirlingshire
Printed and bound in Great Britain
by MPG Books Ltd, Bodmin, Cornwall

FSC
Mixed Sources
Product group from well-managed
forests and other controlled sources
Cert no. SGS-COC-2953
www.fsc.org
© 1996 Forest Stewardship Council

In memory of my grandfather,
Carlo Bonicelli,
a shoemaker

CONTENTS

CHAPTER 1 LEONARD'S OF GREAT
             NECK   1
CHAPTER 2 166 PERRY STREET   37
CHAPTER 3 GREENWICH VILLAGE   62
CHAPTER 4 GRAMERCY PARK   100
CHAPTER 5 FOREST HILLS   144
CHAPTER 6 THE CARLYLE HOTEL   184
CHAPTER 7 SOHO   214
CHAPTER 8 MOTT STREET   253
CHAPTER 9 THE HUDSON RIVER   283
CHAPTER 10 AREZZO   320
CHAPTER 11 LAGO ARGENTO   346
CHAPTER 12 THE ISLE OF CAPRI   373
CHAPTER 13 DA COSTANZO   401
CHAPTER 14 58TH AND FIFTH   455

ACKNOWLEDGMENTS   501

CHAPTER 1

LEONARD'S OF GREAT NECK

I'm not the pretty sister.

I'm not the smart sister either. I am the funny one. I've been called that for so long, for so many years, in fact, that all of my life I thought it was one word: *Funnyone*.

If I had to die, and believe me, I don't want to, but if I had to choose a location, I'd want to die right here in the ladies' lounge at Leonard's of Great Neck. It's the mirrors. I look slimsational, even in 3-D. I'm no scientist, but there's something about the slant of the full-length glass, the shimmer of the blue marble counters, and the golden light of the pavé chandeliers that creates an optical illusion, turning my reflection into a long, lean, pale pink swizzle stick.

This is my eighth reception (third as an attendant) at Leonard's La Dolce Vita, the formal name for our family's favorite Long Island wedding factory. Everyone I know has been married here, or, at least everyone I'm related to.

My sisters and I made our debut as flower girls in 1984 for our cousin Mary Theresa, who had more attendants on the dais than guests at the tables. Our cousin's wedding might have been a sacred exchange of vows between a man and a woman, but it was also a *show*, with costumes, choreography, and special lighting, making the bride the star and the groom the grip.

Mary T. considers herself Italian-American royalty, so she had the Knights of Columbus form a crossing guard for our entrance into the Starlight Venetian Room.

The knights were regal in their tuxedos, red sashes, black capes, and tricornered hats with the marabou plumes. I took my place behind the other girls in the procession as the band played 'Nobody Does It Better,' but I turned around to run away as the knights held up their swords to form a canopy. Aunt Feen grabbed me and gave me a shove. I closed my eyes, gripped my bouquet, and bolted under the blades like I was running for sane.

Despite my fear of sharp and clanging objects, I fell in love with Leonard's that day. It was my first Italian formal. I couldn't wait to grow up and emulate my mother and her friends who drank Harvey Wallbangers in cut-crystal tumblers while wearing silver sequins from head to toe. When I was nine years old, I thought Leonard's had class. Never mind that from the passing lane on Northern Boulevard it looks like a white stucco casino on the French Riviera by way of Long Island. For me, Leonard's was a House of Enchantments.

2

The La Dolce Vita experience begins when you pull up to the entrance. The wide circular driveway is a dead ringer for Jane Austen's Pemberley and also resembles the valet stand at Neiman Marcus, outside the Short Hills mall. This is the thing about Leonard's: everywhere you look, it reminds you of elegant places you have already been. The two-story picture windows are reminiscent of the Metropolitan Opera House, while the tiered fountain is strictly Trevi. You almost believe you're in the heart of Rome until you realize the cascading water is actually drowning out the traffic on I-495.

The landscaping is a marvel of botanical grooming, with boxwood sheared into long rect-angles, low borders of yew, privet hedges in cropped ovals, and bayberry sculpted into twirly ice-cream-cone shapes. The manicured shrubs are set in beds of shiny river stones, an appropriate pre-motif to the ice sculptures that tower over the raw bar inside.

The exterior lights suggest the strip in Las Vegas, but it's far more tasteful here, as the bulbs are recessed, giving the place a low, twinkling glow. Topiaries shaped like crescent moons flank the entrance doors. Beneath them, low meatball bushes serve as a base for the birds-of-paradise, which pop out of the shrubs like cocktail umbrellas.

The band plays 'Burning Down the House' as I take a moment to catch my breath in the ladies' lounge. I'm alone for the first time on my sister Jaclyn's wedding day and I like it. It's been a long one. I'm holding the tension of the entire family

3

in the vertebrae of my neck. When I marry, I will elope to city hall because my bones can't take the pressure of another Roncalli wedding extravaganza. I'd miss the beer-battered shrimp and the pâté rillettes, but I'd survive. The months of planning this wedding nearly gave me an ulcer, and the actual execution bestowed on my right eye a pulsating tic that could only be soothed by holding a frozen teething ring I bogarted from cousin Kitty Calzetti's baby after the Nuptial Mass. Despite the agita, it's a wonderful day, because I'm happy for my baby sister, who I remember holding, like a Capodimonte rose, on the day she was born.

I hold my martini-shaped evening bag covered in sequins (the wedding-party gift from the bride) up to the mirror and say, 'I'd like to thank Kleinfeld of Brooklyn, who knocked off Vera Wang to strapless perfection. And I'd like to thank Spanx, the girdle genius, who turned my pear shape into a surfboard.' I move closer to the mirror and check my teeth. It ain't an Italian wedding without clams casino dusted in parsley flakes, and you know where those end up.

My professional makeup job provided (at half price) by the bride's best friend's sister-in-law, Nancy DeNoia, is really holding up. She did my face at around eight o'clock this morning, and it's now supper time but I still look fresh. 'It's the powder. *Banane* by LeClerc,' my older sister, Tess, said. And she knows: she was matte through two childbirths. We have the pictures to prove it.

4

This morning, my sisters, our mother, and I sat on folding chairs in front of Mom's Golden Age of Hollywood mirror in the bedroom of their Tudor in Forest Hills, pretty (almost) maids all in a row.

'Look at us,' my mother said, lifting her face out of her neck, like a turtle. 'We look like sisters.'

'We *are* sisters,' I reminded her as I looked at my actual sisters in the glass. My mother looked hurt. '. . . and you . . . you're our teen mother.'

'Let's not go *that* far.' My sixty-one-year-old mother, named Michelina after her father, Michael (everyone calls my mom 'Mike'), with her heart-shaped face, wide-set brown eyes, and full lips glazed the color of a terra-cotta pot looked smugly into the mirror. My mother is the only woman I know who arrives fully made up for the makeup artist.

The Roncalli sisters, minus our eldest sibling and only brother, Alfred (aka the Pill), and Dad (called Dutch), are an open-all-night, girls-only club. We are best friends who share everything, with two exceptions: we never discuss our sex lives or bank accounts. We are bound together by tradition, secrets, and our mother's flat iron.

The bond was secured when we were small. Mom created 'Just Us Girls' field trips; she'd schlep us to a Nettie Rosenstein retrospective at FIT, or to our first Broadway show, *'night, Mother*. As Mom hustled us out of the theater, she said, 'Who knew she'd kill herself at the end?' concerned that she'd scarred us for life. We saw

5

the world through Mom's elegant opera glasses. Every year, the week before Christmas, she took us to the Palm Court at the Plaza Hotel for holiday tea. After we filled up on fluffy scones smothered in clotted cream and raspberry jam, we'd take our picture, in matching outfits, including Mom's, of course, under the portrait of Eloise.

When Rosalie Signorelli Ciardullo started selling mineral powder makeup out of her trunk, guess who Mom volunteered as traveling models? Tess (dry), me (oily), and Jaclyn (sensitive). Mom modeled for the thirty to thirty-nine age group, never mind that she was fifty-three years old at the time.

'All great artistes begin with a blank canvas,' Nancy DeNoia announced as she applied pancake makeup the color of Cheerios to my forehead. I almost said, 'Anyone who uses the word "artiste" probably isn't one,' but why argue with the woman who has the power to turn you into Cher on the reunion tour via the tools in her hand?

I kept quiet as she patted the sponge on my cheeks. 'We're losing the schnoz . . . ,' Nancy said, exhaling her spearmint breath as she applied small, deliberate strokes to the bridge of my nose. It felt exactly like the firm pressure applied on an ice bag by Sister Mary Joseph of the MASH unit at Holy Agony when I was hit by a line-drive baseball in seventh-grade gym. For the record, Sister Mary J. said she never saw so much blood come out of one person's head in her life, and she would know, as she had a hitch as a nurse in Vietnam.

Nancy DeAnnoying, like an architect, stood back and surveyed my face. 'The nose is gone. Now I can salvage.'

I closed my eyes and pretended to meditate so Nancy might take the hint and stop the play-by-play of my crap features. She picked up a small brush, dipped it in ice water, and swirled it around on an inky chestnut brown square. I felt my eyebrows tingle as she painted on tiny hairs. I grew up on Madonna, and when she plucked, I plucked. Now I'm paying for it.

My face felt cold and painterly until Nancy dipped a Kabuki brush into the powder and buffed my skin in small circles, like the wax-finish feature at Andretti's car wash. When she was done, I resembled a newborn puppy, all big, wet eyes and no nose.

In the ladies' lounge, I'm taking one of many lipstick time-outs because I actually *eat* at weddings. After weeks of dieting to fit into my dress, I figure I deserve a round of pink ladies, all the passed hors d'oeuvres I can throw back, and enough cannolis to leave a dark crater on the lazy Susan in the center of the Venetian table. I'm not worried. I'll work all this food off dancing to the long-play version of the *Electric Slide*. I fish the tube of lipstick out of my purse. There is nothing worse than bare lips with a suction-cup tattoo of plum pencil around the rim. I fill in between the lines where the color has faded.

My sisters and I have played a game since childhood; when we weren't dressing up as brides, we

7

played Planning Our Funerals. It's not that my parents are morbid, or that anything particularly horrible happened to us, it's that we're Italian, and therefore, tit for tat, it's the law of the Roncalli universe: for every happy thing, there has to be a sad thing. Weddings are for young people and funerals are the weddings of old people. Both, I have learned, take long-term planning.

There are two unbreakable rules in our family. One is to attend all funerals of any known persons with whom we have ever come in contact. This mandate includes people we are related to (blood relatives, family by marriage, and cousins of family by marriage) but also extends beyond close friends to encompass teachers, hairdressers, and doctors. Any professional person who has rendered an opinion or given a diagnosis of a personal nature makes the cut. There is a special category for those who deliver, including 'Uncle Larry,' our UPS man who went quickly on a Saturday morning in 1983. Mom pulled us out of school the following Monday to drive us to his funeral in Manhasset. 'Respect,' she said to us at the time, but we knew the real reason. She just likes to get dressed up.

The second rule of the Roncalli family is to attend all weddings and dance with anyone that asks you, including icky cousin Paulie who was kicked out of Arthur Murray for groping the instructor (the case was settled out of court).

There's a third rule: Never acknowledge Mom's

1966 nose job. Never mind that her remodeled nose is a dead ringer for Annette Funicello's, while we, her biological children, have the profiles of Marty Feldman. 'No one will ever guess . . . unless you tell them,' my mother warned us. 'And if anyone asks, you simply say that your father's nasal gene was dominant.'

'There you are!' My mother bursts into the lounge like a frapped tangerine, all chiffon and feathers, as though someone stuffed her ensemble into the blender and hit Crush. 'Aren't these mirrors amazing?' Mom turns away from the mirror and then looks over her shoulder to check the back of her dress. Satisfied, she says, 'I'm a sylph. Don't let anybody tell you otherwise, Jenny Craig works. How's your table?'

'The worst.'

'Oh, come on. You're at the Friends' table. You're supposed to' – and I hate when she does this, but she does it anyway, makes two fists and egg-beats them – 'liven things up.'

'Mom, please.'

'That toxic attitude is holding you back. It's spilling out of you like offshore oil.' My mother looks at me as she applies her lipstick without looking in the mirror. She snaps the silver cylinder shut. 'You should have brought a date if you didn't want every couple we know offering up their single sons to you like meatball skewers.'

'The Delboccios want to set me up with Frank.' I lean against the wall and cross my arms because

God knows I can't actually sit down in this dress. The Spanx would crush my spleen.

'Fabulous news! See, it was kismet to seat you at the Friends' table.'

'Ma, Frank is gay.'

'Oh, you girls. You use that gay card every chance you get. So what if the man's forty-three and never married and takes his mother's entire mah-jongg club to the islands every spring? That doesn't automatically mean he's gay. Maybe he's just a straight man who happens to smell good, knows how to dress, and talks to old people like they matter. Do me a favor. Date Frank. Go dancing! Go to museums! Restaurants! You'll be dressed up and out on the town and having fun with a good-looking fella who knows how to treat a woman! *Party hearty* – now that's the true meaning of the word *gay*.'

Mom looks at me, and whatever expression she sees on my face melts her heart, and it has since I can remember. She's on my side and I am always aware of that. 'You have so much to offer, Valentine. I don't want you to lose out. You're a winner! You're funny!' My mother gives me a big hug. 'Now, let me look at you.' Mom puts her hands on my face. 'You're a total original. Your big, beautiful brown eyes are set just far enough apart. Your lips, thank God, take after my side of the family. The Roncalli lips are so thin they need Velcro to chew. And your nose, despite what Nancy said today—'

'Ma, I'm okay.'

'She was rude. But I bit my tongue because there

are two people you should never argue with: makeup artists and plumbers. Either can ruin you. And your nose is perfect. You've got a sleek bridge, which is lovely in profile, and it's straight, whereas mine had a bump.'

I'm stunned that my mother refers to The Operation. 'It did?' I've never even seen her old nose. There's only one photo of Mom's face with the old nose in existence, but it's a group shot of her high school French Club and her head is so small, it's hard to see.

'Oh yes, there was a hideous bump. But you know, I looked at that bump for exactly what it was. A glitch I could fix. There are things in this life that you can fix. So fix them, then move on.'

'Are you saying I need a nose job?'

'I wouldn't touch it. Plus, a tall person can carry a nose. So be grateful that you got all the tall in the family.'

'Thanks, Ma.' In the general population, five foot eight is hardly tall, but in my family, I'm a giant redwood.

Mom opens up her sequined martini purse and takes out an atomizer of Dolce & Gabbana red cap and sprays it on the back of her neck. 'Want some?' she offers.

'Nah. I think I'll go with my natural musk at the Friends' table.'

Mom raises her arm high and spritzes above her hair, a croissant-shaped upsweep dotted with coral sequins, which, depending upon your latitude and longitude under the dance floor lights, could blind you for life.

When I was little I'd watch her transform in front of the mirror before a night out with Dad. Efficient and organized, she stood at her makeup table and surveyed her tools. She'd snap open compacts, unscrew the tops off tubes, and shake vials. Then she would think as she twisted the eyeliner pencil in the sharpener. Eventually, a waxy chocolate brown *S* would fall into the waste-basket. She'd take the pencil and smudge it under her eye in preparation for the broad strokes. She would select a brush and dip it into a palette of powder, and then, as if she were Michelangelo painting the eyelash of a saint on the ceiling of the Sistine Chapel, she'd make tiny brushstrokes on her brow bone.

'Is something wrong, Valentine?'

'No. I just love you. That's all.'

'I can't wait—,' my mother begins, then stops to think. 'You know what, if you're my only child who remains single until old age, I will stand proudly with you all the days of your life. *If* that's what you want.'

This might be what I like most about her. Mom believes being single is an infirmity, the equivalent of missing a hand, but she never makes me feel I have to agree with her. 'Mom, I'm happy.'

'You could be happier.'

'I guess that's true.'

'Aha!' She points her finger at me. 'You can

12

reinvent your life on your own terms. You don't have to live with my mother and make shoes.'

'I love my job and I love where I live.'

'I'll never understand it. All I ever wanted to do was move away. And I never wanted to be a shoemaker.'

Mom and I walk arm in arm back into the reception, looking like two asteroids, one pink, the other bright orange, skimming through this Tiepolo-blue sky. Then I realize that's not why the guests are watching us. It must look like I'm holding my mother up – therefore she's either had too much to drink or, God forbid, she's old enough to need assistance. I can practically hear the gears in my mother's brain spin as this real-ization dawns on her, too. Mom lets go of my arm with a flourish, and does a full 360-degree pirouette in the center of the empty dance floor. I bow from the waist as though we planned the move. Mom gives me a youthful wave as she sashays over to the Parents' table, leaving me to return to the tyranny of the Friends.

My sister's brand-new mother-in-law, Mrs McAdoo, wears a fussy corsage of purple roses, which hangs off her lilac crepe dress like a ruby red tire. Mrs McAdoo's pale skin blends into her hair, cut to her chin in a simple bob. My mother would never allow a strand of white hair on her head. The only gray you will ever find in direct proximity to my mother's person is the terrazzo floor in the foyer of our family home.

'Matrons belong in prisons! Besides, I don't believe in going gray,' my mother would say. 'It's an advertisement for death. Go gray and you might as well say' – as she beckons off in the distance – 'come and get me, Grim Reaper!' No, Mom is rich sable brown, now and forever (or for however long L'Oréal makes it).

I look around the room, 312 guests strong. Last night they were a bunch of Post-its on a board in my mom's kitchen, and today, they're at the table they have earned in our version of Italian-American hierarchy. First tier: Parents, Close Friends, Professionals, Coworkers, Cousins, Kiddies. Second tier: In-laws. And third: the Island (relatives we aren't speaking to because something bad went down, never mind that we don't remember what); Rude (late responders); and Dementia (don't ask).

I must look lonely on the dance floor. Why didn't I bring a date? Gabriel offered, but I didn't want him to feel obligated to flap to the chicken dance with cousin Violet Ruggiero in this heat. How can it be that out of all the people in this room, I remain the only single person under forty? Sensing the inert shame, my brother, Alfred, takes my hand as the music starts. It's a little weird to waltz with your only brother, with whom you share a strained relationship, to 'Can You Feel the Love Tonight,' but I make the best of it. He is, after all, a dance partner, even if he is a blood relative. We take what we can get. 'Thanks, Alfred.'

'I'm dancing with all of my sisters,' he says, as if he's ticking off a to-do list for the mechanic at Midas mufflers.

We sway for a few moments. I have a hard time making conversation with my brother. 'You know why God invented brothers in Italian families?'

He takes the bait. 'Why?'

'Because He knew that the single sisters needed someone to dance with at weddings.'

'You'd better come up with a better joke for your toast.'

He's right, and I'm not happy about it. My brother is thirty-nine years old, but I don't see a middle-aged father of two, I only see the persnickety boy who made straight A's and had no friends in school. The only time his cranky mood would lift was when the cleaning lady came on Thursdays and he'd help her scrub the tile. This was when Alfred was the happiest – when he had a brush in his hand and ammonia in a bucket.

Alfred still has the same cowlick on the crown of his head and the same serious countenance of his youth. He also has Mom's old nose and the thin upper lip of Dad's side of the family. He doesn't trust anyone, including family, and he can talk for hours about the evils of the Media and the Government. Alfred is at the ready with a doomsday report any day of the week. He's the first to call when a house is burning live on New York 1 and the first to send mass e-mails when the bedbug infestation on the East Coast is announced.

15

He's also an expert on all diseases that run in families of Mediterranean descent (autoimmune disorders are his specialty). We spent last Christmas dinner listening to his tutorial on prediabetes, which really made the baba au rhums go down smoothly.

'How's Gram doing?' he asks.

I look over at our grandmother, my mother's mother, Teodora Angelini, who got stuck at the Dementia table so she might sit with her cousins and her last living sister, my great-aunt Feen. While Gram's peers are hunched over their plates, sorting through the walnuts on top of the salad, she sits upright, with military posture. My grandmother is the lone red rose in a garden of gray bramble.

With her bright red lipstick, two-piece red linen summer suit, coiffed white hair, and large octagon-framed glasses in jet black tortoise, she looks like a gracious Upper East Side lady who has never worked a day in her life. The truth is, the only thing she has in common with those society matrons is her tailored suit. Gram is a working woman who owns her own business. We've made custom wedding shoes in Greenwich Village since 1903. 'Gram is doing great,' I tell him.

'She can hardly walk,' Alfred says.

'She needs knee replacements,' I tell him.

'She needs more than that.'

'Alfred. Except for her knees, she's in excellent shape.'

'Everything is always rosy with you,' Alfred sighs.

'You're in denial. Gram is almost eighty years old and she's slowing down.'

'That's ridiculous. I live with her. She runs rings around me.'

'That wouldn't be hard.'

And there it is. The Jab. I don't want to fight at my sister's wedding, so I let go of him, but he goes on.

'Gram won't be around forever. She should retire and enjoy the kids. There's a nice assisted-living place out by us.'

'She loves the city. She'd die in the suburbs.'

'I'm the only person in this family who can face the truth. She needs to retire. I'm willing to buy her a condo.'

'Aren't you generous.'

'I'm not thinking about myself.'

'Then it would be the first time, Alfred.'

The law of the sibling jungle springs into effect. Alfred's tone, the look on my face, and the fact that we've stopped dancing sends a silent alert out to my sisters. Tess, sensing a fight, has come to the edge of the dance floor and locks eyes with me. She shoots me the *Need me?* look.

'Thanks for the dance.' I turn my back on Alfred to make my way to the Friends' table, which is now empty because everyone over the age of sixty stampedes the dance floor for an up-tempo version of 'After the Lovin'.'

I squeeze past Mom and Dad in the stampede. 'It's our song!' Mom chirps as she holds Dad's hand high in the air, like a May Day ribbon. They pull each other close as Mom plants her cheek on Dad's. They look like Siamese twins joined at the blush line. Engelbert Humperdinck used to be my mother's favorite singer, until Andrea Bocelli provided the first emotional catharsis of her life. She listens to Bocelli in the car, drives around Queens, and weeps. Through her tears, she says, 'I don't need therapy because Andrea taps my grief.'

I sit down at the empty Friends' table, pick up my fork, and stab my salad. I've lost my appetite. I put the fork down and survey the crowded dance floor, which, when I squint, looks like a pointillist painting of sequins, jet beads, and Swarovski crystals on a canvas of lamé.

'What did Alfred say to you?' Tess says, sliping into the chair next to me. Tess, my older sister by a year and a half, is a busty brunette with no hips. The bridesmaid gown gives her the shape of a champagne glass. Despite her bombshell physique, she is the brainiest of the three sisters, perhaps because Alfred used her as his flash-card moderator from the time she was four years old. Tess has Mom's heart-shaped face, and the second best nose in the family. Her wavy black hair matches eyelashes so thick she never has to wear mascara.

'He implied I'm a loser.' I yank up the front of my dress like I'm pulling a full Hefty bag out of a trash can.

'He told me that I'm a bad mother. He thinks I let Charisma and Chiara run wild.'

I look over at the Venetian table, where seven-year-old Charisma pokes a hole in a cannoli and hands it to five-year-old Chiara, who blows out the filling. Tess rolls her eyes. 'It's a party. Let them have some fun.'

'Alfred wants Gram to retire.'

'He's on a campaign.' Tess checks her lipstick in the butter knife. 'You know, those assisted-living places can be really nice.'

'Don't tell me you agree with him!'

'Hey, I'm on your side,' Tess says gently.

'Every time Alfred brings it up, it's like he stabs me.'

'That's because you care about Gram.' Tess dips the knife in a butter rosette, then spreads it on what remains of Bob Silverstein's dinner roll. 'And the shoe company is your livelihood.' My sister looks weary, which tells me she had the same discussion with Alfred and got nowhere.

I don't want to ruin the reception, so I change the subject. 'How's your table?'

'Why did Ma spread us out like UN peace-keepers? Doesn't she get that we actually *like* each other and want to sit together? Okay, maybe put Alfred and Clickety Click at the Stuck-up table—'

'Call her Pamela. You want an in-law war?' I look around to make certain there aren't any in the area. Alfred has been married to Pamela for thirteen years. She's four feet eleven and wears five-inch stilettos, even at the beach and, rumor had it, during labor. We named her Clickety Click because that's the sound her heels make when she walks in rapid little steps. 'The petite inherit the earth. Nothing is more alluring to a man than a woman who can fit in his wallet.'

'I'd love to be tall like you,' Tess says supportively. 'At least you have gusto. Pam has no gusto. Anyhow, they're completely suited for each other. Alfred is shut down and Clickety is positively bloodless. This spoon' – Tess holds it up – 'has more personality.'

Tess looks over at Charisma and Chiara, who have taken black olives out of the crudité dishes and placed them over their eyes. The girls laugh as the olives roll off their faces and onto the floor. Tess motions for them to stop. The girls scamper off. Tess waves to her husband, Charlie, to watch the girls. He's stuck at the Rude table listening to the guests gripe about their lousy seats near the kitchen.

'Look at Alfred's boys,' I tell Tess.

Our nephews, Alfred Junior and Rocco, look like miniature bankers with their bow ties and the crisp napkins on their laps.

'I heard Pamela sent them to the Good Manners and Me class at Our Lady of Mercy. So well behaved.' Tess sighs.

'Do they have a choice?' I yank up the front of my gown again. I check my watch. It feels like it's been fifteen years between the soup and the salad. 'Mr Delboccio put his hand on my ass.'

'Disgusting,' says Tess.

'To tell you the truth, with the Spanx on, I couldn't even feel it. I could sit on a hot griddle and I wouldn't know it.'

'So how do you know he took a feel?'

'The look on Mrs Delboccio's face. I thought she was going to pick up the candelabra and beat him.'

'He probably had too much to drink. And it's so hot out. The liquor just goes right to the brain and pickles it. Promise me you'll get married in a blizzard.'

'I promise. I also promise to get married at city hall on a Tuesday.'

'C'mon, you'd miss out on all of this.' Tess turns in her chair and looks out at the sea of our relatives. She turns back around. 'Okay, city hall is fine. We'll wear suits. Day suits and wrist corsages.'

The tuxedoed waitstaff pours out of the kitchen and through the galley doors like chocolate chips into cake batter. With one hand, they carry enormous silver trays loaded with plates covered in metal hats. With their other hand, they snap open metal racks and place the trays on top of them. In quick succession, dinner plates filled with succulent beef tenderloin, a delicate purse of whipped potatoes, and spears of fresh asparagus are placed on the table. At the sight of the food delivery, the dance floor empties instantly. The guests return to their tables like a football team heading for the locker room at halftime. Tess gets up. 'Gotta go. It's the entrée.'

The Friends take their seats and nod approvingly at the plates. The tenderloin is pricey, thus demonstrating a level of opulence, which Italian Americans appreciate more than the dissolution of the cold war and tubes of anchovy paste on demand.

'So, how's it going at the shoe shop?' Ed Delboccio asks. His bald head looks like the sterling-silver platter hats the waiters have stacked in the corner. 'Tell me this. Does anybody even want handmade shoes anymore?'

'Absolutely.' I try not to snap, but I must have since everyone at the table looks up at me.

'Don't take offense,' Mr Delboccio says and smiles. 'It's just a query for discussion's sake. Why would anybody order custommade shoes when you can buy them cheap at those outlet malls? Shirley here is a regular at those warehouse sales. KGB—'

'DSW,' his wife corrects him.

'Whatever. The point is, I've saved a lot of wampum at those discount joints, believe me.'

Mrs Delboccio nudges him. 'For God's sake, Ed, it's a different thing altogether. You don't buy shoes from Valentine like you buy them from Payless. They're deluxe. And Valentine works with Teodora, she's . . .' She waves her fork at me, searching for a word.

'She's a master and I'm her apprentice.'

'You take care of your grandmother, too, don't you?' Mrs Mrs Delboccio says.

'She takes care of herself.'

'But you live with her, which is so nice. You're giving up your freedom to take care of Teodora. That's very generous.' Mrs Delboccio smiles, her lips pulled tight, like the zipper on a change purse. Her magenta hair is piled high on her head and sprayed to a shiny finish. She adjusts her bold *stampato* gold necklace. Her purple nails match her gown, which matches her shoes.

'In this day and age, it's rare to find a kid who will take care of an old person,' Mr Delboccio says, leaning toward me and breathing. His breath is a mix of cinnamon and headcheese. Not awful, just refrigerated. 'That's why I'm saving up. I'm going for one of those assisted-living condos. I'm gonna have to pay for what my parents and Shirl's here got for free. When the time comes, God forbid, I don't think our kids will take us in.'

Mrs Delboccio shoots him a look.

'Well, they wouldn't, Shirl. Face it.' Mr Delboccio takes his knife and pushes some potato onto the meat already on his fork and pops it into his mouth. 'They've got their own lives. It's not like our generation. We took in all family members, regardless of their mental status. I can't see our kids doing the same.'

'Why did you become a shoemaker?' Mrs La Vaglio asks. She's a tiny blonde with the Linda Evans haircut from *Dynasty*. Still. The La Vaglios live in Ohio, so I guess my story didn't spread to the Midwest.

23

'I was teaching high school English in Queens—,' I begin.

'And then you had that bad breakup with your boyfriend. How many years did you go with him?' she interrupts. I guess my story seeped into Ohio after all.

'College and then some.' I'm not going to give these people a timeline. They'd brand an *L* for Loser on my forehead with the olive paste.

'Your first love,' Mrs Delboccio says and looks at her husband. 'Ed and I have the same story, except we have a different ending. I met him when I was eighteen. We were married at twenty-four. And here we are.'

'You're an inspiration to all of us,' I say, over-salting my salad.

'Thank you,' Shirley says smugly.

'At the time, your mother was so worried about you.' Sue Silverstein reaches over and pats my hand.

'There's nothing to worry about. I love the twists and turns my life has taken.' This is lovely. When my parents' friends have too much to drink, they tell me things my mother won't.

'A positive attitude is everything,' Max Silverstein says, shaking his fork at me.

'You know, our son Frank is totally available.' Mrs Delboccio sips her wine. 'He's not gay,' she says quickly. 'He's just picky.'

'Well, I'm looking for picky.' I force a smile.

Mrs Delboccio squeezes her husband's thigh

24

under the table so he'll remember that I said some-thing positive about Frank.

'How long ago were you dumped?' Mr Delboccio asks.

'Ed!' his wife shrieks.

'Three years,' I mumble.

Mr Delboccio whistles low. 'Three years of your prime time.'

'Are you seeing anyone now?' Mrs La Vaglio asks.

'If she was, she'd have brought him to the wedding.' Mrs Delboccio talks about me as if the wine I'm guzzling is a magic potion that has made me invisible.

'She could get a date. Look at her.' Mr Delboccio looks at my breasts as though they are two exotic fish swimming in opposite directions in a tank. 'She must want to fly solo.'

'Let's not worry about me,' I say, gritting my teeth. 'I'm fine.'

'Nobody said you weren't.' Mr Delboccio finishes his bourbon and iced tea and clonks the glass down on the table like an ax. I look around to the waitstaff. Somebody cut this guy off, will you? The waiter interprets my signal and brings a gravy boat of *jus* instead. Mr Delboccio takes it and douses what's left of his meat. 'Valentine, here's the thing. As a woman, you got a window. A window of opportunity where you got the face and the figure and the pep to attract a man. Ergo, you got to grab a guy while the window is open, because once it closes, bam, you've lost your

25

chance, and you're in an airless closet. Alone. Okay? Oxygen is cut off. No man can survive in there. Got it? Tick. Tock. A man can always find a woman, but a woman can't always find a man.'

'Ed, no more bourbon for you.' Mrs Delboccio moves his glass. She looks at me apologetically. 'Valentine has a lot of life in front of her.'

'I never said that she didn't. But you remember my sister Madeline, who moved in with Ma when Ma got the brain tumor? My poor mother afflicted with a tension headache that turned into a cancerous mass overnight. Anyhow, how old was Mad back then? Thirty at the most. She moved in, took care of Ma until she died, may she rest in peace, and then Madeline stayed, where was she gonna go? She was the spinster aunt.' Ed looks for his roll to butter. He's already eaten it so he reaches over and takes his wife's. 'Every Italian family has one of you.'

I open my mouth to disagree, but no words come out. Maybe he's right. I imagine my future in an old-folks' home for single women. The TV room in the Roncalli Home for Singles would have the heads of Phyllis Diller, Joan Rivers, and Susie Essman mounted over the fireplace. Big-game catches for girls who deliver big laughs. The way this evening is going, I may have to reserve my room sooner than I thought.

'Madeline was a saint. She took the burden off the rest of us. Of course, we were raising children and had our own lives,' Mrs Delboccio says, smoothing the napkin in her lap.

'Being single *is* a life,' Mrs La Vaglio pipes up.

The table falls to dead silence as the Friends saw their meat. I look down at my watch. Anyone who believes time flies should come and sit at the Friends' table where the main course has lasted longer than the Peloponnesian War. I'd do just about anything to be stuck at the Rude table right now.

Mr Delboccio leans over, practically peering down my gown. 'God meant for man and woman to pair off.' I lean back and pull my dinner napkin up over my bodice and around my neck like a dickey.

'How many shoes do you make a year?' Mr Silverstein wants to know, God bless him.

'Last year we made close to three thousand pairs.'

'How big is the staff?'

'Three full-time and four part-time.'

'Wow, that's a pretty healthy operation.' Mr Silverstein smiles approvingly.

The band plays the opening riff of 'Good Vibrations'; the Friends drop their knives and forks. 'Hi-yo, it's the Beach Boys medley!' Mr Silverstein announces. They get up; the women adjust the waists, hips, and rears of their dresses, then head to the dance floor with the husbands in tow.

I stretch out at the empty table and put my feet up. Tess slips into the seat next to me as Dad deposits Aunt Feen at the Dementia table. Dad surveys the room and then walks toward us at a clip. He's only five feet six but well proportioned, so he seems taller. He has a thick head of salt-and-pepper hair, the prominent Roncalli nose, and the tense lips of his people.

'Jesus crimancee, I'm broiling.' Dad adjusts his bow tie as though it's a dial on an air conditioner. 'I just took Aunt Feen out for a cigarette and I thought she was gonna have a stroke.' Dad sits down next to Tess. 'You know she still smokes a pack a day? Her lungs must look like a spaghetti strainer. How you girls holding up?'

'Great,' we lie.

'Your mother wants me to sing "Butterfly Kisses" to your sister, but I don't know the song at all.'

'Cut off her liquor. Or else she'll sing "You Gotta Get a Gimmick" from *Gypsy* like she did at your twenty-fifth,' Tess says.

'She had sciatica for months afterward,' my father says and nods, remembering.

'Don't try and sing, Dad. Tell them to play the CD and you can dance with Jaclyn instead,' I suggest.

'That's what I said, but you know your mother, she thinks weddings are an opportunity to hold auditions for *American Idol*. I work for the parks department, not Simon Cowell. Any Roncalli, Angelini, or Coo-cootz off the street is expected to get up there and sing. Any minute my brother's gonna get up and perform the first act of *Man of La Mancha*. Trust me. He's one gin and tonic away from "The Impossible Dream."'

28

Our sister Jaclyn is breathtaking in a simple strapless bridal gown with a fluffy tulle skirt. Her tiny waist twists as she threads through the tables looking like an electric-mixer beater dripping with white frosting.

Mom suggested that Jaclyn's white peau de soie bodice be piped with an iridescent mint-colored ribbon to bring out her green eyes. It was a brilliant move. Gram made Jaclyn a beautiful pair of leather pumps in petal green. I buffed the leather until the green was almost completely rubbed away, leaving only a hint of antiqued patina. From head to toe, my baby sister glitters like a citrine.

Jaclyn plops down in Mrs La Vaglio's chair. She is a true beauty, her delicate features in perfect proportion, framed by her shiny black curls. 'Was your meat tough?'

'No, no, no,' Dad, Tess, and I chime.

'I needed a chainsaw on my filet.' Jaclyn fans herself with the engraved menu card. 'Valentine, you're gonna have to kill with the bridal toast.'

'No pressure here,' Tess says wryly as she surveys the guests.

'Do me a favor. Make sure everybody at Gram's table has their Miracle-Ears turned on.' I feel sweat bead on my forehead.

'Don't let this bother you, but my mother-in-law hates everything.' Jaclyn takes a sip of my ice water, then puts the glass against her cheek. 'Always with the comments. Like the Irish know how to tell a funny toast. Please.'

Tess and I look at each other. The Irish invented the toast, not to mention the well-told story, and they happen to be very good at them.

'Watch yourself, Jac. Mrs McAdoo is family now,' Dad says. 'Be kind. The most important thing in life is getting along with other people. Without other people, you're alone. And when you're alone, you're alone.' My father whisks his index finger on the inside of his shirt collar like he's getting the last bit of face cream out of a jar.

'Everything will work out. It usually does,' says me, the voice of optimism. Meanwhile, I'm biting my lip so hard, it's giving me a headache.

'Valerie! You're on!' The bandleader points to me.

'Valentine!' Tess and Jaclyn shout to correct him.

'Whatever!' He waves the microphone at me like a drumstick.

I look across the dance floor. The best man is by the drum set chugging a fuzzy navel with a group of frat boys.

'Knock 'em dead!' Dad says cheerfully. Jaclyn and Tess give me a thumbs-up with smiles peeled so wide open, they look like they're having their teeth bleached. I look over at Alfred, who is giving a dissertation on gluten allergies to the Cousins' table.

'Good evening, family and friends.' I slip the microphone into its stand and adjust the height. I'm five feet eleven in these three-inch heels. I'm not sure, but I may be taller than the groom. I know for certain I'm taller than anyone at the

Friends' table due to spinal disk collapse and hipbone deterioration, which they discussed freely during the soup course.

The chatter in the room dulls to a few lone voices, then suddenly falls to silence. The only sound I hear is the whistle between Aunt Feen's dentures and her gums as she breathes. 'I'm Valentine Roncalli, a sister of the bride.'

'We know who you are!' Lorraine Pinuccia shouts from the remote Island table, so far away her wave resembles a distress signal.

Tess rises up out of her chair slightly and shoots Pinooch a dirty look. I look over at my mother, who has a smile of support plastered to her face identical to the one she had when I blew my line as the 'Gloria in Excelsis Deo' angel in the kindergarten Christmas pageant in 1980. 'You can't help me now, Ma,' I want to shout to her, but she looks embalmed.

'Well, thank you, Cousin Pinooch. You know we're now the Roncalli-McAdoo family and maybe the McAdoos haven't met us all yet,' I explain. It could be the sweat in my eyes, but I think Boyd McAdoo, the thrice-divorced electrician brother of my new brother-in-law is leering at me, another reason to cut this short. 'God was in his heaven,' I begin, 'and decided that it was time to create a country . . . he wanted to create a great country, with gorgeous vineyards, and lush fields, and glorious sunsets—'

'The first country!' My father bellows as he

31

makes a number one in the air with his pointer finger.

'Dad. Please. You might want to save your upper register for "Butterfly Kisses."' I dive back into the story. 'God knew He wanted to call it Italy.' My dad's brother, the eternally inappropriate Uncle Sal, yanks a rose from the centerpiece at the Parents' table and stands, waving it like a flag. '*Viva Italia sempre!*' he cries.

Mr McAdoo stands and yanks another rose from the centerpiece. 'To the Emerald Isle!' he counters.

'E pluribus pizzazz!' my mother heckles.

'To the world!' I raise my arm high in the air to include all global humanity.

Tess applauds. Alone. 'Anyhow . . . ,' I continue, 'God had to fill Italy with people, and He wondered, "Shall I create woman first? Or shall I create man first?" The debate went on for several months until He decided. "I shall create women first so they can have dinner ready for the men."'

Gram, Tess, Jaclyn, Mom, and Dad wait a beat then look around, and finally, in solidarity, they force their laughs. The remaining guests sit in a blue pool of silence lit by low votive candles, which makes them look like out-of-work circus performers in a Fellini movie.

'All right then.' I regroup. 'Do you know why God created brothers in Italian families? Because he knew their single sisters needed somebody to dance with at weddings.' The self-deprecating humor goes over worse than the pointed joke.

I am dying up here. It's so quiet in this room, I can hear the ice melt in Len Scatizzi's rum and Coke.

Mr Delboccio, the fanny feeler, shouts, 'I asked you to dance, Valentine.'

'She said her feet hurt,' his wife pipes up. 'Of course, why would a shoemaker's feet hurt? Doesn't make sense.'

'Regardless, I'm not gonna force,' Mr Delboccio retorts.

'You should never force,' Mrs Delboccio snipes back.

'Okay, you two. Let me hang up this routine so you can get back out on the floor and show us youngsters how it's done. I believe the Neil Diamond medley is next.' And then I do the very thing I hate, I make two fists and egg-beat them. Just like Mom.

'Youngster? Where? At thirty-three years old, you're no spring chicken,' Aunt Feen shouts from the Dementia table. Then she makes a hissing sound with her upper plate for punctuation. She looks around the room, her eyes rolling around in their sockets like frantic golf balls. And then she bellows, 'Thirty-three! *Madonna!* That's how old Jesus was when he died on the cross.'

'People only lived to be forty back then,' Tess hollers back.

'What the hell does that have to do with anything?' Aunt Feen's thick white eyebrows twist into one lone tube sock across her forehead.

33

'That's even worse. That means at thirty-three she's *really* got one foot in the grave and the other on a rag rug.'

'All right. Stop it. Or we're cutting off your sidecars. Here's the best I got. A couple of weeks ago my dad went to the doctor. He took Mom along to do the talking . . .'

A few giggles rise from the tables.

'. . . and the doctor says, "Dutch, you've got bursitis. Now, I can do one of two things. I can give you a shot of cortisol. But you don't need it. Your body produces it naturally." "It does?" My dad was amazed. The doctor said, "All you have to do is have sex." My father and the doctor look at my mother and she says, "Doc, I'm not the one with bursitis."'

The room bursts into applause. 'Please raise your glasses.' I realize that I don't have a drink. The best man slaps his sweaty half-empty fuzzy navel into my hand.

I raise the tumbler high. 'Tom, welcome to our family. Jaclyn, you are beautiful and we love you and we're here for you. *Salute! Cent'anni!*' I take a sip, defying my better judgment and standing orders from the board of health. 'And, folks, don't forget the goody bags. There's Aramis cologne for the men and Li-Lac chocolates for the girls!'

'Chocolate? In this heat?' Monica Spadoni barks from the Rude table. 'They should give us miniature stadium fans. Of course, we're back here by the kitchen where they're broiling meat!'

I ignore her, slip the microphone out of its stand,

34

and give it to the best man, who looks through me, as boys do when a spinster is chaperoning a sock hop. After a few more toasts and the cake cutting, I go to the Dementia table where Gram is dipping a biscotti into her espresso. I lean over the back of her chair and whisper in her ear.

'Are you having fun?'

'Ready when you are. Let me just say good night to the kids.' Gram puts her beaded clutch on the table and pushes her chair back.

I go to the cake trolley and stand next to my mother. I put my hand on her shoulders. 'Ma.'

My mother the mind reader frowns. 'You're leaving?'

'Gotta get Gram home.'

'So soon?'

'Ma. All we'll miss is the great aunts forming a line like Vestal virgins in a Charlton Heston movie to fight over the centerpieces.' Tomorrow every grave of my forefathers from Bayshore to Sunnyside will be decorated with wedding flowers. Italians never waste a floral arrangement. It's a sin.

'Thank you.' Mom takes me in her arms. 'I love you, Valentine. Thank you for taking such good care of my mother.'

'Do me a favor,' I ask her.

'Anything,' she says.

'Don't make Dad sing "Butterfly Kisses."'

Mom throws her shoulders back. 'You people are no fun.'

Gram comes up and gives Mom a quick kiss.

Mom tucks a piece of wedding cake wrapped in a napkin into my purse. Alfred, Jaclyn, and Tess gather round, taking turns saying good-bye to Gram. Finally, after we've kissed the last cousin twice removed we are free to go.

Gram and I make our way out of the Starlight Venetian Room to the lobby, through the grand foyer with its vaulted ceiling, past walls covered in cranberry-and-gold-flocked wallpaper, past the inlaid marble fireplace, and finally, under the twinkling chandeliers to the entrance foyer.

Gram takes a goody bag off the table for me and then takes one for herself. We hear the sexy, opening swing chords of 'Oh, Marie' as the band plays us out into the balmy night. We climb into our car and settle back in the seat. The driver turns and looks at us. 'Early night, girls?'

Gram says, 'Manhattan please.'

We look at each other and smile. At last, we're going home.

CHAPTER 2

166 PERRY STREET

The limousine swerves around potholes as we approach the entrance of the Queens Midtown Tunnel. Gram and I share the Li-Lac chocolate sampler as the skyscrapers of Manhattan loom ahead like giant piano keys, black and white against a silver sky.

Once we're out of the tunnel on the city side, we turn down Second Avenue. The East Village looks like the old Greenwich Village I remember as a child. Tonight, it's a late-summer carnival of dense crowds lit by pale pink lights and blue neon. As we make our way west into the heart of Greenwich Village, we leave the high-rises and nightlife behind us, and enter the hushed sanctuary of winding streets lined with charming brownstones, their window boxes stuffed with geraniums lit by antique lamplights.

From my bedroom window in Queens, as Madonna's 'La Isla Bonita' played on repeat, I'd imagine the glamour and sophistication of Manhattan just a few stops away on the E train. I couldn't wait for Sunday dinners in the Village with my grandparents. When Dad would make the turn onto Perry Street, and drive over the cobble-stones, we'd bounce around in the backseat like tennis balls. The cobblestone streets signaled that we were almost there, the place where magic lived: the Angelini Shoe Company.

'Where is it?' our driver asks.

'The corner building. See that blue-and-white-striped canopy? That's us,' I tell him.

The driver pulls up to the sidewalk and stops the car. 'You live all the way over here?'

'Since the day I was married,' Gram tells him.

'Hot neighborhood,' he says.

'Now.' Gram smiles.

I help Gram out of the car. She fishes for her keys by the light of the streetlamp. I look up at the original sign, over the door. It used to say:

Angelini Shoes
GREENWICH VILLAGE
Since 1903

but years of rain have washed away the last three letters. Now it says:

Angel Shoes
GREENWICH VILLAGE
Since 1903

The *l* in Angel is shaped like an old-fashioned ankle boot, in off-white with teal buttons. When I was a little girl, I longed for a pair of boots just

38

like the one on the sign. Gram would laugh and say, 'Those spats haven't been in style since Millard Fillmore.'

The spicy scent of new leather, lemon wax, and the oil from the cutting machine greets us in the entry. I bypass the frosted-glass paneled door, etched with a cursive *A*, which leads to the workshop, hike up my gown, and climb the narrow stairs. I reach the first floor, one large room that combines the kitchen and the living room.

'Go ahead and turn on the lights,' Gram says from below. 'With these knees, I'll be up by Tuesday.'

'Take your time,' I tell her.

I flip the switches for the track lighting over the kitchen counter. The open galley kitchen extends the length of the back wall. A long black-and-white-granite bar separates the kitchen from the dining area. Four bar stools covered in red leather with bronze tacks are tucked under the counter. I remember Gram hoisting me onto the stool when I was a child. How strange that here I am, in my thirties, turning on lights and making sure everything is safe for her, as she always did for me.

In the center of the room is a long farm table that seats twelve. The straight-backed chairs have floral crewelwork seats, embroidered by my mother. We share meals, meet with customers, and make our business plans at this table, the center of our family life.

An opulent Murano glass chandelier hangs over

the table, dripping with bunches of crystal grapes and draped with beads of midnight blue. There's a vase filled with fresh flowers in the center of the table year-round. Gram is a regular at the Korean market on Charles Street. Fresh flowers are delivered every Tuesday, and Gram makes it her business to go and choose the best of the bunch. This week, orange tiger lilies are stuffed into an antique crock.

Beyond the counter, in the living area, a long, comfortable sofa covered in beige velvet, with throw pillows of apple green and fire engine red, is situated under the front windows. Gram has a black leather recliner with a matching ottoman in the corner. The floor lamp next to it has a stem of clear, pressed glass, with a black-and-white-striped silk shade. A television set rests on a small table in front of the sofa. Sheer eggshell curtains hang from the windows, letting in light, while offering some privacy from the busy street below.

Gram stands in the entrance of the living room and puts her hands on her hips. 'I could use a nightcap. How about you?'

'Sure.' I slip out of my shoes. 'Did you water the tomatoes before we left?'

'I completely forgot! And it was so hot today.'

'No problem. I'll go up.' I yank up the skirt of my gown and climb the steps to the third floor.

I stop in Gram's room at the top of the stairs to turn on the small lamp on her dressing table, and notice the stack of books by her bed.

Gram is a big reader. Once a month she heads over to the public library on Sixth Avenue and fills a tote bag with books. The stack includes: *The Ten-Year Nap* by Meg Wolitzer, *What Happened on the Boat* by Angela Thirkell, *Hold Tight* by Harlan Coben, *Women & Money* by Suze Orman, and David Bach's *Smart Women Finish Rich*.

My mother's old bedroom, opposite Gram's, is decorated for an only child reared in the 1950s. The look is fussy, a prim wallpaper with bunches of violets tied with gold ribbons, a small desk and chair painted white to match the bed, which is covered in a ruffled, lavender organza spread with matching round pillows placed along the carved headboard.

My room, which used to be the guest room, is next door to Mom's. When Gram was lonely after Grandpop died, Aunt Feen lived here for a while. Ten years have passed, but her nearly empty flask of Bonne Nuit remains on the dresser, a thin puddle of amber perfume at the bottom of the bottle. A simple double bed with a headboard and a white coverlet is positioned between two windows with white cotton Roman shades.

There's an old writing desk against the wall on one side, and on the other, a wingback chair, slip-covered in white corduroy. This room has the best closet in the house, a walk-in, with shelves in three-quarter surround. We played Big Business in it when we were kids. Tess and I were secretaries, while Alfred was chairman of the board.

41

I turn on the air conditioner. Gram can't sleep in the cold, and I can't sleep without it. I close my bedroom door behind me so the cool stays in. I pass the bathroom that has the original four-legged tub and forest-green-and-white-checked tile my great-grandfather installed when he bought the building.

Outside the bathroom, at the very end of the hallway, is a primitive set of stairs made of rough-hewn oak that leads up to the roof. My grandfather built the steps after years of using an old ladder to get to the hatch. There are endless discussions about these stairs, and my mother sends workmen over to fix them or to replace them with regulation steps with treads, but Gram sends them away. She refuses to change them. Gram is determined to squeeze the last bit of purpose out of every gizmo in this house, whether it's these stairs, the 1940s alarm clock on her nightstand, or the body she lives in.

I unlock the screen door to the roof garden and push it open. There was a time when there was no bolt on the door, but now we lock every window and door.

I stand and close the door behind me, surveying the most beautiful garden in the world. There's just enough light from the streetlamps on Perry to blanket the roof in blue. It's our official *outdoor space*, which is what you call anything that has open air around it in Manhattan. In the summer,

Sunday dinner is moved to the roof, where we push the furniture against the side walls so the grandchildren have their run of the space.

Through the fall and winter, Gram and I often take our coffee breaks up here, bundled in our coats and gloves. We've had some of our best talks under this city sky, just the two of us. Even though we spent a lot of time together when I was growing up, it was never one-on-one. When we're on the roof, the workshop, the pressures of business, and our family problems seem miles away.

The décor of the garden hasn't changed since I was a girl. In the south corner, there's a large, circular, wrought-iron table painted white, with matching chairs. The table is flanked by three miniature evergreens in terra-cotta pots. The water fountain features a bronze Saint Francis holding a water jug, a small bird perched on his shoulder.

Along the fence line, in full surround, is our official garden, a series of plain wooden boxes four feet deep planted with dense, green tomato vines. We alternate the dependable big boy tomatoes with the heirloom style, which have proved trickier for us to grow. Our vines are planted in the same wooden boxes my grandfather built, their branches tied with remnants of ribbon from the shop, on the same stakes he used.

We cultivate around thirty plants a year, yielding enough tomatoes to can sauce for the entire family, with plenty of tomatoes left over to eat like apples all summer long.

A two-foot chicken-wire fence is attached to the fence line of the roof above the plants. It's partly for safety, but also to train the tomato vines to follow a straight path as they grow toward the sun. The dense, fragrant leaves create a spicy green wallpaper that lasts until the end of summer.

Growing tomatoes is all about patience and process. We place the plants carefully in rich mulch in late spring. Soon, the tender vines fill with white blossoms. Weeks later those flowers become waxy clusters which, in turn, become small green orbs that grow larger before turning orange, finally ripening to a robust red before we pick them. In full harvest, the fat red tomatoes hanging from the green vines look like rubies dangling on a charm bracelet.

I lean against the front wall and look past the West Side Highway to the Hudson River. The streetlamps throw bright pools of yellow light the color of butterfly wings onto the walkway by the water's edge.

In all the years I have watched the Hudson River from this roof, it has never been the same color twice, nor has the sky overhead. One day the sky is a mottled-gray leopard print, then blazing streams of white on hot orange, then a light blue expanse with a smattering of smoke-colored clouds. Just like the sky, the river's mood changes in an instant, like a temperamental lover with a short memory. Sometimes there's a wild surf, and other times it's calm, with waves like the rippled flutes on a teacup. Tonight, the river rolls out like a bolt of silver organza, past the Statue of Liberty and under the Verrazano Narrows Bridge, where it drops off into a midnight blue pit of ocean. It seems to go on forever, and that reassures me.

It's a slow summer night with only a few cars on the West Side Highway. There aren't the usual sounds of truck brakes, car horns, and sirens; tonight it's quiet, as if all of Manhattan is drenched in honey. The sky overhead has turned teal blue, with a border of pale white light that looks like lace over the clutter of buildings across the Hudson on the Jersey side. I can't find the moon, but the Circle Line sails toward the shore of Manhattan, glittering in the dark night like a smoky topaz.

'Sorry, guys,' I tell the bright red tomatoes as I press them, their tough, glassy coats in need of the morning sun to ripen fully. The earth under the vines is as dry as sawdust. I unloop the old green hose from its stand and crank the water dial. Warm pulses of water turn cold as it gushes. I turn to water the plants. My bridesmaid's gown is so tight it won't move with me, so I put down the hose and unzip the back of the dress and slip out of it. My instinct is to save the dress, but for what? I look sickly in taffy colors and I can't imagine any scenario in which I'd put this thing on again.

The gown stands before me like a stiff pink ghost. I turn the hose in its direction. Drenched, the sateen turns the color of a fizzy cranberry cocktail, the exact shade of the paint wash on Palazzo Chupi, Julian Schnabel's West Eleventh Street creation that looms behind our building like a Tuscan villa. Now *that* shade of red would have looked good on me.

All that remains on my body is the Spanx, which looks like a salmon-colored bathing suit from the 1927 Miss America pageant. The boy legs grip my thighs like bandages. My midriff is bound so tight, you'd think the fabric was setting a broken rib. My breasts look like two pink snowball cupcakes sealed in plastic wrap. There's not a ripple on me as I douse the vines along the front of the building, feeling free of the dress, the shoes, and the role of bridesmaid.

As I stand making rain over the tomato vines, the air fills with the scent of black earth and the slightest aroma of coffee. We put our coffee grounds around the roots, an old gardening trick of my grandfather's. I think about him, and how Gram has a whole different view of the man I remember and loved. There seem to be some issues under the crisp white tablecloth he demanded be draped over the table at every meal. Maybe Gram will open up to me someday and tell me the story of their marriage, which is also the history of the Angelini Shoe Company.

My grandparents' shoe shop, and this building, is one of the last holdouts from the old days in this neighborhood. The past ten years have transformed the riverfront from a slew of factories and garages to fancy restaurants and spacious loft apartments. The shoreline of the Hudson River has changed from a flat, forbidding wall of stone to a gleaming array of modern buildings made of glass and steel. Gone are the dangerous docks, black pilings moored with barges, and piers infested with grimy trucks. They've been replaced with green parks, brightly colored jungle gyms in safe playgrounds, and manicured walkways speckled with blue guide lights that pull on at the first sign of nightfall.

Gram handled the changes just fine until the big guns decided to alter our view forever. When three glass-box high-rises, designed by the famous architect Richard Meier, were built next door, Gram threatened to enclose our roof garden with a tall wooden fence covered in hardy ivy to keep out prying eyes. But she hasn't had to yet, because there doesn't seem to be anybody moving into the crystal towers. For months I came up on the roof dreading the neighbors. But, so far, our roof garden looks directly into an empty apartment.

I pull the nozzle close to my face, dousing myself with cold water, I feel the itch of the LeClerc powder as it washes away. Soon, all of Nancy DeAnnoying's handiwork is gone, leaving nothing but clean skin. My hair tumbles out of its chignon under the force of the water. Wet, the Spanx chokes my body like a vine. I look around. I put the nozzle down. Then, I pull the bandeau of the Spanx down, give the bodice a yank, and roll the Lycra down over my waist and hips, pushing it down my thighs and calves. I step out of it. As it rests on the black tar roof, the full girdle looks like the chalk outline of a body at a crime scene.

I close my eyes and hold the nozzle high, dousing my body, like the plants. The cool water feels heavenly against my bare skin. I close my eyes; I relive a similar hot summer night long ago, when my sisters and I stood in a blue plastic pool while Gram spritzed us with the hose.

Suddenly, a blaze of light fills the roof. At first, I'm confused. Is there a police helicopter overhead using giant searchlights to ferret out drug deals? I can see the headline now: NUDE WOMAN FROLICS IN SPRINKLER DURING CRACK BUST. But the sky is clear! I look to the right. Not a bit of movement across Perry Street. I look to the left. Oh no. The lights in the usually empty fourth-floor apartment of the Richard Meier crystal tower are blazing.

I look directly into the eyes of a woman in a summer suit who looks right back at me. She is surprised to see me, but she is not alone. There's a man with her, a tall, kind of gorgeous man with intense black eyes, wearing shorts and a T-shirt that says CAMPARI. We make eye contact but then his eyes move lower, darting back and forth like he's reading incoming flights on an airport screen. It's then that I remember I'm naked. I dive behind a tall row of tomatoes.

I crawl toward the screen door, but as I do, the

hose goes wild, like a wily snake throwing a jet stream of water willy-nilly up into the air and all over the roof. I crawl back to it, cursing as I go. I grab the nozzle and then, staying low, move to the spigot where, from a very difficult angle, I crank until the water finally shuts off. As I crawl to the door and back to safety, the light from the apartment goes out, leaving our roof and what seems like most of lower Manhattan in darkness. I slowly lift my head. The apartment is empty now, a crystal box in the dark.

Downstairs, Gram sits in her recliner with her feet up. Her red patent leather pumps rest, pigeon-toed, by the table, while her suit jacket hangs neatly over the back of a chair. A frosty glass of limoncello waits for me on the counter. 'You took a shower.'

'Uh-huh.' I tie a knot in the sash of my bathrobe. I'll spare Gram the details of my display of public nudity on the roof.

'Your cocktail. I made it a double. Mine, too.' She toasts me. 'The oil pretzels are on the table.' She points to her favorite snack, puffy Italian versions of popovers. I take one and snap it in half.

'I had a talk with your brother at the wedding. He wants me to retire.'

I've held in my anger all day. Now, I've had it. I snap, 'I hope you told Alfred to mind his own business.'

'Valentine, I am eighty years old on my next

49

birthday. How much longer can I . . .' She stops and reconsiders what she is trying to say. 'You do most of what needs to be done around here in the shop, in the house, and even in the garden.'

'And I love it so much I'll be a burden to you all of your life,' I joke. 'The last single woman in our family sleeping in your spare room.'

'Not for long and not forever. You will fall in love again.' She raises her glass to me.

My grandmother has a way of encouraging me that is so gentle, it is only when I'm alone and reflective that I am able to recall her small turns of phrase that eventually shore me up and help me move forward. When she says, *You will fall in love again*, she means it, and also recognizes that I was once in love with a good man, Bret Fitzpatrick, and it was real. I had planned a future with him, and when it didn't work out, she was the only person in my life who said it wasn't supposed to. Everyone else (my sisters, my mother, and my friends) assumed he wasn't enough, or maybe he was too much, or maybe ours was a first love that wasn't meant to go the distance, but no one else was able to put it in perspective so I might make it a chapter in the story of my life, and not the definitive denouement of my romantic history. I rely on Gram to tell me the truth, and to give me her unvarnished opinion. I also require her wisdom. And her approval? Well, that's everything.

'I worry that I hold you back. You should be young when you're young.'

50

'According to Aunt Feen, I'm ancient ruins.'

'Listen to me. Only an old lady can say this. No one else will have the guts to tell you the truth. Time is not your friend and it's, well . . .' Gram looks at her hands.

'What?'

'Time is like ice in your hands.'

I put down my drink. 'Okay, now I'm completely panicked.'

'Too late. I'm doing the panicking for the both of us.'

'What's the matter?'

'Oh, Val . . .'

The tone of her voice scares me.

She looks at me. 'I've made a mess of things.'

'What do you mean?'

'When your grandfather died, he had a couple of loans against the building. I knew about them at the time, but when I went to the bank to settle, the loans were more than I knew. So instead of paying them off, I borrowed more to keep the shop going. Ten years ago, I felt like I could turn the place around to make a profit, but the truth is, we were just getting by.'

'And now?'

'And now, we're in trouble.'

My mind reels. I think of us, working day in and day out and often on weekends. I can't imagine that we aren't making money. I take a sip of the limoncello, hoping it will fortify me. Gram and I never talk about the business side of shoemaking, the profits or losses, the expenses of making shoes. She is in charge of everything relating to the business. She handles the pricing of the stock, the number of orders we take, and the ledger. She uses an outside company to do the payroll for the employees. At one point, I thought of offering to take over the books, but had enough work to do in the shop. I've dedicated the past four years to learning how to *make* shoes, not how to *sell* them. I draw a modest salary from the business, but beyond that, Gram and I never discuss money. 'How . . . how did this happen?'

'I'm the worst kind of businessman. I live in hope.'

'What does that mean exactly?'

'It means that I mortgaged the building to keep the business going. The bank called when they adjusted the mortgage, and I tried to refinance, but couldn't. In the new year, our mortgage payments double, and I don't know how I am going to pay them. Your grandfather was a great juggler. I'm not. I put all my energy into making the shoes, thinking the business would take care of itself. When you came to work for me, I felt like I had the help I needed to pull me out of the hole I got us in. But we're a small operation.'

'Maybe we should think about expanding, making more shoes, and hiring people to help us grow.'

'With what?' She looks at me.

'I've got it!' I clap my hands together. 'I'll make a sex tape! I'll sell it on the Internet! Works for the starlets. Maybe it will only bring in a couple of bucks and a MetroCard, but it's worth a shot.'

'Let's hold off on the desperate measures,' Gram laughs.

I get up and embrace my grandmother. 'There's a solution to every problem.'

'Who told you that?'

'The Norman Vincent Peale of our family, my dear mother.'

'Mike invented upbeat.'

'Yeah, well, this is one time we should follow her lead.'

'Okay, okay,' Gram says and lets go of me.

'Gram?'

'Yes?'

'It's only moncy.'

'It's *a lot* of money.'

'We'll figure it out,' I promise her.

Gram's eyes fill with tears. She lifts her glasses and wipes her eyes. Gram is not a weeper, it's rare that I see her cry.

'You're not alone, Gram. I'm here.'

Gram makes her way upstairs while I close down the house, rinse our glasses, pull the drapes closed, and turn out the lights. As I do my chores, I review all the business questions I have for Gram. I climb the stairs to find out more about exactly what is going on around here.

Gram sits up in bed, reading the newspaper in her fashion. The *New York Times* is folded into a book-size rectangle. She leans on one shoulder into her pillow, holding the paper up, close to the lamplight as she reads.

Gram's face is oval, with a smooth forehead and an aquiline nose. Her even lips have the faintest touch of coral left from her lipstick. Her deep brown eyes study the paper intently. She adjusts her eyeglasses and then sniffles. She pulls a tissue from the sleeve of her nightgown, wipes her nose, returns the tissue to its spot, and continues reading. These are the things, I imagine, that I will remember about her when she's gone. I will remember her habits and quirks, the way she reads the paper, the way she stands over the pattern table in the shop, the way she uses her entire body as she places her hand on the lid of a mason jar to seal it shut when we can the tomatoes. Now I have a new picture to add to the pile: the look on her face this evening when she told me the Angelini Shoe Company is in hock up to the rooftop garden. I played it cool and calm, but the truth is, I feel as though I'm on life support, and I haven't the guts to ask the doctor how long I've got.

'You're staring,' Gram says, looking at me over her glasses. 'What?'

'Why didn't you tell me about the loans?' I ask.

'I didn't want to worry you.'

'But I'm your apprentice. Translated from the French it means "to help."'

'It does?'

'Not really. The point is, I'm here to help. From

54

the moment I became your apprentice, *your* problems became *my* problems. *Our* problems.'

Gram begins to disagree. I stop her.

'Now, don't argue with me. I want to master making shoes because I want to design them someday and I can't do it without you.'

'You've got the talent.' Gram looks at me. 'You definitely have the talent.'

I sit down on the edge of the bed and turn to face her. 'Then trust me with your legacy.'

'I do. But, Valentine, more than the success of this business, in fact, more than anything in this world, I want peace in my family. I want you to get along with your brother. I want you to try and understand him.'

'Maybe he should try and understand us. This isn't 1652 on a Tuscan farm where the firstborn son controls everything and the girls do the dishes. He's not our padrone, even though he acts like it.'

'He's smart. Maybe he can help us.'

'Fine, first thing tomorrow I smoke the peace pipe with Alfred,' I lie. I'm not going to do one more thing to put me into deeper indentured servitude, emotional or financial, to my brother. 'You need anything before I go to bed?'

'Nope.'

The phone rings on Gram's nightstand. She reaches for it. 'Hello,' she says. '*Ciao, ciao!*' She sits up in the bed, waves good night to me. '*Il matrimonio è stato bellissimo. Jaclyn era una sposa straordinaria. Troppa gente, troppo cibo, la musica era troppo forte, ed erano tutti anziani.'* She laughs.

I stand and walk toward the door. I can make out phrases here and there. Nice wedding. Pretty bride. Loud music. Gram's vocal tone has changed, her crack Italian words tumble over one another and she hardly takes a breath, like a gossipy seventh-grader after her first dance. When she speaks Italian, she's lighter, down-right girly. Who is she talking to? I glance back in her direction, but Gram covers the mouthpiece.

She waves me off. 'It's long distance. My tanner from Italy.' Then she smiles and goes back to her call.

On the way to my bedroom, I turn the hallway lights off. Lately, these calls from Italy have become more frequent. Leather must be a hilarious subject between shoemakers and tanners, judging by the way Gram jokes on the phone. Whoever she's talking to has a lot of pep for 5 A.M. Italian time. But how can she laugh when the wolf is at the door with a lien and a buyout? I go into my room, which is about seventy degrees cooler than the hallway. I close the door behind me so the cold air doesn't waft down the hallway and give Gram a chill.

I am so upset, I cannot get in bed, so I pace. What a day. A wedding day so hot that when I danced with Jaclyn's father-in-law he left a wet handprint on my dress. The humiliation of the Friends' table, explaining myself, my *life* to a bunch of people I see only at weddings and funerals, which should tell me something about their place in my universe. Then I return home to bad news which, deep down, doesn't surprise me as much as it should, if I'm completely honest with myself. I have noticed a shift in Gram's mood in the shop. I preferred to ignore it, which is a mistake I won't make again. From now on, I'm not going to pretend everything is fine when it's not. I'm angry at Gram for mishandling the business. I'm angry that she assumed Grandpop's debts without restructuring, or bringing in professionals to advise her. She has set the wheels in motion to close the shop, or maybe this is her way of letting the decision to retire be made for her. I can see it all now: Alfred will close the shop, sell the building, I will be on the street, while Gram goes off to live in one of those cold, impersonal condos, and someday her great-grandchildren will look at photographs of the shoes she made, like relics under glass in a museum.

I should have sat down with her when I came to work here and had her explain everything, not just the history of our family business, or the mechanics of the craft, but the hard facts, the numbers, the truth about what it takes to keep a small, independent company thriving in this era of mass merchandising and cheap foreign labor. I skirted all that because I was beholden to her for making me her apprentice and allowing me to learn how to make shoes. I was indebted to her, and now I will pay the price.

I would have handled things differently if my mentor wasn't my grandmother. I never felt I could ask questions because who was I to ask them? But now, I know. I should have asked. I should have asserted myself! I wasted so much time. And there it is, the root of my anger and frustration, so obvious I should have thought of it sooner. I took my time until my thirties to find my calling, and then I waltzed in assuming that the details would take care of themselves. I should have come to work here full-time when I was young and my grandfather was alive. I should have become their apprentice right out of college instead of being sidetracked by Bret and by a career as a teacher, which I was never completely committed to. Then maybe we wouldn't be in this fix.

I'm a late bloomer, and knowing a little bit about plants the way I do, sometimes late bloomers don't bloom at all. I may never become the artisan I hope to be because there won't be a master to teach me, or a place for me to perfect my craft. The Angelini Shoe Company will close, and with it will go my future.

I waded into becoming a shoemaker when I should have jumped in. I'd show up on weekends and help trace patterns, buff leather, dye silk, or cut grommets; but it wasn't a calling for me at first, it wasn't as if I was compelled to be a shoemaker. I just wanted an excuse to spend time with Gram.

Then, as these things go, I had an epiphany.

One Saturday morning, when I was still teaching English at Forest Hills High School, I came over to help. I draped a gorgeous piece of embroidered velvet over the cutting table. I picked up a pencil and traced around the edges, marking where the seams of the shoe would eventually go. I had traced the pattern instinctively, without breaking the flow of the line, as though something or someone was guiding me. I had an effortless connection to the task, it came as naturally as breathing. I had found my calling. I knew that was *it*, no more teaching. I would leave behind that career and my life in Queens, and sadly, Bret, who had his own life plan configured, which didn't include a struggling artist with student loans, but rather a traditional life, the center of which would be a stay-at-home mother who would raise the children while he took Wall Street by the horns. I didn't fit in his picture, and he didn't fit in mine. Love, I decided then, had to wait while I started over.

I pull my sketchbook off the nightstand and wiggle the pencil out of the wire. I flip the pad open and leaf through my sketches of vamps, insoles, heels, and uppers, drawn tentatively at first, then with a stronger hand. *I'm getting there*, I think as I look at the sketches. I'm getting better, I just need more time.

As I flip through the pages, I reread the notes I've scribbled in the margins: try kid leather here? how about elastic there? velvet? Throughout the pages, knowledge imparted by Gram offers me the instructions and facts that I need daily, ideas to revisit and refer to in the day-to-day operation of the shop. Finally, I flip to a clean white page. I write:

How to Save the Angelini Shoe Company

I am completely overwhelmed. I add:

Since 1903

A hundred and four years have come and gone. The Angelinis were educated and clothed and sheltered with the profits of their shoe shop, a life made and financed by the labor of their own hands. I cannot let the business die, but what does this business mean now, in a world where hand-crafted shoes are a luxury? We make custom wedding shoes, in a world where shoes are manu-factured and mass-produced in minutes and assembled by cheap labor in factories in corners of the world no one has heard of, or worse, pretend that they don't exist. Making shoes by hand is an antiquated art form like glass blowing or quilting or canning tomatoes. How do we survive in a contemporary world without losing everything my great-grandfather built? I write:

Sources of Revenue

I stare at the words until my eyes blur. The only people I know with a real knowledge of money and how to gain access to it are Bret and Alfred, two men I'd rather not ask for help. I flip the pad closed, shove the pencil back into the wire, and drop it onto the floor. I turn out the light. I flip over and pull the blanket close. *I'll make this happen*, I promise myself. *I have to.*

CHAPTER 3

GREENWICH VILLAGE

BuonItalia is an Italian grocery in the Chelsea Market, an old, converted warehouse on Fifteenth Street filled with specialty shops that sell everything from party cakes in the image of Scarlett O'Hara (with antebellum hoop skirts made of frosting) to live lobsters.

The rustic, brightly lit building is a mini-mall of great eating, but nothing tops BuonItalia, as they carry a bounty of all my favorite imports, direct from Italy. You can find everything from jumbo jars of Nutella, a chocolate whip made with hazelnuts (there's nothing else like it spread on a fresh croissant); Bonomelli's chamomile flower tea; Molino Spadoni *farina* (the only kind Gram will put in soup; I've been eating it since I was a pup); to big tins of *acciughe salate*, anchovies straight from Sicily, which we stuff into hot peppers and eat with hot bread.

At the back of the store, a series of open refrigerator bins are filled with fresh, handmade pasta. There's a special on one of Gram's favorite noodles, *spaghetti al nero seppia*, a thin linguine made with the black ink of squid. In the package it looks like licorice whips dusted in cornmeal. I'll prepare it with fresh lemon, butter, and garlic.

I pick up a package of arugula, some firm white mushrooms, and some roasted red peppers to make a salad. Gram loves Zia Tonia's dark chocolate curls on vanilla ice cream, her own version of *stracciatella gelato*, so I pick up a container of that, too. On the way out, I stop at the Wine Vault and buy a bottle of hearty Sicilian Chianti.

As I walk along Greenwich Street, on my way back to the shop, I remember when I was small and my mother wouldn't allow us to go north of Jane, where the old Meatpacking District merged with the residential West Village. Mom believed that if the speeding meat trucks didn't kill you, the exposure to the drug peddlers would.

There was some discussion in the early 1980s about Gram and Grandpop selling the shop and getting out of the neighborhood. There were unsolved murders on the docks of the Hudson River and all-night parties in clubs on the West Side Highway named after places you only hear about during a colonoscopy. So many of my grandparents' contemporaries and neighbors feared the worst, sold their buildings for rock-bottom prices, and left for Long Island, Connecticut, or the Jersey shore. Gram still stays in touch with the Kirshenbaums, who owned a printing press on Jane Street and now live in Connecticut. Friends who hung on until the gentrification of the 1990s fared much better. My grandparents stuck it out, and now Gram will reap the benefits. This strip along the Hudson has become some of the most desired and expensive property on the island of Manhattan.

I remember a more homespun village from my childhood, a working-class neighborhood with a small-town feeling. Gardens weren't manicured. It was pure luck if you had something green growing on your stoop. Buildings were maintained, not renovated. Redbrick walls were chipped and cracked, beaten by the wind and rain to a dull pink, while concrete steps had chunks missing, like the ears worn away by weather on ancient Greek statues.

There used to be big gray garbage drums locked with chains in front gardens, and bicycles hanging off the chain-link fences. Now those same gardens hold marble urns spilling over with exotic plants, and the bikes have been replaced by decorative vines of orange bittersweet berries loaded with blossoms in the spring and berries in the fall. Magazine prettiness has replaced real life.

The poets and musicians who wandered these streets have been chased away by wealthy ladies from the Upper East Side in black town cars shopping for European couture. They haven't paved over the cobblestones yet, but you get the feeling that's coming. How many limousines will have to bounce over them, tossing rich people around in the backseat, before someone objects? As long as there are cobblestones, I will have proof of my childhood. Once those are gone, I won't be so sure about where I came from.

I push the door open. I take a quick look in the shop. The leather Gram cut this morning is laid out on the worktable. The back windows are cracked open; a soft breeze blows over the pattern paper, making it rustle slightly. 'Gram?' I call out to her.

The powder-room door is open, but no sign of her there. There's a note on the cutting table from June Lawton, our pattern cutter: 'Finished up. See you in the A.M.'

I climb the stairs with the grocery bags. I hear a man's voice in the apartment. He talks about food.

'*Quando preparo i peperoni da mettere in conserva, uso i vecchi barattoli di Foggia.*'

He says he cans peppers.

'*Prendo i peperoni verdi, gli taglio via le cime, li pulisco, dopodichè li riempio con le acciughe.*'

Now, he's saying something about stuffing the peppers with anchovies.

'*Faccio bollire i barattoli e poi li riempio con i pepperoni ed acciughe.*'

The voice still isn't familiar.

He goes on, '*Aggiungo aceto e spicchi di aglio fresco. All'incirca sei spicchi per barattolo.*'

'*Così tanti?*' Gram says to him.

I walk into the apartment with my bags.

Gram is seated at the kitchen table. The man

sits at the head of the table with his back to me. Gram looks up at me and smiles. 'Valentine, I'd like you to meet someone.'

I take the bags into the kitchen and place them on the counter. I turn around and extend my hand. 'Hi . . .' The man stands up. He is instantly familiar to me. I know him from somewhere. I shuffle through my memory bank, all the while smiling, but my mental hard drive is coming up with nothing. He's good-looking, sexy even. Is he a supplier? A salesman? He's not wearing brown, so he's definitely not the UPS man. He's not wearing a wedding ring either, so chances are he isn't married.

'I'm Roman Falconi,' he says. The way he introduces himself tells me that I should know his name, but I don't.

'Valentine Roncalli.' I extend my hand. He takes it. I release my grip. He doesn't. He stands and smiles with an expression of knowingness. Maybe he went to school at Holy Agony? I'd remember that. Wouldn't I?

'Nice to see you again,' Roman says.

Again? Nice to see you again? I roll his words around in my head and then suddenly it hits me. Oh no.

This is the guy from the apartment. The Meier building. Last night. The guy in the Campari T-shirt. This is the man who saw me naked. I run my hands over my clothes, relieved that I'm wearing them.

Roman Falconi towers over me. He's definitely taller in person than he seemed in the apartment. Of course, in a glass building, when it's dark out, with distance and the angle, he looked small to me, like one of those bugs trapped in resin for science class.

His nose makes the schnozolas in my family seem demure, but again, everything on his face seems larger up close. He's got thick black hair, cut in longish layers, but it doesn't look coiffed. It would be wonderful if he were gay. A gay man would have looked at my nudity as a study in light, contrast, and form. This guy looked at me longingly, like a ham sandwich and a cold soda accidentally found in the glove compartment on a long car trip with no place to stop and eat for miles. He is not gay.

His eyes are deep brown, the whites around them pale blue – this is genuine Italian stock here. He has a wide smile, excellent teeth. I wiggle my hand out of his grasp. He has a look of surprise on his face, as if to say, *What woman has the temerity to ever let go of my hand?* Big egos go with big hands.

'Valentine is my granddaughter, and the apprentice in the shop.'

'Do you take care of the garden on the roof?' This time his smile is, well, dirty.

'Sometimes.'

Gram interjects. 'Valentine is up there all summer. Every day. She's the real gardener in the family. I don't know what I'd do without her. The stairs are getting to be too much for me.'

'You're just fine, Gram.'

'Tell that to my knees. Valentine is a lifesaver.'

I wish Gram would stop bragging about me. With every word she says, he buys time to remember the woman on the roof as compared with the one standing before him. This man has seen me naked, and believe me, there are states I wouldn't enter if I knew that were true of any of its inhabitants. I like a little control in the nudity department; I prefer to be naked on my own terms, and in circumstances when I have a say over the lighting.

'Last night, I was looking at some ground level real estate next door for a potential restaurant space. The broker asked me if I wanted to see an apartment upstairs for fun. She was hard-selling me on the view of the river. And while the river was a knockout, I saw a woman on this roof who definitely beat that view.'

'Who?' Gram looks at me. 'You?'

I shoot her a look.

'Who else could it have been?' she says and shrugs.

I cross my arms over my chest, then uncross them and place them on my hips. This guy has seen everything anyway, and he hardly needs X-ray specs to see through my arms to my breasts. 'If you'll excuse me, Roland . . .'

'Roman.'

'Right, right. Sorry. I have . . . some things to do.'

'What? We're done for the day,' Gram says.

'Gram.' Now I'm annoyed. I give her the same play-along face that we give each other when we're trapped by annoying customers. 'I have other things to do.'

'What?' she presses.

Roman seems to be enjoying this. '*A lot* of *things*, Gram,' I tell her.

'I'd like to see the roof,' Roman says not so innocently.

'Valentine can take you. Take him up,' she barks. Gram gets up and moves to the stairwell to go upstairs. 'I have to call Feen. I promised to call her before supper. Roman, it's been a pleasure.'

'All mine, Teodora.'

What happened to the grandmother who didn't want company above this floor? What happened to the woman who guards her privacy like the savings bonds hidden in a rusty tin box under the kitchen-table floorboards? She's awfully quick to abandon her house rules in the face of this *paisano*. There's something about this guy that she likes.

'Excuse me,' I tell Roman. I follow Gram into the stairwell and whisper, 'Gram, what the hell is going on? Do you *know* this person? We're two women living alone here.'

'Oh, please. He's all right. Pull it together.' She grabs the railing and takes a step. Then she turns back to me. 'It's been too long for you, young lady. You have no instincts anymore.'

'We'll discuss this later,' I whisper. I return to the living room.

Roman has turned his chair out from the table, crossed his legs, and has his hands folded in his lap. He's waiting for me. 'I'm ready for my tour.'

'Don't you think you've seen enough around here?' I say.

'You think?' he says, grinning.

'Look, I don't know you. Maybe you're just some weirdo who goes around charming old ladies, speaking crappy Italian . . .'

'Hey, that hurts.' He puts his hand on his heart.

This makes me laugh. 'Okay, not so crappy. In fact, I think you speak Italian very well. And I know that because I don't.'

'I could teach you.'

'Okay. Fine. If I ever decide to . . .' Where have my words gone? He's reeling me in here, and I'm trying to resist. '. . . learn how to speak better Italian.' There. I said it. Why is he looking at me like that, with an almost squint? What's he looking for?

'Listen,' he says. 'I'd like to make you dinner.'

'Thank you, but I'm not hungry.'

'Not now, maybe. But, eventually, you're gonna get hungry.' Roman stands. 'And when you do, I'm your man.'

Roman fishes in his back pocket and takes out his wallet. He pulls a card from his wallet and places it on the table. 'If you change your mind about that meal, give me a call.' Roman turns to go. 'You really shouldn't be ashamed of your body. It's lovely.' I hear him whistle as he goes down the stairs. The front door snaps shut as he leaves. Curious about the tall stranger, I go to the table and pick up his business card. It says:

> ROMAN FALCONI
> *Chef/Proprietor*
> *Ca' d'Oro*
> 18 MOTT STREET

Here's the thing about a business card with a man's phone number on it. It moves through life with you if you let it. First, I put Roman's card on the fridge, as if we'd actually order in from the place one night. Then, I moved it to my wallet, where it sat for a couple of days next to the Bloomie's coupons I'd saved from a mailer. Now, it's in my pocket, on my way to my room, where I'll leave it in the crook of the mirror over my dresser, joining the school pictures of my nieces and nephews and a discount coupon for a deep-conditioning treatment at the Eva Scrivo Hair Salon.

Gram convinced me that we needed to bring Alfred into the know about our precarious financial situation. She's invited him over this afternoon to turn over our records and books. And because we are first and foremost Italian women, we are making his favorite dish, tomato-and-basil foccacia, to soften him up and appeal to his sense of duty to family while attempting to swing things our way.

Alfred peels an orange as he sits in Grandpop's chair at the head of the table. He places the peels neatly on a cloth napkin. Gram's handwritten ledgers, her business checkbook, his laptop computer, and a calculator are spread out in front of him. He wears a suit and tie; his oxblood Berluti wingtips are buffed to a glassy burgundy finish. He studies the figures on the computer screen as he absentmindedly drums his fingers.

Gram and I have cleared the granite counter and are using it for a cutting board. I have made a well of flour into which I crack an egg. Gram adds another. I add yeast to the mixture and commence kneading the flour and eggs into dough. Gram sprinkles flour on the counter as I fold and refold the mixture until it's a smooth ball. Gram takes the ball, and with her hands places it on a greased cookie sheet and with her thumbs makes small indentations in the dough. She pulls the edges of the dough into a rectangle, which eventually fills the pan. I scoop fresh-sliced tomatoes out of a bowl and layer them in the folds of the dough. Gram shreds fresh basil onto the tomatoes, then she drizzles the pans with gold olive oil. I hoist the foccacia into the hot oven.

'Okay, Gram, Valentine, sit down.'

Gram and I take our seats at either side of the table, across from each other. We turn our chairs to face him. Gram twists a striped moppeen around her hand and rests it in her lap.

'Gram,' Alfred begins, 'you've done a good job

of keeping the shop running. What you haven't done is make money.'

'How can we—,' I begin, but Alfred holds up his hand to stop me.

'First we have to look at the debt.' He goes on, 'When Grandpop died, instead of going out and getting a partner to help finance the operation, which would have been wise at the time, you borrowed against the building to keep your shop up and running. Now Grandpop had loans of about three hundred thousand dollars on the business. You kept his loan, but unfortunately, you've only paid the interest, so ten years later, you still owe the bank three hundred thousand dollars.'

'Even though she's been paying all this time?'

'Even though she's been paying. Banks know how to make money, and that's how they do it. Now, Gram, here's where you got into trouble,' he says. 'You used the only equity you had to borrow more money. You mortgaged the building. The real problem is that they gave you a balloon mortgage – cheap to pay up front, but then, just as the name implies, it balloons. And now the marker has come due. Your payments double in the new year. Again, the banks were smart. They know your property value only increased in this area, and they're making money on the fact that you will when you sell the building.'

'She doesn't want to sell,' I interject.

'I know. But Gram used the building as her leverage. Once Grandpop was gone, Gram

73

couldn't pay off any new debt. She was saddled with the old debt. The business can only produce what it can produce in any given year.'

'I tried to turn out more product,' Gram sighs.

'But you can't. It's not in the nature of a hand-crafted product. They're supposed to be unique, right?' Alfred looks at me.

'That's what we're selling. Exquisite shoes. Handcrafted. One of a kind.' My voice breaks.

Alfred looks at me with all the compassion he is capable of. 'Okay, here's what I recommend. It's highly unlikely, with the cost of goods in the shop, and your ability to meet your orders, that you will make money. So, basically, the shoe shop is a financial wash.'

'But couldn't we figure out a way to produce more shoes?' I ask him.

'It's impossible, Valentine. You'd have to make ten times what you're producing now.'

'We can't do that,' Gram says quietly.

'There is one way to solve all your problems. You could sell the building and relocate to a cheaper location. Or not. Maybe it's time to close the company entirely.'

My stomach turns. And here it is, in plain language, the scenario that will end my partnership with Gram and destroy any hopes I have of taking our shoe company into the future. Gram knows this, and so she says, 'Alfred, I'm not ready to sell the building.'

'Okay, but you understand that this building is

your greatest asset. It can set you free from the debt, and give you plenty to live on for the rest of your life. At least let me bring brokers through so we can assess what it's worth—'

'I'm not ready to sell it, Alfred,' she repeats.

'I understand. But we need to know what the building is worth so that at the very least, I can go to the bank and refinance your mortgage and restructure your debt.'

I look over at Gram, who is weary from the discussion. Usually, she looks youthful to me, but today, having to own up to her past mistakes by the harsh light of the balance sheet on Alfred's computer, she looks exhausted. The scent of pungent basil fills the air. I jump out of my seat. 'The foccacia!' I run to the oven, look in the window, grab the oven mitts, and rescue the golden dough, its edges turning deep brown from the heat; I lift the pan out and onto the counter. 'Just in time,' I say, fanning it with my oven mitt.

'Don't worry, Gram,' I hear Alfred say. 'I'll take care of everything.'

Alfred's quiet promise to Gram sends a chill through me. Someday, I will look back on this and remember it as the moment Alfred made his play to control the Angelini Shoe Company.

What he will never know is that as determined as he is to sell, I am equally determined to stay and fight. My brother has no idea what I'm made of, but he's going to find out.

★　★　★

The cold rain that brings the first chill of autumn to New York City woke me this morning. The boiler kicked on as the temperature dipped below fifty-five. The scent of fresh paint on the radiators, mixed with steam, signals winter on the way. As I pass Gram's bedroom, she's still asleep. How things have changed. Gram was up and in the shop before dawn. I was never an early riser, but now, with a mission in mind, I'm up with the sun.

I push open the glass door to the shop, prop it with a wedge of old wood, then set my mug of hot milk and espresso on an old rubber cat's-paw heel and begin my rounds, flipping switches to turn on the work lights. Since our meeting with Alfred, I have savored every moment in this building. Each pair of shoes that we finish, pack, and ship galvanizes me to try and hang on to this shop. I can't imagine a world where 166 Perry Street is anything but the Angelini Shoe Company, and anything but home. But there are moments when I am filled with despair about the fate of my future, and feel as though my dreams are slipping away, carried down the Hudson River and out to sea like a paper boat.

Our workshop is one enormous room, with areas assigned to particular tasks. There's a half bath in the back that was once a closet. The workshop is spacious because it's actually two stories high. There are windows on all four walls, very rare in a city building, giving us light throughout the day.

When the storm clouds are low and dark, as they are this morning, it's as if we are cloaked in gray chiffon. The light is muted, but it still breaks through.

The bay windows that face the West Side Highway create an old-fashioned storefront, turning us into a kind of aquarium for passersby who observe us as we work. Strangers often become mesmerized as they watch us press, hammer, and sew. We are so fascinating that PS 3 considers us a mandatory field trip every spring. The kids get a firsthand view of old-world craftsmanship, manual labor from centuries past. They find us as mesmerizing to watch as the seals at the Central Park Zoo.

I lift the key ring off the hook in the alcove by the door. I begin at the front, unlocking the folding metal gates that secure the windows. I roll them off to the side and throw a large latch around them to hold them in place. About twenty years ago, Grandpop installed the gates because the insurance company told him they would raise his rates if he didn't. Grandpop argued that the building had been safe since his father bought it in 1903, and why should he change? The insurance adjuster said, 'Mr Angelini, your building hasn't changed since 1903, but people have. You need the gates.'

When my great-grandfather arrived here, he built wooden storage closets all the way around the room. The wood grain is a mix of anything he could find – planks of oak, ends of mahogany, and strips of tiger-eye maple. The patchwork colors and texture of the wood are a reminder that my grandfather built the shop out of remnants from the Passavoy Lumberyard, which used to operate on the corner of Christopher Street. The closets reach to the ceiling. When we were kids, we used to play hide-and-seek inside them.

We store our tools, fabric, leather, and supplies in the closets. The organization of the goods has not changed since the shop opened. Great-grandpop built within the cupboards slanting shelves where we store the carved wooden models of various sizes of feet, called *la forma*. We build the structure of the shoe around these lasts, which were brought from Italy when my great-grandfather emigrated.

Another closet has a series of wooden dowels that hang horizontally from ceiling to floor. We use a stepladder to reach the wide bolt of sheer, gray-blue pattern paper at the top. Beneath it is a thick bolt of plain muslin, followed by a sumptuous selection of fabrics that alter as the seasons change. There's double-sided white satin jacquard stitched in harlequin checks; embroidered cream silk patterned with loose flower petals in relief; eggshell velvet that shows a pale gold sheen in a certain light; sheer beige organza as stiff as fondant icing; and milky cotton linen textured with nubs of thread that give it the look of raw dotted swiss. Finally, at the very bottom of the closet, a dowel holds skeins of satin ribbon on small wheels in every shade from the palest pink to the deepest purple.

I remember when my sisters and I would hit Gram up for swatches to make dolls' clothes. Our Barbies wore some first-class hand-cut Italian goods. And their accessories? With Gram's supply of jet beads, ball fringe, and marabou feathers, our dolls were swathed in haute couture.

The leather, stacked in sheets, is stored in the largest of the closets. We keep squares of clean flannel between the patent leather sheets, and thin layers of pattern paper between the calfskin. The shelves in this closet are kept well oiled with lemon polish to keep the environment around the skins hydrated. The rich scent of leather and lemon wafts through the shop every time we open a closet door.

We keep by the entrance a small table and straight-backed chair that function as a desk. The phone, an old black model with a rotary dial, sits next to a red-leather-bound appointment book. Over the desk is a bulletin board covered in pictures of the grandkids, and a collage of our customers wearing our shoes in their full wedding regalia. The classic bridal photo comes in two varieties. It's either a full shot of the bride lifting her hem to show her shoes, or she is barefoot and carrying them in her hands at the day's end.

A small wooden statue of Saint Crispin, the patron saint of shoemakers, anchors the invoices on the desk. The statue was blessed by Gram's priest in 1952. Shortly thereafter, the church renounced Crispin's sainthood, and the statue was demoted from the breakfront upstairs to a paperweight in the shop.

Besides a stackable washer and dryer, there are three large machines in the back of the shop. The roller is a long apparatus with large, sleek, metal cylinders that stretch and smooth the leather. The buffer is about the size of a washing machine and features large hemp brushes, which polish the leather, breaking down the grain to give it a sheen. *La Cucitrice* is an industrial sewing machine used to stitch the soles and seams.

There's an old ironing board with a blue paisley cover, and it has more than its share of coffee-colored burns, lots of them my doing. The iron itself is small and heavy, a triangle wedge with the metal handle covered in rattan. It, too, came from Italy with my great-grandfather. The iron takes a good ten minutes to heat up, but we wouldn't think of buying a new one. My great-grandfather rewired it for electricity when he was a young man. Prior to that, they simply put the iron in the fireplace on an open grid to heat it.

Pressing is the first job an apprentice must learn. You'd be surprised by how long it took me to press fabric without having the edges curl. I thought I knew how to iron, but like every skill involved in making shoes, the stuff you thought you knew has to be relearned and refined. Everything we do is about pulling the construction elements together so that each shoe is perfectly molded to the foot of the individual customer. There can be no rough edges, wrinkles, bunching, or gathering. This is the luxury aspect of wearing a custom-made shoe. No one else could wear yours.

I look at my to-do list for the day. I have to sew beading on a pair of sateen pumps for a fall wedding; Gram has finished the shoe proper, now it's mine to festoon. I go to the powder room to wash my hands.

My grandfather started a tradition of wall-papering this room with headlines that made him laugh from the New York daily newspapers. His favorite? From 1958: BABY BORN WITH FULL SET OF TEETH. I taped up TYING THE NUT when a fickle movie star married for the third time two summers ago. Gram added CROOK ASTOR when philan-thropist Brooke Astor's son was indicted for taking money from her estate prior to her death.

I go to the worktable to organize my day. I savor rainy days, and I especially love to work when there's a storm. The rhythm of the drone of the rain as it hits the shop windows is a natural accompaniment to delicate handwork.

'Jesus, it's a monsoon-a-roonie out there,' June Lawton bellows from the entry. She shakes out her black umbrella and props it open by the door. Then she unbuttons her khaki trench coat and hangs it on a hook over the radiator in the hall. 'Too bad it's not raining men, or we'd be in the chips, sister.'

81

June, Gram's oldest and dearest friend, is now in her early seventies. She's an Irish beauty, with sky blue eyes and a swan neck, which she accentuates with plunging V-shaped necklines, elaborate ropes of beads, and long, loopy chains. June is the original West Village bohemian, and proud of it. Sometimes on a summer afternoon she joins me on the roof when I water the tomatoes. She doesn't come up just for the sun; from time to time she likes to smoke pot on her coffee breaks. June would hold up the hand-rolled cigarette and say, 'Occupational hazard,' referring to her days when she sang with a small jazz combo called Whiskey Jam. Gram used to go and catch her shows at Village clubs in the '50s and '60s.

June has the fiery ginger hair of her youth and the smooth skin of someone half her age. I once asked June her beauty secret (it's not the pot) and she told me that, since she was eighteen years old, she would lather her face and neck with soap and water and then gently buff her skin with a wet pumice stone. Then she'd rinse and apply a thin layer of Crisco vegetable shortening. So much for expensive face creams!

Greenwich Village is filled with women like June who moved to the city when they were young to work in the arts, had some success, and squeezed out a living. Now retired, living in rent stabilized apartments that provide a low overhead, they're looking for something interesting to fill their time. June loves to work with her hands and she has great taste, so Gram convinced her to come and work in the shoe shop. My grandfather trained June fifteen years ago, and in that time, she's become an excellent pattern cutter.

'Where's Teodora?' June asks.

'She's not up yet,' I tell her.

'Hmm.' June opens a cabinet, pulls out a red corduroy work smock and puts it on. 'You think she's okay?'

'Yeah, sure.' I look at June. 'Why do you ask?'

'I don't know. She seems tired lately.'

'We've been staying up late watching the Clark Gable DVD boxed set.'

'That'd do it.'

'Last night it was *The Call of the Wild*.'

June whistles low. 'Gable was sex on a stick in that one.'

'Loretta Young was pretty great, too.'

'Oh, she was a true beauty. And it was all real. Those were her lips and her bones. She fell in love with Gable when they were making that picture, you know. She got pregnant, kept it a secret, had the baby, and gave her up for adoption. Then guess what she did? She adopted her own baby back, named her Judy, and pretended for years that the girl wasn't biologically hers.'

'Seriously?'

'Back then you couldn't have a child out of wedlock. It would have ruined her. These stars today? Even bad acting can't ruin them.' June pours herself a cup of coffee. 'This is when I miss

83

smoking. When I get myself worked up.' June drops a teaspoon of sugar into her cup. 'How are you?'

'I need six million dollars.'

'I think I can float you.'

We laugh, then June's expression turns serious. 'What do you want with that kind of money?'

I haven't told a soul that I've been going online to research real estate comparables in the neighborhood. Since Gram gave permission to Alfred to call brokers, I decided I needed my own set of numbers so I could figure out some strategy outside my brother's. The results of my search are staggering. I can trust June, so I confide, 'I'd like to buy the shop. The building with the business.'

June sits down on one of the stools with roller feet. 'How are you going to do that?'

'I have no idea.'

June smiles. 'Oh, what fun.'

'Are you kidding?'

'Valentine, that's what's delicious about being young. Try everything. Reach. Really *reach*. Six mil, or six bucks, what's the difference when you're young and you just might get it? I love the salad days, hell, the salad years! You can't know this now, but the struggle is thrilling.'

'I can't sleep at night.'

'Good. That's the best time to figure out a strategy.'

'Yeah, well, I'm not finding any answers.'

'You will.' June puts down her coffee and stands.

84

She pulls pattern paper off the reel and places it over the duchess satin on her table. She pins the paper to the fabric. 'What does your grandmother think?'

'She doesn't say.'

'Why don't you ask her?'

'June, this is all so touchy. You've known her a long time. What do you think she's thinking?'

'Your grandmother is my best friend, but she is an enigma to me in many ways. I'm very open about what I want, but she never has been. She's a brilliant woman, you know. But she holds a lot in.'

'She's the only person in our family who does.'

June smooths the pattern paper with one hand. 'I think she's been better since you've worked here.'

'You do?'

'You're a good team. She gets a kick out of you, too. That helps.'

'Has she ever said anything about retirement?'

'Never,' June replies, which I take as a very good sign.

Gram pushes the door of the shop open. 'Morning, ladies.'

'Coffee is fresh,' I tell her.

'You should have woken me up, Valentine.' Gram goes to the desk, picks up her notes, reads them, and sighs. Lately, Gram is like the shoemaker in the fairy tale. I think she half-expects that some morning, she'll wake up, come down the stairs, and magically, elves will have done our work for us while we dreamed; splendid new handmade shoes will be assembled and ready to wear. 'I could have used the early start.'

'We've got everything under control,' I tell her.

'Besides that, you were hardly wasting time up there. Weren't you dreaming of Gable?' June says, smiling.

'How do you know?' Gram asks her.

'Who doesn't dream of Gable?' June shrugs.

I pull the finished shoes off the shelf. Gram has wrapped them in clean, white cotton. I unwrap the shoes gently, like taking a blanket off a newborn baby.

I place the left shoe on my work pedestal, smoothing the satin carefully. I marvel at Gram's needlework around the border of the vamp. The stitches are so tiny they are practically invisible.

There is a loud banging at the door. I look up at June, who is at a point in her cutting that can't be interrupted. Gram is making notes on her list. 'I'll get it,' I tell them.

I open the entrance door. A young woman, around twenty, stands under a flimsy black umbrella. She is soaking wet and carries a clipboard. She wears a backpack and a headset around her neck, which leads to a walkie-talkie hooked to her belt.

'Do you guys fix shoes?' She pushes the wet hood of her zippered sweatshirt off her head. Her long red hair is secured with a navy-and-white bandanna tied in a bow. Her creamy skin has a sprinkling of freckles across the bridge of her nose, but not a single one elsewhere.

'Sorry. We don't do repairs.'

'It's an emergency.' The girl looks as though she might cry.

The girl props her umbrella in the corner of the vestibule and follows me into the shop.

'Who are you?' Gram asks politely.

'My name is Megan Donovan.'

'You're Irish,' June says without even looking up. 'I'm a lass myself. We're outnumbered here. You can stay.'

'What do you need?' Gram asks her.

'I'm a PA on the movie shooting over at Our Lady of Pompeii Church . . .' Her voice goes up at the end of the sentence, like a question, but she's not asking one.

'That's my parish.' Gram sounds surprised that they'd be making a movie where she attends mass, got married, and baptized my mother.

'They didn't check with you first?' June continues to pin fabric, but this time she looks up. 'Call the Vatican,' June says with a grin.

'What's the movie about?' I ask Megan.

'Well, it's called *Lucia, Lucia*. And it's about a woman in 1950 in Greenwich Village. Anyhow, we're filming the scene of her wedding and her heel broke. And I Googled wedding shoes in Greenwich Village and found you guys. I thought maybe you could fix it.'

'Where's the shoe?'

Megan drops the wet backpack off her shoulders, unzips it, and lifts out a shoe, which she hands to Gram.

I join Gram behind the table to assess the damage. The heel has completely ripped away from the shaft.

'It can't be fixed,' I tell her. 'But this is a size seven. Our samples are sevens.'

'Okay, let me tell them.' Megan whips out a BlackBerry and types rapidly with both thumbs across the keypad. She waits for a response. She reads. 'They're on their way.'

'Who?' Gram asks.

'My bosses. The costume designer and the producer.'

'We can't fix this shoe,' Gram says firmly.

Megan looks flustered. 'This is my first movie and these people are real perfectionists. When the heel broke, they all started screaming. They gave it to me and said, "Get it fixed," like they'd kill me if I didn't. They're serious about every freakin' thing. I mean, totally picky. The bride couldn't just carry white roses; it had to be a certain kind of white roses. I was at the flower market this morning at three AM to get some Ecuadorian rose that blooms, like, once a year.' Megan wipes her eyes with her sleeve; I don't know if she's wiping away tears of frustration or rain.

Gram pours Megan a cup of coffee. Megan dumps cream and sugar into the mug until the

88

coffee is the color of sand. She grips the mug with both hands and sips.

'Well, now we know where the craftsmanship in America has gone. It's in the movies.' Gram smiles.

'Here, give me your sweatshirt. I'll throw it in the dryer,' I tell Megan. She peels it off and hands it to me. Her black T-shirt with bold white letters that say ADDICTED is, amazingly, dry.

'This place is really old.' Megan looks around and drinks in the operation.

'Yes it is.' Gram nods. 'How do you like making movies?'

'I'm so low on the ladder, you don't need a step to reach me.' Megan sighs.

There is another loud knock at the door. 'That's them!' Megan panics, puts her coffee down, and goes to the door.

Megan returns followed by two women who talk rapidly to each other and at the same time seem preoccupied. 'This is Debra McGuire, our costume designer.' Megan almost curtsies.

Debra's long, dark brown hair is worn in a loose braid to her waist. She wears bright red lipstick, and has half-moon-shaped brown eyes that squint around the room as she takes in our operation. She peels off her black patent trench coat. Underneath, she wears turquoise sari pants tucked into yellow patent leather wellies, a short pink silk skating skirt over the pants. On top, she wears a yellow-and-white-pin-striped band jacket that looks like she stole it off the body of Sergeant

Pepper. It's hard to say how old she is. She could be in her thirties, but she has the presence and command of a woman of fifty. 'Have you fixed the shoe?' she snaps at Megan.

'No,' Gram interjects. 'And who are you?' Gram turns to the woman standing beside Debra.

'I'm Julie Durk, the producer.'

Julie is in her thirties, with pale skin and blue eyes. Unlike the demanding Debra, she dresses like me, in faded denim jeans and a black turtleneck and black suede boots. Julie also wears a navy blue baseball jacket that says *LUCIA, LUCIA* in red where the team logo would go.

'Where are we?' Debra looks around the shop and then at Megan, more annoyed than curious. Before Megan can speak, Gram interrupts.

'The Angelini Shoe Company,' Gram tells her. 'We make custom wedding shoes.'

'I've never heard of you.' Debra circles around the cutting table to get a view of the pattern June is working on. 'Do you know Barbara Schaum?'

'The sandal maker in the East Village? She's wonderful,' Gram says. 'She's been around since the early sixties.'

'This shop has been here since 1903,' I say, hoping this woman will get the hint to be respectful to my grandmother.

'Not many of you left.' Debra moves over to study the shoe I've been working on. 'You guys do what again?'

'We make wedding shoes.' Now I'm peeved.

'Ms McGuire has a lot on her mind,' Megan apologizes for her boss.

'Please.' Debra waves her hand at Megan dismissively. 'Now why can't you fix my shoe?'

'It's beyond repair,' I tell her.

'We have to do reshoots, then,' Julie says, biting her lip.

'It's a fashion film,' Debra snaps. 'We have to get it right.'

'Who made this shoe?' Gram holds up the broken model.

'Fougeray. He's French.'

'If you talk to him, tell him it's better to use titanium in the heel.'

'He's dead, but I'll tell his rep,' Debra says sarcastically.

'Young lady, I'm busy. I don't need your attitude,' Gram continues, unfazed. 'The shoemaker glued the shaft.' She lifts up the heel. 'That's inferior workmanship.'

'They were very expensive.' Julie sounds apologetic, but I'm not sure if it's directed to Gram or to Debra.

'I'm sure they were. But they're poorly made, no matter how much they cost.' Gram raises her eyebrows. 'So how much of the shoe do you see in the scene?'

'The shoe *is* the scene. There's a close-up, a tracking shot—' Debra puts her hands on the cutting table and bows her head to think.

'Maybe—,' Julie begins.

Debra stops her. 'If they can't repair it, they can't repair it. We'll have to reshoot with a different shoe.'

'Would you like to see our collection?' Gram asks. Debra doesn't answer. 'We're not French, but we're experts.'

'Okay, okay, let's see what you have.' Debra sits down on a work stool and rolls to the table. 'You dragged me over here.' She looks at Megan. She folds her hands on the pattern paper. 'So dazzle me.' She looks at us.

'This place is a wonderland of possibilities,' Megan says, looking at Gram and me with hope.

'It's a custom shoe shop,' Gram corrects her. 'Valentine, bring out the samples, please.'

'What are you looking for, exactly?' June asks Debra.

'It's a Cinderella moment.' Debra stands and dramatizes the scene. 'The bride runs out of the church and her shoe falls off.'

'Bad luck,' Gram says.

'How do you know?' Debra says.

'It's an old Italian wives' tale. Is the movie about an Italian?'

'Yes. A grocer's daughter in the Village.'

'Megan said it takes place in 1950.' Gram looks at Megan, who smiles gratefully for including her in the professional conversation. 'One of our styles was designed in 1950 by my husband.'

'I'd love to see it,' Debra says, smiling with feigned enthusiasm.

I line up on the worktable the boxes from the sample closet. Gram takes a soft flannel cloth and wipes down the outside of the boxes before opening them. This is a habit, since we work with pale shades of fabric that can stain and scuff on touch.

'We offer six styles of wedding shoes. My father-in-law named his designs after his favorite characters in operas. The Lola, inspired by *Cavalleria Rusticana*, is by far the most popular,' Gram begins. 'It's a sandal with a stacked heel. We often embellish the straps with small charms and trims. It's usually made with calfskin, but I have made it in double-sided satin.'

Debra looks at the shoe. 'It's lovely.' She puts it down on the table. 'But it's too light and airy. I need substantial.'

Gram opens the next box. 'This is the Ines from *Il Trovatore*.'

Debra examines the classic kid pump with its sleek heel. 'Getting there, but not quite right.'

'The Mimi from *La Bohème* is an ankle boot most often ordered in satin faconne or embossed velvet. I add delicate grommets and grosgrain ribbon laces.' Gram places the boot on the table.

'Gorgeous,' Julie says. 'But a boot would never fall off.'

'The Gilda from *Rigoletto* is an embroidered mule with a stiletto heel, though we've often made it without the high heel.'

'That's my favorite,' June pipes up.

'The Osmina from *Suor Angelica* is a Mary Jane with buttons. The bride's choice of a double or single strap, or a T-strap.'

Debra squints at the shoe. 'No.'

'The Flora from *La Traviata* is fairly new. I designed this style in 1989.' Gram shows them a calfskin ballet flat with ribbons that crisscross over the ankle and go midway up the calf. 'I got tired of sending brides over to Capezio, so I decided to get a piece of that market with this shoe. It really was the only style we were missing from the original collection.'

'If I was getting married again, I'd wear those in a heartbeat.' Debra points to the Flora. 'But this isn't about what I like. It's about our character.' Debra picks up the Gilda. 'I think it's this one. It's breathtaking. And a mule could fall off.'

'That's the one my husband designed in 1950. So you are historically accurate.'

'And you, Mrs Angelini, are the best-kept secret in shoes.' Debra smiles for the first time. I don't know if it's from relief or the shoes, but she's pleased.

Gram has a look of complete satisfaction on her face. Nobody messes with Gram when it comes to shoes. She is the expert.

'These are size sevens,' Debra says, looking inside the shoe. 'How much do we owe you?'

'I'm afraid we never sell the samples.'

'Well, you have to.' Debra's smile disappears. 'This is an emergency.'

'Actually, maybe you could just loan them to us? We would fully acknowledge your services in the film's credits,' Julie offers.

'That would be fine.' Gram shakes Julie's hand.

'Megan, wrap them up and meet us at the costume trailer,' Debra commands. 'Mrs Angelini, we'll need you to come to the set, too, of course.'

'Me? Why?' Gram is confused.

'We're shooting the scene now. If there are any problems, you'll need to be there to address them. I can't take a chance with that' – she points to the Fougeray – 'happening again.'

Gram looks at me. 'May I bring . . .'

'Bring, bring,' Debra says impatiently. 'Megan will show you the way.' Debra pulls on her coat as they move to the door. They go as quickly as they came, like the lightning from the storm that pierces the room in a flash and then is gone. I grab Megan's sweatshirt out of the dryer. She pulls it on.

'I could find Our Lady of Pompeii with my eyes closed.' Gram throws her hands up. 'Grab my kit, Valentine. Let's go.'

There's always some television show or movie filming on the streets of Greenwich Village. The forty-seven versions of *Law and Order* are shot in Manhattan, so it's rare when there isn't a crew somewhere, filming something. We've become accustomed to waiting on corners until the cameras stop rolling, then tiptoeing over snakes of cables and wires, past trailers as crew members talk into headsets and check their clipboards.

When Gram was young, there was a magical place called Hollywood where movies were made. Now, movie stars walk our neighborhood streets like ordinary people. It ceases to be magic when I see Kate Winslet three people in front of me in line at the Starbucks on Fourteenth Street, so close I can see she wears Essie's Ballet Slippers nail polish. They're not icons when you can bump into them while running errands. Gram never saw Bette Davis at her bodega or Hedy Lamarr at the hairdresser's.

'Follow me,' Megan says, motioning to us as Gram and I enter Our Lady of Pompeii Church. She turns and smiles shyly. 'I forgot. You guys know this place better than me.'

The scent of spicy incense hangs in the air from last Sunday's High Mass. The polished marble floor is covered by boxes of lighting instruments and wheels of cable. The table where the Sunday bulletins are fanned is filled with bagels, plastic coffee urns, and heaps of snacks. How strange to see the old Gothic church so out of context. Its rich carved pews, stained-glass windows, and baroque altar went from being a house of God to being a movie backdrop in no time.

'I can't believe Father Prior let them use the church,' Gram whispers.

'Even the Catholic Church likes good publicity,' I whisper back. 'And a hefty rental fee.'

I pick out the star of the movie because she's wearing a wedding gown.

'That's Anna Christina,' Megan tells us. 'She's an unknown until this movie comes out, then she's Reese Witherspoon after *Legally Blonde*.'

Anna Christina appears to be barely twenty years old. She is tiny, with an hourglass figure. Her oval face is framed by waxy black curls that create a startling contrast against her flawless skin. Her lips are cherries in the snow, a true red that says 1950. Debra is on her knees next to her, fussing with the shoes.

'They're too big.' Debra stands, looking like she's about to blow. Standing next to me, I can practically feel Megan's blood pressure skyrocket.

'Let me see.' Gram sails through the chaos toward the actress, but needs to grip Debra's arm in order to kneel down. 'Damn knees,' I hear her say as I thread through the crowd and kneel next to her. Gram presses the toe and the vamp of the satin mule then gingerly slides it off Anna Christina's foot. Gram looks at Debra. 'Which shoe comes off in the scene?'

'The right one.'

'Give me the cotton batting,' Gram says to me. 'We're going to sew it in.'

Gram unspools the cotton and cuts a square gently with a small pair of gold work scissors. I thread the needle and make a quick knot. Gram places the batting in the toe of the shoe and slips it back on Anna's foot. It's still loose. Gram takes another square of cotton batting and makes an arch in the vamp of the shoe. After another quick fitting, Gram hands me the shoe and the batting. 'Sew it.'

I push the delicate needle through the fabric and into the cotton from the vamp to the toe. I stitch a tiny seam anchoring the cotton. I do the same on the other side of the shoe, in essence, making a shoe within a shoe. Gram takes the slipper and places it back on the actress's foot.

'Now it's too snug!' Debra cries. 'It will never fall off.'

'We aren't done,' Gram says in a tone of voice I haven't heard since she caught Tess and me drawing on her bedroom walls when I was five. The set falls into a hushed silence. I look up and see the director, a young man in a baseball cap and a down vest, pacing as though he's awaiting the birth of quadruplets. Gram hands the shoe back to me. 'Make a gusset on the left side.'

I sew a seam, tightening the fabric over the instep. I hand it back to Gram.

'Give me the wax pencil, Val.'

I give Gram the pencil from the kit. She slides the wax over the interior of the insole, softening the leather and making it pliable. Gram slips the mule back on Anna's foot. 'Now, Anna, when it comes time to lose the shoe, just lift your toes and pull your foot out. It should slide right off. Try it.'

Anna does as instructed, lifting her foot off the

floor and pressing her toe against the top of the vamp. The shoe slides off. 'It works!' Anna says, smiling, her relief as palpable as my own.

Suddenly, the crew, who were standing around sending poison rays of worry our way, spring into action. They move to their positions, shouting orders, as the director settles into his seat and stares into the monitor.

Megan pulls Gram and me back into the shadows. We watch Anna Christina as she pushes the mahogany church doors open with two hands, then runs in her duchess-satin wedding gown through the vestibule, and outside, onto the landing of Our Lady of Pompeii. On cue, she loses the rigged Gilda mule as she steps onto the top step.

'It's a tracking shot,' Megan explains. 'One continuous movement.'

In what seems like the tenth time they film the sequence, the shoe falls off on cue, as it has every time. Gram and I breathe again. A man standing next to the director hollers, 'Cut. Moving on.' The crew fans out, toting, lifting, pushing equipment all around us. Debra goes to the director, who has a few words with her. 'You saved our asses,' Megan says, smiling. 'He's telling her he got the shot.'

Debra pats the director on the back and comes over to us. 'Fougeray out, Angelini in.'

CHAPTER 4

GRAMERCY PARK

I spritz some classic Burberry cologne (a gift from my mother during one of her Brit literary benders) on my neck then pump some into the air overhead where it settles on me in a fragrant peach-and-cedar mist. I lean into the mirror over the dresser and check my makeup. The gold-leafed mirror in my bedroom is so old the paint behind the glass has peeled into swirls of sepia, which gives my complexion an alabaster sheen. This magic mirror is my Restylane on the wall. Roman Falconi's business card rests in the crook of the mirror, and for whatever reason, I tuck it in the pocket of my evening coat. Maybe I'll get hungry enough to check out his restaurant sometime.

I grab my evening bag off the bed and open it, checking for my wallet, MetroCard and my emergency makeup trifecta: mauve lipstick, pale pink lip pencil, and concealer. I pass Gram, in her room, slipping out of her work clothes and into her housedress.

'Gabriel's waiting for you,' she calls after me as I go down the stairs.

'Gram says you know Roman Falconi,' Gabriel

says as I enter the living room. Gabriel is a compact version of Marcello Mastroianni with the coloring of Snow White. We met on the first day of college, waiting in a long line to sign up for theater-arts courses. The first thing he said after introducing himself was, 'I'm gay.' And I said, 'That won't be a problem.' We've been best friends ever since. 'How about a glass of wine before we go?'

'I need it,' he says.

I go into the kitchen and pull a bottle of Poggio al Lupo out of the wine rack. 'So do you think you can get us into Ca' d'Oro?' Gabriel sits down at the counter.

'You've heard of it?'

'You really don't get out much, do you?'

'Only when you invite me.' I pour Gabriel a glass of wine, then one for myself.

'*New York* magazine called it the season's hottest Italian debut. I've been trying to get a reservation since he opened. Will you please call him?'

'I'm not calling him.' I toast Gabriel. '*Salute*.'

Gabriel toasts me. 'Why?'

'I came home from grocery shopping and he was sitting here at this table speaking Italian to Gram, who was completely besotted with him. Let *her* call him.'

'You can trust a man who reveres women of a certain age.'

'I don't know about that. He wasn't here to relive Gram's memories of postwar Manhattan.

He wanted to meet the woman he saw naked on the roof.'

Gabriel's eyes widen. 'He's the guy who saw you?'

'Yeah, yeah, yeah. He probably thinks I'm an exhibitionist.'

'Well, he must have liked what he saw.'

'You will do anything to get a table at his restaurant.'

Gabriel puts his hands in the air. 'I'm a foodie. It's serious to me. Okay, so-what's he like?'

'Attractive.'

'What a tepid word.'

'Okay. He's tall and dark and straight on, he could even be considered handsome. But from a certain angle, his nose looks like he's wearing Groucho Marx glasses, the ones with the plastic nose and the eyebrows.'

'The Italian profile. The occasional curse of our people.'

'How do I look?' I ask Gabriel, revealing my dress under my coat in a Suzy Parker pose.

'Appropriate,' he decides.

'And you thought *attractive* was a tepid word! *Appropriate* is worse!'

'That is to say, you look just right to see an ex-boyfriend whom you almost married who is now married to someone else. I like the ruching.'

'This is Gram's dress.' I straighten the rosettes of silk ruffled across the hem.

'She looks better in it than I ever did,' Gram

102

says as she comes in from the hallway. 'What's this fancy party you're going to?'

'Bret Fitzpatrick's company party on the roof of the Gramercy Park Hotel.'

Gabriel smooths his thick bangs off to one side. 'It's a private club now. I'm glad Bret figured out how to wheel and deal to become whatever it is that he is. What is he again?'

'Some fund-management thing.' I place a small canister of mints into my evening bag. I have two reasons for going to this party tonight. First, I'm still thin from Jaclyn's wedding. Second, I need Bret's help figuring out how to finance my future. I don't trust my brother to have my best interests at heart as he restructures our debt. Bret could be a big help. 'Bret is a vice president of something. To be honest, I don't understand what he does.'

'Why would you? You're a cobbler and me, I'm the maître d' at the Café Carlyle. Let's face it. We're service people, while your ex-lover Bret . . . Sorry, Teodora.'

'Gabriel.' I stop him before he can dig himself in any deeper. I pour Gram a glass of wine and give it to her.

'I'm happy to hear that my granddaughter is a woman with a full life.'

'Do you need anything before I leave?' I ask.

'No, thank you, I'm going to heat up the penne, drink this wine, and watch Mario Batali on the food channel.'

'Did you know your boyfriend Roman Falconi has a hot restaurant?'

'He knew all about tomatoes,' Gram says proudly. 'And he spoke beautiful Italian.' Grams folds her hands gratefully, as if in prayer. 'I thought he was wonderful.'

'You're a sucker for an accent,' I remind her.

'So am I,' Gabriel says longingly.

'I just wish you'd be careful about who you let into the house.'

'Valentine, relax. Roman is Barese. I knew his great-uncle Carm a hundred years ago. He was a regular at Ida De Carlo's, on Hudson Street. And I'll bet you weren't nice to him, were you?'

'Nice enough to get a dinner invitation.' I give Gram a quick kiss. I follow Gabriel out the door and down the stairs.

The roof of the Gramercy Park Hotel is a posh indoor/outdoor living room, with glazed walls filled with immense, colorful paintings; thick Persian rugs; low, lacquered furniture; and a fireplace, blazing in the cool autumn night. A chandelier of green glass foliage and twinkling white lights hangs over the aerie like a canopy in a fairy forest. The cityscape seems to fall away in the distance, and from here, the skyscrapers look like black velvet jewelry boxes strewn with pearls.

This isn't old New York, where club hopping included the Latin Quarter and El Morocco. This is brand-new New York, where hoteliers are impresarios, and their elegant salons compete for a wealthy, connected clientele to adorn their whimsical yet priceless settings. We're in the thicket of new posh. My ex-boyfriend Bret Fitzpatrick holds court as the Chrysler Building looms behind him like a platinum sword. How appropriate, as this man was once my knight in shining armor.

'Valentine!' Bret excuses himself and comes right over to us. He kisses me on both cheeks. Then he gives Gabriel a big hug. 'It's a reunion!'

'Don't use that word.' Gabriel gives Bret a good slap on the back before letting go of him. 'We sound old when you use that word.'

'Well, I'm older than you, so I can call it whatever I want,' Bret says, smiling. 'It's great to see you guys. Thank you for coming.'

'Who are all these people?' Gabriel looks around.

Bret lowers his voice, 'Clients and their friends. One of our partners in the hedge fund is a member here.' He looks at me. 'I thought you'd get a kick out of this.'

'It's something else,' I tell him.

'You look great, Valentine,' Bret says as Gabe heads to the bar to get us each a drink.

'So do you.' And he does. Bret looks like a successful Wall Street financier who has earned his place at the top. His custom-made suit shows off his height, while his Ferragamo dress shoes show his good taste. His light brown hair is thinning, but it doesn't matter. He has eyes the color of gray flannel, the expression in them full of warmth. He has a face you can trust. His selfconfidence is apparent, but not in any way arrogant. Bret is self-made, and he carries himself with the grace of a man who has earned it. The stoop of the shoulders of his youth is gone now, replaced with an upright military posture. He has acquired the thing that children born of privilege seem to possess at birth, and the rest of us must develop – it's called *polish*.

When I first met Bret, he was a brilliant working-class kid from Floral Park, with a burning ambition to make it. He used to mow the lawn for a big Wall Street broker who promised Bret a job if he went to college and got a degree in finance. Bret did even better. He was valedictorian of his class at Saint John's and then went to Harvard Business School. In ten years, Bret shed the old life and slipped into a new one, which fit him like a tailored shirt from Barneys. There's a lot of history between us, but it's never awkward. Bret excuses himself as he is pulled away by a distinguished-looking older man in a suit.

Gabriel returns with my drink. 'It's a hee-toe,' he says, giving me the glass.

'What's that?'

'I don't know. Mow, glow, flow, something – hee-toe. Everything you drink now is a hee-toe.' Gabriel takes a sip.

'Or a teeny. A Gabetini, Valentini. Brettini.' I try

the drink. 'This hotel is not as I remember it.' I look over the edge of the roof to the treetops of Gramercy Park, a deep green island filled with beams of gold light from the old-fashioned streetlamps. The park is enclosed by a wrought-iron fence, and is placed in the center of a square composed of traditional brownstones and grand prewar apartment buildings. 'I remember when my friend Beáta Jachulski got married here. It was before the Europeans bought it. It used to be so cozy and the food was delicious. That was before the Age of Enlightenment. Did you see the paintings in the lobby?'

'If you think this hotel has changed, how about our Bret?' Gabriel whispers.

'He had to.' I lean against the wall enclosing the roof and look out over the crowd. 'These are the people Bret has to impress. It can't be easy.'

'You're so forgiving.' Gabriel takes a sip of his drink. 'It makes me sort of sick.'

'I'm really just proud of him,' I say. Gabriel looks at me with a mixture of understanding and suspicion. Five years have come and gone since Bret and I broke up. Tonight is proof that he would never have fit into the new life I cobbled together, like patches of leather from the workshop floor. He was destined for *this*.

'Well, maybe I'm just hurt because the three of us were always *us*, and now Bret is a *them*. He's the only *them* I know.' Gabriel fishes a maraschino cherry out of his drink. Two more roll around the bottom of his glass.

'How'd you get three cherries?' I want to know.
'I asked.'

I watch as Bret moves from his clients over to the corner of the roof where three pretty girls in their early twenties sip cocktails and smoke. It's chilly out, but they wear no stockings on their tanned legs, and their feet are stuffed into pumps revealing toe cleavage and a slight gap on the buttress that supports their four-inch heels. These girls buy shoes for fashion, not fit.

'I'm going to nab the sofa by the fireplace. This fancy out-door living room is all well and good until winter sets in,' Gabriel says. 'I'm so cold you could Zamboni my ass.'

'I'll be over in a minute,' I tell him, but I keep my eyes on Bret and the girls.

Two of the young women peel away, leaving one shivering blonde with a drink in her hand. Bret leans in and says something to her. They laugh. Then she reaches forward and adjusts the flap on his tie. The intimate gesture forces Bret to take a slight step back.

A breeze kicks up on the roof, and the white lights of the chandelier dance, throwing small beams onto the floor. The girl tilts her head toward Bret. Their conversation has turned earnest. I watch them for a few moments, and then, with the cold night wind at my back, I move toward them.

I extend my hand to the girl, interrupting their conversation. 'Hi, I'm Valentine, an old friend of Bret's.'

'I'm Chase.' She looks up at him. 'One of Bret's many assistants.'

'He has many?'

'I exaggerate,' Chase says and smiles. She has the peridontically perfect teeth of a girl who grew up with all the dental advances of the 1990s, including whiteners, lasers, and invisible braces.

'Boy, you have gorgeous teeth,' I tell her.

She seems taken aback. Clearly, she's used to compliments, but no one mentions her teeth as her first and best attribute. 'Thanks,' she says.

I cross my arms and hold my drink in the crook of my elbow like a potted plant.

When she realizes I'm not going anywhere, she says, 'Well, I guess I'll go and get something to eat.' Her eyes linger on Bret. 'Can I get you something?' She doesn't ask this question like an assistant. Bret catches her tone, looks at me, then says in a very businesslike voice, 'No, I'm fine. You go and enjoy the party.'

Chase turns and goes while Bret looks off over the roof, past the East River.

'You can see Floral Park from here.' I point toward the hinterlands, the borough of Queens, from whence we came.

'No, you can't,' he says.

'It would be great if you could.' I hand him my drink and he takes a sip. 'Maybe you'd remember where you came from.'

'Is that a dig?'

'No. Not at all. I think you've done amazing

things with your life.' My sincerity is obvious, and Bret turns to face me. 'So, what's going on with that girl?' I ask him.

'You are so Italian,' he says.

'Don't dodge the question.'

'Nothing. Nothing is going on.'

'She thinks so.'

'How do you know?'

'How long have we known each other?'

'Years and years.' Bret squints and looks over in the direction of Queens as if he can see us there, two teenagers sitting on the rectory fence on Austin Street as we talked until night came.

'Uh-huh. Since *I* had braces. Plus, I happen to be a woman, so I know that she's interested in more than fetching you a lobster dumpling.'

Bret takes a deep breath. 'Okay, so what do I do?'

'You're going to tell her you're married to a lovely woman and that you have two beautiful daughters named Grace and Ava. Of course she knows your family because she answers the phone at the office. Or is she the assistant that actually answers the phone? Anyhow, then you're going to tell her that she deserves a nice guy of her own. She'll argue with you, and when she does, you're going to tell her she's too young. That's a turnoff when you're actually young.'

Bret laughs. 'Val, you're funny. Are you done teaching me a lesson?' He turns to face me.

'All done. Now you can teach me one.'

In a shorthand only old friends with a history have, he asks, 'What do you need?'

'Will you help me save our shoe company?'

'What's the problem?'

I go into a rambling explanation about Alfred, the debt, Gram, and me. Bret is patient and listens carefully. 'Let me look into it,' he says. Then he says the very thing that brings me peace of mind, always did and always will, 'Don't worry, Val. I'm on it.'

I huddle in the cold taxi next to Gabriel like he's a radiator blowing hot steam. The cab cuts through the busy intersection at Union Square.

'I'm never going to another rooftop party after August. That fireplace was for show. It threw off no heat whatsoever. It was like warming myself on a Bic lighter.'

'It was cold up there but I'm glad we went.'

'What were you and Bret talking about? Is he dumping his wife and you two are getting back together?'

'If you'll come and work as our nanny.'

'Forget it. I hate children.'

'My nonna Roncalli was right about men. No matter how old they are, you gotta watch 'em like a hawk. Like a hawk!'

Gabriel rolls his eyes. 'Just a little. You're mean. That poor girl didn't dare go near Bret the rest of the night. It's like you sprayed him with something. How long do you think that Swiss miss cried in the bathroom?'

'She cried?'

'She didn't cry, but she would have liked to take one of those stone tiki-sculpture things and clock you with it.' Gabriel leans back. 'Of course, she would have needed help lifting it. Those sinewy types have very little upper-body strength. And to be smoking in the new millennium. They're morons.'

'They're twenty-two years old. What do they know?' I remind him. 'I liked the food.'

'A little too much fig. Everybody is using fig now, in everything. Fig paste on foccacia, fig slices in the arugula, mashed fig in the ravioli. You'd think figs were a major food group.' Gabriel sighs.

'Her name was Chase.'

'Who?'

'The girl interested in Bret.'

'Chase like the bank?' Gabriel shakes his head. '*There's* a value system at work for you. Who's her daddy? The Monopoly Man?'

'You never know. Her friend's name is Milan.'

'Like the city?' Gabriel asks.

'Like the city *and* the cookie.'

'Whatever happened to going to the Bible or long-running soap operas for good names?' Gabriel clasps his hands together. 'Give me a Ruth or a Laura any day. Now people name their children after places they've never been – it's madness.'

'A Ruth or a Laura would never hit on her boss. A Chase would.'

'You know, I think Bret misses you.' Gabriel looks at me.

'I miss him, too. But when I was with him, I really didn't think about my life very much. I sort of built what I was doing around him. When we broke up, I had to figure out what made me happy.'

'I don't know, Valentine. Sometimes I think you traded taking care of Bret for taking care of Gram. You should fall in love again and have a life.' The cab pulls over to the curb on the far corner of Twenty-first Street, in Chelsea.

'I have a life!' I tell him.

'You know what I mean.' Gabriel gives me a kiss on the cheek. He stuffs a ten-dollar bill in my hand and jumps out.

I roll down the window and wave the ten. 'It's too much.'

'Keep it.' Then Gabriel waves. 'Call the chef.'

I instruct the driver to take me to Perry and the West Side Highway. I lean back and watch as Chelsea blurs into Greenwich Village, the weekend carnival of the Meatpacking District in full tilt. A rambling gray warehouse is now a dance club, with strips of hot yellow and purple neon over the old loading dock, and a red-roped entrance for all the little pretty ones who await admittance. A rustic factory is now a hot restaurant, the interior decorated with red leather banquettes and floor-to-ceiling mirrors painted with the menus in cursive, while the exterior windows are covered in awnings that look like flouncing red capes in the wind.

Through my taxi window, young women like Chase walk in small packs through the pale blue beams of streetlight, like exotic birds behind glass. Rushes of color jolt the black night as they move; one wears a blouse of peacock blue, another a trench coat in Valentino red, and another a skirt of metallic lamé whose hem ruffles along her thighs as she walks. In full stride, their long legs resemble the reedy stilts of cranes. As they cross the street, they laugh as they hang on to one another for support, making sure the metal tips of their spike heels hit the center of the cobblestones, avoiding the mortar in between. These girls know how to walk on dangerous terrain.

I bury my hands in my pockets, slump down into the seat, and wonder how much of my youth is actually left. And how am I spending these precious days? Is this what my life is going to be, hard work, early to bed and up at the crack of dawn, day in and day out for the rest of my life? Is Gabriel right in assuming I've become a caretaker, burying myself in work and worry at the expense of my thirties? Is there even a chance he's right?

At the bottom of my pocket, I feel the business card. I pull it out. The cab stops at the light. I study the card as though it's a free pass to the rides at Coney Island and it's my seventh birthday party. Ca' d'Oro. Someplace new. Roman Falconi. Somebody new. I don't meet men at work, I don't even have a commute home to meet a nice guy on the train. I won't do match.com because I look better in real life than I do in photographs, and how would I ever describe what I'm looking for when I'm not even sure what I want? Besides, there is very little risk involved in calling Roman Falconi. He gave me the card. He wants me to call him. I fish my cell phone out of my evening bag. I dial the number on the card. It rings three times and then—

'Hello,' Roman says into the phone. I hear background din. Voices. Clangs. The rush of water.

'This is Valentine.'

More noise.

'Valentine?' His vague manner says he doesn't remember me at all. I picture him handing out business cards to strange women all over town with a wink and a smile and a promise of a hot plate of braciole. I'm about to snap the cell phone shut when I hear him say, '*My* Valentine? Teodora's granddaughter?'

I put the open phone back up to my ear. 'Yes.'

'Where are you?'

'I'm in a cab on Greenwich Street. You sound busy.'

'Not at all,' he says. 'I'm about to close. Why don't you come over?'

I hang up and lean into the partition to speak to the driver. 'Change of plans. Can you take me to the corner of Mott and Hester, in Little Italy?'

The cabbie crosses lower Broadway and swings onto Grand Street. Little Italy sparkles in the night, like emerald and ruby chips on a diamond drop earring. No matter what time of year you come to this part of town, it's Christmas. The white lights strung over the thoroughfare, anchored by medallions of red and green tinsel, form an Italian coat of arms across Grand Street. Like my mother, my people require year-round glitz, even in their street decorations.

We pass the open marts selling T-shirts that say, PRAY FOR ME! MY MOTHER-IN-LAW IS ITALIAN, and coffee mugs that proclaim, AMERICA, WE FOUND IT, WE NAMED IT, WE BUILT IT. Framed vintage black-and-white photographs of our icons are propped against storefronts, like statues in church: a determined Sylvester Stallone runs through Philadelphia as Rocky, a dreamy Dean Martin toasts the camera with a highball, and the incomparable Frank Sinatra wears a snap-brim fedora and sings into a microphone in a recording studio. A poster of a six-foot-tall Sophia Loren in black thigh-high hose and a bustier, from *Marriage Italian-Style*, hangs in the doorway of a shop. *Bellissima*. Jerry Vale belts 'Mama Loves Mambo' from speakers rigged on the corner of Mulberry Street, while the drone of a hip-hop beat pulses from cars at the intersection. I pay the driver and jump out of the cab.

Well-dressed couples saunter through the intersection, the men in open-collared shirts with sport jackets, and the women, all versions of my own mother, in tight skirts with fluted hems and fitted peplum jackets. Their spangly high-heeled shoes have toes so pointy you could pound a chicken cutlet with them. Every now and again, a hint of a leopard or a zebra print flashes on a purse or a boot or a barrette. Italian girls love an animal print – clothes, furniture, accessories, it doesn't matter, we answer to the call of the wild in every aspect of our lives. The wives grip the crooks of their husbands' arms as they walk, tottering against them to shift the weight their stiletto heels can't tolerate.

As I look around, any of these folks could be in my family. These are Italian Americans out for a night in the city, eating dinner in their familiar haunts. At the end of the meal, and after a stroll (the American version of *la passeggiata*) they'll go to Ferrara's for coffee and dessert. Once inside, the wives will take seats at the café tables with gleaming marble tops while sending their husbands to the glass cases to choose a pastry. When they've had their espresso and cookies, they'll return to the cases and select a dozen or so pastries to take home: soft seashells of honey-drenched sfogliatelle, moist baba au rhums, and feather-light angel-wing cookies, all delicately placed in a cardboard box and tied with string.

Ferrara's doesn't change, its décor is just as it was when my grandparents were young lovers. We've changed though, the Young Italian Americans. As my generation marries outside our group, our children don't look as Italian as we do, our Roman noses shorten, the Neapolitan jaws soften, the jet black hair fades to brown, and often directly to blond. We assimilate, thanks to the occasional Irish husband and Clairol. As the muse of southern Italian women, Donatella Versace, went platinum blond, so went the Brooklyn girls. But there are still a few of us left, the old-fashioned *paisanas* who wait for curly hair to come back in style, can our own tomatoes, and eat Sunday dinner together after church. We still find joy in the same things our grandparents did, a night out over a plate of homemade pasta, hot bread, and sweet wine, which ends with a conversation over cannolis at Ferrara's. There's nothing small about my Little Italy. It's home.

I check the numbers as I walk along Mott Street. Ca' d'Oro is tucked between the bustling ravioli factory, Felicia Ciotola & Co., and a candy store called Tuttoilmondo's. There's a bold black-and-white-striped awning over the entrance of the restaurant. The door has been faux marbleized with streaks of gold paint on a field of cream. *CA' D'ORO* is carved simply in cursive on a small brass plaque on the door.

I enter the restaurant. It's small in size, but beautifully appointed in the Venetian style by way of Dorothy Draper. A long bar topped with charcoal-colored slate runs the length of the right wall. Attached bar stools are covered in silver patent leather. The tables have been carefully arranged to maximize the space. The tops are

118

black lacquer, while the chairs are done in a gold damask with black scrollwork. It's difficult to pull off baroque in a small setting (or on a pair of shoes for that matter), as it requires an open field to repeat the lush patterns of the period. Mr Falconi pulls it off.

Two couples remain, paying their checks. One pair holds hands across the table, their faces soft in the candlelight as they hover over their empty wineglasses; all that's left of their meal is a hint of pink wine against the crystal.

The bartender, a beautiful girl in her twenties, cleans glasses behind the bar. She looks up at me. 'We're closed,' she says.

'I'm here to see Roman. I'm Valentine Roncalli.'

She nods and goes back to the kitchen.

A mural fills the back wall of the restaurant. It's a scene of a Venetian palace at nightfall. Even though the palazzo looks like one of the wedding-cake samples in the window at Ferrara's, with its ornate arches, open balconies, and crown of gold metallic crosses along the roofline, it is haunting rather than kitschy. Moonlight pours through the palace windows, lighting the canal in the foreground with ribbons of powder blue. It's primitive in style, but there's plenty of emotion in it.

'Hey, you made it.' Roman stands in the doorway that leads to the kitchen. His arms are folded in front of him and the expanse of his chest in the white chef's jacket looks enormous, like the sail of a ship. He seems even taller this time; I don't know what it is about him, but he seems to grow each time I see him. He has a navy blue bandanna tied around his head and, in this light, it gives him the cocky air of a pirate on a rum bottle.

'You like the mural?' He keeps his eyes on me.

'Very much. I like the way the moonlight shines through the palace and onto the water. The palazzo, I mean. Or home of the doge,' I correct myself. After all, if this guy can seduce Gram with his Italian, the least I can do is throw around the only official architectural terms I know.

'It's the Ca' d'Oro, on the Grand Canal in Venice. It was built in 1421 and took about fifteen years to complete. The architects were Giovanni and Bartolomeo Bon, a father-and-son team. They designed it to show the traders who came in from the Orient that the Venetians meant business. Glamorous business. Lots of big egos in Venice, center of world trade and all that. You know how that goes.'

'It's impressive. Who painted it?'

'Me.'

Roman turns and goes into the kitchen, motioning for me to follow. I catch my reflection in the mirror behind the bar and instantly relax the number elevens between my eyes. As I follow Roman back to the kitchen, I make a mental note to ask my mother to pick up a box of Frownies for me, those stickers you moisten and place on wrinkles while you sleep. My mother used to go to bed with beige puzzle pieces adhered to the lines on her face, and she woke up with a complexion as smooth as Formica.

The kitchen is so tiny it makes the dining room seem grand. There's a butcher block island (so small it should be called a sandbar) in the center. Overhead, about thirty pots of varying sizes hang on hooks on a large aluminum frame.

The far wall is covered with an aluminum backsplash for the wide, flat grill. Next to the grill are four gas burners in a row, not front and back like a stove in a home. The corner next to the gas burners is filled with a series of four ovens, stacked one over the other, looking like a mini-skyscraper with windows.

There's a deep triple sink on the opposite wall. I stand next to three floor-to-ceiling refrigerators. A large dishwasher is tucked into an alcove by the back door, which is propped open, revealing a small terrace, fenced in with old painted lattices. The steam rises from the dishwasher, making fog in the cold night air.

'Are you hungry?' Roman asks.

'Yeah.'

'My favorite kind of woman. A hungry one.' He smiles. He helps me take off my coat, which I place on a rolling stool next to the door and anchor with my purse.

'There's an apron on the hook.'

'I have to work for my supper?'

'That's the rule.'

Behind me, sure enough, there's a clean white

121

apron. I pull it over my head; it has the scent of bleach and has been pressed with starch. Roman reaches around me and crosses the strings in the back then reaches around to the front of my waist, tying the ends in a tight bow. Then he pats my hips. I could have done without the hip patting, but it's too late. I'm here and he's patting. 'Go with it,' I tell myself. Roman places a large wooden spoon in my hand.

'Stir.' He points to a large pot on a low flame. Inside, a mound of soft, golden risotto glistens, a fragrant mist of sweet butter, cream, and saffron rising from the pot. 'And don't stop.'

The soles of my sandals stick to the matting on the floor, a series of open rubber rectangular sheets placed around the work areas.

Roman drops to one knee and unties the ribbons on my evening sandals, silver calfskin in a gladiator style with flat white ribbons that lace up past my ankle. As he slips the sandal off my foot, the warmth of his hand sends a chill up my spine.

'Nice shoes.' He stands.

'Thanks. I made them.'

'Here.' He pulls a pair of red plastic clogs like his own from under the island. 'Wear these. I didn't make them.' Then he removes my left sandal and slips on the other clog, just like the prince in *Cinderella*.

I take a step in them. 'I'm a delicate size nine. What are these? Fifteens?'

'Twelve and a half. But you don't have to do a

lot of walking in them. You'll be stirring for the duration.' He takes my shoes and dangles them on the hook where the aprons go. 'I'll be right back,' he says and goes out into the restaurant.

As I stir, I look down at my feet, which now remind me of the feet of the kid on the Dutch Boy paint billboard in Sunnyside, Queens. They also remind me of my father's big shoes, which I used to wear when I was a little girl. I'd stomp around in them, pretending to be all grown up.

Now that I'm alone, I give the kitchen a real once-over. My eyes travel up over the sink to a framed picture of a naked woman in profile, with huge hooters, leaning against a pile of dirty dishes. She winks at me. The caption reads: A WOMAN'S WORK IS NEVER DONE.

'That's Bruna,' Roman says from behind me.

'That's quite a stack of dishes.'

'She's the patron saint of kitchens.'

'And chefs?' I'll keep my eyes on the risotto from now on.

He takes the spoon from me. 'So, why did you decide to call me?'

'You asked me, and I have excellent manners, so I did.'

'I don't think that's it.' He puts a tiny amount of salt in his hand and sprinkles it into the pot. 'I think you might like me a little.'

'I'll be able to tell you for sure after I taste your cooking.'

'Fair enough.' Roman shakes his head and grins.

The busboy enters from the restaurant with a large pan of dirty dishes. He places them in the sink. They converse in Spanish as Roman reaches into his pocket and gives him several twenty-dollar bills. The busboy thanks him, peels off his apron, and goes.

'Roberto has another job, at another restaurant,' Roman explains. 'Someday he'll have his own. I started out washing dishes, too.'

'How many employees do you have?'

'Three full-time, me, the sous-chef and the bartender. Three part-time, the busboy and two waiters. The restaurant seats only forty-five, but we're booked up every night. You must know what it's like, running a small business in New York City. You're never off the clock. Even when I don't have a room full of customers, there's prep, or I'm up early going to the markets, or I'm here, working on additions to the menu.' As Roman stirs the risotto, I notice how clean his hands are and how neatly his nails are filed. 'And it's an expensive business. Some days, I feel like I'm just getting by.'

I move to the sink and turn my back on Bruna. 'You must be doing a little better than getting by. You were looking at an apartment in the Richard Meier building.'

'The broker was showing me a potential restaurant space on the street level. Then she offered to show me an apartment.' He smiles. 'I was curious. That's when I saw you.' Roman takes the spoon

124

from me and stirs the risotto. 'That's some building your grandmother owns.'

'We know.'

The bartender, wearing a coat and hat, leans in the doorway. 'I'm leaving.'

'Thanks, Celeste. Say hello to Valentine.'

'Nice to meet you,' she says and goes.

'She's lovely.'

'She's married.'

'That's nice.' Interesting. Roman makes a point that his pretty bartender is married.

'You're a fan of marriage?'

'Good ones.' I slip up onto the clean work counter next to the sink. 'How about you?'

'Not a fan,' he says.

'At least you're honest.'

'Have you been married?' he asks.

'No. Have you?'

'Yes.'

'Do you have children?'

'No.' He smiles.

'I hope you don't mind that I ask questions like a census taker.'

He laughs. 'You have an unusual style.'

'I'm not going for style. If I were, I would have discounted you when I saw you in the Campari T-shirt and the striped shorts that looked like the pantaloons the security guards wear at the Vatican.'

'Oh, so you have something against bright colors.'

'Not really. I just like to see a man wearing something besides action wear.'

Roman grates a wedge of aged parmesan over the risotto. 'And, if memory serves, your outfit that night was spectacular.'

I turn the color of Saint Bruna's ruby red stilettos.

He laughs. 'Now why should you be embarrassed?'

'If I saw you naked on a roof, I'd pretend I hadn't. That's just good manners.'

'Fair enough. But let's say I met you on the street and you were wearing a lovely dress like the one you have on tonight. Don't suppose I wouldn't be imagining what you'd look like without it. So I'd say we've just skipped a step.'

'I don't skip steps. In fact . . . ,' I blurt out, 'I don't go out with Italians.'

He puts the spoon down and takes the bottom of his apron, and using it as hot pads, lifts the pot off the stove.

'May I ask why not?'

'The cheating.'

He throws his head back and laughs. 'You're kidding. You dismiss an entire group of men for something they haven't done but you think they might do? That's completely prejudiced.'

'I'm a believer in DNA. But let me explain this on a culinary level. About ten years ago, there were all these articles about soy. Eat soy, drink soy, and stop eating dairy foods because they'll

126

kill you. So I stopped eating regular cheese and milk and ate the soy stuff. Well, it made me sick but I persisted because everything I read said soy was good for me, even though my body was telling me it wasn't. When I told Gram about it and she said, 'At no point in our history did Italians ever consume soy. Cheese and tomatoes and cream and butter and pasta have been in our diet for centuries. We thrive on it. Get rid of the soy.' And I did. When I started eating the food of my forefathers again, I felt like a million bucks.'

'What does that have to do with dating Italian men?'

'The same principle applies. Italian men have built thousands of years of romantic history on the notion of the Madonna and the whore. They marry the Madonna and they have fun with the whore. You'd have to go back to the Etruscans, with Dr Phil in tow, to change the way Italian men think. And I say it is impossible to change the fundamental nature of our people, in particular the nature of our men. The risotto is done.'

'I've set a table for us.' He motions to the door. 'Please.'

I follow him into the dining room, where the balloon shades in the front window have been lowered halfway. There must be fifty white candles of all different sizes and shapes placed around the restaurant, throwing sheer nets of pink light up the walls. Rows of flickering votive candles in etched crystal holders are placed in small stone

127

alcoves under the mural, their tiny orange flames forming a choir.

I check my watch. It's two o'clock in the morning. I rarely eat past seven. I haven't been out this late since I moved to the Village. I can't believe it. I'm actually having *fun*. I catch my reflection in the mirror, and this time, miraculously, no number elevens appear between my eyes. Either I've been transformed by the youth-enhancing steam facial from the risotto pot, or I like how this evening is going.

'Go ahead. Please. Sit down,' he says.

'This is beautiful.'

'It's just a backdrop.' Roman places on the table a platter of delicate fried pumpkin blossoms that have been dipped in a light batter.

'For what?'

'For our first date. Lose the apron.'

I pull the apron over my head and drape it over the back of a chair at the next table. I unfold the napkin on my lap, and reach for a pumpkin blossom. I take a bite. The delicate leaf, dipped in this crispy batter, is as light as organza.

Roman goes back into the kitchen and comes out with a hot loaf of bread, wrapped in a bright white cloth, then returns to the kitchen.

While he's gone, I notice the table setting, each detail proper and deliberate. I've never seen this china pattern, so I flip the bread plate over and check the seal. The plates are Umbrian, a bold design called Falco, which shows hand-painted white

128

feathers on a vivid green field. The pattern provides a splash of color on the black lacquer tabletop.

Roman returns with a small tureen that he places on the table. He loosens the cork on a bottle of Tuscan Chianti and pours wine into my glass, then his own. He sits down at the table. He picks up his wineglass. 'Good wine, good food, and a good woman . . .'

'Oh, yes. To Bruna!' I raise my glass.

As Roman ladles the risotto onto my plate, a buttery cloud floats up from the dish. Risotto is a tough dish to pull off. It's labor intensive, you must stir the rice grains until they puff up or your arm falls off, whichever comes first. It's all about timing, because if you stir too long, the rice will turn into a goop of wallpaper paste, and not long enough – you've got broth.

I take a taste. 'You're a genius,' I tell him. He almost blushes. 'Where'd you learn how to cook?'

'My mother. We had a family restaurant in Chicago. Falconi's, in Oak Lawn.'

'So why did you come to New York City?'

'I'm the youngest of six boys. We all worked in the family business, but my brothers never saw beyond the fact that I was the baby of the family. Even in my thirties, I couldn't break that birth-order rap. You know what that's like, don't you?'

'Alfred is the boss, Tess is intelligent, Jaclyn is the beauty, and I'm the funny one.'

'So you get it. I'd been working for the family

since I was a teenager. My mother taught me how to cook, and then I went to school and learned some more. Eventually, I wanted to take what I'd learned and make some changes in the restaurant. It soon became apparent that they liked the restaurant just the way it was. After a lot of wrangling, and nearly drowning in my mother's tears, I left. I needed to make it on my own. And where better to make your name as an Italian chef than here in Little Italy.'

Roman refills our glasses. There's a lot of common ground between us. Our backgrounds are similar, not just the Italian part, but the way we are treated in our families. Even though we've both made some bold choices and gotten real-life experience, our families haven't changed their perceptions of us.

'So how did you decide to join the family business?' he asks. 'Not too many shoemakers out there these days.'

'Well, I was teaching school, ninth grade English, in Queens. But on weekends, I'd go into the city and help Gram in the shop. Eventually, she began to teach me things about making shoes that went beyond packing and shipping. After a while, I was hooked.'

'There's nothing like working with your hands, is there?'

'It takes everything I've got – mentally, physically. Sometimes I'm so bone tired at the end of the day I can hardly make it up the stairs. But the work itself is just part of it. I love to draw, to sketch the shoes and come up with new ideas, and then figure out how to build them. Someday, I want to design shoes.' This wine has put me in a cozy place. I just confided my dreams to a man I hardly know in a way I rarely ever admit, even to myself.

'How long have you worked with your grand-mother?' he asks.

'Almost five years.'

Roman lifts another pumpkin blossom from the plate. 'Five years. So that makes you about . . . ?'

I don't even blink. 'Twenty-eight.'

Roman tilts his face and looks at mine from a different angle. 'I would have guessed younger.'

'Really.' I've never lied about my age, but being almost thirty-four years old seems like a good time to start.

'I got married when I was twenty-eight,' he says. 'Divorced at thirty-seven. I'm forty-one now.' He rattles off the numbers without the slightest hesitation.

'What was her name?'

'Aristea. She was Greek. To this day, I've never seen a woman more beautiful.'

When a man tells you that the most beautiful woman in the world is his ex-wife, and he's been looking at your face for over an hour, it sets like a bad anchovy. 'Greek girls are Italian girls with better tans.' I sip the wine. 'What went wrong?'

'I worked too much.'

'Oh come on. A Greek would understand hard work.'

'And – I guess I didn't work hard enough on the marriage.'

I look at Roman's handiwork – the mural, the candles, the feast on the table – and then I look in his eyes, which I'm beginning to trust. I can talk to this man. It's almost effortless. I feel badly that I lied about my age. This could be the first date of many; now what do I do?

'I'm glad you called me—,' he begins.

'There's something I need to tell you,' I interrupt. 'I'm thirty-three.' My face turns the color of the red pepper slices in the crudité dish. 'I never lie, okay? I just did because, well, thirty-three seems almost thirty-four, and that seems like a number that's getting up there. You should know the truth.'

'No worries. You don't go out with Italians. Remember?' He smiles. Then he gets up from his chair and comes over to me. He takes my hands in his and pulls me up to stand. We look at each other in that way people do when they're deciding whether or not to kiss. I feel guilty that I told Gabriel Roman's nose was like the one with the Groucho Marx glasses. From this angle, his nose is lovely, straight and absolutely fine.

Roman takes my face in his hands. As our lips meet for the first time, his kiss is gentle and sensual, and very direct, like the man himself. I might as well be on the Piazza Medici on the isle of Venice, as his touch takes me far from where I stand and off to someplace wonderful, a place I haven't been in a very long time. As Roman slides his arms around me, the silk of my dress makes a rustling sound, like the dip of an oar into the canal in the mural behind him.

The last man I kissed was Cal Rosenberg, the son of our button supplier from Manhasset. Let's just say it didn't leave me wanting more. But this kiss from Roman Falconi, right here in this sweet restaurant on Mott Street in Little Italy, with my feet in gunboat clogs, makes me feel the possibility of a real romance again. As he kisses me again, I slide my hands down his arms to his biceps. Chefs, evidently, do a lot of heavy lifting, whereas button suppliers and hedge fund managers don't.

I bury my face in Roman's neck, the scent of his clean skin, warmed by amber and cedar, is new, and yet familiar. 'You smell amazing.' I look up at him.

'Your grandmother gave it to me.'

'Gave you what?'

'The cologne.'

I can't believe my grandmother gave Roman the free men's-cologne sample in the goody bag from Jaclyn's wedding. I don't know whether to be embarrassed that she gave it to him, or embarrassed for him that he decided to use it.

'She said either I had to take it, or she'd unload it on Vinnie the mailman. You don't like it?'

'I love it.'

'That's a strong word, *love*.'

'Well, that's a strong cologne.'

The sound of laughter from the street breaks the quiet of the restaurant. Through the windows, I can see the feet of a group of Saturday-night party hounds on their way to the next stop. Their shoes, a mix of polished wingtips, suede ankle boots, and two pairs of high-heeled pumps, one ruby red leather and the other black mock croc, stop in front of Ca' d'Oro. 'Closed,' I hear a woman say in front of the entry door.

Not for me. Roman Falconi kisses me again. 'Let's eat,' he says.

For all the extensive construction going on here on the Manhattan side of the Hudson River, there is plenty happening across the water as well. Construction cranes, dangling with cords hoisting parcels of wood, pipes, and cement blocks play in the far distance like marionettes on a stage. The rhythmic chuff of the pile driver softens as it crosses the water, reminding me of the sound of a coffee percolator.

I lean over the railing on the pier outside our shop and wait for Bret to meet me on his lunch break. A painting class is in full swing under the permanent white tents on the pier. Twelve painters with their backs to me and their easels facing east are painting the landscape of the West Village riverfront on white canvases.

I watch the students as a teacher silently moves through the easels, stepping back to observe their work. She touches the shoulder of one painter. She points. The artist nods, leans back, squints at his canvas, and then takes a step forward, dips a small brush on his palette, and paints a slim white seam along the top of an old factory building he has painted in detail. In an instant, the gray sky in his painting, hovering over the rooftops like old cotton, is suffused with light, changing the entire mood of his cityscape. Gram taught me about the power of contrast, using a light trim to heighten the vamp of a shoe, or a dark one to define it, but I've never seen the concept come alive with such a subtle placement of color. I'll remember it the next time I choose a trim.

Bret works at a brokerage house within walking distance of our shop. When we were together, he'd sometimes come and help on weekends when he needed a break from studying for his MBA. I admired that he never forgot his working-class roots and was able to roll up his sleeves and do good old-fashioned manual labor when it was called for. I think if we needed help with an order and we asked him to come over today, he would still pitch in for old times' sake.

In the distance, I see him, walking briskly toward me in his suit, his beige Burberry trench flapping open in the breeze. Bret finishes the last bite of an apple and tosses the core into the Hudson River. I'm genuinely proud of him and all he's accomplished; but I also worry. He's the only man I know who has it all, but the man who has it all can top himself only one way: by getting *more*. I think of Chase and her dazzling smile. Is she *more*? When Bret reaches me, he gives me a kiss on the cheek. 'So fill me in. Tell me everything about the business.'

'Gram has been borrowing against the building to keep the business afloat. Alfred looked at the books and said she needs to restructure her debt.'

'How can I help?'

'I think Alfred is using this as an excuse to have Gram retire and sell the building. He'd be cashing in on sky-high real estate, but it would mean the end of the Angelini Shoe Company. Which would leave me—'

'Without a place to work. Or a home.'

'Or a future,' I add bluntly.

'What does Gram want to do?'

'She told him she's not ready to sell. But, between you and me, she's scared.'

'Look, she's sitting on prime real estate. We have guys who handle that.'

'I don't want you to help her sell it. I want you to help me buy it.'

Bret's eyes widen. 'Are you serious?'

'You know how much this business means to me. It's everything. But I don't have much money saved, nowhere near what it would take. I have no collateral. And while I'm close to being a master, there are still things I'm learning from Gram.'

'Val, this is tough. Alfred has your grandmother's ear.'

'I know! But I do, too. If I had an alternative plan, I think she'd consider it.'

'So you're looking for investors who would keep you in business while you figure out a way to buy the business outright?'

'That sounds good. I mean, I don't know anything about finance.'

'I know,' he says, smiling.

'But *you* do.'

'You know I'm here for you. Let me figure this out.' He takes my arm as he walks me back to Perry Street.

'Are you behaving yourself?' I ask.

'Like a conscientious altar boy. I know what I have at home, but thanks for reminding me.'

'Hey, that's why I'm here. I'm a foghorn for fidelity.'

Tess twirls in the stylist's chair to check the back of her brand-new haircut in the mirror. I lured my sister to Eva Scrivo's, the chicest hair salon in the Meatpacking District, with the promise of hip, modern hair.

Black leather chairs are lined up in front of floor-to-ceiling mirrors, filled with customers in the various stages of cut and color. One woman wears a headdress of massive fronds of tinfoil painted with bleach; another woman, with short, swingy champagne-streaked strands is getting a blow out, her hair pulled tight on the end of a round brush; another customer has her roots saturated with a purplish brown mixture while the ends of her hair stand away from her scalp like bike spokes.

'You were right, Val. I needed this. I was a boring soccer mom with that blunt cut.' Tess smiles. 'Not that there's anything wrong with soccer moms, because I *am* one.'

Scott Peré, the master of curly hair, fluffs Tess's chunky layers with one hand while looking at her reflection. 'I'm only gonna say this once, so listen up. Layers after thirty, girls. Layers.'

'I can think of a lot of things a woman needs after thirty, and layers aren't even in my top ten,' I tell him.

'Rule amendment,' he says. 'With your gorgeous skin you've got until forty.' Scott takes his comb and moves on to his next customer, who sits under a drying contraption that throws heat on her pin curls as it slowly gyrates around her head like a swirling metal halo.

I poach some smoothing cream from Scott's station and flip my head over and work it through. My cell phone rings in my purse. 'Grab that for me, Tess. It's Gram wondering where we are.'

'Hello.' Tess listens for a few moments. I put my hair in a topknot. 'This isn't Valentine. I'm her sister.' Tess hands me the phone. 'It's a man.'

'Hello?'

'I thought it was you. Sorry,' Roman says.

'Roman?'

138

'Sexy name!' Tess says approvingly as she takes her purse and goes to the counter to pay.

'I was calling to thank you for the other night,' Roman continues. 'I got your note. I carry it in my pocket.'

'I'm dreaming of that risotto.'

'Is that all?' He actually sounds disappointed. 'I was wondering when we could see each other again.'

'Do you need a haircut?' I ask him.

'No,' he laughs.

'Too bad. There's an open chair here and I'm pretty good with scissors.'

'I'm going to pass on the haircut, but not on you. Okay? But here's the hard part. I'm pretty much chained to this place.'

'It's the same for me in the shop. How about I call you for coffee? After lunch sometime?'

'That's good.'

I close the cell phone and slip it into my pocket. I meet Tess outside the salon. She motions to me as she talks to her husband. 'No special night. Absolutely not. You tell Charisma to stay away from that canned frosting, and Chiara is not allowed to sleep in our bed. Okay, honey. I'm going back to Gram's with Val. I'll be home by bedtime. Love you.' She hangs up her phone. 'Charlie has his hands full. Charisma was playing on his cell phone and called his boss by accident.' Tess looks at me. 'Well?'

'I had a date.'

'And?'

'And he's very interesting.'

'A Poindexter?'

'Not at all. He's hip.'

'Complicated?'

'Aren't they all?'

'Even my Charlie. Complicated even in his simple demands. He likes pasta every Tuesday, a movie on Fridays, and sex on Saturdays.'

Tess has never mentioned sex with her husband. Obviously, the haircut has freed her. I laugh. 'That's a doable schedule.'

'I'm not complaining. But you gotta watch out for the routine. You need to keep a man on his toes. Charlie's getting close to forty, and you know what happens. New car, new wife, new life.'

'That will never happen to you,' I promise my sister.

'It happened to Mom.'

'Yeah, but that was the eighties. Back then, it happened to everyone's mother.'

'History has a funny way of repeating itself.' Tess buries her hands in her pockets as we walk. 'Even Gram had her *problem* with Grandpop.'

I stop and face my sister. 'What?'

'Yeah, Mom told me that Grandpop had a . . . friend.'

'Are you serious?'

'I don't know her name or anything, but Mom told me about it before I got married.'

'And you didn't tell me?'

'As if tales of infidelity are some sort of heirloom we need to share like the family silver?'

'Still.' I feel bad that Gram hasn't confided this to me. 'Gram's never mentioned it.'

'You idolized Grandpop. Why would she?'

I unlock the front door to our building. Tess and I go into the vestibule. The door to the shop is propped open, the worktables are bare, and the small desk lamp throws off the only light in the room. There's a note on the desk in Gram's handwriting. 'Meet me on the roof – the chestnuts are in.'

We race up the stairs, out of breath as we reach the top. 'In my next life,' I gasp, 'I want to live in one of those fabulous lofts, all the space without the stairs.'

'The original assisted living,' Tess pants.

I push open the door to the roof. Gram has the grill going, with two large frying pans covered in tinfoil over the red charcoal flames. The smoke from the charcoal offsets the scent of sweet chestnuts as they roast, a delicious smell of honey and cream.

'They're good this year. Meaty,' Gram says, shaking the pan, gripping the handle with an oven mitt. She wears a kerchief over her hair, and her winter coat is buttoned to the top. 'Oh, Tess, I love your hair.'

'Thanks.' She tosses her head. 'Scott is very good. You should go to him, Gram.'

'Maybe I will.' Gram lifts the spatula off the hook on the side of the grill. She lifts the foil off one pan with her oven mitt, then she whacks the chestnuts with the flat side of the spatula, cracking them open. She scoops them onto a stainless-steel cookie sheet. Tess and I sit down on the chaise longue and take the tray. We blow on them, and then take one apiece, pulling the sweet, translucent chestnut out of its burnished shell. We pop them in our mouths. Heavenly.

'My mother hated chestnuts,' says Gram. 'When she was growing up in Italy, money was tight and they made everything with chestnuts – pasta, bread, cakes, fillings for ravioli. When her family emigrated, she vowed she'd never eat another chestnut. And she never did.'

'It just goes to show you, sometimes you can't shake the things that happened to you in childhood.' Tess looks off toward New Jersey, where her husband is probably locked in a garage while Charisma and Chiara paint the automatic doors with frosting.

'I'd like to shake some of the things that happened to me in adulthood,' I say as I crack open another chestnut.

The door to the roof swings open. 'Don't be alarmed, it's just me,' Alfred says as he places his briefcase by the door. He goes to Gram and gives her a kiss.

'This is a surprise,' says Tess as our brother kisses her on the cheek and then me.

'Gram called and said the chestnuts were in,' Alfred says stiffly.

'I'm glad you could make it.' Gram beams at

her only grandson with enough love to fill the boat basin on Pier 46.

'I've been to the bank,' he says, drawing a deep breath. 'They want some numbers, a new appraisal on your property.'

'Do you think we're going to be okay?' I stand up.

'I don't know yet, Valentine. There's still a lot of information to gather. The more I dig, the more I believe you should think about selling the building.'

'Oh, so you didn't come for the chestnuts, you came here to nail up a For Sale sign,' I tell him.

'Val, you're not helping,' Alfred says.

'And *you* are?' I shoot back.

Gram moves the chestnuts around with her spatula. 'Bring the brokers through, Alfred,' she says quietly.

'Gram . . . ,' I protest but she cuts me off.

'We have to, Valentine. And we're going to.' Her tone tells me the subject is closed. Alfred takes a chestnut from the tray Tess holds, cracks the shell, and eats it. I look at Tess, who looks at me. Then Tess says, 'Just don't forget Valentine, Gram. She's the future of the shoe company.'

'I think of my grandchildren first.' She takes the tray from Tess. 'All of you.'

CHAPTER 5

FOREST HILLS

There isn't a soul on the E train as Gram and I board at the Eighth Street station to go out to Queens. It's a quiet Sunday morning, but the evidence of a wild Saturday night is visible as we skirt empty liquor bottles and soda cans. As we push through the turnstile, the subway platform is filled with the pungent scent of motor oil and Dunkin' Donuts. I've never understood how the doughnut smell can waft down from street level but the fresh air can't.

A train pulls into the station, its dull gray doors open wide, and I quickly step in and scan the car to make sure it's *a good one*. A good car has no abandoned food on the seats, odd riders, or mysterious moisture on the floor. Gram chooses two seats in the corner and I sit down next to her. As the train lurches out of the station, Gram pulls the Metro section of the *New York Times* out of her purse and begins to read.

'You know this is a setup,' I tell her. 'We're going for Sunday brunch, but there's something else brewing. I'm very intuitive about these things.'

144

'Aren't we going to see the pictures from Jaclyn's wedding and watch the video?'

'That's only part of the agenda.'

Gram folds the newspaper into a square. 'Well, what do you think they're up to?'

'Hard to say. What do *you* think?'

I attempt to be direct with Gram, who is known to keep important details to herself, only to drop the bomb when there's a room full of relatives. When she doesn't answer me, I try another tack. 'Alfred called. What did he want?'

'He had a question about quarterly taxes. That's all.'

'I figured he already sold the building and the Moishe brothers were on their way to pack us up.'

She sets the paper down on her lap. 'You know, Valentine, I'm just trying to do the right thing for my family.'

I'd like to tell Gram that this time the right thing for her family is the wrong thing for the two of us. I've met with a real estate agent in the village, and there's simply no place to move the Angelini Shoe Company that we can possibly afford in the vicinity of Perry Street. The real estate agent found an empty loft space way out in Brooklyn, in an industrial area surrounded by auto-repair shops, a steel factory, and a lumberyard. The thought of moving our shop away from the Hudson River and the energy of Greenwich Village made me so sad, I never even went to look at the space.

'You understand why I'm on edge.' I look out the window.

'Nothing has happened yet.'

I nod. This is vintage Gram, and the very attitude that got us into trouble in the first place. And, I'm afraid I'm just like her. Denial provides temporary comfort, cushioned with hope and bound by luck, it's a neutral, an emotional state that goes with every-thing. Years may pass as we wait for the other shoe to drop, and in the meantime? Well, we're *fine*. We wait in hope. Denial does no damage until the last minute, when it's too late to salvage a situation. 'I'm sorry. I'm just nervous, that's all,' I tell her.

As the train pulls into the Forest Hills station, I help Gram stand. Her grip is strong, but her knees are unreliable, and lately, they're getting worse. It takes her longer to climb the stairs at night, and she's all but stopped her walks in the Village. I cut an article out of the *New York Times* about knee replacement and left it by her morning coffee, but when Gram read that there's a six-week recupera-tion period, it killed any possibility that she'd actually go in for the surgery. 'My knees are good enough,' she insisted. 'They got me this far, they can get me to the finish line.' Then she dropped the article into the recycling bin.

We take the escalator up to the street. I don't know what we would have done if she had to climb the stairs. I might've had to throw her on my back like the shepherd carrying the sheep in our Christmas crèche.

146

We emerge on the sidewalk facing Our Lady Queen of Martyrs Church where I attended mass every Sunday until I went to college. Gram takes my arm as we walk the two blocks to my family homestead.

'You know, sometimes I can't believe I grew up here,' I say as I take in the old neighborhood.

'When your mother told me that she was moving to Forest Hills after she got married, I almost died. She said, 'Ma, the fresh air.' Now, I'm asking you – is this air any better than our air in Manhattan?'

'Don't forget her pride and joy – her garden and her very own attached garage.'

'That was your mother's highest aspiration. To park her car where she lived.' Gram shakes her head sadly. 'Where did I go wrong?'

'She's a good mother, Gram, and a fine member of the Forest Hills bourgeoisie.' I take Gram's arm as we cross the street. 'Did she ever rebel?'

'I wish!' barks Gram. 'I hoped she'd become a hippie like all the other kids her age. At least that showed some moxie. I told your mother that every generation should take their culture by the collar and shake it. But the only thing your mother wanted to shake were martinis. To tell you the truth, I don't know where she came from.'

I know what Gram means. I used to pray for a feminist mother. My friend Cami O'Casey's mother, Beth, was a lean broomstick of a woman, with gray hair at thirty-six, who wore Jesus sandals and pounded her own oatmeal. She worked in a government agency in Harlem and wore cool buttons that said things like KILL YOUR TV SET and I LOVE YOU WITH ALL MY KIDNEY. Instead, I got Hollywood 'Mike,' with her wiglets and her tackle box full of makeup and that damned dressing room mirror surrounded by Greta Garbo lightbulbs. Cami's mother marched for peace while my mom sat around and waited for fishnet hose to come back in style.

To this day, my mother holds up current fashion trends like barbells. She knows when to shelve lime green because purple is the color of the moment. When big hair was huge in the eighties, Mom went for perms. She'd come home kinked, frizzed, and puffy, and when the curls weren't big enough, she'd throw her head upside down and spray her hair from the roots out until it stood away from her scalp like the rays over the head of Jesus on the Holy Sacrament tabernacle. Sometimes her hair was so big we worried that she might not fit into the car.

I prayed a novena in 1984 so my mother wouldn't get emphysema from all the hairspray she used. I did a science project on the devastation caused by aluminum chlorofluorocarbons, the powdery stuff in aerosol cans, especially Aqua Net. I showed my mother scientific proof that her beauty regimen could actually kill her. She just patted me on the head and called me 'My little Ralph Nader.'

When I wasn't praying to God to spare her life, I prayed my father wouldn't get asthma or worse from the secondhand hair-spray inhalation. I imagined the entire family dead from the fumes and the police finding us on the floor like a clump of Lincoln logs. When I told my mother my deepest fear, she said, 'But when the authorities find us, I bet my hair looks good.'

'Your mother's been landscaping again,' Gram says as we stand at the foot of the front walk of 162 Austin Street. 'It looks like Babylon came to Queens.'

The Roncalli Tudor is freshly painted and shel-lacked with chocolate brown and off-white trim over the entry porch. There are three brand-new, glossy holly bushes on either side of the entrance. There are two small English-style flower beds where plain grass would ordinarily grow. The plots are crammed with decorative pumpkins, squat autumn cabbages, and the last of the purple im-patiens, hemmed in by a slanting brick border on either side of the walk. Three hanging baskets spilling with shiny green leaves are suspended from the portico like the chickens in Chinatown. Over the front windows there's a United States flag unfurled next to the flag of Italy. The window boxes beneath them are stuffed with red, white, and green foil pinwheels that spin in the breeze. Cars are to Queens Boulevard what flora, fauna, and foil are to my mother's front yard. Everywhere you look, something is growing or spinning or swaying. My father may be a retired urban park ranger, but my mother has yet to allow him to put down his trowel.

'She doesn't know when to stop.' Gram takes a step onto the walkway. 'I wonder what she spends a year on Miracle-Gro.'

'A lot. The Burpee seed catalog is my mother's porn.'

'Hi, kids!' Mom pushes the front door open and runs down the sidewalk to greet us. 'Ma, you look like a jillion.'

'Thanks, Mike.' Gram gives Mom a kiss on the cheek. 'Your garden looks—'

'You know I hate grass. It's too country.'

Mom wears a long, white, raw-silk tunic with matching white slacks. The deep V neckline of the tunic is studded with flat turquoise beads. Her brown hair is blown straight to her shoulders, revealing extra large, silver hoop earrings. Her shoes, winter white suede mules with four-inch chunky heels, show off her slim ankles. Her left arm, from wrist to elbow, is covered in silver bangle bracelets. She jingles them. 'Very Jennifer Lopez, don't you think?'

'Very,' I tell her.

'I'm making custom omelets. Daddy is doing the French toast thing,' Mom tells us as we climb the stairs. 'Everybody is here.'

The interior design of my parents' home is an homage to the glory of the British Empire and a direct poaching of every room ever depicted in the Tudor style in *Architectural Digest* since 1968. Anything English is coveted by Italian Americans, because we respect whoever got there first. As a result, my mother adores cheery chintz, braided rugs, ceramic lamps, and oil paintings of the British countryside, which she has yet to visit.

150

Gram and I follow Mom to the kitchen, with its mod white appliances and white marble counters trimmed in black. Mom calls the color scheme 'licorice and marshmallow,' as nothing in Mom's life could ever be referred to as black and white.

Jaclyn has spread the photos from her wedding on the kitchen table. Alfred sits at the head of the table, but it's Tess, who sits on his right, who captures my attention. Her nose is red; she's been crying.

'Come on, you can't look that bad in the photos,' I tease Tess, but she looks away.

Amid the commotion of double cheek kisses and hellos, I motion to Tess to meet me in the bathroom. We stuff ourselves into the half bath, off the kitchen, that used to be a pantry. The floor-to-ceiling wallpaper in pink, green, and yellow polka dots in this tiny space makes me feel as though I've landed in a bottle of pills. 'What's the matter?'

Tess shakes her head, unable to get the words out.

'Come on. What is it?'

'Dad has cancer!' Tess begins to wail. My mother opens the door to the powder room, revealing Dad, Mom, Gram, Alfred, and Jaclyn crammed in the doorway as though we are in a moving train and they're on the platform saying good-bye.

One look at Dad's face tells me it's true.

'Air, I need air!' I shout. They disperse as we fan out into the kitchen. Dad grabs me and hugs me hard. Soon, Tess and Jaclyn are embracing him, too. Alfred stands back and away from it all with a grim expression on his already pinched face. Mom has her arm around Gram, big tears rolling down her face, yet miraculously, her mascara doesn't run.

'Dad, what happened?'

'I don't want you to worry. It's not a big deal.'

'Not a big deal? It's cancer!' Tess fights to regain her composure, but she can't. The tears continue to flow.

'What kind?' I manage to call out over the weeping.

'Prostate,' Mom answers.

'I'm so sorry, Dutch.' Gram takes my father's arm. 'What does the doctor say?'

'They caught it early. So, I'm weighing my options. I think I'm going to go with the seeds implanted in the nuts scenario.'

'Dad, do you have to call them . . . nuts?' Big tears roll down Jaclyn's face.

'I didn't want to say scrotum in front of your grandmother.'

'It's better than nuts,' Mom says.

'Anyway, evidently about seventy-five percent of men who reach my age have prostrate issues.'

'*Prostate*, honey.' From the tone of my mother's voice, I can tell she's been correcting Dad's phonics since the diagnosis.

'Prostate, prostrate, what's the damn difference? I'm sixty-eight years old and something's gonna get me. If it isn't a shit ticker,' Dad says, thumping his chest, 'it's gonna be cancer. That's the truth. I wanted you, my progeny, to know what I'm up against. And I wanted to tell you all in person, without spouses or the kids, so you could ingest the information firsthand. Naturally, I was also worried I'd scare the kids talking about my private areas. How the hell could I tell them that Grandpop has a problem in his pee-pee? It didn't seem right.'

'No, it wouldn't be right,' I whisper. I look at my father, who is the funniest person I know but doesn't have any idea he's funny. He's worked all his life as head of the parks department here in Forest Hills, until he retired three years ago and went to work for my mother as the family gardener/dustman. He scrimped and saved and put us all through college. He's been a willing costar to my mother, the lead, in the movie of their marriage. I never imagined anything bad happening to him because he was so stable. He wasn't a saint, but he was solid.

My mother puts her hands in the First Communion position. 'Look. We are facing this as a family, and we will beat it as a family.' The expression on her face is pure Joanna Kerns in the climax of *My Husband, My Life*, a TV weeper running in the repeat cycle on Lifetime. Mom takes a breath, hands still in the prayer position. She continues, 'The doctor tells us it's stage two . . .'

'. . . on a sliding scale of four,' Dad adds.

Mom continues, '. . . which is very good news. It means at his age, your father could easily outlive the cancer.'

I have no idea what my mother's explanation means, and neither does anyone else, but she forges on.

'I am galvanized. He is equally galvanized. And thank God for Alfred, who is on top of getting Daddy the top medical care in the country. Alfred is going to call his friend at Sloan-Kettering to get your father the A team.'

Alfred nods that he will make the call.

'We have magnificent children . . . grand-children' – Mom waves her arms around – 'a lovely state-of-the-art home, and a beautiful life.' She breaks down and weeps. 'We're young and we're gonna beat this thing. And that's that.'

'Good deal, Mike.' Dad claps his hands together. 'Who wants French toast?'

I drank way too much of the autumn-blend hazelnut coffee Mom served in the ornate sterling-silver urn with the spigot shaped like a bird's head. (Heirloom, anyone?) There's something about Mom's delicate Spode teacups and the bottomless urn that tricks you into believing you're consuming less caffeine than you really are. Or maybe I drank so much coffee because I was looking for an excuse to get up from the table from time to time, so I wouldn't cry in front of my father.

We managed to keep the patter light through breakfast, but occasional silences descended on us as our thoughts wandered back to Dad's terrible news. Conversation did not flow, it ricocheted

154

around the room, exhausting us. Attempting to be chipper in the face of my father's illness, a man who has never been sick a day in his life, is a tall order even for *Funnyone*.

The girls have cleared the brunch dishes from the table and are now sorting through the wedding pictures. Dad and Alfred are watching a football game in the den. The male bonding is evidently necessary after viewing wedding photos.

I've escaped to the backyard for air, but it's actually claustrophobic because the only open space is on the stone footpath that leads to an outdoor living suite of English cottage furniture. And that's not all. Artfully placed amid the dense landscaping is a clutter of traditional lawn ornaments including a sundial, a birdbath, and statuary of three Renaissance angels playing flutes. The reflection of my face in the blue medicine ball on a pedestal looks like a Modigliani, long and horsey and sad.

'Hey, kid,' Dad says from behind me.

'Why does Mom overdecorate *everything*?' I ask. 'Does she think if she keeps landscaping in the English style, Colin Firth is going to come over that wall and take a dip in the birdbath?'

I sit down on the love seat. Dad squeezes in next to me. We are sharing rear-end space the size of a single subway seat. 'This is the original Agony in the Garden.'

Dad laughs and puts his arm around me. 'I don't want you to worry about me.'

'I'm sorry, Dad, but I do.'

'I've been very blessed, Valentine. Besides, the big C ain't what it used to be. People walk around with cancer like good bridgework. It becomes a part of you, the doctors tell me. Remission can last until you're dead, for God's sake.'

'Well, I'm glad to see you have a positive attitude.'

'Besides, I haven't been a saint, Val. I probably had this coming.'

'What?' I turn and face my father, which, on this Barbie dream house of a love seat is not easy.

'*Mezzo-mezzo.*' He makes his hand into a flat wing and tips it. 'I mean I've tried to be a good father and a decent husband. But I'm human and sometimes I failed.'

'You're a good man, Dad. You failed very little.'

'Ah . . . enough for the marker to come due.'

'You didn't get cancer because you made mistakes in your life.'

'Of course I did. Look at the evidence. I didn't get lung cancer because God was mad I smoked. I get the cancer down below because I . . . you know.'

The mention of *you know* leaves us to our separate silences and memories. My dad remembers 1986 one way, and I remember it as a time when the very core of our family was shaken by my father's midlife crisis, and my mother's ability to negotiate it.

'I don't believe in a vengeful God,' I tell him.

'I do. I'm an old-fashioned Catholic. I believed

156

everything the nuns taught me. They said that God was watching me every second of every day, and that I'd better examine my conscience and beg God to forgive my sins before I went to sleep because *if* I accidentally suffocated during the night, without cleansing my soul, I'd go straight to hell. Then, when I became a teenager, they told me if I was even going to think about sex, I'd better marry her. And I did. But somewhere along the way, I started to think about God, and who He really is, and I came to the conclusion that He wasn't watching me, day in and day out, like the nuns said.'

'So what was He doing?'

'I figured He gave me life and then waved sayonara, saying, "You're on your own, Dutch." The rest was up to me. It was my job to live a good life and do the right thing. A soul is like an Etch A Sketch. When you screw up, it's like you're writing on it. But you have a chance to say you're sorry, turn it over, and shake it until the bad thing disappears. That's the notion of confession in a nutshell. The trick is to hit the finish line without a mark on your soul. I mean, you could say cancer is a good thing because it's giving me a chance to prepare. At least I'm being given the gift of a set time period. Most people get a lot less.'

My eyes fill with tears. 'I never want you to die, Dad.'

'But I'm gonna.'

'But not now. It's too soon.'

'I want to be ready, though. Then, if there's

actually a judgment day like the nuns promised, I'll have minded my p's and q's. God will show up at the end as He did in the beginning, and check to see if I've done okay. What more can a man ask for? I wouldn't mind seeing the face of God. What the hell.'

'Dad, I think you're a Buddhist.'

My father has never been eloquent, especially where his feelings are concerned. But no matter what he didn't say, I knew he loved us, and he loved us deeply. But I never knew that he had a spiritual philosophy. I figured he didn't need one because he didn't have a bad bone in his body. 'Dad, you've never talked about God to me.'

'I left that up to the church. We hauled you to mass every week for a reason. Those people are in the redemption business. Let's face it,' he says, crossing his hands on his lap and continuing, 'I'm not a holy man by a long shot, but I did have to ask myself the big question: What about me, Dutch Roncalli, is eternal?'

'And what's the answer?'

'The acre forest at park 134. When I was made an urban park ranger in 1977, I was given the responsibility of planting and maintaining a two-acre green space in the center of the park with a natural pond and a surrounding grove of fir trees. It can never be sold, just like the land in Central Park. By law, the natural habitat must be maintained in perpetuity. So, it's my little gift to the future generations of the borough of Queens. Small stuff, but to me, eternal.'

'That's great, Dad.' I take a deep breath. 'But don't you think your children are your legacy?'

'I can't take credit for what you and Tess and Jaclyn and Alfred have become. You kids are like those hamsters you had to raise in the second grade. You're strictly loaners. I just took care of you until you could take care of yourselves.'

'But you loved us, too.'

'Absolutely. And, as fathers go, I look damn good on paper. None of you on drugs, none of you gamblers or bookies. Nobody with a tic. But that's to your mother's credit. All of you are successful in your fields. And you, taking up the shoemaking and taking care of your grandmother. That says a lot about you. You will be repaid, Valentina.'

My father is the only person in my life who puts an *a* on the end of my name, and to hear him say it brings me great comfort.

Then he says, 'Somebody's gonna take care of you when you're old. Payback.'

'I hope you're right.'

'Some guy would do the Watusi for a shot at such a good wife.'

'Me?'

'You. You've got a big heart. Of all the kids, you're the most like me. You didn't spring out of the womb knowing all the answers, like Alfred. You didn't have a master plan, like Tess. And you never relied on your pretty face, like Jaclyn. You've worked hard for everything you've ever gotten. That's why you're funny. You needed a sense of humor when things didn't work out the way you hoped. And the same is true for me. Things didn't always go my way. But I never gave up. And I don't want you to give up.'

'I won't.' I squeeze my dad's hand.

'I want you to find a nice guy.'

'Know anybody?'

Dad puts his hands in the air. 'That's up to you. I don't get involved in those matters.'

'To tell you the truth, I've met somebody.'

'Really?' Now it's Dad's turn to shift in the tiny seat and get a jab in the hips. I adjust to make room for his 360 degrees. 'What does he do?'

'He's a chef. Italian.'

'Real Italian? Or is he Albanian or Czech? You know, nowadays they come over here with an accent and open pizza parlors like they're authentic sons of Mama Leone when us real Italians know the truth.'

'No, no, he's real Italian, Pop, from Chicago.'

'So, what do you think about this *paisano*?'

'I don't know, Dad.'

'You know what? You don't have to know everything. Sometimes, it's better not to.'

A Forest Hills Sunday-afternoon quiet descends on the garden, like old fog. The arm of the love seat pinches my thigh, but I don't shift. I want to sit next to my father as long as I can, just the two of us, he with his theories of religion, love, and the eternal nature of trees, and me, hoping that he'll be around for the turns my story will take.

I reach out for my father's hand, something I

haven't done since I was ten years old. He grips it tightly, as though he will never let go. Dad looks off into the Buzzacaccos' yard, with its fire engine red picnic table, shriveled hedges, and crumbling statue of the Venus de Milo (with arms). I look up at the house. My mother stands in the kitchen window watching us with a face so sad, now she's the Modigliani.

The wheels on the brush machine whirl as I crank the pedal. I put my hand in a cotton mitt and then place a soft pink leather pump over the mitt. I brace the heel with my free hand and place the shoe between the round brushes. I buff the vamp of the shoe until the leather looks like an iridescent pink seashell.

One of the joys of working with leather is finding the patina. Sheets of new leather from the tanners are lovely, but new leather without a cobbler's expertise is just a hide. In the hands of a craftsman, the same animal flank becomes art. Hand-tooled leather develops its own personality; etching and embossing give it a pattern, while buffing gives it character. And character makes it one of a kind.

Sometimes it takes days of resaturating the leather with dye, letting it dry, then polishing and buffing for hours to acquire a shade that pleases the eye and is appropriate for the shoe. Then I give the leather a pearlized depth by manual brushing. I can see grades and tones in the surface that change in the light; deep veins in the fiber give a look of age, and the sheen provides a layer of energy for the final product. My grandmother has taught me that the palette for leather and suede is limitless, like musical notes. One persnickety bride wanted her shoes dyed Tiffany blue to match the box her engagement ring came in. It took me a month to get the right saturation of color, but I did it.

I place the second shoe on my left hand, guiding it under the brushes with my right. I hear a tapping on the front window of the shop. Bret waves to me and I motion for him to meet me at the entrance.

'You're up early,' he says as I hold the door open and usher him in.

'That's the shoemaker's life. And evidently the same is true for the barons of Wall Street.' I check the clock. It's 6:30 A.M. I've been working in the shop since 5:00.

'I've got some information for you.' Bret sits down on the rolling stool at the cutting table. I sit down next to him. He opens a file. 'I've done some digging. Let me start out by saying that you're in the worst possible profession to get investors.'

'Great.'

'Fashion is a wild card. Many more failures than successes. Completely dependent upon the whims of the marketplace and individual spending habits. Designers are artists, and therefore considered unreliable in the business world. In a word, hand-crafted anything is on shaky ground for investment purposes.' I find it odd that anything as necessary to human beings as shoes could be viewed as risky, but Bret continues, 'Unless you're Prada, or some other venerable family company that the conglomerates are looking to buy.'

'Does it matter that the business has been here since 1903?' I ask.

'It helps. It shows a level of quality and craftsmanship. That's good. But it also says *rarified* to the investor.'

'What do you mean?'

'It means that your name has exposure to a very small audience, and that wedding shoes are luxury items. Given the current economy, investors aren't looking at luxury goods for a return on their money. Right now, in fashion, it's all about trends and a low sticker price. That's why you see so many celebrities with clothing lines. Target, H & M, even Wal-Mart, all have a stake in low-priced high fashion. They're the guys financing the trend.'

'Well, we don't do what they do.'

'What you could do, and what all major designers do eventually, is lease your name and your designs. You get them mass-produced and you get a portion of the revenue stream. But even then, somebody has to believe there's a market for you.'

'All the major wedding designers have used us from time to time. Vera Wang used to send girls down here regularly until she started manufacturing shoes with her own name on them.'

'That proves my point exactly. Traditional designers are getting the portion of the business you *should* be getting when they start their own affordable secondary lines. Val, if we're going to get Angelini Shoes back in the black by finding a team of investors to make you more liquid, then you need a product that is stylish but can be mass-produced for maximum sales and profit.'

'I don't even know if Gram would let me sell our designs. I mean, they're my great-grandfather's.'

'Then you'll have to design something new. Something that reflects the Angelini brand, but is your own creation. Then you wouldn't even need Gram's permission. The hard truth is that nobody is interested in a shoe shop that can produce three thousand pairs a year. The profit margin is too small. But your classic wedding shoes can become the flagship items in a broader portfolio. You can continue to make one-of-a-kind shoes. As a matter of fact, you have to – that's the Angelini hook. But you also need a product that can be mass-merchandised to pay off your existing debt, meet your balloon mortgage payments, and allow you to maintain a living and working space in one of Manhattan's fastest gentrifying neighborhoods. This is a tall order, Val, but if Angelini Shoes is going to make it in the twenty-first century, there's no other way.'

Bret leaves a file behind, full of research about luxury goods made by long-standing family businesses and how they work in the new century. There are spreadsheets filled with figures, and columns with comparisons, and graphs showing the growth of certain products in the last twenty years, as well as a chronicle of failed ventures. Family-owned businesses like Hermès, Vuitton, and Prada are cited. There is a section about buyouts of small enterprises by conglomerates (which seems to be the way of the world in fashion). I look around our shop, with its machinery from the turn of the last century, and our hand-drawn patterns on butcher paper, and wonder if it's even possible to make the Angelini Shoe Company a viable name in the age of mass-produced, machine-made goods. And even if it is, am I the one to do it?

The November sky over the Hudson River is a menacing lilac with a low row of Jasper Johns – style charcoal clouds threatening rain. Occasionally, the pumpkin-colored sun peeks through to throw light on the choppy river, its whitecaps showing teeth like the edge of a serrated knife. I pull the belt on my wool coat tight, yank the brim of my baseball cap down, and tuck my long chenille scarf inside my collar.

'Here.' Roman gives me a cup of hot coffee from the deli as he sits down on the park bench, propping his vintage black leather Doc Martens on the railing in front of us. He wears faded jeans and a chocolate brown leather motorcycle jacket that looks to be at least twenty years old, and on him, it's twenty years of sexy. Roman leans back on the bench as a runner with a chapped pink face jogs by. Roman puts his arm around me.

'It was nice of you to call,' I tell him.

'Between your shoes and my gnocchi, I only see you about half as often as I would like to.'

Roman came over when I told him I was taking a coffee break on the river. He could tell something was bothering me when I went over to the restaurant and helped him prep a supply of eggplant, and today, while we were talking on the phone, I finally told him about my father's diagnosis. I hadn't wanted to tell him because there's nothing worse than bad news when a romance is in full bloom. One of us (him) would wind up being in charge of cheering up the other one (me). Who needs that?

Roman sips his coffee. 'What kind of man is your father?'

I look across the river as though the answer lies somewhere on the shores of lower Tenafly. Finally, I say, 'He's Tuscan leather.'

Roman laughs. 'What does that mean?'

'Tough hide, soft underside. Not glamorous. Durable. But very versatile. A lot like me. When he learns a lesson, he learns it the hard way.'

'Give me an example.' Roman pulls me closer, partly for warmth and partly because when we're together, we can't hold each other enough.

'Dad was an urban park ranger in Queens and he went to a convention in upstate New York in the summer of 1986. When he was there, he met a woman named Mary from Pottsville, Pennsylvania.'

'Seriously?'

'I know. *Pottsville*. My mother would have much

preferred he fool around with a woman from fancy Franklin Lakes or ultraglam Tuxedo Park, but when you're the wife, you don't get to choose. Anyhow, my dad came home from the convention and everything seemed normal, except he suddenly grew a mustache and got contact lenses. I was only a kid but I kept looking at him and thinking, "That mustache looks like a mask. What's Dad hiding?"'

'How did your mom find out?'

'She got an anonymous phone call one day while he was at work. When she hung up, she turned the color of iceberg lettuce, went into her bedroom, closed the door, and called Gram. But even as kids, we knew that my mother would never share bad news with us. So Tess, my older sister, wisely listened on the extension. When Mom hung up the phone, she put a plan in place. She very quietly packed us up and moved us right here to Perry Street with Gram and Grandpop. Of course, Mom never said she was leaving Dad. She simply invented a whole story about taking the summer to "rewire the Tudor," leaving Dad in Queens to "oversee the electricians."'

'So everyone was pretending.'

'Exactly. Mom told Gram she needed time to think. But no one ever addressed with us kids what was actually going on, so we just lived in a total fog.'

'Did your father ever explain what was happening?'

'He came into the city every Sunday to have

dinner with us, but Mom would disappear somehow, you know, make an excuse about running an errand or meeting a friend or something. Now I know she couldn't bear to see him. I found out recently that she went to the movies every time Dad came to see us. She saw *Flashdance* nine times that summer. It spawned her lifetime love of off-the-shoulder sweaters.'

'I really can't wait to meet your mother,' he says wryly.

'Then, after a couple of months, Mom regrouped. She pulled a George Patton and began to strategize how to save our family. It turns out Dad is a security junkie. He's all about safety. He checks every single window and door before he goes to bed. Mom was the adventuress. Dad was the responsible one. Mom knew that he would never give up the security of a wife for the unknowns of Mistress Mary in Pottsville.'

I take a sip of coffee before continuing. 'She never mentioned the affair. Ever. She just removed herself from Dad's world and let him experience life without her for a while. Believe me, if you knew my mom and suddenly she was gone, you'd miss the sheer force of her. She was deeply hurt, but she also knew that if she disappeared from his life, he would remember why he fell in love with her in the first place.'

'Did it work?'

'Absolutely. And I got to watch my parents fall in love for the second time. Trust me. There's a reason parents are romantic figures *before* their children are born – it's because the children can't take it. I'd catch my mother on my father's lap when I came home from school. Once I even caught them making out in the kitchen. My mother was so adorable and easygoing and present in the relationship that Dad couldn't resist her. Suddenly, Mary from Pottsville was, well, Mary from Pottsville. She could never be Mike from Manhattan.'

'I never saw my parents romantic with each other.'

'Why would you? Your poor mother was exhausted from the family restaurant. Who feels romantic after twelve hours of making meatballs, frying smelts, and baking bread? I wouldn't.'

'And Mom is still killing herself in that kitchen, while my dad wears a suit and chats up the customers. He's the old-school restaurateur. But it works for them.'

'You know what Gram said to my mother after she got back with my father?'

'What?'

'She said, "Keep him on a long leash, Mike." In other words, don't make him pay for a mistake for the rest of his life. Let him go, trust him. And Mom did.'

'You know what?' Roman says. 'I like the idea of a long leash.'

'I figured you would.' I put my arms around his neck. As we kiss, I think about the many times I've walked the riverfront alone and seen couples kiss on these benches, and turned away because I wondered when and if I'd ever find someone to share a kiss and a coffee break with on a cloudy day. Now he's here, and I wonder what he's thinking.

'I'm marinating a flank-steak special,' he says as he stands.

I throw my head back and laugh. He pulls me up from the bench. 'What is so funny?'

'I must be some kisser for you to be dreaming of marination.'

He pulls me close and kisses me again. 'You have no idea what I'm dreaming about,' he says, taking my hand. 'Come on. I'll walk you back.'

'What'd I miss?' I hang up my coat in the entry and enter the workshop, which is in full shipping mode. Gram is tucking peau de soie pumps into our signature red-and-white-striped shoe-boxes. June covers the shoes in a rectangle of red-and-white-striped tissue paper, places the lid on top, and affixes our logo, a gold crown with simple foil letters stamped ANGELINI SHOE COMPANY.

'Seventy-five pairs of eggshell beige pumps to Harlen Levine at Picardy Footwear in Milwaukee,' June says as she loads a box into a crate. 'And now, I could use a beer.'

'Autosuggestion.' I pull my work apron on.

'We're expecting the Palamara girl any minute,' Gram reminds me. 'I'm going to have you measure her for the pattern.'

'Okay.' This is a first. Gram usually does the measurements. I look at June, who gives me an enthusiastic thumbs-up.

There's a knock on the entrance door. The wind off the river is so strong, the bride-to-be practically blows into the shop when I open the door for her.

Rosaria is twenty-five years old, with a full face, black eyes, a small pink smile, and straight blond hair. Her mother had her wedding shoes made here, and Rosaria is carrying on the tradition. 'I'm so excited.' She rummages in her purse. 'Hi, every-body,' she says without looking up. Then she pulls a magazine article, stapled to a larger sheet of paper with a hand-drawn sketch of the dress, out of her purse.

'Here's my gown. I copied an Amsale.'

'Lovely.' Gram hands the picture and sketch to me. 'Valentine is going to make your shoes from start to finish.'

'Great.' Rosaria smiles. The sketch shows a simple empire-waist gown in silk faille. It has a square neck and a sheer cap sleeve. 'What do you think?'

'It's very *Camelot*,' I tell her. 'Have you ever seen *Camelot*?'

She shakes her head that she hasn't.

'Don't you watch old movies with your grand-mother?'

'Nope.'

June laughs. '*Camelot* is not an old movie.'

'It's old to them. It's forty years ago,' Gram says, continuing to pack shoes into the boxes.

171

'You're getting married next July. Were you thinking of a sandal?'

'I'd love a sandal.'

I pull a book off the desk to show her the variations of the Lola design. She shrieks and points to a sleek linen sandal piped in pale pink with crisscross straps. 'Oh God, that one!' she says, pointing.

'You got it. Take off your shoes and we'll take the measurements.'

Rosaria sits down on a stool and removes her shoes and socks. I take two precut pieces of butcher paper off the shelf and write her name in the upper-right corner of both pieces. I place them on the floor in front of Rosaria, then help her step onto the center of each piece of paper. I trace around her right foot, making a pencil mark between each toe. I do the same for the left foot. She steps off the paper. I cut two pieces of thin twine off the wheel on the desk and measure the strap length for the top of her foot. I do the same for the ankle strap. I mark the string and put it in an envelope with her name on it. 'Okay, now the fun part.' I open the closet of embellishments for Rosaria, who looks at the shelves and the clear plastic bins like a little girl who has landed in a treasure chest full of jewels and can choose anything she wishes.

We are very proud of the components we use to make shoes. Gram travels to Italy every year to buy supplies. When you cook, it's all about quality ingredients, and the same is true for making shoes. Sumptuous fabrics, fine leather, and hand-tooled

172

embellishments make all the difference and define our brand. Loyalty plays into Gram's work ethic also. She buys our leather and suede from the Vechiarelli family of Arezzo, Italy, the descendants of the same tanner my great-grandfather used.

Most cobblers have farming in their background. The Angelinis were farmers who became butchers. Butchers often got into the tanning business because it was more profitable to sell the prepared leather instead of selling the skins. My great-grandfather made the leap from butcher to shoemaker as a result of timing.

Early in the twentieth century, a movement occurred in Italy in which artisans (shoemakers, jewelers, tailors, potters, silver-and goldsmiths, glass makers) taught young men who desperately needed work the trade of their choice. The masters would go into small villages and teach classes in their area of expertise. The apprentice system is a mainstay in the working life of Italians, but this particular movement was as political as it was artistic, born of the need to lift the Italians out of poverty after the war. The movement spread, thus the proliferation of handcrafted Italian goods, some of which still exist today. For the families who trained together, and opened their own businesses, branding was born.

Gram buys the leather for our shoes in Arezzo, and the nails and binding from La Mondiale, the oldest cobbler supplier in Italy. For embellishments, she goes down to Naples, where she works with a young, creative team, Carolina and Elisabetta D'Amico, who create handmade jeweled ornaments for shoes. Gram often provides a rough sketch of what she wants, as well as choosing from their extensive stock. The D'Amicos make buckles and ornaments inlaid with gleaming crystals – white-hot rhinestones; dazzling faux emeralds, rubies, and cabochons. Their costume-jewel embellishments are so opulent, we call them *Verdura* for the feet, as they could easily be mistaken for the real thing.

We also carry a wide selection of handmade fabric ornaments, including velvet bows so delicate we position them on the thin leather straps with tweezers before sewing them on. We carry silk-flower embellishments, bold calla lilies made of raw silk, innocent daisies of organza and tulle, and silk rosettes in every color combination, from ruby red to deep purple spiked with moss green velvet leaves. We have a selection of tiny numbers and letters, cut out of metallic gold, silver, and copper leather, which we often sew into the shaft of the shoe. We often place the bride and groom's initials or the date of the wedding inside the shoe for an heirloom touch.

Rosaria looks with wonder at the clear plastic trays of rosettes. First she picks up the cornflower blue roses, because that's the color her bridesmaids are wearing. She is intrigued by the strips of round-cut clear crystals on satin streamers, but decides they are too disco for her taste. After much deliberation, she settles on the antique cream rosettes. Then she calls her mother for her approval.

I give the sketches of Rosaria's feet to June, who places the patterns in her bin. I pull an index card from the desk drawer and make notes. I put all of the dimensions of Rosaria's feet on the card, then staple the fabric swatch and bin number of the rosettes. I staple the envelope with the string measurements to the card as Rosaria, giddy with delight, tells her mom every detail. She is as excited about the shoes as she is about her gown. Rosaria hangs up with her mother and turns to Gram. 'I feel so proud that I'm carrying on my mom's tradition.'

'When is your final fitting?' I ask.

'May tenth, at Frances Spencer's, in the Bronx.'

'I know it well. Best knock-off seamstress in the five boroughs. I'll be there with your shoes so they can do the final hem with the heel you'll be wearing.'

'Thank you.' Rosaria gives me a hug, takes her purse, and goes.

I jot down Rosaria's fitting date on the card and then open the file case on the desk.

'I'm giving Rosaria the shoes as my gift,' Gram says, not looking up from her work. 'No charge.'

'Okay.' I mark the receipt. This is a bad time to be giving away shoes. 'Are you sure?'

'I'm sure.' Gram takes the shoes she has been working on and wraps them in cotton.

'You know, with Alfred checking our numbers . . .'

'I know. But Alfred isn't running this business. I am.'

June looks at me and raises her eyebrow as if to say, *Don't argue with her*.

I tack up the order. On the bulletin board, I see a note in Gram's handwriting. It says: 'Meeting with Rhedd Lewis at Bergdorf's, on December 5, 10 A.M. Bring V.'

'Gram, what's this?'

'You remember that costume lady from the movie? Debra McGuire? Well, she may have been prickly, but she liked us. So she recommended us to Rhedd Lewis at Bergdorf's, who asked to meet with us.'

'Did she say why?' I can hardly contain my excitement.

'She didn't. Maybe she's getting married and needs shoes.'

'Or maybe she wants to put our shoes in the store!' My mind reels with the possibilities of supplying the most elegant department store in New York City with our shoes. This is exactly the kind of break Bret was hoping we would get. We need the big guns to recognize and support our brand. 'Can you imagine? Our shoes in Bergdorf's?'

'I hope not.' June puts her hands on her hips and turns to Gram. 'Remember when your husband put the shoes in Bonwit Teller's? It was a disaster. We hardly sold any stock. The word came back that brides didn't want to spend on their shoes when they had spent a pretty penny on their gowns.'

'That turned us off to department stores,' Gram admits. 'That was our first and last foray into big business.'

'Maybe it will be different this time. Look in any fashion magazine. Upscale shoppers are spending two grand on a purse without batting an eye. That makes our shoes look like a bargain. Maybe there's an opportunity here.'

'Or maybe you just go to the meeting, see what she says, and then go to the Bergdorf café and have the deviled eggs,' June says practically as she takes her shears and cuts a pair of size-eight soles from the pattern paper. June looks at me and smiles supportively, but she's been around this company long enough to know that it is highly unlikely Gram will change a thing about the way she conducts her business, even if it means she could lose the entire operation.

'Gram, I think we should go to the meeting with an open mind. Right?'

She doesn't answer me as a long, black limousine pulls up in front of the shop. It seems to stretch from the corner to the lobby door of the Richard Meier building. As it parallel-parks, I see BUILDBIZ on the license plate.

A man in a crisp navy blue suit with a red tie hops out the back door followed by my brother. The wind kicks up their silk ties like kite tails as they head for our entrance.

'What's Alfred doing here?' I ask.

'He called while you were out with Roman. He's bringing a broker by to see the building.'

I look at June. Our eyes meet but she looks away quickly.

'Hello, ladies,' Alfred says as he comes into the shop. He goes to Gram and kisses her on the cheek. Gram beams with pride as Alfred turns to the man and introduces her. 'This is my grandmother Teodora Angelini. Gram, this is the broker I told you about, Scott Hatcher. We went to Cornell together.'

Gram shakes his hand. Alfred puts his hands on his hips and looks around the shop as though June and I aren't there. It's a wonder to me how gregarious my brother is when he is around his peers. With family, he's morose. But at work, when he's on his game and personality plus is required, he's a pistol.

The broker is about six feet tall, a better-looking version of Prince Albert of Monaco, with a full head of hair. His eyes are wide and green, and he has the warm, fixed smile of a salesman.

'We're going to take a look around, Gram.' Alfred flashes her the fake businessman smile.

'Go right ahead,' she says.

'Let's start on the roof.' Alfred leads Scott up the stairs.

I sit down on my work stool. 'Well, the day I dreaded is here.'

'Now, don't be this way,' Gram says softly.

'How should I be?' I pick up the laces for my boot and take them to the ironing board. I plug in the iron and bury my hands deep in my pockets as I wait for it to heat.

June puts down her shears and says, 'I need a coffee. Can I bring you girls anything?'

'No thank you,' I tell her.

June slips on her coat and dashes out the door.

'June can smell a fight,' Gram says quietly.

'I'm not going to fight with you. I just wish you'd get your game on.'

'Bergdorf's isn't going to save us. The one thing I'm certain of is that there's no magic solution in business. You're climbing a mountain here, pick, step, pick, step.'

Suddenly, Gram's old aphorisms sound ancient and irrelevant. Now I'm angry. 'You don't even know what the meeting is about. You didn't ask. Why don't we just put a Closed sign on the door and give up?'

'Look, I've been down every road with this business. We've been on the brink of closing more times than I can count. Your grandfather and I almost lost it after his father died in 1950. But we held on. We survived the sixties, when our sales dipped to nothing because the hippie brides went barefoot. We made it through the seventies, when manufacturing overseas quadrupled, and then we rode the wave of the Princess Di years in the eighties when everybody went formal with their weddings and required custom gowns and shoes. We brought the business out of debt, and went into profit – and I designed the ballet flat to hang on to the market share we were losing to Capezio.' She raises her voice. 'Don't you dare imply that I'm a quitter. I've fought and fought and fought. And I'm tired.'

'I get it!'

'No, you don't. Until you've worked here every day for fifty years, you can't possibly know how I feel!'

I raise my voice and say, 'Let *me* buy the business.'

'With what?' Gram throws her hands in the air. 'I pay your salary. I know what you make!'

'I'll find the money!' I shout.

'How?'

'I need time to figure it out.'

'We don't have time!' Gram counters.

'Maybe you could give me the same courtesy you show your grandson and give me time to counter-offer whatever he comes up with.'

Alfred comes into the shop. 'What the hell is going on?' he says sharply as he motions toward the hallway where Hatcher is inspecting the stairs.

'I want to buy the business and the building,' I tell my brother.

He laughs.

The sound of his cruel laughter goes through me, devastating my self-confidence, as it has all my life. Then he says, 'With what? You're dreaming!' He waves his arms around like he already owns the Angelini Shoe Company and 166 Perry Street. 'How could you possibly afford – *this*? You couldn't even buy the iron.'

I close my eyes and fight back the tears. I will not cry in front of my brother. I won't. I open my eyes. Instead of buckling, as I always do, I find the deepest register of my voice and say definitively, 'I am working on it.'

Scott Hatcher appears in the entry, puts his hands in his pockets, and looks at Gram. 'I'm prepared to make you an offer. A cash offer. I'd like to buy 166 Perry Street, Mrs Angelini.'

I pull my knit hat down tightly over my ears, which sting from the cold. As I walk through Little Italy on this Tuesday night, the streets are empty, and the twinkling arbor over Grand Street looks like the last tent pole left to strike before the traveling circus leaves town. I turn onto Mott Street. I push the door to Ca' d'Oro open. The restaurant is about half full. I wave to Celeste, behind the bar, and go back to the kitchen.

'Hi,' I say, standing in the doorway.

Roman is garnishing two dishes of osso buco with fresh parsley. The waiter picks them up and pushes past me to go into the dining room. Roman smiles and comes over to me, kissing me on both cheeks before pulling the hat off my head. 'You're frozen.'

'It's gonna get worse when I'm jobless and home-less.'

'What happened?'

'Gram got an offer on the building.'

'Want to come and work with me?'

'My gnocchi is like Play-Doh and you can't count on my veal. It's rubbery.'

'I take back my offer then.'

'How do you do it, Roman? How do you buy a building?'

'You need a banker.'

'I have one. My ex-boyfriend.'

'I hope you ended it nicely.'

'I did. I'm not one for drama in my personal life. Which is a good thing given how much drama there is in my professional life.'

'What did your grandmother say?'

'Nothing. She heard the offer, put down her work, went upstairs, got dressed, and went to the theater.'

'Did she actually tell the guy she'd sell him the building?'

'No.'

'So maybe she's not going to do it.'

'You don't know my grandmother. She never gambles. She goes with the sure thing.'

Roman kisses me. My face warms from his touch, it's as though the warm Italian sun has come out on this bitter-cold night. I feel a draft from the back door, propped open with an industrial-size can of San Marzano crushed and peeled tomatoes. I put my arms around him.

'Have you noticed that since our first date, I've brought nothing to the table but bad news? My father got cancer and I have business problems?'

'What does that have to do with us?'

'It doesn't seem to you like I'm walking bad luck?'

'No.'

'I'm just standing here braced for more bad news.

Come on. Lay it on me. Maybe you're married and have seven screaming kids in Tenafly.'

He laughs. 'I don't.'

'I hope you're careful when you cross the street.'

'I am very careful.'

The waiter enters the kitchen. 'Table two. Truffle ravioli.' He looks right through me, and then, impatiently, at his boss.

'I should go,' I say, taking a step back.

'No, no, just sit while I work.'

I look around the kitchen. 'I'm good at dishes.'

'Well, get to it then.' He grins and turns back to the stove. I take off my coat and hang it on the hook. I pull a clean apron from the back of the door and slip it over my head, tying it around my waist. 'I might like you more than Bruna,' he says.

I catch my reflection in the chrome of the refrigerator; for the first time today, I smile.

CHAPTER 6

THE CARLYLE HOTEL

Gram and I are right on time for our meeting with Rhedd Lewis at Bergdorf Goodman. Gram gets out of the cab and waits for me on the corner as I pay the driver. I scoot across the seat and join her on the corner of Fifty-eighth Street and Fifth Avenue.

Gram wears a simple black pantsuit with a chic, oversize sunburst pendant on a thick gold chain around her neck. The hem of her pants breaks in a soft cuff on the vamp of her gold-trimmed black pumps. She holds her black leather shoulder bag close to her. Her posture is straight and tall, like the mannequin posing in a Christian Lacroix herringbone coat directly behind her in the department store window.

The exterior of Bergdorf's is stately; it was once a private home, built in the 1920s, with a soft gray sandstone exterior accented with lead-glass windows. It was one of several grand residences built in Manhattan by the Vanderbilt family. This corner lot is one of the most prestigious in all of New York City, as it overlooks the grand piazza of the Plaza Hotel to the north, while it faces Fifth Avenue to the east.

Gram smiles at me, her bright red lipstick applied beautifully. 'I love your suit.'

I'm wearing a b michael, a navy silk-wool cropped jacket with a generous pilgrim collar and matching wide-leg trousers. I made the designer a pair of shoes for his mother, so this suit is a barter deal. 'You look great, Gram.'

We enter the store through the revolving door at the side entrance. This part of the store resembles a solarium except that the glass cases are filled with designer handbags rather than exotic plants. The blond wood-parquet floor is lit by a chandelier drenched in honey-colored prisms. Gram and I head straight for the elevators and our meeting. I have high hopes, and Gram has done her best to temper my expectations.

As we get off the elevator on the eighth floor, it's quiet, even the phones ringing on a soft pulse. There is no hint of the shopping bustle happening below us, in fact, it feels like we're in a tony Upper East Side apartment building rather than a suite of offices. The tasteful décor is a wash of neutrals, with the occasional pop of color in the furniture and artwork.

I check in with the receptionist. She asks us to wait on the love seat, covered in apple green moiré and trimmed in navy blue. The coffee table is a low, modern Lucite circle, with copies of the Bergdorf

185

winter catalog featuring resort wear fanned across its surface. I'm about to pick it up and peruse it when a young woman appears in the doorway. 'Ms Lewis will see you now. Please follow me.'

The young woman leads us into Rhedd Lewis's office, which has the subtle fragrance of green tea and pink peonies. The desk is a large, simple, modern rectangle covered in turquoise leather. The sisal carpet gives the room the fresh feel of a Greek villa by way of Fifth Avenue. The lacquered bamboo desk chair is empty. Gram and I take our seats on Fornasetti chairs, two sleek modern thrones with caramel brown cushions. Gram points to the park, beyond the windows. 'What a view.'

I rise up out of my chair. With the last of the autumn leaves gone, the bare treetops in Central Park look like an endless expanse of Cy Twombly gray scribbles.

'It must've been a dream to live in this grand house,' a woman's deep voice says from behind us. I turn around to see Rhedd Lewis in the doorway. I recognize her from her profile on Wikipedia. She's tall and willowy, wears red cigarette pants with a black cashmere tunic and a necklace that could only be described as a macramé plant hanger from the seventies. Somehow, the strange piece works. On her feet, she sticks with the classics, black leather flats by Capezio. She walks to the front of her desk, practically on tiptoe.

Rhedd Lewis is around my mother's age, and her upright posture and grand carriage are the tip-off that she was a dancer in a former life. Her honey blond hair is cropped short in wispy layers, with a fringe of long bangs that sweeps across her face like drapery. 'Thank you for slumming uptown.' She smiles, extending her hand to Gram. 'I'm Rhedd Lewis.'

'I'm Teodora Angelini and this is my partner, Valentine Roncalli,' Gram says. 'She's also my granddaughter.'

I hide my delight at Gram's announcement that I'm her partner (this is the first time she has ever said it!) by thrusting my hand toward Rhedd as if I'm handing her a flier for a sofa sale at Big Al's in the East Village.

'I love a family business. And when a young woman takes up the mantle, it thrills me. The best designers inherit the skill set. But don't tell anyone I said that.'

'Your secret is safe with us,' I tell her.

'And here's another one. When it comes to craftsmanship, there's nothing like the Italians.'

'We agree,' Gram says.

'Tell me about your business.' Rhedd leans against her desk, crosses her arms, and stands before us like a professor posing a challenge to her class.

'I'm an old-fashioned cobbler, Miss Lewis. I trust the old ways. I learned how to make shoes from my husband, who learned the trade from his father. I've been making wedding shoes for over fifty years.'

'How would you describe your line?'

'Elegant simplicity. I was born in December 1928, and my work is influenced by the times I grew up in. In the world of design, I like traditional trendsetters. I'm a fan of Claire McCardell. I admire the whimsy of Jacques Fath. When I was a girl in the city, my mother took me to the salons of designers like Hattie Carnegie and Nettie Rosenstein. It was a thrill to actually meet them. I didn't end up making hats or dresses, but what I observed became important when I set out to make shoes. Line, proportion, comfort, all these things matter when you're an artist making clothes.'

'I agree,' Rhedd says, listening intently. 'Who do you like now?'

Gram nods. 'In the shoe business, you can't beat the Ferragamo family. They get it right every time.'

'And your inspiration?' Rhedd smooths the necklace around her neck.

'Oh, I'd say – my girls.' Gram smiles.

'And who would they be?'

'Let's see. Jacqueline Kennedy Onassis, Audrey Hepburn, and Grace Kelly.'

'Simplicity and style,' Rhedd agrees.

'Exactly,' Gram says.

Whenever Gram makes cultural references, she refers to her holy trinity of style for women of a certain age: the First Lady, the movie star, and the princess. Born around the same time as Gram, their lives, while they didn't mirror her own, gave a context to her work. Jacqueline Onassis was all

188

about cut and line, built from the finest fabrics; Audrey Hepburn was a waif, her style influenced by dance, then exalted in theatrical evening wear that was embroidered and beaded; Grace Kelly had the cool classicism of the debutante turned working girl, gloves, hats, A-line dresses, tweed coats.

Gram points out that her muses wore the fashions, the fashions didn't wear them. Gram believes a woman should invest wisely and prudently in her wardrobe. Her philosophy is that you should own one gorgeous coat, one great pair of evening shoes, one good pair for day. She can't understand why women my age power-shop, as she, Gram, believes in quality over quantity. However, in other ways, my generation is a lot more like hers than she knows.

Gram's peers were born at the end of the Jazz Age. They had a certain inborn confidence in their abilities that my mother's generation had to struggle to find. Even though my mom's generation of women were rowdy feminists, Gram's group really blazed the path for them in the workplace; of course they would say that they *had* to. Gram's group included the young women who went to work in mills, factories, and shops when the men went off to fight in World War II. The jobs they held during the war went back to the men when they returned. Gram says that's how women ended up back in the kitchen in the 1950s. She went back to the kitchen, too, but it was up a flight of stairs after a full day of work in the

189

shoe shop. Gram was a working mother before that was a label. In her day, she said, she 'helped her husband,' but in fact, we know the truth – she was his full partner.

Rhedd circles around her desk, sits down, and leans forward. She adjusts the Tiffany clock and the ceramic pencil cup before her. Her computer screen is recessed into the wall next to her desk. Her screen saver is a black and white 1950s photo of the great model Lisa Fonssagrives, smoking a cigarette in a New Look gown at the intersection where Gram and I got out of the cab a few minutes ago.

'Ladies, my good friend Debra McGuire told me about you. Debra has a great eye. She brought me the shoes you gave her for the movie. I was very impressed.'

'Thank you,' Gram and I say at once.

'And it gave me an idea.' Rhedd gets up and goes to a tea cart under the windows. She pours herself a glass of water, and then two more, one for me and one for Gram. As she serves us, she says, 'We work about a year in advance on our holiday windows. And when I saw the shoe you made, it gave me an idea for the 2008 windows. I want to do brides. And a Russian theme.'

'Okay.' Gram thinks. 'Cut velvet, boots, calfskin, fleece.'

'Maybe. I'm looking for a one-of-a kind fantasy shoe, something that would be shown exclusively in *my* windows.'

'Interesting,' Gram says, but I can hear the skepticism in her voice. 'But you should know that we work from our company designs—'

'Gram, every pair of shoes we make is custom,' I interrupt and look at Rhedd. 'We've done fantasy styles for weddings. We did a pair of riding boots in white calfskin and black patent leather for a bride and groom who were married on a horse farm in Virginia.'

'That's true,' Gram admits. 'And we did a pair of mules in fire engine red satinet for a bride who was married to a fireman on the Lower East Side.'

'And there was the bride who married a Frenchman and we did a Madame Pompadour pump with oversize silk bows.'

'To be perfectly honest,' Rhedd says, 'I haven't had much luck with small shops like yours. Small companies, exclusive custom shoemakers, stay small for a reason. Usually, they know what they know and they're uncomfortable in a bigger venue. They lack a worldview, a vision.'

'We *have* a vision,' I assure her. I don't look at Gram as I make my point. The salesman in me comes out. 'We know we have to grow our brand, and we are taking a hard look at how we can do that in today's marketplace. We approach every customer as an opportunity to reinvent our designs. However, and you should know this, we are proud of our legacy. Our shoes are the finest made in the world. We believe that.'

Rhedd looks off toward the closed door behind

us as though she's expecting some big idea to walk into the room, but lucky for me, I think she heard it already. 'That's why I want to give you a chance.'

'And we appreciate it,' I tell her.

'A chance for you and for other shoe designers to give me what I need.'

'There are others?' Gram leans back in her chair.

'It's a competition. I'm meeting with several other designers, a custom shop from France, and a few well-known names who manufacture on a grand scale.'

'We're up against the big guys?' I take a sip of my water.

'The biggest. But if you're as good as you say' – her eyes narrow – 'you'll prove you have the talent and execution to pull this off.

'My creative director is going to come up with some sketches for the backdrop of the windows, the settings, if you will. I will select the wedding gowns for the tableaux, and from that group, we will choose one gown to send to you and the other designers. You will each design and build a pair of shoes for that gown. And then I will choose my favorite, and that designer will be brought on to do the shoes for all the gowns in the windows.'

My heart sinks a little. I was hoping that whatever she was going to offer us would be real, and timely. She's not an idiot, and she senses my disappointment.

'Look, I know this feels like a long shot, but if

you do what you say you can do, you have as good a chance as anyone to get the job.'

'That's all we need, Ms Lewis.' I stand and extend my hand to her. Gram rises and does the same. 'A chance. We'll show you how it's done.'

After our meeting with Rhedd Lewis, I sent Gram home to Perry Street in a cab, while I took the crosstown bus over to Sloan-Kettering to meet Mom. I BlackBerried my sisters with a cc to Alfred about the Rhedd Lewis meeting, telling them of the competition. Tess is good for a novena (we really need the prayers now), Jaclyn will be supportive, and the cc to Alfred was to show him that I do have a vision about the future of the company. I included a snapshot of Gram in front of the store for Mom, who likes a visual with her news.

The sliding doors of the hospital open as I approach. Once inside, I see my mother sitting on a couch by the windows facing a sunlit sculpture garden, typing on her BlackBerry like a wild game of Where Is Thumpkin. Her sunglasses are perched on her head like a tiara, and she is dressed from head to foot in baby blue, with a wide swath of beige cashmere thrown across her chest like a flag.

'I'm here, Mom.'

'Valentine!' She stands and embraces me. 'I'm so happy when it's your shift.' Mom has decided, that instead of all of us showing up for every single one of Dad's appointments, she would put her children on rotation so we wouldn't burn out. Of course, she is in attendance at every poke, prod, and MRI.

My mother has never suffered from burnout, nor does she shy away from a project before it's completed. I never saw her energy flag when it came to her family; she was and is eternally peppy, whether it was French-braiding three little girls' hair before school, negotiating through the mayhem of the holidays, or pouring concrete to form a new front walkway, she is up for anything. These days, it's getting my father well.

'I loved the picture. How did it go at Bergdorf's?'

'We're entering a competition to design a pair of shoes to win the holiday windows for Christmas 2008.'

'Fabulous! What a coup!'

'It's a long way to winning, Ma. We'll see what happens.' It doesn't even dawn on my mother that we might not win. Another reason to love her. 'So, how's Dad?'

'Oh, it's just boring test day. They're going to put the seeds in after Gram's birthday.'

Mom and I sit down. Instinctively, I put my head on her shoulder. Her skin has the scent of white roses and white chocolate. Her hoop earrings rest against my cheek as she talks. 'He's going to be fine.'

'I know,' I tell her. But I really *don't* know.

'We stay positive and we pray. That'll do the trick.'

I love that Mom thinks cancer is a trick that can be turned at will with a smile and a Hail Mary. When I lie in bed and think about my father and the future, I think of his grandchildren, and how, at the rate I'm going, he'll never meet my children. Sometimes I swear Mom can read my thoughts, and she asks, 'How's it going with the fella you're seeing?'

I lift my head off her shoulder. 'He's tall.'

'Excellent.' My mother nods her head slowly. In the pantheon of male attributes, my mother admires tall above full pockets or a full head of hair. 'Handsome?'

'I'd say so.'

'That's wonderful. Dad said he's a chef. I love that name, Roman Falconi. Sexy.'

'He owns his own restaurant down in Little Italy.'

'Oh, I'd love a chef in the family. Maybe he could teach me how to make those fancy foams they're doing at Per Se. I read about them in *Food and Wine*. Imagine the infusion of new ideas!'

'He's got a lot of those.'

'When is the unveiling?' Mom asks.

'I'm bringing him to Gram's birthday party at the Carlyle.'

'Perfect. Neutral ground. Well, my only advice in general is to take it easy. Don't force it.' My mother bites her lip.

'I won't.'

'I only hope you find the abiding happiness I

have with my Dutch. Your father and I are nuts about each other, you know.'

'I know.'

'We've had our troubles, God knows, all kinds of storms and rough waters on high seas. But somehow, we rode through it all and made it back to shore. Sometimes we even crawled, but we made it back.'

'Yes, you did.'

'I can say that we prevailed.'

'You did.'

'And, you know? *That's* what it's all about. A great philosopher said, something like, you know I can never remember jokes or the exact words of philosophers, but basically, he said that love is what you've been through together.'

'It was James Thurber. The American humorist and author.' Sometimes my BA in English comes in handy.

'Well, whoever. My point is, it seems to me we keep going through it.'

'You do, Mom.'

'Your father wasn't a saint. But I'm not the Blessed Mother either, am I?'

'I think you have more jewelry.'

'True.' She laughs. 'But I know he never wanted to hurt me, or you children. He just lost his mind for a while. Men go through their own version of the change in their forties, and your father was no exception.'

'Roman is forty-one.'

'Maybe he went through it last year, before you met him,' Mom says brightly.

'We can hope.'

Mom goes into her purse; when she snaps it open, a clean whoosh of peppermint and sweet jasmine fill the air. Sticking out of the pocket where the cell phone goes is a clump of perfume testers from the Estée Lauder counter. That's another of Mom's elegant-living tricks, she tucks paper bookmark perfume samplers in lingerie drawers, evening bags, purses, and car vents, wherever ambience is needed, and evidently, in my mother's view, you need ambience everywhere.

She finds the tinfoil sleeve of gum among the cancer pamphlets, punches a red square, hands it to me, then pops one in her own mouth. We sit and chew.

'Mom, how did you know you could get Dad back after the . . . incident?'

'I didn't do a thing.'

'Sure you did.'

'No, really, I just left him alone. The worst punishment you can give a man is to isolate him. I've never seen one who can handle it. Look at what being alone did to our priests. Of course, that's another subject entirely.'

'I remember when you and Dad fell in love again.'

'We were lucky, we got it back. Most people don't.'

'How did you do it?'

'I had to do what a single girl in your position has to do when she likes a guy. Never mind that I had four children and a college degree collecting dust. I had to make myself desirable again. That meant I had to show my best self to him at all times. I had to figure him out all over again. I had to redo the world we lived in, including the house and my wardrobe. But mostly, I had to be sincere. I couldn't stay with him for you, or for my mother, or for my religion, I had to stay with him because I wanted to.'

'So how did you know when you had succeeded?'

'One day, your father came home with a bag of groceries from D'Agostino's. You kids were at school. It was a few weeks after we got back together. Big week. First week of school . . .'

'September 1986. I was in the sixth grade.'

'Right. Anyway, he comes into the kitchen. And I was sitting there, filling out some form for one of you kids for school and he opens the fridge and unloads food into it. And then he lights up the burner on the stove and puts a big pot of water on the flame. Then he gets out a saucepan and starts cooking. He's chopping onions, peeling garlic, browning meat, and adding tomatoes and spices and all. After a while, I said, "Dutch, what are you doing?" He said, "I'm making dinner. I thought lasagna would be good." And I said, "Great."'

'That's how you knew he loved you?'

'In eighteen years, he had never made a meal. I mean, he'd help if I asked. He'd cut up melon for a fruit salad for a buffet or he'd pack the Igloo with ice for a picnic or he'd set up the bar for the holidays. But he had never gone to the store and bought the ingredients without asking and then come home and cooked them. That was left to me. And that's when I knew I had him back. He had changed. You see, that's when you know for sure somebody loves you. They figure out what you need and they give it to you – without you asking.'

'The without asking is the hard part.'

'It has to come from the heart.'

'Right,' I say and nod.

Mom and I watch the people move through the lobby, patients on their way to appointments, staff returning from break, and visitors jostling in and out of the elevators. The sun bounces off the windows in the pavilion that faces the lobby, and drenches the tile floor with a gleam so bright, I close my eyes.

'Have I upset you?' Mom asks me.

I open my eyes. 'No. You're a font of wisdom, Mom.'

'I can talk to you, Valentine.' She fiddles with the gold post in the back of her hoop earring. 'I just—' And then, to my complete surprise, she breaks into quiet sobs. 'Why the hell am I crying?' She throws her hands up.

'You're scared?' I say softly.

'No, that's not it.' Mom fishes through her purse until she finds the small cellophane pad of tissues. She yanks one out. 'These' – she holds up the tiny square – 'are worthless.' She dabs under her eyes with the small tissue. 'I just don't want it all to have been a waste. We've come so far and I was hoping we'd grow old together. Now, time is running out. After all *that*, we don't get the time? That would *kill* me. It's like the soldier who goes off to war, dodges gunfire and bombs and grenades, makes it out of the war zone, only to return home and slip on a banana peel, fall into a coma, and die.'

'Have a little faith.'

'That's coming from the least religious of my children.' Mom sits up straight. 'I don't mean that as a judgment.'

'I mean faith in *him*.'

'In God?'

'No. Dad. He's not going to let us down.'

Our family, like all the Italian-American families I know, is big on Excuse parties: birthdays and anniversaries that end in a zero or a five. We even have special titles for them, a twenty-fifth anniversary is *A Silver Jubilee*, a thirtieth birthday is *La Festa*, a fiftieth anniversary is called *A Golden Jubilee*, and a seventy-fifth anything is a miracle. So, imagine how thrilled we are to toast Gram, in good health, still with excellent vitality, in fine physical shape save for those knees, and having

200

'all her marbles,' as she calls them, on this, her eightieth birthday.

I also thought, knowing my immediate family would be in full attendance, that this would be the perfect opportunity to introduce them to Roman. I know I'm taking a chance here, but I have learned, when it comes to my family, it is best to introduce a new boyfriend in a crowded public venue where there's less possibility of a gaffe, slip, or chance that someone will reach for the photo albums and show pictures of me buck naked, wearing only angel wings, on my fourth birthday.

We offered Gram the standard big bash at the Knights of Columbus Hall in Forest Hills, with a DJ; a ceiling of silver balloons; the stations of the cross on the walls, covered with streamers of crepe paper; and a custom sheet cake with Gram's age embossed on it. But she opted for this party instead, a chic night out, dinner and a show at the Café Carlyle. She'd seen enough and plenty of the extended family at Jaclyn's wedding, plus, Gram's favorite singer of all time, Keely Smith, the great song stylist and comedienne, is the headliner at the Carlyle. When Gabriel, my friend the maître d', told us that she was appearing, we reserved a table.

Keely Smith and her music have a special place in Gram's life. When my grandparents were young, they used to travel around to catch Keely singing with her then husband Louis Prima, backed by

Sam Butera and The Witnesses. The act was a swinging cabaret alternative to the orchestras of the big band era. Gram will tell you that they personified *hip*.

Italian Americans revere Louis Prima, as we are married and buried to his music. Jaclyn, Tess, and Alfred danced to Louis's chart of 'Oh, Marie' at their weddings, and my grandfather was buried to Keely's version of 'I Wish You Love.' Prima is primo with the Roncallis and the Angelinis.

I check my lipstick in the cab on the way to the Café Carlyle, the Krup diamond of cabaret rooms. When a Village girl crosses Fourteenth Street and heads north, she had better be Upper East Side chic. Also, I want to look good for Roman, who hasn't seen me gussied up since our first date. How can I look glamorous when I run over to the restaurant kitchen to help him make pasta by hand or shuck clams for chowder? Tonight, he's getting the best version of his girlfriend.

I'm wearing a midnight blue coatdress with a wide embroidered belt that belonged to my mother. I've had my eye on it for years, and this summer, when she purged her closet, I got lucky. There's a picture of Mom holding me at my baptism in the fall of 1975 and wearing this coatdress. Her long hair is secured with a headband, which is attached to a fall, giving her cascading curls to her waist. Mom looked like a Catholic Ann-Margret with one foot in the sacristy and the other on the Vegas strip.

I wear the coatdress with pants, as it's much shorter on me. My mother wore it as a dress with sheer L'Eggs stockings, and I know that for certain because we used to collect the plastic eggs her hosiery came in and play farm.

Tess, Jaclyn, and I happily accept Mom's second-hand clothes because we know how much she treasured them the first time around. Tess ended up with a few structured St John jackets from the eighties, appropriate for PTA meetings, while I opted for coats and dresses she had made by a seamstress for special occasions. Jaclyn, with her tiny feet, inherited Mom's collection of Candy platform sandals in every shade of fake python that was available during the Carter adminis-tration. Yes, tangerine snakeskin exists. Mom says that you know you've been around awhile when you own every possible variation of a heel in your shoe collection. She still has the Famolare Get There sandals with the wavy bottoms. My mother never needed the recreational drugs of her era, she just put on those sandals and swayed.

As the cab makes a quick turn off Madison and onto East Seventy-sixth Street, I see Gabriel outside the hotel entrance, talking on his phone. I pay the cabbie and jump out.

Gabriel snaps the phone shut. 'You've got the best table ringside.'

'Great. Is Gram here yet?'

'Oh, she's here all right. She's on her second scotch and soda. I hope the show begins soon, because there will be a show, just not the one you're paying to see.'

'Gram's tipsy?'

'June is worse. The woman can put it away. Evidently, her legs are made of sea sponge. And your Aunt Feen looks stoned. What's the deal with her anyway? Lipitor with an Ambien chaser? Do me a favor. Check her meds.' Gabriel motions for me to follow him inside. 'Is Roman on his way? I hate latecomers.'

'Yep.'

'Have you had sex yet?'

'No.' I yank my belt tightly. Tonight may be the night, but I don't have to tell Gabriel.

'You bore me. What are you waiting for?'

'I'd like to spend more time with him before I take him on my magical mystery tour. Our relationship is building beautifully, thank you.'

'Who said anything about a relationship? I'm talking about sex.'

'You know they are coffee and cream to me.'

'Go ahead. Have your high standards and enjoy them alone. Follow me, darling.'

I follow Gabriel through the lobby of the Carlyle Hotel. Art Deco mirrors conjure up a sophisti-cated era, a time of rumble seats, speakeasies, clean gin, and elbow-length satin evening gloves. The chandeliers dazzle, like open cigarette cases, sunbursts of silver, gold, and daggers of crystal glowing overhead. Every detail of the lobby is lustrous – the brass doorknobs, the hinges, and

204

even the patrons gleam. The polished marble floors look like sheets of ice, pale silver marble in the center with crisp black hems of granite.

Gabriel leads me through the bar, where the frosted sconces throw low lights over the soft mushroom-colored walls. The neutral background shows off the stylish William Haines club chairs, covered in peach velvet and grouped around marble-topped bar tables.

We enter the Café Carlyle through etched glass doors. The room resembles a luxurious leather train case lined with sage green and pale pink bouclé. A series of murals painted by Marcel Vertes shows beautiful women flying, dancing, and leaping through the air, in a carousel of color; shades of strawberry, cream, sea green, magenta, and grass green fill the room in endless summer. The ceiling, painted dark blue, hangs overhead like a night sky. The neutral-patterned leather booths with a print of small circles, airy bubbles, seem inspired by Gustav Klimt. Small tables are grouped downstage, draped in crisp, midnight blue linens.

Gram and June chat shoulder to shoulder at our table, a large banquet shape to accommodate our family. Aunt Feen sifts through the mixed nuts in a silver dish, while June swishes the cherry in the bottom of her cocktail around like a pinball as the band members filter in and take their places onstage. A glossy black baby grand Steinway fills the small stage. A microphone and stand rests in the curve of the piano. Keely will literally be three feet from our table.

'You made it,' Gram says when she sees me, toasting me with her scotch. I give her a quick kiss.

'Happy birthday!'

'I love your ensemble,' June says.

'Thank you. And you look spectacular.'

'To old broads!' Gram raises her glass to June.

'We certainly are!' June touches her glass to Gram's.

'Thanks to the cream at Elizabeth Arden, I am about a week younger than I was when I walked out of the house this morning.' Gram takes my hand and squeezes it. Tess, Jaclyn, and I treated Gram to a day of beauty at the Elizabeth Arden salon. She's been pummeled, plucked, and primped since morning. 'Thank you. It's been a marvelous day, and now, we get Keely.'

Mom throws her arms around her mother from behind. 'Happy birthday, Mama,' she cries in her black sequin tank with matching silk georgette palazzo pants and a wide hammered-gold chain-link belt that drips down her thigh with a fringe of rhinestones. She wears strappy gold sandals to complete the Cleopatra effect. Dad wears a black-and-white-pin-striped suit with a gray dress shirt and a wide black-and-white silk tie. They match, but of course, they always do.

June stands and gives Dad a hug. 'Dutch, you look fantastic.'

'Not as good as you, June.'

'How's your cancer?' Aunt Feen brays.

'My numbers are improving, Auntie.'

'I put you on the prayer wheel at Saint Brigid's.'

'I appreciate it.'

'The last guy we prayed for died, but that wasn't our fault.'

'I'm sure it wasn't.' Dad throws us a look and sits down next to Aunt Feen for more abuse.

Tess waves from the check-in desk, in a strapless red cocktail dress. She makes an entrance worthy of my mother and is followed by Charlie, who wears a matching red tie. There are some inherited traits not worth fighting.

Tess gives Dad a hug. 'Hey, Pop. How are you feeling?'

Before he can answer, Aunt Feen says, 'How should he feel? The man's full of cancer.'

Charlie reaches down and squeezes my shoulder. 'Hey, sis,' he says. 'Can't wait to meet the Big Man tonight.' Charlie smiles supportively. It's funny that Charlie would call Roman the Big Man when it's Charlie who's big. He looks like Brutus in every Hollywood Bible epic ever made. He's also Sicilian, so he tans in twelve minutes and takes twelve years to forgive a slight.

'I can't wait for you to meet him. Be nice.'

'I'll be adorable,' Charlie says and sits down next to Tess.

Gabriel brings Jaclyn and Tom to the table. Jaclyn wears a short cream-colored wool skirt with a matching cashmere sweater and pearls. Tom, in his Sunday suit, looks like he's been spit-polished for his First Communion. As Jaclyn and Tom take their seats, Alfred and Pamela join us.

Pamela turns forty next year, but she looks about twenty-five. She's slim and has long, sandy blond hair, with a few pieces bleached the color of white chalk around her face for contrast. She's a mix of Polish and Irish, but she's picked up on our Italianate details when it comes to prints, sequins, and the size of her engagement ring. Tonight she wears a long, flowing, orchid-print evening wrap dress.

Alfred plants his arm firmly around her. He came straight from work, so he's wearing a Brooks Brothers suit with a red Ronald Reagan tie. Pamela greets everyone with a kiss, but she's not comfortable doing it. After thirteen years of marriage to my brother, whenever we all get together it's as if it's the first time she's met us. We've made repeated attempts to make her feel a part of things, but our efforts don't seem to take. Mom says Pamela has an 'aloof personality,' but Alfred told Tess that we're 'intimidating.'

My sisters and I don't think we're scary. Yes, we're competitive, opinionated, and discerning. And yes, at family gatherings, we yell, talk over one another, interrupt, and basically become the children we were at the age of ten minus the hair pulling. But intimidating? Must be. Pamela sits at the table gripping her evening clutch in her lap

208

like it's a steering wheel, staring at the Steinway with a patient, if plastered-on, smile as Alfred orders her a glass of white wine.

The waiters arrive, filling our table with hors d'oeuvres, delicate crab cakes, tiny potatoes with buttons of sour cream and caviar, clams casino on the half shell on an artful bed of shiny seaweed, oysters on ice, and a silver platter of baby lamb chops. Aunt Feen stands up, reaches across the table, and grabs a lamb chop, holding it like a pistol. She takes a bite before sitting back down in her chair. She chews. 'Succulent,' she says through the meat.

The lights in the café dim, and the crowd applauds and whistles. I look to the door, hoping to see Roman rush in to take his seat next to me. I scan the crowd, and there's no sign of him. The band strikes up, into a fizzy intro, and the applause escalates as Gabriel announces, 'Ladies and gentlemen, Keely Smith!'

The glass doors push open and Keely enters the room, looking exactly like the cover art on her albums. Her hair is bobbed and jet black, with two signature spit curls on her cheeks. Her pale pink skin is flawless, her black eyes shine like jet beads. She wears simple gold silk pants topped with a bugle-beaded Erté jacket. The three-quarter-length sleeves reveal chunky Lucite bracelets that offset a diamond ring the size of a cell phone.

Keely weaves through the crowd like a bride at

her third wedding, greeting the patrons with warmth, but just a touch blasé. Her manner is casual and familiar, as though she's getting up to sing a few songs in her living room after dinner. She takes the microphone and scans the crowd, squinting at us as if to examine who we are and why we came. 'Any Italians here tonight?'

We whistle and cheer.

'Louis Prima fans?'

We applaud loudly.

'We're Keely fans!' Gram hollers.

'Okay, okay. I see I'm gonna have to work tonight.' She looks to her conductor, behind the piano, and says, 'Here we go . . .' The band launches into a high-energy rendition of 'That Old Black Magic.'

Keely stands before the microphone in the curve of the baby grand piano and taps the beat on the waxy finish with her long red fingernails as she sings. She makes time with her feet in gold stiletto sandals with inlaid tiger's-eye straps. Her toenails are painted maroon. She notices that I'm staring at her feet, and smiles. The song ends, the crowd bursts into applause. She takes a step down-stage and looks at me. 'You like my sandals?'

'Yes. They're gorgeous,' I tell her.

'A woman cannot live by shoes alone. Though there have been times in my life when I had to. I've walked many miles in my lifetime. I'm going to be eighty years old.'

A ripple goes through the crowd.

Keely continues. 'Yep. Eighty. And I owe it all to . . .' She points heavenward.

'Me, too!' Gram waves to her.

'Today is her birthday,' Tess shouts.

'It is?' Keely says and smiles.

'Yes it is.' Gram didn't need the creams at Elizabeth Arden, she's getting a total rejuvenation right here. 'You're my gift.'

'Stand up, sister,' Keely says to Gram.

Gram stands.

Keely shields her eyes from the stage lights overhead and looks down at Gram. 'You know the secret, don't you?'

'You tell me,' Gram says, playing along.

'Never go gray.'

My mother whoops. 'Tell her, Keely!'

'And the big one: younger men.'

'I hear you!' June, three straight-up whiskeys down, waves her napkin like a flag of surrender, to whom I'm not sure, but she keeps waving.

Keely points to June. 'Now, not for the reason you think, Red. Although that's important.' She continues, 'I like a younger man because the men my age can't see to drive at night.'

The drummer snares a rim shot. 'I want to sing something just for you. What's your name?'

'Teodora,' Gram tells her.

'Hey, you really are a *paisan*.' Keely makes the international sign for 'I'm Italian,' making a slicing motion with her hand without a knife. 'You got a boyfriend?'

Her grandchildren answer for her. 'No!' we holler. Then, a man wearing trifocals, at the next table, whistles like he's hailing a cab. 'Lady didn't say she was looking,' Keely chides him. 'Tay, you got a man?'

'I'm with my family tonight,' Gram says with a giggle.

'And the less they know, the better. Take it from me.' Keely smiles and waves her hands over us like she's a priest giving the final blessing. 'Anybody who gets in the way of Grandmom's fun will have to deal with me.' Then she extends her hand forward to Gram. 'This one's for you, kid. Happy birthday.'

Keely sings 'It's Magic.' Gram leans forward, puts her elbows on the table, and props her face in her hands and closes her eyes to listen. My father puts his arm around my mother, who nestles into his shoulder like it's an old pillow. Tess looks at me with tears in her eyes, Jaclyn reaches across and squeezes Tess's hand. Their husbands smile, sip their drinks. Pamela sits ramrod straight and blinks as Alfred picks the parsley off the mini crab cake before sampling it. My phone vibrates in my purse. As the magic song ends, the crowd bursts into applause and Gram stands and throws Keely a kiss. I look into my purse and check my BlackBerry. The text message reads:

Flood in the kitchen. Can't make it.
So sorry. Kiss Gram.
Roman

Tess leans over and whispers, 'Are you okay?'

'He's not coming.'

'I'm so sorry.'

I feel my cheeks flush. I built up this whole evening in my mind. I pictured Roman sailing in to meet my family, handsome and glib, charming them, and pulling my father aside to tell him how much I mean in his life, and then later, my father would tell me that he's never been more impressed with a suitor, and I'd have that feeling of security in the pit of my stomach, the kind that allows you to surrender to love when it comes your way. Instead, I'm embarrassed. No wonder Alfred believes I'm unreliable. It seems things never work out the way I plan. Of course the kitchen flooded, and of course Roman had to stay and take care of it, but to read the words: CAN'T MAKE IT means so much more than *Can't make it tonight*. Can we ever make it? At all? Will Ca' d'Oro always come first?

Keely sings 'I'll Remember You,' Gram's eyes fill with tears, June gets misty, and even Aunt Feen's face relaxes in a smile as she goes back in time to her youth. A tear rolls down my face, but as good as she is, it's not because of Keely. Tonight, I could cry her a river on my own terms, and it would not have to be set to music.

CHAPTER 7

SOHO

Gram and I stand on the corner of Jane and Hudson, surveying the Christmas tree selection as we inhale the cold night air, filled with the invigorating scent of crisp pine and clean cedar.

There's nothing like December in Manhattan when the Christmas trees go on sale. Every other street corner becomes an outdoor garden, as freshly cut trees are stacked and displayed in their corridors of evergreen. Peels of pungent pine bark fall onto the sidewalk as the sellers trim the trunks and wrap the trees in their umbrellas of webbed plastic before delivery. Glossy wreaths with red velvet bows and sprays of holly tied with gold mesh ribbons hang on roughhewn stepladders, ready for pickup. You cannot help but close your eyes and believe in the possibility of the perfect Christmas.

I arrange for delivery of our blue spruce as Gram chooses a wreath for the shop door. Mr Romp places our ten-foot tree on a turnstile and gives it the umbrella treatment. Gram takes my arm as we walk back to the shop.

'Are you inviting Roman to Christmas dinner?'

'Think he's ready for us?' I joke.

The truth is, I've prepared Roman. The good news, he's from a crazy Italian family, too, so he gets it, we have a shorthand. I worry about that though, a romance at our stage of things should feel solid. Our feelings are clear, but scheduling the time? That's the tricky part. That, and I live with my grandmother. I've never brought a man home to stay. I wouldn't even know how to ask. I suppose I could do what Italian girls have done for decades: sneak. But when?

Maybe this is the state of romance for two self-employed people over thirty. Between his schedule at the restaurant, and mine in the shop, our communication is like a stack of unread mail; we get to it and each other when we can. It all began with a slow, delicious meal at Ca' d'Oro; I thought it was the ultimate to have a man cooking for me, feeding me, pleasing me. But the truth is, the last time we ate together we had take-out cold sesame noodles from Mama Buddha on a park bench on Bleecker Street before I had a shoe fitting with a customer.

'Roman has to do *something* for Christmas,' Gram says, pushing the door to the vestibule open. 'He'd liven things up.'

'Just what we need.'

Gram goes into the kitchen to make us a dish of spaghetti marinara for dinner. I climb the stairs to take the Christmas decorations out of storage in my mother's old bedroom closet. I flip on the small bedside lamp and pull cardboard cartons full of ornaments out of the closet and stack them on the bed. Boxes labeled SHINY BRIGHT are filled with vintage gold-glass teardrops, and silver, green, red, and blue balls embossed with stripes or flocking, each loaded with meaning and memory.

The old Roma lights, oversize bulbs of ruby red, navy blue, forest green, and taxicab yellow, are the only lights my sisters allow on Gram's tree. Tess and Jaclyn may have the small, mod twinklers in their own homes, but here at Gram's, the tree has to be exactly as we remember it: a live blue spruce loaded with smoky glass ornaments that have been around since my mother was a girl. We cherish the ornaments that are a little the worse for wear, the felt reindeer with an eye missing, the plastic choirboys in faded red flannel cassocks, and the tinfoil-star tree topper that Alfred made in kindergarten.

The bed is now covered in boxes. I look for the extension cord with the foot pedal for turning the tree lights on and off. I can't find it. 'Gram?' I holler from the top of the stairs.

'What is it?' She appears on the landing a flight below.

'Where are the extension cords?'

'Look in my room. Check my dresser. It's got to be in one of those drawers,' she says, heading into the kitchen.

I flip on the light in Gram's room. Her perfume

216

lingers in the air, freesia and lilies, the same scent that you catch when Gram pulls off her scarf or hangs up her coat.

I pull open her dresser drawer and search for the extension cords. Gram is a pack rat, like me. Her drawers are well-organized but are filled with stuff. The top drawer holds stacks of her lingerie anchored by stockings still in their packages. I lift them carefully, looking for the cords.

An unopened bottle of Youth Dew perfume sits on top of a stack of pressed antique handkerchiefs, which she still uses in evening bags on special occasions. I lift out a box of lightbulbs in their flimsy carton. Searching under it, I find a shoe box of receipts, which I carefully place back where I found it.

I look in the second drawer. Her wool cardigans are folded neatly. In an open plastic bin, there's a flashlight, a bottle of holy water from Lourdes, and an envelope marked 'Mike's report cards.'

I open the last drawer. Gram's purses and evening bags are neatly stacked in felt bags. I lift a cigar box filled with small metal gizmos, wheels, latches, and hook replacements for repairing the machines in the shop. Under the box, there's a black velvet pouch lying flat against the bottom of the drawer. I pull out a heavy gold picture frame.

Inside is a picture of Gram from about ten years ago. The background is unfamiliar and rural. Gram stands next to an olive tree with a man who is not my grandfather. She must be in the hills of Italy. The man has thick white hair brushed to the side, crackling slate blue eyes, and a wide smile. His skin is golden, as is hers, tawny with summer.

The hills behind them are in full bloom with sunflowers. The man has his arm around Gram's waist, and she is looking down, smiling. I quickly shove the photograph into the pouch and bury it at the bottom of the drawer with the small box of machine parts on top of it. I see the cord for the Christmas lights hidden in the far corner. 'I found it!' I call out to her. I close the drawer carefully and turn out the light.

'Maybe it's one of her cousins,' Tess whispers as we wait for my parents to arrive in the vestibule of Our Lady of Pompeii Church on Carmine Street for Christmas Eve mass. Garlands of fresh greens hang from the columns leading to the altar, covered with gold-foil pots of red poinsettias. A series of small trees with tiny white lights forms a backdrop for the ornate gold tabernacle.

'He didn't look like a cousin.'

Gram is seated inside, with the grandkids and Alfred, Pamela, Jaclyn, and Tom, while Tess and I wait for our parents while they park.

'Who could it be?'

'It looked romantic to me.'

'Oh, come on! You're talking about our grandmother.'

'Older people have relationships.'

218

'Not Gram.'

'I don't know. She gets a lot of phone calls from Italy, and remember what she said to Keely Smith about having a boyfriend.'

'She didn't say she had one. She was just playing along for the show. Gram is not the type,' Tess insists.

'The picture is hidden in a velvet pouch in her dresser, like it *matters*.'

'Okay, I'll tell you what. When we go back, you keep her busy in the kitchen and I'll go up and check it out. I'm sure it's nothing.'

'It's a mob scene out there,' Dad says as he and Mom enter the church.

Tess, Mom, and Dad follow me to the side aisle. We squeeze in next to Charlie and the girls. Gram sits on the far end of the pew, next to Alfred. She leans forward and checks to make sure every member of our family is in place. She smiles happily as she surveys the lot of us before turning her eyes back to the altar. Maybe Tess is right. Gram is not the type to have a life outside of the family she loves. She's eighty years old. That ship has definitely sailed.

Gram's kitchen was designed with holidays and the preparation of big meals in mind, so there is no such thing as too many chefs in this kitchen. The long marble counter is a crack workstation, while the fully loaded galley kitchen can accommodate several of us as we reheat and arrange the platters. Christmas Eve dinner is exactly as it was when we were kids, except now, instead of Gram doing all the cooking, we pot-luck the food.

Gram made her traditional wedding soup with spinach and mini meatballs made of veal, Tess brought her homemade manicotti, Mom roasted a loin of pork with sweet potatoes, and prepared a second entrée of breaded chicken cutlets with steamed asparagus. Jaclyn made the salad. I'm in charge of the starters, which feature the traditional seven fishes: smelts, shrimp, sardines, oysters, baccala, lobster, and scungilli.

'What did Clickety Click bring for dessert?' Tess asks after looking around and making sure Pamela is out of earshot.

'They went to DeRoberti's,' I tell her. Pamela brought cookies, cannolis, and mini cheesecakes, but we don't mind the store-boughts, because at least she goes to a great Italian bakery.

'It's Christmas and I want peace in the valley,' Mom says firmly.

'Sorry, Mom,' Tess apologizes.

'Never mind you. Look at my chicken cutlets,' Mom says proudly as she arranges them on a platter. 'I pound them until they are as thin as paper. Before I bread them, you can see right through them. Jaclyn, your salad looks delish.'

'It's from my Nigella Lawson cookbook,' Jaclyn says. 'I figure with the name Nigella, she's got to have some Italian in her, right? We got her entire collection at our wedding.'

220

'Her entire collection? Is that all?' Gram asks as she joins us in the kitchen. 'When I got married, there was only one cookbook given to brides.'

'And now I have it. Ada Boni's *The Talisman*.' Mom garnishes the cutlets with spikes of fresh parsley.

'It's the best. Whenever I make Charlie meatballs, recipe number two, out of that book, he'll do whatever I want. I made them last month and he retiled the half bath.'

'Well, at least you know what motivates him,' I tell Tess.

'You know, I try to do what Ma did when we were growing up. A fresh, home-cooked meal every night and dinner with the family. Not easy to pull off these days.'

'Thank you for acknowledging my contribution. I hoped my children would appreciate the little things I did and the big meals I prepared. I think Saint Teresa of the Little Flower said it best, "Do small things in a big way," or was it "Do big things in a small way"? I can't remember. Doesn't matter. I worked hard all of my life' – Mom lifts the steamer full of asparagus off the stove, removes the lid, and lifts the asparagus out with tongs – 'inside my home. I don't like the delineation of career in the office versus homemaking. Work is work. And I worked for my family, to the exclusion of my own goals. You four children were my job. My performance evaluation came when each of you graduated from college and fled the nest able to take care of yourself. I gave up my own life, but I'm not complaining. It's just the way it was. And by the way, it was fabulous!' Mom places the platter on the table.

When we were growing up, my friends would tell me that their moms would threaten them into behaving by saying things like, 'I hope your children ruin your life the way you've ruined mine!' or 'If you don't shape up, I'll kill myself and then what will you do, you little bastards!' or 'This time next year I'll be dead, so you can go ahead and have your pot parties!' Mom never said anything of the like to us. She would never threaten suicide because she's a genuine life junkie.

No, when Mom really wanted to scare us, she'd say, 'That's it! I've had it! I'll go out and get *a job*! You heard me! *A job!* Then you'll see what it's like with no mother around here to wait on you hand and foot!' Or the big jab delivered loud and singsongy, 'I'm going back to work!' Never mind that my mother never had a job outside our home. She graduated from Pace with a teaching degree and never used it. 'When would I have gone back into the classroom?' she used to say. 'When?' As if the classroom were this mythical place that swallowed women with teaching certificates whole in the land that time forgot.

The truth is, my mother had other plans. She was busy building Roncalli Incorporated. She had Alfred ten months after she married Dad. Then Tess was born, followed by me, and finally Jaclyn, and *we* became her high-powered career. Lee Iacocca had nothing on my mother. Motherhood was her IBM, her Chrysler, and her Nabisco. She was the CEO of our family. She woke early every morning, 'put on her face,' and dressed like she was going into an office. Mom made lists, organized six lives on a giant eraser-board calendar, got us to and from wherever we needed to be, and never complained, well, not much. One year for Christmas, we made up business cards for her that said:

MICHELINA 'MIKE' RONCALLI
Mother Extraordinaire
Available 24/7
Forest Hills, Queens, New York, USA

She was so proud of those cards she handed them out to strangers, like she was running for borough president. She could've handled that job, too, believe me. Mom is a born leader, a taskmaster and a visionary. She also toots her own horn, which doesn't hurt in politics.

'How are the boys doing on the roof?' Gram brings the soup bowls to the counter.

'I'll check.' I head up the stairs to the roof.

'And call the kids please,' Mom calls after me. 'We're ready.'

I climb the stairs two at a time to the third floor. I do a quick check of the bedrooms. I stop and check the clock in Gram's room. Where is

Roman? He said he'd be here fifteen minutes ago. Now I'm worried Tess and Jaclyn are beginning to think he's a phantom. I put it out of my mind; he'll be here.

The kids are scattered everywhere, playing dress up and hide-and-seek, or maybe Charisma is calling Japan like she did the last time she was here (twenty-three bucks on the long-distance bill). Whatever they're up to, no one appears to be bleeding or crying so I breeze past them and go up to the roof.

The men are in charge of preparing a fire in the charcoal grill on the roof. After dinner, we bundle up in our coats and head to the roof to roast marshmallows. This was my grandfather's Christmas chore, and it's not lost on us that it takes Dad, Alfred, Charlie, and Tom to do what Grandpop did by himself.

I step out onto the roof and into the cold night air to check the grill. The charcoals are still black, their edges turning deep red. In an hour, they'll be just the right temperature for the marshmallow roast. A swirl of gray smoke rises from the fire as Alfred holds court in his Barneys topcoat.

My brother points to buildings on the West Side Highway. He's conducting what sounds like a tutorial on real estate, with Pamela at his side shivering in a fur capelet. Charlie, Tom, and my father listen carefully, rapt at his knowledge. He points to a building on the corner of Christopher Street. He rattles off the asking price, followed by the recent sale price, like he's reciting the names of his children. I stand in the cold long enough to hear him drop some big numbers.

'Dinner is ready,' I interrupt.

'Do you need any help down in the kitchen?' Pamela asks.

'We're okay.' I smile at her. 'Could you help corral the kids?'

'Sure.' She follows me down the stairs. I almost ran to the Home Depot on Twenty-third Street and bought those rubber step guards because I knew Pamela was coming and I was afraid she'd take a tumble off those five-inch stilettos and somersault down three flights of stairs, winding up in the workshop in a bloody heap.

'I like your dress, Pamela,' I tell her, genuinely admiring her red silk-shantung shift with a matching bolero and red ankle-strap sandals. 'You look as young as you did the day you met my brother.'

She blushes. 'Your brother told me that change was nonnegotiable.'

'What?'

'Well, he said, no matter what, he didn't want me to change from the day he met me.'

'Isn't that sort of impossible?'

'Well, maybe. But I'm trying to keep up my end of the deal. Plus, his eyesight keeps getting worse, so it all evens out.'

As Pamela gathers the kids for dinner, I return to the kitchen. Mom, Gram, and my sisters place garnishes on the platters for the Christmas Eve Feast of the Seven Fishes. I'm about to tell my sisters about Alfred's No Change Clause and kvetch about how controlling our brother can be, but decide not to. Pamela, after all, is only doing what we tried to do for all these years – make Alfred happy. If that means she has to wear her jeans from 1994 and fit into them for the rest of her life, so be it. I feel sorry for my sister-in-law. When I picture Pamela at family parties, I see her on the outside, peeking through twists of crepe-paper streamers as if they're prison bars. She never participates at weddings when we form a soul-train dance line, or joins the card games we throw together after Sunday dinner. She sits in a corner and reads a magazine. She's just not one of us.

The buzzer sounds.

'Are we expecting someone?' Mom asks.

'Who could it be? Last-minute FedEx?' Tess teases, looking at me, knowing full well that I've been waiting for Roman to arrive so I can put him on display like the radish rosettes in the crudité dish. 'A testy bride maybe?'

'On Christmas Eve? Never,' Gram answers. 'Or any other day, for that matter.'

'It's probably June. You invited her, didn't you, Gram?' Jaclyn plays along with Tess; after all, it's Christmas, so let's have some fun with *Funnyone*.

'She's with her wild East Village friends eating a seitan turkey and smoking weed,' Gram says and shrugs. 'You know those show people.'

226

I press the button on the monitor. 'Who is it?'

'Roman.'

'Come on up,' I say cheerfully into the intercom. I turn to my sisters. 'Behave yourselves.'

Tess claps her hands together. 'Your boyfriend! We're finally going to meet him!'

'I wonder what he's like!' Jaclyn trills.

'Girls, let's not put pressure on Valentine.' Fully aware of the power of the first impression, my mother checks her lipstick in the chrome reflection of the toaster. Then she adjusts her posture, throws back her shoulders, lifts her neck, and parts her lips ever so slightly to show off a shallow dimple in her left cheek. Now she's ready to meet my boyfriend.

Roman comes into the kitchen carrying a large baking pan covered in foil and then Saran Wrap. He wears a tailored black cashmere overcoat that I've never seen before. 'I thought you could use dessert. Cobbler. Merry Christmas,' he says.

I give Roman a kiss. 'Merry Christmas.'

I take the pan from Roman and place it on the counter. He unbuttons his coat and hands it to me. 'You look pretty,' he says softly in my ear.

'Introduce us please, Valentine.' Mom looks Roman up and down like she's studying the statue of *David* on a group tour. She actually goes up on her toes, craning for a better look at him.

'Ciao, Teodora.' He kisses both of Gram's cheeks before turning to shake my mother's hand.

'This is my mother, Mike.'

'Merry Christmas, Mrs Roncalli,' he says warmly.

My mother offers her cheeks, and Roman picks up on her cue and gives her the European double-kiss action, too. 'Please call me Mom. I mean Mike. Welcome to our Christmas celebration.'

'This is my sister Tess.'

'You have two daughters, right?' Roman asks as Tess extends her hand and he shakes it.

'Yes, I do.' Tess is impressed that the stranger has retained any biographical information about her whatsoever.

'And this is my baby sister, Jaclyn.'

'The newlywed?'

'Yes.' Jaclyn shakes his hand and squints at him like she's surveying stew meat in the butcher department at D'Agostino's.

'Well, Roman, what did you make for us?' Mom bats her eyelashes at him.

'It's a cobbler of blackberry and fig,' he says, just as I hear my niece pipe up from the stairs.

'Who's that guy?' Charisma points at Roman.

'Charisma. Come over here and say hello.' Tess looks at Roman. 'I'm sorry. She's seven. She hates all boys. This is Aunt Valentine's friend.'

Charisma squints at him. 'Aunt Valentine doesn't have friends.'

'Well, not in a long time, but now she does and we're all happy for her,' my mother explains as I contemplate jumping headfirst out of the kitchen window.

228

'We're just about to sit down to dinner.' Mom makes a sweeping gesture with her arm toward the table. My mother's body language shifts from slight wariness to full receptivity of Roman Falconi. 'You must meet my husband and the boys.'

'Our brother, Alfred, his sons, and our husbands,' Tess explains as she puts her arm around Jaclyn in a united, don't-mess-with-us fashion.

'You're forgetting Pamela,' I remind them.

'And Pamela. My only daughter-in-law. She's so tiny you almost miss her.' My mother waves her hand in the air and laughs.

My father and the boys come downstairs and Mom, now in full command of Roman Falconi, introduces the remaining family members. Alfred's sons extend their hands in greeting, like gentlemen in the drawing rooms of old. Chiara, with all the charm of her older sister, makes a face at Roman, and runs to join her sister at the table.

Gram motions to us to help her in the kitchen. Pamela stands up to come with us, but Tess says, 'Don't worry, Pam. We've got it.' Pamela shrugs and goes to the table.

'You complain that Pamela doesn't help and then you don't let her,' Gram whispers.

'If we gave her a platter to carry, she'd collapse under the weight and her stilettos would sink into the floorboards like penny nails.' Tess puts a pepper grinder under one arm and picks up the water pitcher with the other. Gram, Jaclyn, and I grab the last of the platters and join the family at the table.

My father takes his place at the head of the table. He folds his hands in prayer. He makes the sign of the cross, and we follow him. 'Well, God, it's been a helluva year.'

'Dad . . . ,' Tess says softly, looking at the children, who find the mention of hell hilarious in a prayer.

'You know what I mean, dear Lord. We've had trials and tribulations and now we meet a new friend on the journey . . .' Dad pauses and looks at Roman.

'Roman,' Mom pipes up.

'Roman. We give thanks for our good health, my relative good health, Ma's eightieth birthday, and all the rest in between.' Dad goes to make the sign of the cross.

'Dad?'

He looks up at Jaclyn.

'Dad . . . one more thing.' Jaclyn takes Tom's hand. 'Tom and I would like you all to know that we're having a baby.'

The table erupts with joy, the children jump up and down, Gram wipes away a tear, Mom reaches across the table to kiss Jaclyn and then Tom. Dad holds up his hands.

Roman takes my hand and puts his arm around me. I look up at him; he is beaming, which means the world to me.

'My baby is having a baby. Well, this is proof positive that God isn't sinkin' our ship just yet.' Dad puts his hand to his forehead, 'In the name of the Father and of the Son and of the Holy Spirit—'

'Amen!' we shout, the least religious of my mother's children the loudest. I'm thrilled about Jaclyn and Tom's news, and I'm also happy that my first Christmas with Roman is off to a great start.

We crowd onto the roof in our coats, hats, and mittens for the Annual Christmas Marshmallow Roast. Mom follows with a bottle of Poetry wine and a stack of plastic glasses embossed with sexy girls dressed as elves. (Where does she find this stuff?)

Dad and Alfred load the sticks with marshmallows and hand them to the kids, who gather around the grill like little match children, holding the white puffs into the flames. Roman puts his arm around me.

'Time to light the torches!' Mom calls out. 'Ambience inside and out, I say.'

'She's exactly as you described her,' Roman whispers in my ear, then joins Charlie and Tom as they fan out and light the torches on the corners of the roof.

Dad helps Alfred Junior and Rocco hold their marshallows on sticks to the flames. Charisma, a little pyro, lets her marshmallow burst into flames, open like a bomb, and ooze onto the hot coals. Chiara waits patiently, toasting each side of her marshmallow uniformly. My sisters stand behind the girls, guiding them as another holiday tradition is handed down from my generation to the next one.

'Great-gram?' Charisma asks. 'Tell the story of the velvet tomatoes.'

'Great-gram has had too much great wine.' Gram sits down on the chaise and puts her feet up. 'And I'm having some more. Have Auntie Valentine tell the story.'

'Tell the story!' Charisma, Rocco, Alfred Junior, and Chiara jump up and down.

'Okay, okay. When I was six years old, my mother brought me over to stay with Gram and Grandpop when she went to see *Phantom of the Opera* for the eighth time.'

'I love an Andrew Lloyd Webber show,' Mom says unapologetically to Roman, who shrugs.

'Alfred and Tess were at summer camp . . .'

'Camp Don Bosco,' Tess clarifies.

'. . . and baby Jaclyn was in Queens with Dad. I had Gram and Grandpop all to myself. And I came up here to play on the roof. First I had a little tea party, using garden tools for utensils and mud for scones. Then I decided to be like Gram, and I went over to the tomato plants and started to dig around in the dirt. But when I looked up through the vines, there were no tomatoes. So I ran downstairs, right into the shoe shop, and I said,

"Somebody stole the tomatoes." And I started to cry.'

'She almost had a nervous breakdown,' Gram says wryly.

'She was worried! No tomatoes,' Chiara says in my defense.

'Right. So Grandpop explained that sometimes the plants don't bear fruit, that sometimes, no matter how well you take care of them, it's just too rainy for the plants to make tomatoes. The plants are so smart, they know not to bloom, because the tomatoes would come in all mealy and tasteless, and what good would they be?'

'And then I said we might have to wait until next summer for the tomatoes to grow. But Valentine was heartbroken.' Gram lifts her glass of wine.

I pick up the story again, looking at Roman, who is as engrossed as the kids in the fate of the tomatoes, or maybe he's just being polite. 'The next Sunday, everyone came over for dinner, and Gram said, "Go up to the roof, Valentine. You won't believe your eyes."'

'And everybody raced up the stairs!' Chiara says.

'That's right.' I put my hands on Rocco's and Alfred Junior's shoulders. 'We all came up to the roof to see what had happened. And when we got here, there was a miracle. There were tomatoes everywhere. But they weren't tomatoes to make sauce, they were velvet tomatoes, made with red and green fabric, and they dangled from the barren plants, like ornaments. Even the tomato pincushion from the shop was there, hanging from the vine. We jumped up and down like it was Christmas morning even though it was the hottest day of summer. I asked my grandfather how it happened. And he said, "Magic!" And then we all celebrated the harvest of the velvet tomatoes.'

My mom gives me a thumbs-up as the kids eat their marshmallows and we drink our wine. I look around at my family, feeling blessed and full. Pamela remains glued to my brother's hip, like a gun holster, while Gram lies with her feet up on the chaise. Tess and Jaclyn pull Mom away to watch a Norwegian cruise ship make a lazy entrance into New York Harbor. I look at Roman, who seems to fit into this crazy family without too much fuss. The moon peeks out between the skyscrapers looming behind us, looking an awful lot like a lucky penny.

Dad holds up his sexy elves plastic cup of wine. 'I'd like to make a toast. To Dr Buxbaum at Sloan who took my prostrate numbers from north to south. Which is a good thing.'

'To Dr Buxbaum!' we toast. My father is beating prostate cancer and he still can't pronounce it.

'Many, many more years, Dutch,' Mom says, raising her glass again. 'We have lots of sunsets to see, and lots of places to go. You still have to take me to Williamsburg.'

'Virginia?' Tess asks.

'That's your dream trip?' Jaclyn says. 'You can get there in a car.'

'I believe in setting goals that one can achieve. Low expectations make for a happy life. I can die without seeing Bora-Bora. Besides, I love glass-blowing, Georgian architecture, and Revolutionary War reenactors. Aim for doable, kids.'

'I think you mean it.' I swig my wine.

'I absolutely do. I have dreamed of the attainable and the attainable has found me. I wanted a nice Italian boy with good teeth, and that's what I got.'

'I still have all my choppers,' Dad says, nodding.

'You think small things don't matter until you consider teeth,' Gram toasts Dad from the chaise.

We sip our wine as we ponder Dad's bite and Mom's dream of Colonial Williamsburg. The only sound we hear is the faint pop of the marshmallows as they ignite into orange flames, only to turn bright blue before charring to black. Roman supervises the operation and actually seems to be having fun. He looks over at me and winks.

The kids have gone downstairs to play with some of those minuscule Polly Pocket dolls, while the grown-ups remain on the roof, sitting around the old table finishing our wine. A cold wind kicks up as the fire in the grill dies down. I collect the cups, and I'm about to head downstairs to start the dishes when I hear Alfred lean over and say to Gram, 'Scott Hatcher's offer is still on the table.'

'Not now, Alfred,' she says quietly.

I knew this was coming. I could barely look at Alfred all night, knowing he was calculating square footage and interest rates with every mouthful of manicotti. He's made remarks and dropped hints until I'm good and sick of it. So I turn to my brother and say, 'It's Christmas! She doesn't want to talk about Scott Hatcher and his cash offer. And besides, you told us Hatcher was a *broker*, not a buyer.'

'He's both. He sells properties, but he also buys them for investment purposes. Anyhow, what difference does it make?'

'A lot. A broker comes in and gives an opinion. It's a process. After a few months, when you've gathered enough information and gone out to competitors to get the best price, then, and only then, if you want to sell, do you hire your own broker and name your price. But that's not what's going on here. He's a developer.'

'How do you know?' Alfred counters.

'I did my research.' If only Alfred knew how much research. I know more about Scott Hatcher than I ever wanted to. 'It isn't prudent for Gram to sell the building after one offer. That's bad business.'

'And you know from business?' Alfred sneers.

'I've been putting together my own numbers.' My family looks at me. *Funnyone* is artistic, not a numbers person. I've blindsided them.

'You're not serious.' Alfred turns away from me.

'I'm deadly serious,' I say, raising my voice.

Alfred turns back and looks at me, confused.

'Not now, Valentine,' Gram says firmly.

'Anyhow, it's Gram's decision. Not yours,' Alfred says dismissively.

'I'm Gram's partner.'

'Since when?' Alfred yells.

I look at Gram, who begins to speak, but reconsiders.

'Kids, don't get like this,' Dad interjects.

'Oh, we're gonna get like this.' I stand up. When I stand, the in-laws – Pamela, Charlie, and Tom – get up from the table and inch back to the fence line of the roof. Only Roman remains at the table, with a look on his face that says, *Here we go.*

'You two, stop it right now,' Mom chirps. 'We've had a lovely holiday.'

I persist. 'How much was the offer, Alfred?'

He doesn't answer.

'I said, how much?'

'Six million dollars,' Alfred announces.

Shrieks rise from my relatives on the roof, like hosannas at a tent revival.

'Gram, you're mega rich!' Tess exclaims. 'You're like Brooke Astor!'

'Over my dead body,' Gram says, looking down at her hands. 'That poor Astor woman. And I mean poor. May she rest in peace. If you don't raise your children right, all the money in the world doesn't matter. It's the fast track to tumult.'

'Please, Ma, we are *not* the Astors. There's a lot of love here,' Mom says.

'So what's going to happen with the offer?' Jaclyn asks delicately.

'It's a very high offer, a great offer, in fact, and I've advised Gram to sell,' Alfred says, laying out his plan like a road map. 'She can *finally* retire after fifty years of killing herself, get a condo in Jersey out by us, and put her feet up for the first time in her life.'

'She has her feet up right now,' I tell him. I turn to Gram. 'What happens to the Angelini Shoe Company?'

Gram doesn't answer me.

'Valentine, she's *tired*.' Alfred raises his voice. 'And you're pushing her. Stop being selfish and think about our grandmother for a change.'

'Now, Alfred, you know how much I love my work,' Gram says.

'That's right. We've got a great business going here. We make three thousand pairs of shoes a year.'

'Oh, come on. That's hardly viable by any current business standards. You don't have a Web site, you don't advertise, and it's run like it's 1940.' Alfred turns to our grandmother. 'No offense, Gram.'

'None taken. That was a big year for us.'

Alfred continues, 'You use the same tools Grandpop did. At this point, the Angelini Shoe Company is nothing more than a hobby for you two, and the part-timers you employ. It's a financial wash in a good year, but with the debt, it's irresponsible not to consider closing and cleaning up what you owe. Besides, even if we could find somebody to buy the shop, it would not come to one percent of what this building is worth. This building is the gold.'

'It's our business!' I tell him. Doesn't he see that our great grandfather's shoe designs are the gold? Our name? Our technique? Our reputation? Alfred puts no value on our tradition. What are we without it? 'We make our living in this shop!'

'Barely. If you had to pay rent, you'd be in the street.'

Clickety Click moves back to Alfred's side. She threads her arm through his, which tells me that she's heard this before.

'I live within my means. I've never asked anyone for a penny.'

'I helped you when you broke up with Bret and quit teaching.'

'Three thousand dollars. You didn't *give* me that money. I paid it back in six months at seven percent interest!' I can't believe he's throwing this in my face. Then again, of course he's throwing this in my face. He's Alfred! My mother shifts uncomfortably on the lawn chair and Dad stares off at the Verrazano Narrows Bridge as if it's burst into flames like a marshmallow on a stick.

'I think what Alfred is trying to say,' Mom says diplomatically, 'is that my mother is of a certain age now, and in looking ahead, down the road, we should all anticipate changes.'

'Right, Ma,' I challenge her. 'And the road is icy, your tires are bald, and you're skidding. Anything to support your precious and brilliant son, Alfred. What he wants, he gets. If he was truly concerned about Gram and her well-being, I wouldn't open my mouth. But my brother is all about the money. He's only ever been about the money.'

'How dare you! I'm worried about Gram!' Alfred shouts.

'Are you?'

'Your brother loves his grandmother,' Dad interjects.

'Don't speak for him,' I tell my father.

'Don't speak for me,' Alfred tells Dad.

Dad puts his hands in the air in surrender.

'And don't speak for me,' Gram says, standing. 'I will make all the decisions about the Angelini Shoe Company and my building. Alfred, as smart as you are, you have a big mouth. You should never talk numbers. You've thrown everyone into a tizzy.'

'I thought since it was just family—'

Roman looks off, like a guest hoping to disappear from the fray. But he can't move. I catch a flicker of impatience in his eyes.

'Even worse!' Gram says. 'Those kinds of numbers only make people nervous. For God's sake, they make *me* nervous. I'm a private person and I don't want my business ripped into like a

Christmas package for public consumption. And, Valentine, I appreciate everything you do for me, but I don't want you to stay here because you think you have to—'

'I *want* to be here.'

'—and Alfred has a point. I'm not what I was.'

'I didn't mean it to sound like that, Gram,' he says. 'I do believe it's your choice. But I'd like to see you relax for the first time in your life. There's a reason people don't work at a job when they're eighty.'

'Because most of them are dead?' Gram says, giving up and sitting down.

'No, because they've earned a break. And, Valentine, nobody said you couldn't pursue shoe-making as a hobby. It's time for you to have a real career. You're in your midthirties and you're living like a Boho bum. Who's going to take care of you when you're old? I suppose I'll get stuck with that tab, too.'

'You're the last person I'd ask for help.' And I mean it. Clickety Click exhales, one less thing for her to worry about.

'We'll see. So far, I'm the only Roncalli kid who picks up a check.'

'What are you talking about?' Tess wants to know.

'Gram's party.'

'We offered,' Jaclyn and Tess say in unison.

'So did I!' I tell him.

'But I paid! And I've got news for you, I always pay.'

241

'That's not fair, Alfred, you can't pick up a check and then complain about it. That is terrible form!' Tess makes a motion that Gram, the honoree, is listening.

Alfred doesn't care. He goes on. 'Who do you think pays for Dad's doctors? He has insurance, but there's a deductible and there are out-of-pocket expenses. He has to go out of network for some of the procedures. But you girls don't know that! Why? Because you never ask!'

'We will repay you, Alfred,' Mom says quietly.

'If you didn't swoop in and pay for everything, like Lord Bountiful, we would be happy to pay our share,' I tell him. 'You only pay so you can hold it over our heads.'

Alfred turns to me. 'I'm not going to apologize to *you* for being successful. There's a success tax I pay every day in this family. I'm the one who makes money, so I'm the one who pays. And you resent me for it!'

'Because you complain about it! I'd rather be broke and living in a box on the Bowery than in that castle of fear you live in. Just look at Clickety Click . . .' The words are out of my mouth before I can stop them.

Tess and Jaclyn inhale quickly, while Mom mutters, 'Oh no.' In the silence that follows, I swear I can hear the clouds drift past in the sky overhead.

'Who is Clickety Click?' Pamela asks. She looks at me and then up at her husband.

'I don't know what she's talking about,' he says.

'Valentine?' Pamela looks at me.

'It's a—'

'It's a term of endearment really,' Tess says, jumping in. 'A nickname.'

'It's not a nickname if I've never heard it.' For the first time in seventeen years, Pamela's voice hits its upper register. 'Wouldn't I know my own nickname?'

'I'm begging you, girls, get off this subject. It's getting us all nowhere.' Mom pulls the collar on her faux mink up around her ears. 'Come on. It's getting too cold up here. Let's go in and make some Irish coffee. Anyone for Irish coffee?'

'Nobody is going anywhere.' Pamela sets her steely gaze on Mom. 'What the hell does Clickety Click mean?'

'Valentine?' Mom looks at me.

'It's a nickname that—' I begin.

'It's the sound you make when you walk in your high heels,' Jaclyn blurts out. 'You're small and you take short steps and when the heels hit the ground, they go . . . clickety click, clickety click.'

Pamela's eyes fill with tears. 'You've been making fun of me all this time?'

'We didn't mean it.' Tess looks desperately at Jaclyn and me.

'I can't help my . . . my . . . size. I never make fun of you, and there's plenty to laugh at in this crazy family!' Pamela turns on her heel and stomps off. Clickety click. Clickety click. Clickety click.

243

When she realizes the sound she's making, she rises up onto her toes and moves silently en pointe until she reaches the door. She grabs the door frame for balance. 'Alfred!' she barks at him. Then Pamela goes clickety click down the stairs. We hear her calling for the boys.

'You know, I don't care if you're mean to me. But she never did anything to you. She's been a good sister-in-law.' Alfred follows her down the stairs.

'I'm going to wrap up some leftovers for them,' Mom says, following Alfred out.

'You had to blurt it out,' Tess says, throwing up her hands.

I point to Jaclyn. 'You had to tell her?'

'I felt trapped.'

My face is hot from the wine and the fight. 'Couldn't you have made something up? Something glamorous, like the clickety click of an expensive watch or something?'

'That would be Tickety Tock,' Charlie says from his guard position in the outpost by the fountain.

'You'll have to apologize to her,' Gram says quietly.

'You know I'm not supposed to get upset in my condition,' Dad says, adjusting the collar on his car coat. 'These implanted seeds are radioactive. If my blood pressure goes berserk, they're likely to blow like Mount Tripoli.'

'Sorry, Dad,' I whisper.

Dad looks at his three contrite daughters. 'You

know, we got one family here. One small island of people. We're not Iran and Iraq and Tibet, for crying out loud, we're one country. And all of youse, except you, Tom, with the Irish blood, *all* of youse have some Italian, or in the case of Charlie's people, the Fazzanis, a hundred percent Italian including that quarter Sicilian, so we got no excuses.' Dad remembers his manners and looks at Roman. 'Roman, I'm assuming you're a hundred percent.'

Roman, caught off guard, nods quickly in agreement.

Dad continues, 'We should be united, *for* one another, and we should be unbeatable. But instead what do we got? We got rancor. We got rancor coming out our ears and out our asses. And for what? Let it go. Let it all *go*. None of this matters. Take it from your father. I've seen the Grim Reaper eyeball to eyeball and he is one tough bastard. You got one life, kids. One.' Dad holds up his pointer finger and presses it skyward for emphasis. 'And trust your old man, you gotta enjoy. That's all I know. Now if Pamela has short legs and has to wear high heels to read her watch, well, we need to accept that as normal. And if Alfred loves her, then *we* love her. Do I make myself clear?'

'Yes, Dad,' Jaclyn, Tess, and I promise. Roman, Charlie, and Tom nod in agreement.

Gram's eyes are closed as she leans back on the chaise.

'So that's gonna be how it's gonna be. I'm going in.' Dad goes down the stairs.

Charlie and Tom have stepped away from the fray as far as they can go without falling off the roof. They stand with their hands in their pockets, half-expecting more bullets to fly on Christmas. When they don't, Tom looks around and says, 'Is there any more beer?'

Roman helps me into the passenger seat of his car, then climbs in the other side. I shiver as he starts the engine. His seat is pushed back as far as it can go; I push my seat back to his. 'What do you want to do?' he says.

'Take me to the Brooklyn Bridge so I can jump.'

'Funny. I have a better idea.'

Roman drives over to Sixth Avenue and heads uptown. The streets of Manhattan are bright and empty.

'I'm sorry you had to hear all that.' I reach over and hold his hand.

'One time at a Falconi Christmas, we served dinner in the garage; my brothers got into a fight and were so angry they started pelting each other with spare tires. Don't worry about it.'

'I won't now.' We laugh. 'What did you think of Alfred?'

'I don't know yet,' Roman says diplomatically.

'Alfred has very high standards. No one is allowed to fail. After my father's affair, Alfred got very righteous and even thought about going into the seminary to become a priest. But then Alfred was called by a different god. He became a banker. Of course, that's just another way to get back at Dad. My father never made a lot of money, and that's another way for Alfred to be superior. Alfred is morally and financially superior.'

'How about his wife?'

'She's under his thumb. She's so nervous, she eats baby food because she has chronic ulcers.'

'Why is he so hard on you?' Roman asks gently.

'He thinks I'm flip. I changed careers, I live with my grandmother, and I didn't close the deal with the perfect man.'

'Who was he?'

'Doesn't matter. I'm not interested in perfect.'

'What do you want?'

'You.' Roman lifts my hand and kisses it. I'm besotted, and I don't think it's a passing holiday mood. As terrible as the fight on the roof was, I was soothed by Roman's presence. He made it all better without saying a word or doing a thing. I felt protected.

Roman slows down in front of Saks Fifth Avenue and then makes the turn onto Fifty-first Street. He parks the car at the side entrance. 'Come on,' he says. He comes around to my side and helps me out of the car. 'It's Christmas. We gotta do the windows.'

He takes my hand and we walk behind the red velvet ropes. There's a Latino family down the way taking pictures in front of a window with a circus

247

act of snowmen. The father holds up his three-year-old son, near the glass.

Fifth Avenue is hushed as we look at the windows, dioramas of holiday happiness through the ages, a fussy Victorian scene where the family opens a present and the puppy pulls the ribbon from a package over and over again, another of the Roaring Twenties, with girls in bobbed haircuts and short sequin sheaths doing the Charleston in synchronized repetition.

A man with a saxophone appears on the corner of Fiftieth Street, breaking the silence with a jazz riff. Roman holds me close and moves me down the line to the tumbling-snowman window. The man with the horn stops playing, his brass sax dangling around his neck like an oversize gold charm. As we move to the next window, I look at the old man and smile. He wears a beat-up English tweed cap and an old coat. He sings,

> We have been gay, going our way
> Life has been beautiful, we have been young
> After you've gone, life will go on
> Like an old song we have sung
> When I grow too old to dream
> I'll have you to remember
> When I grow too old to dream
> Your love will live in my heart
> So, kiss me my sweet
> And so let us part
> And when I grow too old to dream

248

That kiss will live in my heart
And when I grow too old to dream
That kiss will live in my heart

Roman takes me in his arms and kisses me. When I open my eyes, the floodlights on the dormers of Saint Patrick's Cathedral disappear into the black sky in cones of white smoke. 'You want to stay at my house tonight?' he asks.

'That's about the best Christmas present I can think of.'

Back in the car, Roman looks at me and smiles. I plan to spend the ride to wherever he lives kissing his neck. And I do. He turns on the radio. Rosemary Clooney sings, sounding as smooth as whiskey and whipped cream. All I can think is that we're going to start something wonderful tonight. I bury my face in his neck and wish that this car could take off and fly us to his home.

I am falling in love! My thoughts explode like a coin shower when the winning quarter hits the release lever in a slot machine in Atlantic City. I watch myself in my mind's eye as gold disks pour out all around me by the hundreds, then thousands! I see spinning tops and ribbons unfurled, bluebirds flying out of belfries, church bells ringing, showgirls, rows of them in red sequin shorts, tap dancing at full power until the sound is so deafening you have to cover your ears. I see a bright blue sky filled with red kites, purple and white hot-air balloons, and shooting silver asteroids of fireworks that rain down like Christmas tinsel. I feel a parade coming on! Marching bands, flank after flank, in emerald green uniforms, baton twirlers in white sequin tank suits weaving in and out of formation while polished copper tubas work the street from right to left, braying a tune, my tune! My song! My head is full of sound, my eyes are full of wonder, and my heart is full of old-fashioned, spectacular joy. I open my eyes and look up at the moon, and it's flipping in the sky! A celestial coin toss! I won! I'm in the money, my friends!

Roman pulls his car into a parking garage on Sullivan Street. He leaves the key in the ignition and waves to the attendant, who waves back. We go out onto the street and he kisses me under the streetlight. 'Which one is yours?' I ask him.

'That one.' He points to a loft building, an old factory of some sort, with words carved on the door, but I can't read them. He grabs my hand and we run to the entrance. We get inside and go up in the elevator to the fourth floor, we kiss, and when the car bounces, our lips wind up on each other's noses and we laugh.

The doors of the elevator open onto an enormous floor-through loft with a series of large windows on both sides. The floors are wide planks of distressed oak with polka dots of old nail heads. Four large white pillars anchor the center of the room, creating an open, indoor gazebo. Greek-key plaster molding hems off the cathedral ceiling, while architectural pilasters lean against the wall, giving the loft a feeling of an old museum storage room. There's a large painting on the far wall of a lone white cloud on a blue night sky.

An industrial kitchen, the length of the loft, is behind us. Neat and organized, it's outfitted with state-of-the-art appliances. A wild chandelier of Murano-glass trumpet vines in orange and green hangs over the counter.

His bed, in the far corner of the room, is a four-poster, with a valance behind it of clean white muslin. The silver radiators spit steam into the silent loft. It's got to be 120 degrees in here. I begin to sweat.

'Let's get that coat off you,' he says. He kisses me as he unbuttons my coat. He doesn't stop with the coat. He undoes the tiny pearl buttons on my pale pink cashmere sweater and slips it off my shoulders. For a second, I wonder how I look, then disregard it, good, he's already seen me naked. He touches the damp drops on my forehead.

'Is this the steam heat or us?'

'Us,' I promise. He unzips my skirt. I help him off with his coat. He struggles with the sleeve of his shirt until I pull it off his arm, like a wrapper. We laugh for a moment, but then go back to kissing. I hold his face in my hands, never letting go as we move across the room. We leave a trail of our clothes on the floor, like rose petals, until we make it to his bed. He lifts me up and puts me on the soft velvet coverlet. He reaches across and opens the window. The wind blows in, ruffling the valance like summer laundry on the line. The cool air settles on us as he lies over me.

We make love to the music of the cranky boiler and the whistle of the Christmas wind. We are hot and cold, then cold and hot, but mostly hot as we tangle ourselves in each other. His kisses cover me like the velvet quilt that now lies on the floor like a parachute.

I sink down into his pillows, a spoon in chocolate cake batter.

'Tell me a story.' He pulls me close and rests his face in my neck.

'What kind of story?'

'Like the tomatoes.'

'Well, let's see. Once upon a time . . . ,' I begin. As I'm about to continue, Roman falls asleep. I look to the floor and the coverlet, knowing that sometime in the next few hours, the boiler will rest and I will freeze. But it doesn't, and I don't. The only thing I wear as I sleep are his arms. I'm warm and safe and wanted by a man I adore, who lies beside me like a mystery, and yet, enough is known to sleep deeply and dreamily long into this Christmas night. What a blissful place to rest my once weary heart, patched like the old man's coat pockets, the man who grew too old to dream.

CHAPTER 8

MOTT STREET

'Now that's my idea of a merry little Christmas.' June bites into a jelly doughnut and closes her eyes. She chews, then sips her coffee. 'You know, sex on a holiday is the best. You've had good food, scintillating conversation, or in your case, a family brawl that sets the mood for a roll in the hay. And after a fight, you know, you need it. Gets the kinks out.'

'Sounds like you've been there?' The better question may be, where *hasn't* June been?

'Oh, I could tell you about a Saint Patrick's Day in Dublin that would make your—'

'June.' Gram comes into the shop, wearing her coat and a scarf tied under her chin. She puts down her purse and takes off her gloves and coat.

'I was just about to tell Valentine about that rogue with the brogue who I met on vacation in 1972. Seamus had no shame, believe me. Delightful man.'

'I wish you'd write a book. That way, we might savor the details as a literary experience' – Gram hangs up her coat – 'and we'd have the option of checking the book out of the library . . . or not.'

'No worries. I'll never write a book. I can't be vivid on the page.' June flips the pattern paper on the cutting table like she's a matador twirling a cape. She lays it on the table. 'Only in real life.'

'The sign of a true artist,' I say and fire up the iron.

'What do you think?' Gram removes her head scarf. She turns slowly to model her new haircut and color. Her white hair is gone! Now dyed a soft brown, her hair is cut and cropped, with long layers pushed to the front, and pale gold high-lights around her face where there used to be small, pressed curls. Her dark eyes sparkle against the contrast of her pink skin and warm caramel hair color. 'I used the gift certificate you girls gave me for Christmas at Eva Scrivo's. What do you think?'

'God almighty, Teodora. You lost twenty years on the walk home,' June marvels. 'And I knew you twenty years ago, so I can say it plain.'

'Thank you.' Gram beams. 'I wanted a new look for my trip to Italy.'

'Well, you've got it,' I tell her.

'I mean *our* trip to Italy.' Gram looks at me. 'Valentine, I want you to go with me.'

'Are you serious?' I have only been to Italy on a college trip, and I would love to see it with my grandmother.

In all the years my grandparents traveled to Italy, the trips were strictly business: to buy supplies, meet fellow artisans, share information, and learn

254

new techniques. Usually, they would be gone about a month. When I was small, they went annually; in the later years, they would stagger the trips and go every two or three years. When Grandpop died ten years ago, Gram resumed her annual trips.

'Gram, are you sure you want to take me?'

'I wouldn't think of going without you. You want to win those Bergdorf windows, don't you?' Gram flips through her work file. 'We need the best materials to make them, don't you think?'

'Absolutely.' We are waiting for the dress design that Rhedd Lewis promised us. I'm learning that in the world of fashion, the only people who work on deadlines are the ones making things, not the ones selling them.

June puts down her scissors and looks at Gram. 'You haven't taken anyone to Italy in years. Not since Mike died.'

'I know I haven't,' she says quietly.

'So, what gives?' June pins down her pattern paper on the leather.

'It's time.' Gram looks around the shop, checking the bins for something to do. 'Besides, someday Valentine will run the shop, and she needs to meet everybody I deal with.'

'I wish we were leaving tonight. I'm finally going to see the Spolti Inn, and meet the tanners, and go to the great silk fabric houses in Prato. I've been waiting my whole life for this.'

'And those Italian men have been waiting for *you*,' June says.

255

'June, I'm taken.' Did she even *hear* the cleaned-up version of my Christmas night?

'I know. But it's the law of the jungle. It's been my experience, whenever I have a man, I attract more of them. And in Italy, trust me, the men line up.'

'For tips. Porters, waiters, and bellboys,' I tell her.

'Nothing wrong with a man who can do some heavy lifting for you,' June says and winks.

'Valentine will have plenty of work to do. There won't be time for hobnobbing and socializing.'

'Too bad,' June sighs.

'That's really why I'm taking you,' Gram says to me. 'You'll do the work while *I* hobnob and socialize.'

I think about those late-night calls from Italy that seem to go on for longer than necessary to order leather. I think about the man in the picture buried at the bottom of Gram's dresser. I remember our conversations about time being like ice in her hands. Is she really taking me to Italy for an education so that she might eventually hand off the Angelini Shoe Company, or is something else going on here? I expected Gram to go to Eva Scrivo and come home with a version of her old haircut, short, full, and silver, instead she walks in here looking like the senior-citizen version of Posh Beckham at an assisted-living bingo night. What gives?

There's a knock at the door.

'Let the fresh hell begin,' June says gaily.

'Gram, Bret is here for our meeting.'

'Already?' Gram says in a tone that tells me she would rather not take this meeting at all.

'Gram, I want you to have an open mind. Please.'

'I just changed my hair completely. You can assume I'm open to new things.'

I push the door open. Roman stands in the doorway with a paper cone of red roses in one hand. The other hand is behind his back. 'What a surprise!'

'Good morning.' He leans over and kisses me as he hands me the flowers. 'I was in the neighborhood.'

'They're beautiful! Thank you. Come on in!'

Roman follows me into the shop. He's wearing jeans, a wool bomber jacket, and on his feet: yellow plastic work clogs over thick white socks.

'Aren't your feet cold?'

'Not in my Wigwam socks,' he says, smiling. 'Worried about me?'

'Just your feet. We gotta work on your shoe selection. You're with a cobbler now. You made me give up Lean Cuisine lasagna so I can't let you go around in plastic clogs. I'd love to make you a pair of calfskin boots.'

'I won't say no,' he says, grinning. From behind his back, Roman produces two more bouquets of flowers. He gives one to Gram and the other to June. 'For the babes of Angelini shoes.' They fall all over him in gratitude. Then Roman notices Gram's hair. 'Teodora, I like your hair.'

257

'Thank you.' She waves the bouquet at Roman. 'You really shouldn't have!'

'Valentine's Day isn't for another month.' June inhales her bouquet.

'Every day is Valentine's Day for me.' Roman looks at me in the process. 'Now, how many of your boyfriends have used that line?'

'All of them,' I tell him.

In the powder room, I fill two pressed-glass vases with water and deliver one to Gram and one to June. I find a third vase and fill it with water for my bouquet.

Gram arranges her roses in the vase. 'It's gratifying to see that there are still men out there who know what pleases a lady.'

'In *all* ways.' June winks at me.

Gram places June's flowers in the other vase as the shop falls into deadly silence save for the rustle of the pattern paper as June cuts it. Roman, good sport that he is, spins the brushes on the buffing machine, waiting for someone to say something that isn't related to his/mine/our sex life.

'And you haven't even had my cooking yet,' Roman says to June.

'I can't wait,' June growls.

'Now, June,' I warn her. It's one thing for June to take us on a jazz tour of her love life when it's just us girls, but it's another thing entirely for her to paint the frisky picture of *The Good Old Lays* in front of Roman.

The front door pushes open.

'Good morning, ladies,' Bret calls out from the vestibule. Bret enters the shop in a navy Armani suit, with a splashy yellow tie on a crisp, white shirt. He wears polished black Dior Homme loafers with tassels.

Bret extends his hand to Roman. 'Bret Fitzpatrick.'

'Roman Falconi,' he says, giving Bret a firm handshake.

'I take it you're here for wedding shoes?' Bret jokes.

'What do you got in a thirteen?' Roman looks to Gram, June, and then me.

And here it is, my past and my future in a head-on collision. As I size them up, it's obvious to me that I like tall *and* employed. I am also my mother's daughter, and therefore, critical. Roman's clogs look like giant clown shoes next to Bret's sleek loafers. Given a choice, I would have preferred serious shoes on my boyfriend in this moment.

'Bret's an old friend of ours,' Gram says.

'He's helping us with some new business opportunities here at the shop,' I explain.

Roman looks at Bret and nods. 'Well, I won't keep you. I've got to shove off. Faicco's has some amazing veal shanks from an organic farm in Woodstock. Osso bucco is our special tonight.' Roman kisses me good-bye.

'Thank you for the flowers,' Gram says and smiles.

'Mine, too,' June says.

'See you later, girls.' Roman turns to go. 'Nice to meet you,' he says to Bret.

'You, too,' Bret says as Roman goes.

'That wasn't awkward at all,' June says as she holds a straight pin between her pursed lips. 'Something old meets something new.'

'That's your new boyfriend?' Bret looks off at the door.

'He's a chef,' Gram brags.

'Ca' d'Oro, on Mott Street,' I answer before Bret even asks. When we were a couple, our communication resembled a good game of *Jeopardy!*, and to be honest, sometimes I miss that connection.

'I've heard of it. It's supposed to be very good,' Bret says agreeably.

It's nice to know my old boyfriend isn't one bit jealous of my new one. Though maybe I wish he were. Just a little. 'I highly recommend the risotto.'

Bret sits down and opens his briefcase. He pulls out a file marked ANGELINI SHOES. 'I wanted to run something by you. Have you ladies had a chance to discuss expanding your brand?'

'Valentine mentioned a couple of things—' Gram begins.

'Gram, your hair is different. What did you do?'

'It's a new cut.'

'And a dip in Mother Dye,' June laughs. 'And I know, because I dip myself.'

'Well, you look great, Gram,' Bret says. I'm impressed with Bret's ability to soften up a resistant client. He must kill at the hedge fund.

'June, is it all right with you if we discuss business?'

'Pretend I'm not even here.'

'Valentine was telling me about the concept of branding. Now, you know, we've been in business for over a hundred years, so our brand is known and tested. It is what it is. Here's what I don't understand.' Gram smooths her new bangs off to the side. 'We make wedding shoes from our historical designs. Our catalog, if you will. We make them by hand. We can't make them any faster. How would we serve a larger clientele than we already have?'

'Valentine?' Bret tosses me the question.

'We wouldn't, Gram. Not with our core designs. We couldn't. No, we'd have to design a new shoe, one that could be mass-produced in a factory. We would introduce a more affordable, secondary line.'

'Cheaper shoes?'

'In price, yes, but not in quality.'

'I'll be honest. I don't know how to do that,' Gram says.

'Investors like to know that the product they finance has the potential for wide distribution, therefore a higher profit margin. The way you do that is to come up with something that's both fashionable and affordable and doable for the designer and manufacturer,' Bret says and hands Gram a report that says: BRANDING, GROWTH, AND PROFIT FOR THE SMALL BUSINESS. 'Now, if you

261

follow my logic, I think we can put a fund together that will buy you the time and materials to develop the business in new directions.'

'That makes sense,' I say encouragingly, but when I look at Gram, she seems unconvinced.

'So, investors are looking for you, a venerable institution, with quality brand identification, to come up with something that can be mass-produced.' Bret continues, 'Here's the beauty. It doesn't have to be a wedding shoe.'

'I see.' Gram looks at me.

'I'm thinking about creating something new that is part of our brand, but doesn't forsake the custom work in the shop,' I explain. 'This would be an outside product, created here, developed here, but manufactured elsewhere.'

'China?' Gram asks.

'Probably. Or Spain. Or Brazil. Indonesia. Maybe Italy,' I tell her.

'Are there any American companies that factory-make shoes?'

'A few.'

'Could we use one of those?'

'Gram, I'm checking into that now.' I don't want this conversation to get stuck in the Made in America argument Gram has with anyone who will listen. I have to keep her mind on the bigger picture, and our operation.

'Let's not worry about that aspect of production right now,' Bret says, backing me up. 'Let's focus on the work ahead.'

'Gram, I have to create this shoe first. I'm thinking a casual shoe, but hip. And maybe even accessories. Maybe we'll eventually expand to include those.'

'Oh, God, no. Not belts!' June interrupts. 'I'm sorry. I know I'm supposed to be the hear no evil monkey over here, but sometimes, a girl has to speak up. We tried accessories. What a disaster. Mike made belts and sold them to Saks, and they were returned, remember?'

Gram nods.

'He used a soft leather, a gorgeous calfskin that stretched like Bazooka gum after a couple of wearings. The customers were peeved and Saks was outraged. Every belt was returned.' June shakes her head. 'Every single one.'

'And Mike said "never again." He said we have to stick to what we know.'

'Well, Gram, we don't have that luxury. We have to take a chance, because if we don't, if we don't come up with something that can revitalize our business and take it to the next level, we won't be here in a year.'

'Okay, then,' Bret says, giving me the file. 'You two need to talk, and I'm going to tell my guys that you are putting together a portfolio of ideas for them.'

'You can also tell them we're going to Italy to bring them the latest innovative materials applied to classic design,' I tell him.

'Val, I never thought I'd say this, but you sound like a businessman.'

'I believe in this company.'

'That comes through.' Bret gives Gram a kiss on the cheek, then June, then me. 'Keep it up. You know what you're doing.' Bret leaves the files with us and goes.

'He really believes in you,' June says.

'He knew me when . . . ,' I tell her. 'There's something to be said for that.'

Ca' d'Oro is closed on Monday nights, so for Roman and me, it's date night. Roman usually comes over to Perry Street and I cook, or I go over to his place and he does. Tonight, though, he has invited my family to the restaurant for dinner, in reciprocation for Christmas, and as penance for missing Gram's eightieth birthday at the Carlyle. This couldn't be a more perfect setup, because I want my family to get to know him on his own turf. Ca' d'Oro is Roman's masterpiece; it says who he is, shows the scope of his culinary talents, and demonstrates that he's a real player in the restaurant world of Manhattan.

When I finished work at the shop, I came over, set the long table in the dining room, put out candles and a low vase of greens and violets for a centerpiece. Now, I'm in the kitchen acting as Roman's sous-chef. Preparing food is a respite from making shoes, mostly because I can sample the recipes as he makes them.

'So, *he's* your type?' Roman places a thin sheet of pasta dough over the ravioli tray.

264

I follow him, filling the delicate pockets with a dab of Roman's signature filling, a creamy whip of sweet potatoes mixed with slivers of truffle, aged parmesan, and herbs. 'I wondered how long it would take you to ask me about Bret.'

'He's a businessman in a suit and tie. Successful?'

'Very.'

'You're still friends, so it must not have been an ugly breakup.'

'It was a little ugly, but we were friends before, so why not stay friends after?'

'What happened?'

'A career on Wall Street and shoemaking don't complement each other. I can look back on it and appreciate it for what it was. What worked about us was our backgrounds. One of each.'

'One of each?' Roman places another sheet of pasta dough over the wells of filling. Then he places the cutting press over the dough, and punches out twelve regulation-size ravioli onto the flour-dusted butcher block. He picks the squares up one at a time and lines them up on a wooden tray, and sprinkles them with yellow cornmeal. 'Explain that to me.'

'You should never have two of the same thing in a relationship. Mix it up. Irish – Fitzpatrick, and Italian – me. Nice. Put a southerner with a northerner. Good. A Jew with a Catholic, evens out the guilt and shame nicely. A Protestant with a Catholic? Slight stretch. My parents encouraged us to marry our own kind, but too much of the same thing breeds drama.'

'Two Italians?' he asks.

'Fine if you're from different parts.'

'Good. I'm Pugliese and you're . . . what are you?'

'Tuscan and Calabrese.'

'So we're okay?'

'We're fine,' I assure him.

'Maybe it's the careers that are killers. How about a chef and a shoemaker? Does that work?'

I reach up and kiss him, saying, 'That depends.'

'But what if you're all about the drama? The drama of creativity and risk? What if that kind of passion is the thing that binds you together?'

'Well, then obviously, I would have to revisit my rule.'

'Good.' Roman lays another sheet of dough over the press. I fill the wells carefully. 'Why don't you go out in the restaurant and put your feet up?'

'No thanks. I like to help. Besides, if I didn't, I'd never see you.'

'I'm sorry,' he says tenderly. 'Occupational hazard.'

'You can't help it, and you shouldn't. You love your work and I love that you love it.'

'You're the first woman I ever dated who understands that.'

'Besides, I'm more helpful to you here than you would be to me at the shop. I can't see you sewing pink bows on bridesmaid shoes.'

'I'm lousy with a needle and thread.'

Roman lays a final sheet of pasta dough over the wells, snaps the press shut, reopens it, and a dozen ravioli squares pop out of the trap. He places them on the wooden tray with the others. Then he opens the oven and checks the roast pork and root vegetables, simmering in a wine reduction that fills the kitchen with the scent of butter, sage, and warm burgundy wine. I watch as he skillfully juggles the preparation of the meal. He invests himself in his work; it's clear he is dedicated and puts in the hours. Roman also does the research. He tests new recipes and combinations, trying things out, rejecting ideas, replacing old ones with new.

Despite the depth of my feelings (and his), I sometimes wonder how we can build a relationship when we hardly see each other. I remember reading an interview with Katharine Hepburn. She said that a woman's job in a relationship with a man was to be adorable. I attempt to be a no-fuss, stress-free, supportive girlfriend who is more than aware of the pressures he has at work, so I don't pile on more. To be fair, he does the same for me. I figure as long as we're both in the same place, I imagine this arrangement will work just fine and get us to the next level (whatever that is).

'Hi, kids!' Mom enters the kitchen loaded down with shopping bags. 'I did a downtown shopping blitz. I can't resist a deal, and nobody tops

Chinatown for bargains. Silk slippers for two dollars.' She holds up a bag stuffed with them.

'I know what I'm getting next Christmas.'

'In twelve months, you'll forget I bought these. Your sisters are here. The boys are parking. You're making ravioli?'

'Tonight's special,' says Roman.

'Yum.'

'Where's Dad?' I ask.

'He's making a shaker of Manhattans behind the bar. Is that okay, Roman?'

'Absolutely. Make yourselves at home. This night is all about you,' Roman says and smiles.

'And it's just wonderful! We have our own private chef in his own hot restaurant cooking for us. It's more than we deserve!'

'I'll meet you at the bar, Mom.' Mom goes back out to the dining room as I lift the tray of finished ravioli and place them on a portable shelf on wheels. I pull the shelf toward the worktable. 'You know my mother is very impressed with you.'

'I can tell. You win over Mama and you got the daughter.'

I reach up and kiss Roman. 'Mama doesn't have anything to do with it.'

Roman hands me a basket of homemade bread sticks to take out to the bar.

Mom and Dad sit on bar stools with their backs to the restaurant. Dad's feet, in black suede Merrells rest on the lower bar of the stool, while Mom's, in dark brown calfskin ankle boots with a high wedge heel, dangle above the foot bar, like a child's. Tess and Jaclyn stand next to the bar. Tess is wearing a red cocktail dress, while Jaclyn wears black maternity pants and a matching oversize turtleneck. Jaclyn holds up her hand. 'I know. I'm the size of a bus.'

'I didn't say a word.' I give her a quick hug.

'I saw it in your eyes.'

'Actually, I was thinking how beautiful you look.'

Jaclyn takes the bread basket and pulls a stick from the pile. 'Nice try.' She chews. 'I just hit double digits in pants.'

'I should have your pants play the stock market,' Dad jokes.

'Not funny, Dad,' Jaclyn says as she chews.

'How're you feeling?' I put my hands on my father's shoulders.

'Your mother ran me all over Chinatown like a runaway rickshaw. I'll be dead but she'll have a lifetime supply of slippers.'

'Where are your husbands?' I ask Tess.

'Parking.'

'Thank God the boys like each other.' Mom swirls her burgundy-colored Manhattan around in the tumbler and sips. 'You know that doesn't usually happen with in-laws.'

Tess looks at me.

'Ma, we *know*,' I remind her. Sometimes Mom can be clueless; after all, we've had nothing but frost with Pamela for years. 'Are Pamela and Alfred coming? They didn't RSVP.'

'We're still on the Island,' Tess says and shrugs. 'Pam hasn't spoken to any of us since the blowup at Christmas.'

'Did you call and apologize?' Mom asks her.

'I don't know what to say. Besides, Valentine should call. She's the one who blurted it out.'

'We *all* call her Clickety Click. Besides, she calls us the Meatball Sisters behind our backs and I never got an apology for that.' I sound five years old.

'Mom, you make comments about her size, too,' Jaclyn says as she fishes a cherry out of her ginger ale, pops it into her mouth, and chews.

'About her general size, her smallness, yes, but never specifically her feet.'

'Feet, ass, hands, it doesn't matter,' Dad declares. 'You girls are icky picky and Pamela got her feelings hurt. Now it's up to you to heal the rainbow. Our rainbow has a gaping hole in it right now because you can't keep your opinions to yourselves. Somebody needs to call her and straighten out the situation.'

'Your father is right. We should call her,' Mom says.

'I don't want to call her!' Jaclyn grabs another breadstick. 'I can't! I'm seasick until noon every day, and the truth is, I can't take any more stress. I'm tired of it. She's been in this family for years. Grow a hide already! Yeah, we're a tough crowd, but so what? And while you're at it, eat a sandwich. Clickety Click? It's more like Thin-ety-thin.'

'The pregnancy hormones have arrived,' Mom whispers. 'Must be a boy.'

Charlie and Tom enter the restaurant and greet Mom and Dad. Roman comes out of the kitchen with a plate of fried pumpkin blossoms. He places them on the bar, then shakes their hands.

'I'm giving you four stars already for the parking. It was a slam dunk.' Charlie takes off his coat.

'Parking is a snap in Little Italy,' Dad says. 'Italians know how to attract business, right, Roman? And when we taste your food, we'll tell you if you can keep it.' Dad throws Roman a wink.

Roman forces a smile. My father doesn't notice. Gram pushes the door open and enters. She takes off her hat, shakes out her new hair, and then turns full circle, like a model. Charlie and Tom whistle, while my sisters marvel at her brown hair.

'Ma! You're a brunette again!' Mom claps her hands together joyfully. 'Finally you took my advice!'

Dad spins around on his bar stool. 'Somebody's been throwin' back her Geritol,' he says approvingly.

'Mom, now you can trim another five years off your age,' Tess offers.

'At least! If eighty is the new sixty, that makes me forty!'

'And that makes me a perv.' Dad sips his drink. 'With your fuzzy math, I'm old enough to be your father.'

'Nothing wrong with an older man,' Mom says and shrugs.

'Alfred is on his way,' Gram announces.

'He told me he wasn't coming.' Mom goes behind the bar to pour Gram a Manhattan.

'I told him he *had* to come.' Gram puts her tote bag on a stool by the bar. 'I'm tired of this silly feud. I've seen enough of them in my lifetime. A family fight stagnates, then over time turns into a hundred-year war, and nobody remembers what the argument was about in the first place.'

'My sediments exactly, Ma.'

'*Sentiments*,' Mom corrects Dad.

'Should we wait for Alfred to begin?' Roman asks Gram. 'I'll go ahead and bring the food out,' he says on the way to the kitchen.

'Need me?' I ask him.

'I got it,' he calls over his shoulder.

I catch Roman's exasperated tone. My family has done nothing but complain since they arrived. My boyfriend got a very tired look on his face when my family rehashed the Pamela Christmas tiff. No one should have to live through that twice.

'The sketch of the wedding gown arrived.' Gram hands me a large gray envelope marked BG from her tote. 'Hand-delivered by Bergdorf Goodman.'

The sketch of the wedding gown we are to design a shoe for is rendered in ink and watercolor on a heavy sheet of drawing paper. The silhouette shows shards of chiffon, which look like they've been cut with a steak knife and sewn haphazardly onto a fitted sheath. It looks like a dress made of fine silk that accidentally ended up in the washing machine. It's dreadful.

'Who needs shoes with this gown? You need a coat.' I give the design to Tess.

'One that buttons from neck to ankle.' Gram shakes her head. 'Who is Rag and Bone?'

'Two hot designers,' I tell her.

Mom puts on her reading glasses and peers through them at the design. 'Oh dear, is there some sort of new austerity program in place?' She hands it off to Jaclyn. 'I don't understand why they wouldn't use someone like Stella McCartney. She's classic and romantic and whimsical.'

'And your mother was in love with her father. Paul was her favorite Beatle,' Dad chimes in.

'I'm not going to apologize for my good taste,' Mom says and swigs her drink. Roman brings a tureen of ravioli to the table.

Jaclyn gives me the design. 'Why can't things be pretty? Why does everything have to be so ugly?' Jaclyn weeps, then bangs her hands on the table. 'What is wrong with me? Why am I crying?' she sobs. 'I'm not crying inside my mind – inside my mind, I'm sane! It's just a dress. I don't care about that dress,' she blubbers. 'But I can't stop . . .' Roman goes behind the bar and pulls out a box of tissues. He places them on the table, next to Jaclyn.

'Now, now.' Mom puts her arm around Jaclyn to soothe her.

'God, I wish I could drink! Four more months

with nothing to take the edge off!' Jaclyn puts her head in her hands and cries, 'I need booze!'

Roman exhales slowly as he surveys the table. He has the same look on his face that he did during the fight on Christmas Eve. He's trying not to judge, but he's definitely annoyed. Good food doesn't matter when you're serving it to angry people.

Alfred pushes open the entrance door, bringing a brisk shot of cold air in with him. Alfred extends his hand to Roman. 'Nice to see you again,' he says with a tone as chilly as the winter wind he dragged in.

'I'm glad you could make it,' Roman says pleasantly, but he looks as though he's got six Roncallis too many in the restaurant already.

Alfred doesn't move to take off his coat. Instead, he surveys the tops of our heads, refusing to make eye contact. He finally walks over to Mom and kisses her on the cheek. He shakes Dad's hand. 'I can't stay. Gram asked me to show up and say hello, but I have to get going soon.'

Tess looks down at her empty appetizer plate, while big wet tears drop onto Jaclyn's sweater like dew. 'What's the matter, Jaclyn?' Alfred asks her.

She sobs, 'I don't know!'

'Please, Alfred. Stay at least for the antipasto,' Dad implores him. What can Alfred do? Say no to his sick father?

Alfred pulls out a chair. 'Just for a minute.'

'Great.' Roman forces a smile. 'I've got a fresh antipasto, followed by a specialty of the house, a truffle ravioli, and then we're having pork roast with roasted root vegetables.'

'I'd like to see the menu,' Dad jokes. Everyone laughs except Roman.

We take our seats. Alfred sits on the far end, next to Gram. Dad sits at the head of the table on one end, while Roman takes the seat at the head of the table closest to the kitchen. We dig into a platter of rolled salami, sweet sheets of pink prosciutto, glossy olives, sun-dried tomatoes, hunks of fresh parmesan, and flaky tuna drizzled in olive oil. Roman puts a basket of homemade bread, fresh from the oven, in rotation around the table.

Jaclyn passes the sketch of the dress to Alfred.

'What's this?'

'The Bergdorf dress.'

He looks at it. 'You got to be kidding.'

'It's definitely a design challenge,' I say, forcing a smile.

'You really think that this is going to change the course of the shoe company?' He shakes his head.

'We can only try,' I say evenly, resisting the temptation to snap back at him. I take the sketch from him and slip it back into the envelope, placing it on the table behind me. A dull quiet settles over the table. Roman surveys our plates, making certain his guests have what they need. He stands quickly and replenishes our wineglasses.

'Dad, how are you feeling?' Charlie asks.

'Pretty good, Chuck. You know, I get a burning sometimes, in my nether parts—'

'Not while we're eating, honey,' Mom says.

'Hey, he asked. And I *do* get a burning sensation.'

'When are you going to Italy, Gram?' Alfred changes the subject.

'April. Valentine is going with me.'

'Why?'

'I'm going to meet the suppliers,' I explain.

'April. I love Italy in April,' Roman says as he sits back down.

'You should join us.' I squeeze Roman's hand.

'I just might.'

'I'd invite myself along, but it's planting season in Forest Hills,' Mom says gaily.

'For the record, we can't fit any further flora and fauna on Austin Street.' Dad waves his fork at Mom.

'Honey, you say that, and then, voilà, there's another gorgeous rhododendron or strip of yellow phlox thriving somewhere in the garden.'

'There's always room for phlox,' I say and pass the bread to Jaclyn, who finds the word *phlox* so funny, she can't stop laughing. 'Now what?' I ask her.

'I don't know,' she giggles. 'It's like I had too much sugar and I'm on the scrambler at Six Flags. On the inside, I'm not laughing. I swear,' she laughs. 'Bah-ha-ha.'

'I never had those mood swings when I was pregnant,' Tess says.

'Who are you kidding? It was like Glenn Close with the curly perm moved in. You hid in closets.

You read my e-mails. You swore I was having an affair,' Charlie says.

'I don't remember that at all,' Tess insists. 'But childbirth? That's another story.'

Tess rips a piece of bread in two and butters it. 'They say you forget, but you don't.'

'Tess, you're scaring me,' Jaclyn says. Tom pats her hand.

Roman looks at me and raises both eyebrows. He stands, picks up the tureen, and goes around the table serving the ravioli. I can see he's about to snap, between Dad's burning groin, Tess and Charlie's fussing, and Jaclyn's weeping, this isn't exactly the kind of light dinner conversation that goes well with handmade ravioli. What's the matter with my family anyhow? They almost seem annoyed to be here, as if coming to dinner at a hot Manhattan restaurant was a supreme sacrifice. On top of their surly moods, they seem oblivious to the amount of work Roman has put into this meal for *them*.

I try and make up for my family. 'Roman, the ravioli is scrumptious.'

'Thank you.' Roman sits down.

Why aren't they complimenting his cooking? I kick Tess under the table.

'Ow,' she says.

'Sorry.' I look at her but she doesn't catch my cue.

When Tess was dating Charlie, I knocked myself out to make him feel welcome. I listened to Charlie drone on about installing home-security systems until my eyes rolled back in my head like martini olives. When Jaclyn got serious with Tom, she warned us that he was 'shy,' so we made sure to bring him in on every conversation, to try and include him. He finally told Tess and me to back off, that it wasn't necessary to include him in our dull conversations, he gets enough of that at work. We've failed with Pamela, but it wasn't from lack of trying; she's just not into the stuff we enjoy, like eating, so it's always been a struggle to find common ground. When Alfred was dating her, we were on our best behavior, but once they married, it was too much work.

Now, as I look around the table, reciprocation of my kind gestures toward my sisters and brother when they were bringing someone new into the family has gone out the window. It seems they are just too jaded, disinterested, and old to put on a good face for Roman. He's getting the rent-a-wreck version of my family when the rest of the in-laws got the Cadillac treatment. It's almost assumed that *Funnyone* isn't a serious player in romance, so why bother? Why use the good china on Roman, he won't be around anyway. But they're wrong. They are my family, and they should be on my side and, God forbid, root for my happiness. Tonight, it's clear they couldn't care less. Here they are at a restaurant short-listed in *New York* magazine for Best Italian Eatery and they act like they're grabbing a sweaty hot dog in wax paper out of a bin at Yankee Stadium. Don't they see that this is special? That *he* is special?

'Are you going to tell the chef what you think?' I say so loudly that even Roman is startled. The family does an en masse *hmm, good, great* garble that seems insincere.

And then Alfred says, 'Who's paying for the trip to Italy?'

'We are,' I tell him.

'More debt.' He shrugs.

'We need leather to make shoes,' I snap at him.

'You need to modify your operation and sell the building,' he says. 'Gram, I agreed to come tonight hoping that I might be able to tell Scott what your plans are.'

Now I'm really angry. This dinner was supposed to be a lovely evening about getting to know my new boyfriend, and now it's turned into agenda night for the Angelini Shoe Company. 'Could we talk about this another time?'

'I have an answer for Alfred,' Gram says quietly.

Alfred smiles for the first time this evening.

'I've been doing a little research on my own,' Gram begins. 'I had a long talk with Richard Kirshenbaum. Remember him?' She turns to Mom. 'He used to run the printing factory on the West Side Highway? He and his wife owned it.'

'I remember her well. Dana. Stunning brunette. Amazing fashion sense. How is she?' Mom asks.

'Retired,' Gram deadpans. 'Anyhow, I told him about the offer and he advised me to wait.

He said that Scott Hatcher's offer wasn't nearly enough.'

'Not enough?' Alfred puts his hands on the table.

'That's what he said.' Gram picks up her fork. 'But we can talk about the details another time.'

'You know what, Gram? We don't have to. I can see Valentine and her crazy ideas have gotten to you and you're not thinking clearly.'

'I'm clear,' Gram assures him.

'No, you're just buying time.'

'First of all, Alfred, if I could buy time, I would have done it already. It's the only thing I don't have enough of. Though none of you would understand that, not having reached your eightieth birthdays.'

'Except for me.' Dad waves his white napkin in surrender and continues. 'Time? It's like a freakin' gong in my head in the middle of the night. And then I get the cold sweats of death. I'm hearing the call to arms, believe me.'

'Okay, Dutch, you're right. You're exempt. You would understand this because you have a health situation—'

'Damn right.'

'—that would make you empathetic to old age. But the rest of you are too young to understand.'

'What does this have to do with your building?' my brother asks impatiently.

'I am not going to be pushed into anything. And I feel you're pushing me, Alfred.'

'I want what's best for you.'

'You're rushing me. And as far as Mr Hatcher is concerned, he is looking out for his best interests, not mine.'

'It's a cash offer, Gram. As is. He'd buy the building *as is*.'

'And as it is, today, I'm not selling.'

'Okay. Fine.' Alfred places his napkin next to his plate. He stands and moves to the door. Roman shakes his head in disbelief at my brother's lack of manners.

'Honey!' Mom calls after him. He goes through the door. Mom goes after him.

Dad looks at me. 'See what you started?'

'Me?'

I look to Roman, but he is gone. 'Great. Now dinner is ruined. I hope you're all happy.' I throw down my napkin. 'Now that's something to cry about.' I look to Jaclyn, who suddenly can't muster a tear.

I go into the kitchen. Roman is carefully slicing the pork loin and placing it on a platter. 'I'm sorry.'

'It's okay. It's actually worse in my family. When they're not complaining, they're plotting.' Roman puts down his carving knife, wipes his hands on a moppeen, and comes around the butcher-block table and puts his arms around me. 'Let it go,' he says.

I pretend, for his sake, that I can. But I know, having seen the expression on his face and his abrupt exit to the kitchen, that my family just became a potential deal breaker in our relationship.

281

Roman left Chicago because of this kind of infighting and competition in his own family, why should he put up with it from mine? Why would any man sign on for this kind of nonsense, even when it's achingly familiar?

As complex as Roman is in the kitchen, when it comes to his private life, he is a minimalist. He doesn't clutter his loft with unnecessary furniture, his kitchen with dust-collecting gadgets, or his heart with emotional fracases. He makes quick decisions and clean breaks. I've seen him do it. He is not a fan of drama for the sake of it, and the last thing he wants to do is argue. He wants his life outside work, which is competitive and volatile, to be the opposite: calm and peaceful. My family, even when I beg them, cannot deliver that. Sensing my feelings, he says, 'Don't worry.'

'Too late,' I tell him.

CHAPTER 9

THE HUDSON RIVER

Last week, Gram left for her annual two-week Lenten retreat with the women's sodality of Our Lady of Pompeii. The ladies stay at a convent in the Berkshires during the ides of March, and find inner peace through participation in daily masses, group rosaries, hikes in the woods, and meals so loaded with starch that when Gram returns home she has to juice for a week to clear out the gluten. However, she considers the sacrifice well worth it because, while her body may take a health hit, her soul is cleansed. *Mezzo. Mezzo.*

I'm aiming to have my sketch of the shoe design for the competition at Bergdorf's finished by the time Gram returns. I want to have a clear notion of what we'll need to build the shoes before we go to Italy. While Gram has left the design of the shoe up to me, she promised to weigh in with any refinements or corrections before we turn it into a pair of real shoes and deliver them to Rhedd Lewis. I have become obsessed with the sketch of the dress, studying it so often, I see it when I sleep. I've come to appreciate the design, and the strange charm of it. The Rag & Bone gown has grown on me.

It's helpful to have the house to myself. I'm one of those people who actually savors being alone. I like to get up in the middle of the night, turn on the lights, put on a pot of coffee, and get to work without fear of waking Gram. There is nothing more peaceful than New York City at three A.M. It's the rest period before the madness begins at dawn.

I relish a big space with nobody in it but me. Virginia Woolf celebrated a room of one's own, but I've learned that I require a house of my own. When I'm designing, I fill all available surfaces with offbeat objects that inspire me: a marble bocce ball that's the exact shade of vanilla ice cream, a small watercolor of a cloud that has hues of lavender on a field of white, wheels of paint chips, boards of fabric swatches and skeins of silk trim. I like to create a circus of ideas, which I can walk through and live with, until something speaks to me. Slowly, I winnow out the claptrap until I'm left with just a few things that move me the most. This is how my mind works, several concepts at play at once, all advancing toward an unknown conclusion; disparate pieces becoming a new whole, in this case, a pair of shoes for a wedding gown that may, on the surface, appear to be in tatters, but is actually, after hours of study, a dress design that is forward thinking and new. My laptop is propped open, ready to record any ideas I have, and to provide available research when I need a goose in a particular direction.

The dining table is covered in fabric folded neatly

in rectangles, a few old shoes I've saved from yard sales, a crocheted bride doll that belonged to my mother in the 1950s and a large collage that I've been making since we first met with Rhedd Lewis. I started the collage on an enormous sheet of butcher paper. I pasted images, photographs, scenes, and words from old magazines, then textured the whole by gluing on artful bits of lace, buttons, and loose crystals. Somewhere in this wild stew, which my subconscious directed, lies my design, or at least, the impulse that will guide me through the process of designing our shoe.

Using Rhedd's sketch as a jumping-off point, my collage is a landscape of women, collected from couture photo shoots, advertisements, and newspaper stories, most of whom are in repose or turned away from the camera's lens. I imagine the woman in the Rag & Bone sketch, who she might be and why she chose this particular design above all others to wear on her wedding day. My instincts say this dress isn't for a first-time bride. It's for a woman who has been down the road of true love more than once; she's jaded and even a little ambivalent, hence the unfinished details and frayed chiffon. If the bride is not committed, her gown isn't either.

Gram has taught me that, as custom cobblers, we have succeeded only when we have taken something a client *needs* and turned it into something she *desires*. I have to think like the bride who chooses to wear this gown and design shoes to complement *her* style.

We use line to accent and play up the individual customer's physical attributes, we use balance to make the shoe comfortable and provide a seamless fit, form is mandated by personal taste and silhouette, shape is about taking current trends and making the shoe contemporary, color is about working with the dress design so both elements flow as one, pattern is used to accent the fabric of the gown, while texture is about the overall statement of the shoe. Is the leather or fabric appropriate for the time of year the bride is married, and do all the elements feed seamlessly into the overall presentation?

Gram says to keep it simple but not to be afraid of dramatic elements. These are the arenas an apprentice must master. All these notes must dance in the head of the artist as she creates; one element cannot take precedence over another, rather, the goal is a harmonious confluence of all of them. This harmony creates beauty.

I look at the shards of chiffon on the sketch. I prop it up against the candlesticks on the dining room table and walk to the kitchen and look at it from across the room. It reminds me of something. Something specific. And then I remember. I climb the stairs to Gram's room.

Gram was married in 1948 in an eggshell silk-georgette gown with a scoop neck and sheer, short, puffed sleeves of organza with a wide band of fabric around the upper arm. The natural, fitted waist flowed out to a full circle skirt. There were accents aplenty: ornate handmade Italian cutwork lace was sewn on every seam. There was spider lace on the bodice, facing, and tips of the voluminous ruffles on the hem of the skirt. A photograph of Gram tossing the bouquet shows the gown from the back, where there are wings of tulle fashioned like a capelet, which must have trailed behind Gram like a mist when she walked. It was a typical postwar, pre-New Look ensemble, overtly feminine and deliberately overdone. The war was over and, evidently, one of the great prizes was the sea of femininity that awaited the soldiers as they returned home.

Today the design looks cluttered and home-made, like the crocheted bride doll my mother loved as a girl. Gram's gown has small seed pearls on the bodice, whereas the doll has pearls on the clunky layers of yarn skirt. Gram wears the bright red lipstick and pencil-thin eyebrows of the postwar era, whereas the doll's face is piquant, with red Cupid's bow lips and no eyebrows at all. The look on both faces is pure domestic content-ment. I can even picture Gram the following morning, lipstick matte, eyes sparkling, flipping pancakes, wearing a starched sheer organza apron with a frilly pocket shaped like a heart. A joyful wife the morning after her blissful wedding night begins a new life.

As I flip through the black-and-white photo-graphs of my grandparents' wedding, I look for clues. There's something I remember about these photographs that will help me with the design. I'm just not sure what.

Finally, I find a photograph of Gram's wedding shoes as she lifts the hem of her gown slightly to expose the garter. Gram wears a pair of cream-colored, leather platform sandals. The folds of the leather on the vamp are tufted into diamond shapes accented with small leather buttons.

How interesting: boot buttons on an open sandal.

The gown in the sketch, with its seemingly haphazard layers of ripped material, needs a substantial shoe, but not a boot, to stabilize it. Platforms are out, but hefty straps, large buckles, and bows are in. Somehow, I have to make the eye go to the feet and not to the dress. I'm beginning to understand the point of the Rhedd Lewis challenge. This dress is all about *not* looking at it, but directing the eye to the shoe. And here it is, the epiphany, the beam of clarity, the moment of truth I have been waiting for: make the shoe drive the dress.

I get out my sketchbook and begin to draw my grandmother. I copy the expression on her face in the photo album, her wide eyes, her hair in sausage-roll curls.

Then I take the dress in the sketch and draw it anew, on Gram's body. I create a new silhouette, feminine but strong. Gone is the fussiness, replaced with modern restraint. The wide streamers of ripped chiffon now seem fresh, not haphazard.

I flip the page in my sketchbook. I draw the

shape of the foot, then fill it, with wide straps and a tongue of soft leather anchoring the straps. Then I add texture on the straps, some of smooth leather, others with the striae of silk, a combination of materials that gives it a new-century feeling. I'll worry about how to execute this later. Right now, it's about the freedom of letting the idea loose on the page. The gown exposes leg, so I follow that line down to the ankle of the shoe, creating an oversize bow around the ankle, a touch of femininity that looks powerful, like the boot laces on the Mighty Isis in the comic books I loved as a girl. The condition of the fabric gives me license to create a shoe that uses scraps, pieces of luxe materials, soft leathers, off beat embossing on the leather, whimsical braiding, bold embell-ishments, and oversize pearls on the strap anchors.

I draw and erase and draw and erase. I sketch again. Soon, I take my putty eraser and reshape the heel. It's too definitive, it needs to be more architectural to read *modern*. Right now, it's too similar to Gram's stacked heel in 1948, so I add half an inch to the height of the heel and sculpt it until the heel comes into focus to match the rest of the shoe.

My cell phone rings. I pick it up.

'You online?' Gabriel asks.

'No, I'm drawing.'

'Well, get online. You're on *WWD* flash.'

'No way!'

I pull the laptop over. *Women's Wear Daily* has

an online board that announces changes in the fashion industry, acquisitions and sales.

'Scroll down to "Rhedd Lewis Windows."'

I scroll down:

Rhedd Lewis shook up the Fifth Avenue aesthetes by announcing a contest among handpicked (by her) shoe designers who will vie to have their line in the Christmas windows. Stalwarts include: Dior, Ferragamo, Louboutin, Prada, Blahnik, and Americans: Pliner, Weitzman, and Spade. Tory Burch is also said to be in the running. Custom Village shop Angelino Shoes is also said to be under consideration.

'You made it!'

'Made what? We're misspelled. Angelino?'

'Maybe they'll think you're Latino. That's a good thing. Anything Latino is hot. You know, you'll be *ValRo*. Like *JLo* is JLo. There you go. You're in the moment.'

'We *are* in the moment, Gabriel,' I say, defending my fledgling brand.

'Hey, don't shoot the messenger.'

I hang up and close the screen on the laptop. I put my head down on the table. I liked this process better when I didn't know the competition. Those huge, multimillion-dollar corporations have the resources of the universe at their disposal, and I'm sitting here with rubber cement, some old shoes, and a crocheted doll for inspiration. What was I thinking? That we could *win*? My brother, Alfred, is right. I'm a dreamer, and not a very good one.

I pick up my pencil and go back to work. I started this process, so I must finish it. It's funny. As I shade the buttress, I can see the shoe in completion in my mind's eye. Will my vision carry me through? Or is this a real fool's errand?

The front door buzzer startles me, and I get up to buzz Roman in. The oven clock says 3:34 A.M. I hear Roman's footsteps on the stairs. When he reaches the top of the stairs, he stands in the doorway, leaning against the sashes, propping his body up with both hands.

'Hi, hon,' he says.

I keep sketching. 'I'll be right there.' I want to fill in this heel before I forget what I saw in my mind's eye.

He comes into the kitchen and runs the faucet, filling a glass of water. He comes and stands over my shoulder. I finish the oversize pearl button and put down my pencil and paper. I stand and put my arms around him. He is exhausted, weary from the long hours. I don't even have to ask, but I do anyway. 'How was work?'

'A disaster. I fired my sous-chef. He's just not up to speed, and he's extremely temperamental. I can't have two hotheads in the kitchen.'

He sits down. 'I don't know how my parents have done it, how they've stayed in business this long. Running a restaurant is impossible.' Roman puts the glass down and puts his head in his hands. I rub his neck.

'You'll figure it out,' I whisper quietly in his ear.

'Sometimes I wonder.'

I move my hands down to his shoulders. 'Your shoulders are like cement.'

I continue rubbing his shoulders, feeling the pain in my right hand from sketching for too long. I stop and rub my wrist.

'Come on, let's go to bed.' I lead him up the stairs. He goes into the bathroom while I turn down the covers. I dim the lights in the bedroom. Roman comes into my room, undresses, and climbs into bed. I fluff the covers around him, and he burrows into the pillows. Soon, he's snoring.

I lie back on the pillows and look up at the ceiling, as I have every night since I moved in. My eye travels around the crown molding, here since the place was built, its Greek-key design reminding me of icing on a cake. The spare white center of the ceiling is like a fresh sheet of sketch paper, empty and longing to be filled. I fill the space with the living image of my grandmother in the Rhedd Lewis gown, wearing the shoes I created. She moves across the expanse of white deliberately and willfully. She is wearing the shoes, the shoes aren't wearing her, even though they are ornate and structured, they are also wily and fun, as couture shoes should be.

I exhale slowly, as if to blow the images off the ceiling and erase them from my mind's eye.

I imagine Rue de Something or Another on a sunny day in Paris as Christian Louboutin pores over his winning sketch for Rhedd Lewis surrounded by a team of French geniuses, in their expansive, modern, state-of-the-art design lab. The workers bring forth sheets of soft calfskin. They fill the table with sumptuous fabrics – silk moiré, taffeta, crepe de chine, and embroidered velvet. Christian points out aspects of his brilliant sketch to the workers. They applaud. Of course they win the windows, why wouldn't they? The applause becomes deafening. *I'm screwed*, I think. *I'm screwed*. And my greatest folly was thinking for one second that I could actually compete with the big guns. The *Angelino* Shoe Company. Win? The odds of that are about as good as my father learning to pronounce *prostate*. It will never happen.

I turn over and put my arm around Roman, who has fallen into a deep sleep. I imagined so much more for us with the full run of the house. I dreamed of romantic nights drinking wine on the roof while I point out the hues and shifts of the Hudson River; I imagined Roman making me dinner in the old kitchen downstairs, then making love in this bed in my room. Other nights, where we just relax, he with his feet up on the old ottoman, me next to him while we watch *The Call of the Wild* so I might teach him everything I know about Clark Gable. Instead, he is gone all day, works through supper and into the night, comes home near dawn, bone tired, and crashes. As soon as the sun is up, after a quick cup of coffee, he is gone again.

We don't have the long, intense conversations that I crave. In fact, we hardly talk at length because there never seems to be enough time. The texting, the twenty-second phone calls, while plentiful, make me feel needed, but then I feel abandoned when he hangs up in midsentence. In the rush of it all, I assign him feelings and tenderness he may not have, because there isn't time to find out what he's feeling. When we do scrape together an hour here or there, his phone doesn't stop ringing, and there's always some crisis in the kitchen that only he can negotiate, and usually, it needs his immediate attention. To be fair, I've been consumed with my work, too, with the slate of orders in the shop, trying to find financing to move forward, and the competition for the Bergdorf windows. I'm probably not full of fun because I'm busy, with work and life, worried about my father's health and my future.

Maybe this is what relationships *are*. Maybe this is the work my mother and Gram refer to when they talk about marriage. Maybe I must accept the disappointments because it's nearly impossible to make room for someone in a life crowded with ambition, drive, and deadlines. Now is the time to establish our careers, as the opportunity may not come later. Roman had his wake-up call, so he moved to New York and started his own restaurant. I surely had mine when I found out about the debt, and my brother's determination to sell the building. I'm not just an apprentice anymore. I have to mastermind the future so that I *have* a place to work in the years to come. Roman and I know where we're going in our careers, but where are we headed in our private lives? I touch his face with my hand. He opens his eyes.

'What is it?' he says groggily.

I want to tell him everything. But instead, I don't. I can't. So I whisper, 'Nothing. It's nothing. Go back to sleep.'

'I don't care if it's Lent. A bribe is a bribe and they work,' Tess tells me as she fishes two Hershey kisses out of the bottom of her purse. 'Charisma? Chiara?' The girls clomp down the stairs to the workshop, then burst through the door like two pink bottle rockets.

Tess looks down at them. 'Enough with the running and the jumping and the noise. Young ladies should have some finesse. You sound like a longhorn cattle drive on those stairs.'

'Well, you called us.' Charisma stands before her mother in a shiny pink T-shirt that says PRINCESS and a full tulle skirt that conjures up the lead swan in the ballet. Her black laceless Converse sneaker slips-ons have two rolls of knee socks clumped around her ankles. Chiara is still dressed by my sister, so she wears a pressed pink-striped corduroy jumper, a blouse with a Peter Pan collar, and Stride Rite lace-up boots.

'Cool down. There's a chocolate kiss in it for you if you do. Mommy is trying to talk to Auntie Valentine.'

Charisma and Chiara put their hands out. Tess drops a kiss in each.

'I'm saving mine!' Chiara hollers as she follows her sister back up the stairs.

'I'm the worst mother. I use payola.'

'Whatever means necessary,' I tell her.

'How's it going with Roman?'

'Not so great.'

'You're kidding. What happened to making 166 Perry Street into a love spa while Gram's on retreat?'

'It's so *not* a love spa. I work all day. I sketch all night. He works all day *and* all night, gets here at three in the morning, goes to sleep, and wakes up the next morning and goes. I'm getting a little taste of what a permanent relationship would be like with him, and let's just say that the only permanent thing about Roman is that he's perpetually in motion.'

'That would change if you married him.'

'*Married* him? I can't even get him to commit to go to the movies.'

'You have to make Roman focus on you. When we were dating, Charlie was so invested in his job it scared me. After we got married, his priorities shifted. Our family comes first. Now he goes to work, and when he comes home, life begins.' Tess puts her hand on her heart. 'Us. The part of his life that matters.'

We hear a loud crash upstairs. We run to the vestibule. Chiara appears at the top of the stairs with Charisma.

'What was that?' Tess yells. The hand on her loving heart has turned into a fist that she shakes in the air.

'I spun Charisma in a pas de deux. Don't worry. She landed on the rug.'

'Stop throwing your sister around. Sit and watch your show.'

The girls disappear into the living room.

Tess looks at me. 'Don't look at my children as an example of what yours might be someday. You might have ones who behave.' Tess looks up at the clock. 'Mom can't get here fast enough. She knows how to handle those two.'

June pushes the door open with her hip. She carries two green plastic flowerpots filled with purple hyacinths. 'We need some spring around here,' she says, handing the pots off to Tess.

'Val is going to break up with Roman.' Tess takes the flowers to the sink and runs water into the pots.

'I didn't say that.'

'It sounded like it to me,' Tess says.

'Why on earth would you give him the boot?' June asks.

'We hardly see each other. He's busy, I'm busy.'

'So?' June buries her hands in her pockets and looks at me.

'*So?* It's a pretty big deal that we barely lay eyes on each other.'

'Everybody's busy. Do you think people get less busy as time goes on? It gets worse. I'm busier now than I've ever been, and if I sat down and tried to figure out why, I couldn't. There's no ideal situation out there. A shot of a good man even once in a while is not a bad thing.'

'I hear you,' I say. When it's good with Roman, it's the best it can be. I sometimes think that the good stuff blinds me to reality, sways me to keep trying. But is that enough? Should it be?

'You have a perfect situation.' June pours herself a cup of coffee. 'You see each other, you have fun, then you go your separate ways. I'd be with a man myself right now if they didn't eventually nag me to move in. I don't want somebody in my house twenty-four/seven. I like my own life, thank you.'

'My sister wants a family someday.' Tess puts the hyacinth in the front window where the sun can get to the clusters of starburst petals. 'She's traditional,' Tess says.

'Am I?' I ask aloud. I've never thought of myself as particularly traditional. I guess I appear to be one of my tribe, but the truth is, whenever I have the opportunity to walk the hard line of tradition, I balk.

The entrance door creaks open. 'Hi-yo!' Mom calls out in the vestibule.

'In here, Mom,' I holler.

Mom comes into the shop roaring like a March leopard in a spotted trench coat fit for the random rainstorms of spring. She'd be a March lion but she looks pasty in solid beige, and besides, leopard print is her trademark. Mom wears black leggings, shiny black rubber rain demiboots, and a wide-brimmed patent leather rain hat tied under the chin with a bow. 'Are the girls ready?'

Tess goes to the foot of the stairs and calls for her daughters. They don't answer. We hear her shout, 'Okay, I'm coming up.' Tess goes up the stairs.

'She really needs to get a grip on those children,' Mom says softly.

'She's hoping you will. Where's Dad?'

'Home. He's not feeling so hot today.' Mom forces a smile. 'He's exhausted from the treatments.'

'They're working, aren't they, Mom?'

'The doctor says they are. The radiation team at Sloan is very optimistic.'

For the first time since Dad was diagnosed, Mom looks tired to me. The constant appointments have taken a toll on her. When she's not running my father to the doctors, she's educating herself about his illness. She reads about what he should eat, how often he should rest, and which holistic supplements to take and when. She has to go out and find all the stuff, the organic food and medicinal herbs, then go home and prepare the dishes, strain the tea, and, then, the hardest part of all: force my father to follow the regimen. This is a man who would sprinkle grated cheese on cake if he could. He's not exactly a compliant patient, and it shows on my mother's face. She hasn't had a good night's rest in months, and it's clear to me that she needs a break.

'Mom, you look exhausted,' I say gently.

'I know. Thank God for Benefit's LemonAid. I smear that concealer on the dark circles under my eyes like I'm buttering bread.'

June pours Mom a cup of coffee. Mom takes the mug and is about to put the cup down on my sketchbook. I push it aside and give her a rubber cat's-paw heel for a coaster instead.

'What can you do?' Mom sighs and sips her coffee, holding the mug with one hand and opening my sketchbook with the other. She absent-mindedly flips through it. Then, she focuses and stops on my recent sketch for the Bergdorf shoe. I'm just about to pull the notebook away when Mom says, 'My father was so gifted.' She holds up the sketch and shows it to June. 'Look at this.'

June looks at the drawing and nods. 'That man was ahead of his time. The wide straps, the button details. Look at the heel. Wide at the base, into a spindle at the tip. Completely courant and the man has been dead ten years.'

'That's not Grandpop's sketch.' I take a deep breath. 'It's mine.'

'What?' June takes the sketchbook. 'Valentine. *This* is brilliant.'

'That's the shoe we're going to make for the Bergdorf competition. At least, that's the one I'm going to show Gram, and if she likes it, we'll build it.'

'You really have the gift.' June puts the sketchbook down on the table. 'Wow.'

'Genetics. It's all in the DNA. Good taste cannot be learned or bought.' Mom tightens the belt on her trench coat. 'It is inborn of natural talent and honed with hard work. Valentine, all the hours you're putting in here are paying off.'

'That's quite a shoe,' June says. 'Complex. How are we going to build it?'

'Well, I'm hoping I can find some of the elements in Italy.'

'Good, because we don't have embossed leather like that in this shop. And that braiding – I've never seen anything like it.' June shakes her head.

'I know. I just . . . dreamed it up.'

Charisma and Chiara run into the workroom. 'Aunt June, do you have any candy?'

'What did you give up for Lent?' June, the fallen-away Catholic asks them.

Chiara stares at June. Charisma, no fool, steps forward and answers her, 'Well, we don't give up candy, we just try and do good deeds.'

'And what would those be?'

'I'm nice to the cat.'

'How kind of you.' June opens her purse and gives each of them a peppermint candy.

Charisma makes a face. 'But these are free at the Chinese restaurant.'

'Yes, they are. So stop and thank them sometime,' June says. 'The Chinese are the backbone of civilization. They invented macaroni and flip-flops.'

Unconvinced, Charisma and Chiara, holding their lousy candy, look at each other.

301

'Okay, kids, let's go. Grandpop is waiting at our house.'

Tess helps the girls into their coats. 'Mom, thanks so much for taking them for the weekend.' Mom herds the girls out the door.

June is happy to see them go, though only I would know it. 'Aren't they delightful.'

'Sometimes.' Tess says, pulling on her coat. 'I'm late. I'm going to meet Charlie at the Port Authority. We're taking the bus to Atlantic City.'

'Romantic weekend planned?' June asks.

'His company has a convention. I'm going to play the slots while he looks at the latest smoke alarms,' Tess says as she goes. The entrance door snaps shut.

'Smoke alarms? To put out *what* fire?' June whistles low. 'I say buyer beware and *run*. There's your best advertisement for marriage, Valentine. Take a good look.'

A cold draft from the open window wakes me. I sit up in bed and look out, pulling the cotton blanket and down comforter around me. Snow. Snow in March. The West Side Highway is a carpet of white, with black zippers of tire prints made by the early morning delivery trucks. There's a doily of frost on the windowpane, and a layer of icy flakes on the sash.

I slept peacefully through the night. Alone. Roman was busy with a sold-out seating, and had to finish the prep work for a private party, so he crashed at his place instead of coming over and waking me. Gram comes home tomorrow night, and while I've enjoyed my run of the place, I have to admit I miss her.

I spent most of yesterday cleaning and putting things back where they belong. I did some research for our trip to Italy and found some new suppliers to visit in addition to Gram's old reliables. I found some interesting new-guard talent who make braids and trims. I'm hoping to meet them on our trip, and add them to the roster of suppliers we currently use. I want to deliver a shoe to Bergdorf with embellishments that Rhedd Lewis has never seen before. Italian designers have recently been influenced by the influx of talent from a new sweep of immigrants, so I've come across lots of Russian-, African-, and Middle European–inspired accents in buttons and trim. I can't wait to show Gram the new stuff.

When I finished my research, I scrubbed the bathroom, cleaned the kitchen, and made lasagna. The work in the shop is up to speed. Gram will return home to a clean house and a first-rate operation, with all existing deadlines met and orders filled.

I get up and pull on some comfortable sweatpants and a hoodie, and go into the bathroom. I pat on some of the rich botanical face cream that Tess gave me for Christmas. Might as well have a spa day, as I won't be seeing anyone. It's Sunday, and I have the day to myself.

I go down to the kitchen, take out the coffee press, and put a kettle of water on the stove. I get the milk out of the fridge and pour it into a small pan, putting the burner on low to steam it. I open the wax-paper sack from Ruthie's, at the Chelsea Market, and pull out a soft brioche sprinkled with glassy raw sugar. I place the brioche on a frilly dessert plate and take a cloth napkin out of the drawer. My cell phone is beeping in the charger, so I flip it open and play the message.

'Hi, honey.' Roman's voice is raspy. 'It's me. It's five o'clock on Sunday morning. I'm still in the kitchen. It's snowing. I wish we were together. I miss you. I'll call you later.'

'Yeah, it would have been nice, Roman,' I say aloud. 'But you have a wife. Her name is Ca'd'Oro and she comes first.'

I realize that I'm willing to overlook a lot because whoever is with me has to do the same. But I also remember how Roman made it his business to find out who I was in the very beginning, when the only clue he had was a glimpse of me on the roof. And now that I'm here for him, I might as well be a pair of those clunky clogs he keeps in the restaurant kitchen. Always on hand. Available. Comfortable. Reliable. The hunt is over.

I pour the boiling water into the coffee press, inhaling the rich earthiness of the dark espresso. I pick up the pot of foaming milk on the stove and pour it into a wide ceramic mug. I add the espresso until the milk turns the color of chocolate taffy.

I take my breakfast and climb the stairs to the

304

roof, stopping in my room to pull on my boots, down coat, hat, and gloves. Pushing the door open and stepping out onto the roof covered in fresh snow, it's as if I'm standing in a well of soft white candle wax, the shapes of everything familiar gone, replaced with smooth edges, rounded corners, and drapes of silver ice. I place my coffee and brioche on the snow-covered Saint Francis fountain, shake off a lawn chair, and open it to sit.

The sun, behind the thick, white clouds, has the luster of a dull gray pearl. The river has the texture of old, speckled, forest green and beige linoleum as the wind gently ruffles the surface. The walkway on the river is empty except for a couple of park attendants in their blue overalls sprinkling rock salt along the cross-walk at Perry Street.

A seagull hovers overhead, giving my brioche a studied look. 'Shoo,' I say to him. He flaps away, his gray wings matching the morning sky. I nestle the mug between my hands and sip. I feel a pang of guilt as I remember Sunday mass. A good Catholic girl usually becomes a guilty Catholic woman, but I say a quiet prayer, and any nagging guilt about my whereabouts at the eight A.M. express mass at Our Lady of Pompeii is exhaled and sent out to sea. *Doing the best I can*, I remind God.

Snow begins to tumble down, throwing a white net over lower Manhattan. I pull the hood of my coat up over my head, put my feet up on the wall, and lean back.

Why is it, in the story of my life, that the moments

I remember with the deepest affection are the times when I have been alone? I can line them up like facted perfume bottles on an antique dresser.

When I was ten, I went to work with my father at the park. At the end of the day, when the summer sky over Queens was turning the color of smashed raspberries, he went into the supply shed and left me alone on the swings a few feet away. I had the whole of LaGuardia Park number fifteen to myself. I swung as high and as fast as I could, climbing higher and higher, until I swore I could see the blue lights on the top tier of the Empire State Building.

When I was a nineteen-year-old sophomore in college, I went to check my grade at two o'clock in the morning outside Sister Jean Klene's advanced class, Shakespeare: The Comedies. And I got an A. I stood and stared at that letter *A* until the reality of it set in: I had achieved the impossible. The solid B student had broken the barrier and earned a perfect grade.

And I'll never forget the night Bret dropped me off at my apartment in Queens, before leaving on his first business trip to some outpost like Dallas, Texas. I was twenty-seven years old and he had asked me to marry him. Sensing my uncertainty, he said, 'Don't answer now.' After he left to go to the airport to catch his flight, I felt the great relief that comes with being alone. I needed to seek my own counsel, to think things through. So I made a dish of spaghetti with fresh tomatoes from this garden, olive oil from Arezzo, and sweet white garlic. I made a salad of artichokes and black olives. I opened a bottle of wine. I set my own little table and lit candles. Then I sat down to eat a glorious meal, slowly savoring every bite and sip.

I realized that my answer to his proposal, upon his return, would not be the great moment; the great moment had already happened. He had asked. This was the first time in my life I recognized that I delight in the process and not necessarily the result. I was a good girlfriend, but wife? I couldn't see it. But Bret could. And now, he has it, the life he dreamed of even then. The only difference? He's with Mackenzie, not me.

I don't crave a traditional life. If I did, I assume I'd have one. My own sister thinks I want a life like she has, with a husband and children. How can I explain that my thirties may not be about reaching some finish line everyone seems to be rushing toward? Maybe my thirties are about the precious time I have left with Gram and deciding which path to take in my life. Stability or the lark? Very different things.

When I observe Gram, I see how fragile the notion of tradition can be. If I take my eyes off the way she kneads her Easter bread, or if I fail to study the way she sews a seam in suede, or if I lose the mental image I have of her when she negotiates a better deal with a button salesman, somehow, the very essence of her will be lost. When she goes, the responsibility for carrying on will fall to me. My mother says I'm the keeper of the flame, because I work here, and because I choose to live here. A flame is a very fragile thing, too, and there are times when I wonder if I'm the one who can keep it going.

A wind kicks up. I hear the snap of the old screen door. I turn around, my heart pounding a little faster, hoping for a second that Roman made it over after all. But it's just the wind.

That evening, I'm debating as I pace behind the kitchen counter. Do I heat up the lasagna now or wait until Gram gets home tomorrow night? One of the rules of etiquette my mother insisted upon on is that you never cut a cake before the company comes. You present it properly and whole to the guests, like a gift. The lasagna will become a leftover instead of a welcome-home gesture if I eat a square tonight. So I put it back in the refrigerator.

The buzzer sounds. I press the intercom. 'Delivery,' Roman says. I buzz him in. Then I go to the top of the stairs and turn on the track lights.

'Hi, Valentine.' Roman smiles up at me from the bottom of the stairs.

His face is about the best thing I've ever seen. 'I thought you were working tonight.'

'I'm playing hooky so I can be with my girl.' He climbs the stairs two at a time, wielding an enormous tote bag. He drops the bag when he reaches me, scoops me up in his arms, and kisses me. 'You're surprised?'

I kiss him tenderly on his cheek, his nose, and then his neck, hoping each kiss will make up for the doomed thoughts I had about us on the roof this morning. I'm not a good liar, so I fess up, 'I'm surprised. I totally gave up.'

Roman looks at me, concerned. 'Gave up what?'

'That I'd see you before Gram came home.'

'Ah.' He looks relieved. 'Well, I'm here. And I'm not going anywhere.' He kisses me again. I let the words *I'm not going anywhere* play in my head like a simple tune. Roman picks up the bag and follows me into the living room. 'I'm going to make you dinner.'

'You don't have to. I made a lasagna.'

'I don't think so.' He pulls a bottle of wine out of the bag. 'We're starting with a Brunello, vintage 1994.'

'I wasn't even legal drinking age then.'

'You were plenty old enough.'

Roman laughs as he pulls the cork out of the wine and places it on the counter. He takes two wineglasses from the shelf and fills them. He brings me a glass. He toasts and we sip. Then he kisses me, the lush wine on his lips making mine tingle. 'Like it?'

I nod.

'Get ready. I have a wine for each course.'

'Each *course*?'

'Uh-huh,' he laughs. 'We're having two.'

I pull out the stool under the counter and climb onto it. I watch him as he unpacks the tote, which is like one of those boxes in the circus where you think the last pup in a skirt has danced out, but another jumps out of the box and gets in line. There is box after box, tray after tray, container after container, until most of the counter is filled with unmarked delicacies.

Roman opens the cabinets, pulling out a large skillet, and a smaller one. He puts the flames on low underneath the empty pans. Quickly, he throws butter in one and drizzles olive oil in the other.

He reaches into the tote and hands me a small white box. 'This is for you.'

I shake it. 'Let me guess, a truffle?'

'I'm boring you with my truffle dishes. No, it's not fungi.'

'Okay.' I open it. A branch of coral the color of a blood orange lies on a pad of white cotton. I pull it out of the box and place it in my hand. The solid fingers of the waxy jewel make a lovely shape that curls as it rests in my hand. 'Coral.'

'From Capri.'

'Have you been there?'

'Many times,' he says. 'Have you?'

'Never.'

'Well, I'm taking you for your birthday. I worked it out with Gram. When you fly to Italy next month, you'll get your work done, and then we're going to Capri for a week at the end of your stay. We're going to stay at the Quisisana. An old friend is the chef of the restaurant there. We'll eat and swim and relax. How about it?'

'You're serious?'

'Very.' Roman leans across the counter and kisses me.

'I'd love to go to Capri with you.'

'I'm taking care of everything. Just the two of us, and that ocean and that sky and that place. This will be the first time I'm in love when I've gone there.'

'Are you in love?'

'Didn't you know?'

'I was hoping.'

'I am.' Roman puts his arms around me. 'Are you?'

'Definitely.'

'There's an old trick that I learned from the locals on Capri whcn I was there. Everybody wants to go into the Blue Grotto, and it gets overrun with tourists. So they came up with a sign that says *Non Entrata La Grotto*. When the sign is out, the tour guide tells the people on the boat that the surf is too rough to enter, but in fact, the locals put the sign there to keep the tourists out while they're inside swimming.'

'That's a cheat. What if it's the only time the poor tourists can visit Capri and they miss out on the Blue Grotto?'

'The tour guides circle past the grotto and return later, when the sign is gone, and they row inside.'

'What's the grotto like?'

'I've tried in every place I've ever lived to paint a room that color blue. And I've never found it. And the water is warm. Some old king used it as a secret passageway through the island to the other side. A lot of decadent stuff went on in there.' Roman pulls me close. 'And there will be more of that this spring.'

The kitchen fills with the scent of hot butter. Roman quickly turns and lifts the pan off the stove, throwing in garlic and herbs, swishing them around in the butter, creating a smooth mixture. 'Okay, I'm gonna let this set. First up: caviar. From the Black Sea.'

He snaps open a container and places a wafer-thin pizzelle, which looks like a flat, circular waffle, on a plate. 'You know the pizzelle cookies from when we were kids? This is my version. Instead of sugar, I make these with lemon zest and fresh pepper.' He opens the tin of caviar and scoops a spoonful onto the pizzelle. Roman adds a dab of crème fraiche on top of the Black Sea beads and gives it to me.

I take a bite. The combination of the tart lemon in the pizzelle, the rich caviar, and the rush of sweet cream melts in my mouth.

'Not bad, right?'

'It's heavenly.'

I watch as Roman throws medallions of beef into the large skillet with the olive oil. He chops sweet onions and mushrooms onto the meat, dousing it in splashes of the red wine from the bottle we are drinking. Slowly, he adds cream to the pan, and the sauce turns from golden brown to a pale burgundy.

'I spent a few months on Capri in the kitchen of the Quisisana. Best thing I ever did. They have an open oven outside, behind the kitchen. In the morning, we'd build the fire with old driftwood from the beach and then we'd keep it going all day, slow-roasting tomatoes for sauce, root vegetables for side dishes, you name it. I learned the value of taking time when cooking. I roasted tomatoes down to their essence, the skins turning into silky ribbons, while the pulp turns rich and hearty in the heat. You don't even have to make a sauce out of them, just throw them on pasta, they're that sweet.'

In the small pan, where the herbs are glazed in butter, Roman empties a container of rice, loaded with olives, capers, tomatoes, and herbs. As steam rises off the rice, and the steak sizzles, he sets the counter for dinner.

Roman has the most beautiful hands (people who work with their hands usually do), long fingers that move with grace, artfully and deliberately. It's mesmerizing to watch him slice and chop, the blade rhythmic as it glints against the wood.

'The nights on Capri were the best. After work, we'd go down to the beach and the ocean would be so calm and warm. I'd lie in that saltwater and look up at the moon, and just let the surf wash over me. I felt healed. Then we'd build a big fire and roast langoustines, and have some homemade wine with it. That's my idea of bliss.' He looks up at me. 'I can't wait to take you there.'

Roman is very neat when he works, straightening

the kitchen as he goes, maybe his tidiness coming from the necessity of working in small spaces. Nothing is wasted in Roman's cooking, he respects every stalk, leaf, and bud of an herb that he uses, examining it before mincing it or rubbing it into a recipe. In his hands, common foods become elements of delight, crackling softly in butter, steaming in cream, and drizzled with olive oil.

Roman opens a container filled with finely chopped vegetables – bright green cucumbers, red tomatoes, yellow peppers – and broken bits of fresh parmesan cheese. He sprinkles the vegetables with balsamic vinegar from a tiny bottle with a gold stopper. 'This is very special. It's twenty-two years old. Last bottle! It's from a farm outside Genoa. My cousin makes it himself.'

Roman fills two bowls with the chopped salad. I remember telling him how much I love raw vegetables finely chopped; he remembers and he delivers. He opens a second bottle of wine, this one earthy and hearty, a Dixon burgundy 2006. He turns to the stove and flips the steaks, which make a cloud of steam. A misty cloud rises from the pan of rice. He lifts it off the burner and spoons the hot rice mixture onto the dishes. He throws the moppeen over his shoulder and lifts the other pan. He places the lean steak artfully on top, my dish of rice first and then his. Then he drizzles the sauce from the pan on top of the steak and rice.

'Should we sit at the table?' I ask him.

'No, this is better.' He pulls out a stool and sits down across from me. 'I feel like I'm at a board of directors meeting when I sit over there.'

I pick up the knife to cut the steak, but I don't need it. I break off a piece with the fork. The savory sauce has cooked through the meat in an explosion of flavors that are magnified by the sweet grapes that turn hearty and earthy to taste. I chew the delectable bite. 'Marry me,' I say to him.

'And here I thought you were breaking up with me.'

I put my fork down and look at him. 'Why would you think such a thing?'

'Come on, Valentine. I'm the worst. I really blew it the past two weeks. Teodora is gone, and I planned to come over every night and spend a lot of time with you.'

'It's okay,' I stammer. It's as if that seagull delivered to Roman a message from my epiphany on the roof this morning. He really *can* read my mind.

'No it isn't. I wanted to be with you, but then things went wild at the restaurant and I blew it. That's all there is to it. But I'm sorry about it. I wanted to make this time special for you.'

'I hate that we spend a lot of time apologizing to each other for working hard. It's the way it is. We're both trying to build something.' I love how I was ready to kill him this morning and now, I'm making excuses for him. This surely falls under the category *Be Adorable*, doesn't it?

'I don't know how else to do it. I don't know

how to run a restaurant and not be there twenty-four hours a day. I don't think it's possible. Now, down the line, when it's established and I've paid back my investors, and I find the right chef to replace me in the kitchen, then this becomes a different discussion.'

It's funny that Roman uses the word *discussion*, when we haven't had one. I attempt to be understanding when I say, 'I guess I don't know where I fit in your life right now. And I don't want to ask you to put me first, because that's not fair either.'

Roman folds his arms on the counter and leans forward. 'What do you need to hear from me?'

'Where do you see this going?' There it is. I put it out there. The second it's out of my mouth, I wish I could take it back. But it's too late. The last thing I wanted to do was turn our last night together into one of *those* talks.

'I'm serious about you,' he says. 'I don't have a high opinion of myself when it comes to being a husband, because I tried and failed at it. But that doesn't mean I don't want to try again.'

'How do you feel about my career?'

'I'm in awe of you. You're an artist.'

'And you are, too.' I sip my wine. 'You are also the Emergency Glass Box guy.'

'What's that?'

'At the first sign that we're going down in flames, you break the glass and pull the lever and save the day. Like coming over here tonight. Cooking

316

for me. Taking me to Capri without leaving the dinner table. Kissing me with great wine on your lips. Telling me you're in love with me. That was the crème fraîche on the caviar.'

'I want this.'

'Roman, you have fallen in love with me.'

'I wouldn't waste caviar from the Black Sea on a fling.'

'What does the fling get?'

'Potato chips.'

I laugh. 'So that's how I tell?' I smooth the napkin on my lap. 'The caviar test?'

'There are other ways.' Roman comes around the counter to my side. To be honest, I don't want to stop eating this dinner, but sometimes a woman has to choose between food and sex, and it's the idiot who chooses food. I can reheat the steak later, but letting Roman know that I'm in love with him, too, is a moment that won't come around again. Well, it *might*. But it would be *different*. So, I push the plate away as he lifts me off the stool and into the moment. Desire definitely has a shelf life. Delay love or the expressing of it, and it dies. Take it for granted, and it goes away, like the morning snow on the roof during the ides of March.

Roman carries me up the stairs, marking each step with a kiss. My feet drag along the hallway wall like handles on an old suitcase as he carries me to my room. As we make love, every doubt I have, every question that enters my mind about us, who we are, where we're going, and what we will become, disappears like the quarter moon behind the low clouds of spring.

I have fallen more deeply in love with this man on the very day I was planning to say good-bye to him. I may need my solitude, but I also want to be with him. I may not always see this clearly when he is away from me, but it's what I'm most sure of when we're together.

'I love you, Valentine,' he says.

'You know, I get that a lot.'

'You do?' he asks as he kisses my neck.

'"I love you, Valentine" is actually a popular phrase used in greeting cards.'

'If you were sending me one, what would it say?' he asks.

'I love you, too, Roman.'

And there it is, words that I dread to say and do mean, because with them comes the responsibility of owning it, moving forward together and deciding for real who we are to each other. Now we're not just lovers discovering what we like and sharing what we know. In this mutual declaration, we're accountable to each other. We're in love, and now, our relationship has to build slowly and beautifully in order to hold all the joy and misery that lies ahead.

He places the tip end of his nose on the tip end of mine. I almost feel he's looking so deeply into my eyes, he's seeing the rest of my life play out in slides clicking through on a carousel. I wonder

318

what he's looking for, what he sees. Then he says, 'Our children would be blessed, you know.'

'They would never go without good food or pretty shoes.'

'They'd have brown eyes.'

'And they'd be tall,' I say.

'And they'd be funny. A house of laughs we'd have.' He kisses me.

'That's my dream,' I tell him.

We get tangled up in the down comforter and the pillows that fly around the bed like doors opening and closing, and as we settle in to make love, we begin to make plans. I no longer wonder where this is going. Now, I know.

CHAPTER 10

AREZZO

I pull over on the side of the road on the hilltop above Arezzo and park the rental car. After the hullabaloo at the Rome airport, with customs, the bags, and figuring out the directions on the Italian map, I am happy to actually set foot on Tuscan ground.

We have arrived, and now, our work begins. We must buy supplies to meet our orders, and find distinctive and fresh elements to make the shoes from my sketch for the Bergdorf windows. It's not going to be easy to win over Rhedd Lewis, but I have a greater goal in mind: to distinguish the Angelini Shoe Company as the face of the future in the custom-shoe business. That may sound lofty, but we have to succeed in new ways if we're going to save the old company and reinvent our business.

Gram and I spent most of the flight working on the fine details of the sketch for the competition. There's a problem with the heel I designed. Gram says that I need to refine it, while I feel it needs to be bold and architectural. Her idea of modern and mine are about a half century apart. But that's okay – Gram is encouraging me to use my imagination, and while she likes what I've drawn, she also knows her experience counts when it comes to actually building the dream shoe.

Gram gets out of the car and joins me. The cool April breeze washes over us as the sun, the color of an egg yolk, begins to sink behind the hills of Tuscany. It drenches the sky in gold as it goes, throwing its last bit of light on Arezzo. The houses of the village are built so closely together, the effect is of one enormous stone castle surrounded by fields of emerald green silk. The winding cobbled streets of the town look like thin pink ribbons and I wonder for a moment how we will get the car through them.

All around us, the hills of Tuscany are parceled into contour farms. Sloping dales of dry earth are planted with rows of spindly olive trees next to square beds of bright sunflowers. It creates the effect of a patchwork quilt, bursts of color separated by straight seams. Soft spring colors, chalk blue and cornmeal yellow, spike the fresh green leaves while stalks of wild lavender grow on the side of the road, filling the air with the powdery scent of the new buds.

'This is it.' Gram smiles, exhaling a breath that she seems to have held since we landed in Rome. 'My favorite place on earth.'

Arezzo looks different to me now. I came to Italy during my college years, but I stuck to the touristy stuff. We took a day trip through Arezzo, during which I snapped some pictures for my family and promptly got back on the bus. Maybe I was just too young to appreciate it. I couldn't have cared less about architectural or family history back then, as I had more important matters on my mind, like the hotness of the Notre Dame rugby team, who'd joined our tour group down in Rome.

The Angelini side of my family is originally from Arezzo. However, we didn't have this magnificent view from the mountaintop because we lived in the valley below. We were farmers, descendants of the old Mezzadri system. The padrone, or boss, lived on the highest peak, where, from his palazzo, he would oversee the harvest of the olive trees and the yield of the grapes. The farmers exchanged their labor for food and lodging on the padrone's land, and even the children helped pick the crops. From the looks of this valley, I would have been very happy to be a serf, walking through these deep green fields under a bright blue Tuscan sky.

'Let's go,' Gram says and climbs back into the rental car. 'Are you hungry?'

'Starving.' I slip behind the wheel. I'm driving a stick shift for the first time in twelve years. The last stick I drove was Bret Fitzpatrick's, on his 1978 Camaro. 'I'm going to have biceps of steel when this trip is over.'

I drive carefully into town as there are no side-walks, folks just cross the streets willy-nilly, anywhere they please. Arezzo is a haven for poets. The baroque architecture with its ornate details is the perfect backdrop for artists to gather. Tonight, young writers type on their laptops on the steps of the public square and on tables under the portico of an old Roman bath that now houses offices and small shops. There is a feeling of community here, one I wouldn't mind being a part of.

The incline up to the hotel is steep, so I gun it. As I reach the curve of the road behind the square, Gram asks me to stop.

She points to a small peach-colored stucco store-front with dark-wood-beam accents. 'That's the original Angelini Shoe Company.' The old work-shop is now a *pasticceria* that sells coffee and sweets.

'It was also the homestead. They lived upstairs, just like us,' she adds.

The second story has glass doors that lead to a balcony filled with terra-cotta pots overflowing with red geraniums. 'No tomatoes, Gram.'

She laughs and directs me up the street to park outside the Spolti Inn, a rambling hotel built of fieldstone. I help Gram out of the car and unload our bags. My grandparents stayed at this inn every time they traveled to Tuscany on their buying trips.

The staff of the hotel know Gram, as do the locals. Some even remember her great-aunts and -uncles, Gram tells me. Most custom shoemakers get their leather from Lucca, while Gram insists on Arezzo, where our family has used the same tanner for over 100 years.

As we climb the steep stone steps to the entrance of the hotel, Gram lets go of my arm, pulling in her stomach and straightening her spine. She takes the banister. With her brown hair and peasant skirt, black cotton blouse and sandals, she could be twenty years younger. It's only when her knees give her trouble that you notice her age.

We pass through a small, open breezeway lined with an eclectic mix of marble planters spilling over with edelweiss, daisies, and bluebells.

'Signora Angelini!' the woman behind the desk cries.

'Signora Guarasci!'

The old friends greet each other with a warm embrace. I take in the lobby. The front desk is a long mahogany counter. There's a slotted wooden box holding the room keys on the wall behind it. It could be 1900 except for the computer next to the sign-in book.

A deep sofa, covered in gold-and-white damask, is anchored by two ornate floor lamps and an over-stuffed gold chenille ottoman that serves as a coffee table. The overhead chandelier is white wrought iron with cream-colored linen shades over the bulbs.

Signora Guarasci is a petite woman with small hands and thick white hair. She wears a blue cotton skirt with a pressed white smock over it, gray tights, and open black leather clogs, a more stylish version of the plastic ones that Roman wears in the kitchen of Ca' d'Oro. The signora embraces me as Gram makes my introduction.

While Gram catches up with her old friend, I take our bags, climb the stairs, and find our rooms.

I unlock the door to number 3, place my suitcase by the door, and look over my new surroundings. The spacious corner room is painted sunflower yellow with off-white trim. There's a high, soft double bed with six fat feather pillows and a pressed black-and-white-checked coverlet. There's an antique oak library table under the windows. An old gray rocking chair is positioned near a white marble fireplace, both looking like they have been here for a hundred years. I open the windows and a cool breeze blows through, turning the long white muslin draperies into billowing ball gowns. The walls of the open closet are lined in cedar, which gives the room a green, woodsy scent.

The bathroom that connects my room to Gram's is simple, with black-and-white-checked tile, a deep ceramic tub with a shiny silver handheld nozzle, and a marble sink with an antique mirror over it. A large bay window on the far wall looks out over a garden. Privacy shades are pulled to the top. The signora has left the window open, letting in more of those fresh spring breezes.

I go back out into the hallway, pick up Gram's luggage, and unlock the door to room number 2. Gram's room is twice the size of mine, done in china blue and white, with windows the length of the room, and a full seating area with two low chairs and a sofa covered in white duck fabric.

'How are the rooms?' Gram asks as I skip back downstairs.

'Gorgeous. Now I see why you stay here.'

'Wait until you taste the signora's cooking,' Gram says.

Signora Guarasci enters the lobby and claps her hands together. 'Now, you eat.'

I help Gram up off the very soft sofa. She takes my arm as we go into the dining room.

'When we go home, I'm making an appointment with Dr Sculco at the Hospital for Special Surgery. You're getting your knees replaced.'

'I am not.'

'You are, too. Look at you. You've got mod hair, good skin, and a great figure. Why should you suffer with bad knees? They're the only thing about you that's eighty years old.'

'My brain is eighty.'

'But nobody can see that in a pencil skirt.'

'Good point.'

We take our seats at a table by the windows that overlook a small pond at the back of the house. Every table is set with cutlery, pressed napkins, and small vases of violets even though we are the only patrons in the dining room.

Signora Guarasci pushes through the kitchen door carrying a tray with two ceramic crocks of soup and a basket of crusty bread with a tin of butter. The signora pours us each a glass of home-made red wine from a decanter, then goes back into the kitchen.

'*Perfetto! Grazie.*' Gram raises her glass.

'I like having you with me, Val,' Gram says. 'I think this is going to be a great trip for both of us.'

I taste the minestrone made of pork, root vegetables, and beans in a thick tomato broth. 'This is
de-lish.' I put the spoon down and break off a piece
of the warm crusty bread. 'I could stay here forever.
Why would anyone ever leave?'

'Well, your grandfather had to. He was six years
old when his mother died. Her name was
Giuseppina Cavalline. Your great-grandfather called
her Jojo.'

'What was she like?'

'She was the most beautiful girl in Arezzo. She
was about nineteen when she walked into the
Angelini Shoe Shop and asked to speak with the
owner. Your great-grandfather, who was around
twenty-two at the time, fell in love at first sight.'

'And what about Jojo? Was it mutual?'

'Eventually. See, she had come by to order custom
shoes. My father-in-law, so eager to impress her,
trotted out samples of the finest leather and showed
her the best designs. But Jojo said that she didn't
care if the shoes were fashionable. Your great-
grandfather thought this was very odd. What young
woman doesn't love the latest styles? Then she
turned and walked across the room and your great-
grandfather saw that she had a very pronounced
limp. And she said, "Can you help me?"'

Gram looks out the window, as if to better
remember this story that happened just a few streets
away. She continues, 'He worked six days and six
nights without stopping, and created a beautiful
pair of black leather ankle boots with a stacked

heel. He created a hidden platform on the interior of the shoe that evened out her stride without being visible to anyone else.'

'Brilliant.' I wonder if I could ever build such an ingenious shoe.

'When Jojo came back to the shop and tried on the shoes, she stood up and skimmed across the room. For the first time in her life, her steps were uniform and her posture straight and tall. Jojo was so grateful, she threw her arms around your great-grandfather and thanked him.

'Then he said, "Someday, I'm going to marry you." And he did, a year later. And a few years after that, my husband, your grandfather, was born in the house I showed you.'

'What a romantic story.'

'They were happy for a long time. But when she died of pleurisy ten years later, my father-in-law was so grief-stricken, he took your grandfather and went to America. He couldn't bear to be in Arezzo any longer, to walk in the streets where they lived, or stay in the bed where they slept, or pass the church where they married. That's how deep his grief was.'

'Did he ever find love again?'

'No. And you know, a cobbler can be very appealing to women.'

'Give a woman a new pair of shoes and her life changes.'

'That's right. Well, he was a wonderful man, very funny and bright. You remind me of him in many ways. Michel Angelini was a great designer, in my opinion, ahead of his time. He'd love that shoe you designed, believe me.'

'He would?' This compliment means the world to me. After all, my great-grandfather designed every shoe our company makes. A hundred years later, his work is still relevant.

'He would be happy to know that Angelini Shoes is still in operation. He'd also be thrilled that you are carrying on his legacy. He sacrificed so much for his work. Well, at least his personal life.'

The meaning of his sacrifice is not lost on me. I get it: a creative life is an all-consuming one. If we aren't in the shop building shoes, we are sending them; and if we're not shipping them, we're creating new ones. It's a cycle that never ends, especially when we do our jobs well. 'It's sad he never found another woman to share his life with.'

'My father-in-law was crazy about her. The truth is, no one could ever compare to her. He told me that many times. He missed her right up until the moment he died. And I know that for sure because I was with him.'

'Gram, I've always wondered about something. Why does the sign over our shop say "*Since 1903*" when, in fact, it was 1920 when Grandpop and his father emigrated?'

Gram smiles. 'He met Jojo in 1903. That was his way of honoring her.'

I think about Roman, and if our love will last. It seems the women in my family have to fight for love to sustain it. It doesn't come easily to us, nor does it stay without a battle. We have to work at it. I look over at her. 'Is something wrong?'

'The last trip I took with your grandfather was this time of year, the spring before he died.'

'We didn't even know he was sick.'

'He did. I think he knew that it was the last time he would see Italy. He had a bad heart for years. We just never talked about it.'

Gram breaks a roll open and puts half of it on my plate. I remember Tess telling me about Grandpop having a *friend*. We're far from Perry Street, and Gram is opening up in a way that she never allows herself at home. I'm usually as reticent to discuss these matters as she is, but the moment is here, and the wine is hearty, so I ask, 'Gram, did Grandpop have a girlfriend?'

'Why do you ask?'

'Tess told me that he did.'

'Tess has a big mouth.' Gram frowns.

'Why wouldn't you tell me?'

'What good would it do?'

'I don't know. An honest family history is worth something.'

'To whom?'

'To me.' I reach out and put my hand on hers.

'Yes, he had a girlfriend,' Gram sighs.

'How was that even possible? When would he find the time?'

'Men can always find the time for *that*,' Gram says.

'How? You lived and worked in the same building.'

'This is a buying trip, not a Lenten retreat,' Gram says. 'I save my secrets for the confessional.'

'Pretend I'm a version of Father O'Hara with better legs.'

'What do you want to know?'

'Did you confront him? Did you confront *her*?' I have a vision of my independent grandmother standing up for herself, like Norma Shearer when she takes on Joan Crawford in *The Women*.

She nods. 'After my husband died, I saw her on the street. I told her I knew, and she denied it, which was nice of her. Then I asked her if she made him happy.'

'Did she answer you?'

'She said no, she couldn't make him happy. He wished that he could make it work with me. Well, that got to me. With all our problems, the truth is, I loved your grandfather. We had tough times in our business and that really took a toll on us at home. I was hard on him when he'd try new things and fail, and he grew to resent me.'

'Being an artist is all about trying new things.'

'I know that now. I didn't then. I also learned that when a man resents his wife, he acts on it.'

'You must have been furious.'

'Oh, of course I was. And I did what lots of women do with rage. We bury it. We withdraw. Stop talking. We go to bed angry and we wake up angry. We fulfill our obligations, we keep up the house and the children, but the very act of holding

331

it all together is resentment in a different form. My way of hurting him was to act like I didn't need him.'

Gram lifts off her glasses and brushes away a tear.

She continues, 'I regret that deeply. Maybe, I think, on one of those days when he was taking a break and having a cigar on the roof, I should have climbed the stairs and gone outside and put my arms around him and told him that I loved him. Maybe we could've gotten it back. But I didn't and we couldn't and that was that.'

I'm jet-lagged and can't sleep. I sit in the window of the Spolti Inn and wait for morning. The houses are dark, but the moon is bright, turning the main street into a glistening silver river. The rolling hills fall away in the darkness as the clouds pass in front of the moon like party balloons.

I throw back the coverlet and climb into bed. I pick up Goethe's *Italian Journey*. My bookmark is a photograph of Roman standing in the door of Ca' d'Oro. I close the book and pick up my cell phone. I dial. Roman's phone goes to voice mail. So I text him:

Arrived safely. Bella Italia! Love you, V.

Then I dial home. Mom picks up the phone.
'Ma? We got here.'
'How was the trip?'
'Good. I'm driving a stick shift. Gram and I will

need neck braces after a month in that rental. It bucks like Old Paint. How's Dad?'

'Hungry. But the organic diet seems to be working.'

'Give the man a plate of spaghetti.'

'Don't worry. He sneaks salami, so when he's cured, we can't say it's the bean curd that did the trick. Hey, I put a surprise in your suitcase for Capri. It's in the red Macy's bag.'

'Great.' My mother's idea of a surprise is a 75-percent-off demi-bra and matching tap pants made with a print of dancing coffee beans that have the word *Peppy* embroidered across the rear end.

'Something wonderful is going to happen for you on the Isle of Capri. I'm thinking engagement.'

'Ma, please.'

'I'm just saying, hurry up. I don't want my first face-lift and the first dance at your wedding to co-incide. I'm sinking like a soufflé over here.'

'You don't need any work, Mom.'

'I caught a glimpse of myself looking down in the bathroom tile when I was scrubbing it and I said, "Dear God, Mike, you look like a sock puppet." I'd get the Botox but they aren't saying good things about it, plus, what's my face without any expression? Animation is my thing.'

My mom could talk twelve transatlantic hours in a row about cosmetic enhancement, so I cut her off. 'Mom, how do you know if the guy is *the* guy?'

'You mean if he'll be a good husband?' She pauses,

then says, 'The ticket is for the man to love the woman more than she loves him.'

'Shouldn't it be equal?'

Mom cackles. 'It can never be equal.'

'But what if the woman loves the man more?'

'A life of hell awaits her. As women, the deck is stacked against us because *time* is our enemy. We age, while men *season*. And trust me, there are plenty of women out there looking for a man, and they don't mind staking a claim on somebody else's husband, no matter how old, creaky, and deaf they are.'

She lowers her voice. 'Even *with* the cancer, at sixty-eight, your father is a *catch*. I don't need round two in the infidelity fight. I'm twenty years older and fifteen pounds heavier, and my nerves, let's face it, are shot. Plus, I'll let him make a mistake once, but twice? Never! So, I keep myself nice and smile, even if I'm crying on the inside. *Maintenance!* Do you think I wanted to go to the dentist and have all the silver pried out of my mouth and replaced with enough porcelain to build a shrine and fountain to the Blessed Lady? Of course not. But it had to be done! When I smiled with my old teeth it was like looking into a pickle barrel and that wouldn't do. A woman must endure a lot to keep herself in shape and keep a man . . . intrigued. And don't think I'm kidding about the face-lift. I've got the infomercial on Thermage Tivoed. I've watched it plenty; the only thing is, there are women on that commercial who look better in the *before* pictures and I've yet to figure that out. And show me one woman over sixty—'

Mom gags and coughs. Saying that number actually closes her throat. She goes on.

'—one woman over *that* fence who doesn't know she's got to fight like a tiger and I'll show you a woman who has given up. The only difference between me and the women who let themselves go and wind up looking like Andy Rooney in a wig is my *will*. My fortitude. My determination not to quit.'

'Mom, you're the Winston Churchill of antiaging. "Never, never, never, never, never give up your sit-ups." You make me want to jump out of this bed and do squats.'

'A nimble bride is a happy one, honey.'

Gram grips my arm as we climb the steep hill past the church to Vechiarelli & Son, our tanners for as long as the Angelinis have been shoemakers. The back streets of Arezzo burst with color, red cabbage roses on pink stucco walls, crisp white laundry hanging high against a blue sky, collections of small ceramic pots spilling over with green herbs in kitchen windows, and an occasional wall fountain, in the shape of a face, cascading sparkling water into an urn.

'It's the first shop to the right,' Gram pants once we make it to a level street.

'Thank God.' My heart is racing. 'I'd say we should have driven, but I don't think the car could have made it up this hill. I don't think there's a shift on the stick for straight up.'

Gram stops, adjusts her skirt, smooths her hair, and secures her shoulder bag just so on her arm. 'How do I look?'

'Great.' I'm surprised. Gram has never asked me to comment on her appearance.

'How's my lipstick?'

'You're in the pink, Gram. Coco Chanel pink.'

Gram throws back her shoulders. 'Good. Let's go.'

Vechiarelli & Son is a three-story stone house on the end of the street, with a similar setup to our shop at home. The main entrance, used for business, is a wide wooden door under the portico. On the upper floors, there are double doors that lead to small balconies on each level, the top one propped open with a plant, a throw rug hanging over the balcony, airing out in the breeze.

As we climb the steps to go into the shop, we hear a heated argument at full tilt, two men shouting at each other at the top of their lungs. The fight is punctuated with the sound of something being slammed on wood. They're speaking Italian, and way too quickly for my level of fluency.

I turn to look at Gram, who stands behind me. My expression tells her we should run before the nut jobs inside figure out they've got company. 'Maybe we should have called first.'

'They're expecting us.'

'This is some welcome wagon.'

Gram pushes me aside, lifts the brass door

knocker, and bangs it several times. The fight inside seems to escalate as the voices move toward us. I take a step back. We've kicked over a hornet's nest, and the swarm sounds deadly. Suddenly, the door flies open from the inside. An old man with white hair, navy wool slacks, and a blue-stripped button-down shirt has a look of pure aggravation on his face, but the anger falls away when he lays eyes on Gram.

'Teodora!'

'*Dominic, come stai?*'

Dominic embraces Gram and kisses her on both cheeks. I am standing behind her and I can see that the line of her spine changes as he kisses her. She grows about two inches taller, and her shoulders relax.

'*Dominico, ti presento mio nipote, Valentine,*' she says.

'*Que bella!*' Dominic approves of me. Better that than the alternative!

'Signor Vechiarelli, it's a pleasure to meet you.' He kisses my hand. I get a good look at his face. It's the same face as the man in the photograph buried in the velvet pouch in the bottom of Gram's dresser drawer. I try not to show my surprise, but I can't wait to get back to the hotel and text Tess to tell her.

'*Venite, venite,*' he says.

We follow Dominic into the shop. There's a large farm table that takes up the center of the room. A series of deep shelves filled with sheets of leather line an entire wall, from floor to ceiling.

337

Old-fashioned tin lamps hang low over the table, illuminating the polished wood in spheres of white light. If I close my eyes, the fragrant beeswax, leather, and lemon take me home to Perry Street. A single door leads to a back room. Dominic calls through the open door.

'*Gianluca! Vieni a salutare Teodora ed a conoscere sua nipote.*' Dominic turns to me and raises his eyebrows. '*Gianluca è mio figlio e anche mio socio.*'

'Lovely.' I look at Gram, figuring a bull with flaming nostrils will come galloping through that very door, impale us on his horns, toss us into the air, trample and kill us. Gram motions that all is just fine, but I don't believe her for a second.

'Gianluca!' Dominic bellows again. This time, it's a command.

Gianluca Vechiarelli, Dominic's son and partner (his description) stands in the doorway filling it with his height. He wears a brown apron over work pants and a denim shirt that has been washed so many times it's practically white. It's hard for me to see his face because the work lights are so bright, and he is taller than the lights.

'*Piacere di conoscerla.*' Gianluca extends his hand. I take it. My hand gets lost in his.

'*Come è andato il viaggio?*' Dominic asks Gram about our trip, but clearly he couldn't care less, he's more interested in her arrival here than her departure from America. He pulls rolling work stools out from under the table and invites us to sit. I remain standing while he sits down next to Gram, giving

338

her his undivided attention. It seems he cannot get close enough to her. He doesn't seem even slightly embarrassed that his legs are touching hers, and that his hands have made their way to her knees.

While Gram fills in the details of our trip so far, Gianluca is busy pulling samples of leather off the shelves and arranging them on the table. He breathes deeply as he arranges the squares, squinting at them and then moving them into different positions. I take a peek at his face. He's good-looking, but there's more gray in his hair than black, so I figure he's somewhere in his fifties.

Gianluca has the same nose as his father, straight and fine, with a high bridge. There are deep grooves on the sides of his mouth, which either come from smiling or screaming, and if I were betting, I'd go with the latter. He catches me looking at him. He smiles, so I smile back at him, but it's slightly uncomfortable, as if I've been caught shoplifting.

Gianluca has a slight overbite and deep blue eyes, the exact color of the morning sky over Arezzo. It's common knowledge that Italian men check out American women, but what you never hear is that we return the favor in kind. I study him with the same eye I use to look at the leather. I'm interested in quality, integrity, and texture; after all, fine Italian craftsmanship and the pursuit of it is the reason we climbed this hill, isn't it?

Gram and Dominic have not stopped talking. He says something and she laughs her big laugh, which

I hear only occasionally when we're home. The truth is, I've never seen her like this. If I weren't so enthralled by the exquisite leather Gianluca is laying out on the table, I'd be wondering what the hell is going on here.

'So, you make the shoes?' Gianluca says to me.

'Yes. I'm her apprentice.' I point to Gram. 'I've been training for four years.'

'I've been working with Papa for twenty-three years.'

'Wow. So, is it working out?'

Gianluca laughs. 'Some days good, some days not so good.'

'This morning?' I cover my ears.

'You heard us?'

'Are you kidding? They heard you in Puglia.'

'Papa? Teodora and Valentine heard us argue.'

Dominic makes a motion, like he's brushing a fly off a slice of bread. Then he puts his hand on his thighs, scoots the stool even closer to Gram, and resumes his conversation with her. I almost lean across the table to say, 'Why not sit in her lap, Dom?'

Soon the front door of the shop pushes open, and a gorgeous young woman enters, tossing her purse onto a table. She has long brown hair, and wears a tight, dark brown suede skirt and a sleek black tank top. She pushes her sunglasses up onto her head, anchoring her hair with them. She wears the most exquisite pair of sandals I have ever seen. They are flat, with thin T-straps covered in tiny chocolate brown jewels that lead to a center medallion shaped in a fleur-de-lis made of baguettes of black onyx. She heads straight for Gianluca and gives him a hug. Evidently, this Tuscan air is good for everybody's love life but mine.

Gram turns and looks at her. 'Orsola!'

'Teodora!' The young woman goes to Gram and gives her a hug.

'This is my granddaughter, Valentine.'

I extend my hand to the Tuscan hottie. 'Nice to meet you. You must be Gianluca's wife?'

Gianluca, Orsola, Dominic, and Gram laugh loud and long.

'Did I say something wrong?'

'Gianluca is my papa.' Orsola grins. 'You just made his big ego even bigger.'

'An Italian man with a big ego? That's impossible,' I tell them.

Gram gives me a look that says, *Watch it. Your humor doesn't play in Arezzo.*

She's right, so I quickly cover my tracks. 'Orsola, I've got to know. Where did you get those sandals?'

'Our friend Costanzo Ruocco made them for me on Capri. Every summer we visit on holiday.'

'I'm going to Capri in a few weeks.'

'Oh, you must visit him. I will give you his number and address before you go.'

I was hoping to meet other shoemakers on this trip, as there are artistic questions I have that Gram cannot answer, and sometimes, I have ideas that Gram doesn't like, and it would be nice to run them by a master who has no stake in the argument.

Orsola follows Gram and Dominic to the back of the shop. Gianluca pulls out a few more samples and places them on the worktable. I sit down and begin choosing some for Gram to approve. There's a supple beige calfskin that would be an excellent choice for our Osmina design. My head swims with the possibilities as I look around the shop. Leathers in shades of cream and ebony, embossed with small gold Florentine symbols, others in patterned basket weaves, still more in colors I only dream about: ice blue patent leather, deep ruby red suede and faux leopard on shiny black horsehair.

Gianluca pulled a drawer from the supply closet and set it on the table. It is filled with leather laces in pastel shades of mint green, pink, and gold; white leather buckles; black leather trim; and patent leather bows with hand-cut fasteners. I dump the contents of the drawer on the table, as there doesn't seem to be two of any particular style.

I push the mound around, separating the samples. A metallic glint catches my eye. I pull a braid of gold leather, white satin ribbon, and white calfskin out of the pile. It's very Chanel, braiding you might see on an expensive purse or even as a trim on a leather jacket, but there's an original touch to it, a fourth skein of twisted flat hemp that gives a straw-and-hay effect to the gold.

'Orsola braids the leather,' Gianluca says.

'This is magnificent.' I study the braid of gold

under the light. 'I just designed a shoe this would work on.'

'Orsola can make anything you need.'

'She's very talented. And beautiful. Your wife must be a knockout because your daughter . . .' I whistle.

He smiles. 'Orsola's mother is beautiful. But I'm divorced from her.'

'I thought divorce was illegal in Italy.'

'Not anymore.' He turns and opens a cupboard filled with brightly colored suedes. He lifts a few samples out and places them on the table.

Gram appears in the doorway of the back of the shop and leans in. Her knees don't seem to be bothering her now. 'So, do you see anything you like?'

'We're in trouble.' I hold up a sheet of soft calfskin. 'I like everything.'

Dominic stands behind Gram, placing his hand on the small of her back. 'I don't have too much of that,' he says.

'How much do you need?' Gianluca asks.

'We can get about three pairs per sheet, right, Gram?'

Gram nods.

'Do you have four sheets?' I ask Gianluca.

'We do.'

'We'll take them.' I look at Gram.

She nods her approval. 'Val, why don't you choose the rest?'

'Because I'm not sure what we need?' My voice breaks.

'Yes, you are.'

'Gram, it's an entire year's worth of inventory. You trust me with this?'

'Absolutely.'

Gram turns to face Dominic. 'See my knees?' She lifts her skirt. 'I need new ones.'

'New ones?'

'Titanium. I'm told they'll give me the legs of a showgirl and then I can climb these hills like a goat. But, for now, I'll just have to lean on you.'

Dominic extends his arm, Gram takes it, and they turn to go.

'Uh . . . where are you going?' I call after her pleasantly.

'Dominic's going to show me a new technique he's using to emboss leather.'

I'll bet, I think to myself as they go. Gianluca has moved another large stack of leather from the shelves for me to go through.

I take my sketchbook out of my purse and flip through it to find my list of things we need.

Gianluca stands behind me as my sketchbook falls open to my design of the Bergdorf's shoe.

'This is yours?' he asks.

I nod that it is.

'Bellissima.' His eyes narrow as he looks at it more closely. 'Ambitious, no?'

'Well, it is complicated,' I say, 'but—'

'Si, si,' he interrupts with a smile. 'It's for you to figure out. You imagined it and now you will bring it to life.'

I return my attention to one of the sheets of leather

on the table in front of us. Gianluca watches me as I examine the leather under the lights, checking for patina, finish, and suppleness. I roll the corner of the sheet, as Gram taught me, checking for splits or creases in the leather, but the material is as smooth and luxurious in my hands as dough.

Sometimes tanners will add elements to the finishing solution to cover flaws in the leather. Since our shoes are handcrafted, you can't hide inconsistencies in the materials, as you might with machine-made shoes. We often resew seams as we custom-fit the shoes, so it takes strong, uncompromised leather to sew and resew. I run my hands over the expanse of the buttery suede. No wonder my family has used this company for years. These are first-class goods. I look up at Gianluca and smile in approval.

He smiles back at me.

I lift several sheets of leather off the stack and put them to the side. I return the bulk of them to the shelf behind me.

Gianluca stays in the doorway for what seems like a long time. What's he looking at? I look up at him. He looks amused, which is odd, because I'm not saying anything. Is there something about me that's funny, even when I'm not trying to be? *Funnyone* translates, I guess. That's good to know, but enough already. 'That's okay, I got it.' I wave the braid at him so he is free to go.

'*Va bene.*' He grins and goes. But I think he'd rather stay.

CHAPTER 11

LAGO ARGENTO

I wake to the sound of a soft rain tapping against the tile roof. The clock says it's five o'clock in the morning. I don't want to move from underneath these warm blankets, but I left all the windows open and I can see where the floor is damp from the rain. I get up and close the windows that look out over the pond, then go to close the ones that look out over the town square.

There's a low, thick mist hovering over the village, like tufts of pink cotton candy. Through the fog, I see a woman walking toward the inn. I'm curious to see who might be out and about this early in the morning.

The woman moves slowly, but as she comes closer, I see her tie the ends of her scarf underneath her chin. It's Gram. What is she doing out at this hour? Her trench coat is unbuttoned below the belt, and underneath the coat I can see the moss green skirt she wore yesterday. Dear God. She didn't sleep in her room last night.

I begged off from a late supper at the Vechiarellis' last night knowing I needed to take care of a few e-mails and check my list for the fabric shopping

346

today. But I could also tell that I was a third wheel and that Gram wanted to be alone with Dominic.

I hear the door to her room close softly. When I hear her running water in the bathroom, I seize my moment and tiptoe back to my bed. I pull the covers up around me and close my eyes.

I wake up again at seven. I bolt out of bed, take a bath, do my hair, and get dressed. Then I rap on her side of the bathroom door. She doesn't answer. I pull the door open and peer into her room. Her bed is made. Of course it is! She didn't sleep in it. I grab my tote bag, notebooks, and phone and go downstairs.

Gram is sitting in the dining room reading the paper. She wears a navy blue skirt and a matching cashmere sweater. Her hair is brushed out softly, and she's applied her pink lipstick.

'Sorry, I slept late.'

'It's only seven.' She looks up from her paper.

'But we have so much to do today. That drive to Prato is two hours, right?'

'Yes. I wanted to talk to you about that.' She puts the newspaper down and looks at me. 'Could you go without me?'

'Well, sure, Gram, if you're sure you trust me to pick the fabrics—'

'I do. You did a marvelous job, great, with the leather yesterday. Gianluca will drive you to Prato.'

'What are you doing today?'

'Dominic is taking me on a picnic.'

Signora Guarasci places the hot coffee, steamed

milk, and sugar on the table. She brings a basket of rolls, with a tin of sweet butter and blackberry jam. 'Did you sleep well?' the signora asks.

'Yes,' Gram and I answer together.

'I don't know how you can say you had a good night's sleep, Gram. The thunder was *so loud.*'

'Oh, it was,' she agrees.

'I am surprised you could sleep at all.'

'It wasn't easy,' she says, not taking her eyes off the newspaper.

'All that crashing, and banging and thunder and lightning . . .'

She continues to read. 'It was something.'

'Gram, you're busted.'

'Valentine. What are you getting at?' Gram puts down the paper and looks around. Lucky for her, we're still the only patrons at the Spolti Inn.

'When I woke up this morning around five, it was raining and I went to close the windows and I saw you out walking.'

'Oh,' she says. She picks up her paper again and pretends to scan it. 'I was jet-lagged and I went out for an early stroll.'

'In yesterday's skirt?'

She puts down the paper. 'Now . . .' She blushes. 'That's enough.'

'I think it's wonderful.'

'You do?'

'Absolutely.'

'It's just a little odd . . . ,' she begins.

'For me to learn about this side of you?'

'Well, yes.' She clears her throat. 'And it's not a *side* of me, it *is* me.'

'I approve. In fact, I more than approve. I'm happy for you. I think it's difficult to find love at all in this world, and for you to have a . . .' I can't find the strength to say the word *lover*, so I say, '. . . *friend* is a gift. So why pretend it isn't happening? There's no need for you to come traipsing down the mountain in the morning acting like you stayed here. Pack up your stuff and go over there and stay with him. What happens in Arezzo stays in Arezzo.'

Gram laughs. 'Thank you.' She sips her coffee. 'And that goes for you, too.'

'Hey, I'm taken.' I look out the window and it feels like New York and all our problems are a million miles away. For a moment, I forget the Bergdorf's contest, our mounting debt, and the agony of dealing with Alfred. I even decide to put Roman on the shelf until we get to Capri, because I'm weary of analyzing us. All I see for now is spring unfolding in Italy, with the tiniest buds of green breaking through the gray branches. 'But before you go, I need to know one thing.' I pull out my notebook.

'Yes?'

'How much double-sided duchess satin do you think we need in the shop?'

I wait for Gianluca to pick me up on the sidewalk in front of the Spolti Inn. The morning fog has lifted, leaving the cobblestones clean and wet, and the air brisk.

Arezzo is famous for its windy mountaintop climate, and it does not disappoint. I'm wearing a sleeveless pink wool shift with a matching bolero my mother found for 75 percent off at Loehmann's. Giving credit where credit is due, my mother insists you can find great stuff at Loehmann's *if* you search. The bolero was one of her greatest triumphs as it's a gorgeous, tightly woven cash-mere the color of sand.

Gianluca pulls up and gets out of his car. He comes around and opens the door for me.

'Good morning,' he says.

'Good morning.' I get a whoosh of the scent of his skin as I climb in; it's crisp and lemony. He closes the car door behind me, bracing the outside handle like it's a lock on a bank vault. I'm sure Dominic warned him that if I accidentally fell out of the car while in his care, he'd have to kill him on behalf of my grandmother.

Gianluca goes around the front of the car and gets into the driver's seat. This is an old-model Mercedes, but the interior still has the scent of new leather, while the navy blue exterior is polished to a glassy finish.

Gianluca hits the gas pedal like he's bolting from the first position at the starting gate at NASCAR in the Poconos.

'Whoa,' I say. 'Keep it under ninety miles an hour, will you?'

I scroll through my e-mails. I answer Wendy's about the hotel, Gabriel's about the leather, and Mom's about Gram. Roman writes:

I dream of you and Capri. R.

I text back:

In that order? V.

'You like that thing?' Gianluca points to my phone.

'I couldn't live without it. I'm in constant touch with everyone I know. How could that be a bad thing?'

He laughs. 'When do you *think*?'

'Funny you should ask. I actually turned this off and soaked in the tub last night, and then I did some reading.'

'*Va bene, Valentina.*'

That's funny, only my father ever called me Valentina.

He continues, 'I don't like those things. They interrupt life. You can't go anywhere without beeps going off and silly songs playing.'

'I'm sorry to tell you, Gianluca. But I think these things' – I hold up my phone – 'are here to stay.'

'Agh.' He dismisses the entire contemporary-communication matrix with a wave of his hand.

'Oh, I'm sorry. I'm being rude e-mailing instead of talking to you.' I put the phone on pulse and put it in my purse.

I catch the corner of his mouth turning up in a smile. Okay, Gianluca, I'm thinking, you're Italian. You're a man. This is all about *you*. 'I'm all yours,' I tell him.

To reward me for my undivided attention, Gianluca frequently slows down to show me the exterior of a rococo church, or a roadside shrine to the Madonna placed by a devout farmer, or an indigenous tree that grows only in this part of the world. On the outskirts of Prato, he takes a turn off the autostrada and onto a back road. I grip the handle above the door as we jostle over the gravel roadway.

As Gianluca slows down, I see a lake through the trees. It shimmers like pale blue silk taffeta. The edges of the water are blurred by wild fronds of deep green stalks that bend and twist over the shoreline. I commit the color scheme to memory. How luscious it would be to create an icy blue shoe with a deep green feather trim. I roll down the window to get a closer look. The sun hits the water like a slew of silver arrows.

'This is one of my favorite places. Lago Argento. This is where I come to think.'

The lovely silence is broken by the beep of my cell phone. I'm mortified that I'm spoiling Gianluca's sacred space.

'Go ahead and answer it. I cannot fight progress.'

I look at Gianluca, who laughs, and then I laugh. I reach into my purse and check my phone.

Roman texts:

You first. Forever and ever. R.

I smile.

'Good news?' Gianluca asks.

'Oh, yeah.' I put the phone back in my purse.

The Prato silk-factory building is a modern, rambling complex painted a dull beige, and has a tall steel-ornamental fence enclosing it. Low landscaping around the border gives it a manicured look.

Many great designers come here to shop for fabric. The old-guard, visionary Europeans like Karl Lagerfeld and Alberta Ferretti, to new talents like Phillip Lim and Proenza Schouler, make the trip to Prato. Some designers even take the scraps from the floor and weave them into original fabric designs; evidently, even the chuff of this factory is valuable.

Gianluca shows his ID as we pull up to the guard's gate. They ask me for my passport. Gianluca opens it to the page with my picture and hands it to the guard.

Once we park, I wait for Gianluca to come around and open my door. He was polite about my beeping phone, so I'm not about to undercut his proper Italian manners. When he opens my door, he takes my hand to help me out. When our hands touch, a slight shiver runs down my spine. It must be the spring air, which blows cool under the hot sun.

We go through the entrance where there's a small reception area with a window. Gianluca goes up to the window and asks to see Sabrina Fioravanti. In a few moments, a woman around my mother's age, with reading glasses on a chain around her neck, greets us.

'Gianluca!' she says.

He kisses both her cheeks. 'This is Signora Fioravanti.'

She takes my hands, pleased to meet me. 'How is Teodora?' she wants to know.

'She's doing fine.'

'*Vecchio?*' Signora says. 'Like me.'

'Only in numbers, not in spirit.' I start thinking about what my eighty-year-old Gram is up to this very minute.

I follow Sabrina into the mill, to the finishing department, where the ornate silks are being pressed and mounted onto bolts, which spin the fabric onto giant wheels that fill to the size of tree trunks. I can't resist touching the fabrics, buttery cotton sateen embroidered with fine gold thread, and cut velvet with squares of raw silk.

'Double-sided fabrics you need?' Sabrina asks.

'Yes.' I reach inside my purse for my list. 'And taffeta with a velvet backing, and, if you have it, a silk striate.' I take a deep breath.

'Is there a problem?' Gianluca asks me. He points to the deep lines forming a number eleven between my eyebrows. 'You look concerned.'

'No, I'm just thinking,' I lie. 'And when I think, I get a unibrow.'

'What?'

'You know, worry lines. Ignore them.'

Sabrina returns with a young man carrying a pile of fabric swatches. It will take me the better part of the day to look through them. Now I know why I have the worry lines. This is a big job and Gram isn't here to guide me. She's too busy pitching woo with Dominic under the Tuscan sun to schlep to this factory and sort through hundreds of fabric samples to find what we need. I'm feeling abandoned, that's all. But it's too late, we're here now, and I have to go it alone.

Sabrina goes. I pull up a stool and put my purse on the table behind me. Gianluca pulls up a stool and sits across from me at the worktable. I place my written list on the table and begin to sort through the fabrics.

'Okay.' I look at Gianluca. 'First, I need a durable satin jacquard. Beige.'

Gianluca sorts through a pile and pulls one. He holds it up.

'Not too much pink in the beige,' I tell him. 'More gold.'

I put aside the fabrics that would be too flimsy even if we backed them ourselves. Gianluca follows my lead. Then he begins to make a stack of the heartier varieties. I find a heavy double-sided satin embroidered with filigreed gold vines.

I wonder if we can cut on the embroidery and reluctantly put it aside.

'You don't like that one?' he says.

'I love it. But I don't think I can cut around the pattern.'

Gianluca picks up the sample. 'But you can. You just buy extra, and repeat the pattern across.' He drapes the fabric on the table, then tucks it under. 'See? It's the same with the leather.'

'You're right.'

I place the silk with vines on the top of my buy pile. There are so many to choose from, but the selection is enthralling. I begin to imagine shoes in every sample I pick up: canton crepe, peau-de-soie, matelasse, velveteen, faille, and a silk broadcloth with a tone-on-tone stripe. I throw myself into the fun of it, and the process picks up speed as we sort for a good while.

'You like making shoes?' Gianluca asks.

'Can you tell?' I check another item off my list. 'Do you like working as a tanner?'

'Not so much.' Now Gianluca gets the number eleven between his eyes. 'Papa and I fight. We have for many years. But it's worse since my mother died.'

How long has your father been a widower?'

'Eleven years in November.' He picks up a stack of crisp linen samples from the end of the table. 'Are both your parents living?'

I nod that they are.

'How old are they?' he asks.

'My father is sixty-eight. If you ever meet my mom, you mustn't let on, but she is sixty-one. We have an age thing in my family.'

'What is an *age thing*?'

'We don't like getting old.'

'Who does?' He smiles.

'How old are you?'

'I am fifty-two,' he says. 'That's too old.'

'For what?' I ask him. 'To change careers? You could do that in a second.'

Gianluca shrugs. 'Working with my father is my obligation.' He seems resigned, but not actually unhappy about his situation.

'In America, when something isn't working for us, we change. We go back to school and develop a new skill, or we switch jobs, or employers. There's no need to toil away at something you don't love.'

'In Italy, we don't change. My desires are not the most important thing. I have responsibilities and I accept them. My father needs me. I let him think he's the boss, but his siesta has become longer the older he gets.'

'So do Gram's.'

'You work in your family business.' He sounds defensive.

'Yes, but I chose it. I wanted to be a shoemaker.'

'Here, we don't choose. The dreams of the family become our dreams.'

I think about my family, and how that used to be true for us. It was family first, but now, it seems,

357

my generation has let go of all of that. I could never work with my mother, but it's different with my grandmother. The generation that separates Gram and me seems to bind us to a common goal. We understand each other in a way that works professionally and at home. Maybe it's because she needs the help, and I was here at the right moment to give it to her. I don't know. But my dreams and the dreams of my grandmother somehow met, and blended, creating something new for each of us. Even now, it seems, she is handing the reins over to me; never mind that the horse has a lame leg and can't see, to her the Angelini Shoe Company is worth something, and to me, even with mounting debt and the production of custom shoes in jeopardy, it's a priceless legacy. I only hope that I can hang on to it so I might pass it along to the next generation.

Gianluca and I enter a tall atrium in the center of the complex where the factory workers take their breaks. Some of the younger ones are on their BlackBerries, others chat on cell phones, while the middle-aged employees have an espresso and a piece of fruit. There are workers here close to Gram's age, which is a huge difference compared with back home. Here, the older artisans – the masters – are revered and an integral part of the process of making fabrics. My brother, Alfred, should see this so he might understand why Gram keeps working. The satisfaction a craftsman seeks, after years of work, is perfection itself. A master may not reach it, but after years of study, training, and experience, she may come close. This, in itself, is a goal worth aiming for.

Gianluca brings me a caffè latte, while he carries a bottle of water for himself. 'My wife drank caffè latte, never espresso.'

'My kind of girl.'

Gianluca sits down next to me.

'I feel bad that you got stuck with me. I'm sure you have all kinds of important things to do.'

'I do?' He smiles.

'Sure. You have a daughter and a family in Arezzo. You probably have a hobby or a girlfriend.'

He laughs.

'What's funny about that?'

'There is no subtlety with you.'

'Well, forgive me. I'm just trying to make conversation.'

He swigs his water, and leaves my question lying on the table like the rejected pile of flimsy silk linen. But I *am* curious about this man, I don't know why. I have nothing to lose, so I get personal with him. 'Why did you get a divorce?'

'Why aren't you married?' He answers with a question.

'You first.'

'My wife wanted to move to the city. But she knew I couldn't leave my father. So we agreed that she would live in Florence while I stayed on in Arezzo, and I would visit, or she would come

359

home on weekends. Orsola was going to university, and it seemed like the arrangement could work. We were doing what we needed to do, what we wanted to do. But that doesn't make a marriage.'

'Sounds ideal to me. Very romantic to have two lives that come together once in a while and sparks fly.'

'It's no good. You take each other for granted.'

'I know all about that.' The reasons behind Gianluca's divorce sound an awful lot like the excuses I use when Roman disappoints me. Sometimes I feel that we put our relationship on hold in order to do our work. Somehow, though, I think love fixes all of this. Isn't love the most practical of all emotions? Isn't it a constant? 'Do you still love her?'

'I don't believe you can love someone who doesn't love you.'

'Sometimes you can't help it.'

'I can,' he says simply. 'Now tell me about you.'

My phone pulses. I fish it out of my purse. 'Saved by technology.' I check the phone. 'It's Gabriel,' I say aloud. I'll text him later.

'Your boyfriend?' he asks.

'No, no. Just a friend.' I snap my phone shut and put it back in my purse. 'We should get back to work,' I say.

I follow Gianluca back through the atrium to the hallway that leads to the workroom. There's a set of glass doors that separate the hallway from the atrium. Gianluca dials the security code. I look at the reflection of the two of us in the glass.

'Nice couple, eh?' he says, meeting my eyes in the glass.

I nod politely. I remember something Gabriel told me back in college. He said a man never spends time with a woman unless he wants something. Gianluca is spending an awful lot of time with me. I wonder what he's after. More business? Maybe. But we make only so many pairs of shoes a year. It's not likely I'd double my leather order. It's almost as if he *wants* an excuse to be away from the tannery. I heard the yelling. It isn't all fun and games at Vechiarelli & Son. Maybe I'm his excuse to take some time away from the shop.

We return to the workroom and take our seats at the table. Sabrina left a new pile of swatches on the table.

'It is still your turn,' says Gianluca. 'I want to know about you. Tell me about your boyfriend.'

'Well, his name is Roman. He is a chef in his own restaurant. He makes rustic Italian cuisine.'

Gianluca laughs. 'All Italian food is rustic. We've been eating the same food for the past two thousand years. Will you marry this Roman?'

'Maybe.'

'Has he asked?'

'Not yet.' The look on Gianluca's face annoys me. 'Hey, for the record, I was asked once before.'

'Of course, you had many suitors.'

I just look at him. Is he joking or does he actually

believe I'm a femme fatale? Let him think whatever he wants. My romantic past, my pre-Roman era, seems historic to me now. A woman can reinvent or erase her history entirely when she travels. This is one of the great benefits of leaving home.

'Do you want children?' he asks.

'You know, for the longest time I didn't know. But now, I think I might.'

'How old are you?'

'I'll be thirty-four at the end of this month.'

He whistles low. 'You'd better hurry.'

'Who are you? The fertility police?'

'No, it's that I'm older and I have experience. You need energy to raise children. You should do it soon. It's the best thing I ever did.'

'Orsola is beautiful and has a big heart. You should be very proud of her.'

'She is the best thing to come out of my marriage.'

'Do you think you'll marry again?'

'No,' he answers quickly.

'You've made your mind up about *that*.'

'I have my daughter. What would be the purpose of getting married again?'

'Oh, I don't know. Love, maybe?'

'Love is not what makes a marriage,' he says. 'Love starts one, perhaps, but something else finishes it.'

'Really.' I put down my swatches and lean forward. 'Please. Explain.'

362

'Marriage in Italy used to be about two families coming together,' he begins.

'Yes, and merging their assets,' I say, nodding. 'A business of a sort.'

'Correct. And their beliefs, too, about how to live and how to build a life together. But sometimes, families don't mesh. My wife, I believe, loved me, but she thought I would achieve great things. And when I didn't, she left.'

'What was she expecting?'

He waves his hand in the air. 'A city life.'

'You know, Gianluca, a city life is not so bad.'

'I don't want it.'

'How could you *not*? It's the best. Gram and I live in Greenwich Village in New York City. And we have a roof garden where we grow tomatoes, and sometimes, at night, it's so quiet you'd think you were by the lake you showed me this morning. Really.'

'I don't believe you.'

'Maybe it's because there are so many buildings, and we live so closely together, but we appreciate nature more. Every tree is fascinating. Flowers are treasured. City people love flowers so much they're sold in bunches on street corners year-round.'

'I prefer a field of flowers.'

'Well, you can have that, too, if you take a train ride up to the botanical gardens in the Bronx. You notice the sky more, too. Of course, I don't think you can beat the colors of the Italian sky, but what we have is also very beautiful. The pollution makes for some gorgeous purple sunsets over New Jersey.'

He laughs. 'Just don't breathe it.'

'Best of all, our building looks out over the Hudson River. The river is wide and deep and flows out past Staten Island to the Atlantic Ocean in a grand sweep. When winter comes, the river freezes and creates a great expanse of silver ice. It never freezes all the way across, like a lake – where you could skate on it – instead it breaks into big gray puzzle pieces of ice that bob in the water until the sun melts them. But for days, when it's freezing, you can see these gray blocks of ice bumping up against each other where they used to fit together. And at night, if you walk by the river's edge, the only sound you'll hear is the soft tapping of the pieces of ice as they float on the surface as water rushes underneath.'

'That quiet?'

'Almost silent. During the winter, the parks and the walkway are empty. I take walks over there, and it's all mine. I wonder, how can this view be free? But it is.'

'It belongs to you.'

'I pretend it does. I was walking alone on a pier one morning last winter. The river was frozen, but something new caught my eye. It was a flash of ruby red bobbing on a slab of ice. So I walked out to the end of the pier. Three seagulls had caught a fish, a big one. They had gored it and were eating. The red I saw at a distance was the blood of the fish. I turned away at first. But then I had to look back. There was something so compelling about the palette of the black river, the silver ice, and the maroon blood of the fish. It was horrible, and yet beautiful. I couldn't take my eyes off it.'

Gianluca listens intently to every word I say.

I continue, 'I learned something about myself that morning.'

'What did you learn?' Gianluca leans toward me, waiting for my answer.

'I can find art in the worst moments. I used to believe my art had to be about the things that brought me joy and gave me hope. But I learned that art can be found in all of life, even in pain.'

As Gianluca drives us back to Arezzo, I flip through the swatches of the fabrics we selected at the silk mill. My favorite is a double-sided silk with a repeating pattern of hand-painted calla lilies. I imagine using the fabric to make an elegant slip-on mule with black velvet piping. There are just a few of our old standard choices among the swatches. I hope Gram approves. I took a big step and went ahead and placed the orders. I had a moment of complete exhilaration as I signed my name for the first time on the line on the order form marked DESIGNER.

The sun doesn't so much set here as plunge behind the hills. Twilight seems to last for a few moments, and then the moon appears in the purple sky like a rosette of whipped cream. It's a romantic moon, and it's no wonder my grandmother is under its spell. 'You know, your father and my grandmother—'

Gianluca takes his eyes off the road and looks at me.

I make the international hand signal for sex.

He laughs. 'For many years. Since your grandfather died.'

'*That* long?' How do you like that? I thought I knew all the family secrets.

'They were good friends. Now, there's something more.'

'*A lot* more.'

'My father was good friends with your grandfather also. Very intelligent. Big personality. Like you,' Gianluca says as he takes a turn off the autostrada onto a small side road.

'Another lake?' I ask.

'No. Dinner.' He smiles.

Gianluca takes another quick turn onto another side road. In the clearing ahead, there's a charming stone farmhouse lit with torches at the entrance. A few cars are parked outside.

'This is Montemurlo,' he says. 'We're halfway home.'

After we park, he places his hand on the small of my back to guide me into the restaurant. I find myself quickening my step, but he just takes longer strides to keep up with me. Once we reach the door, Gianluca motions for me to go through the empty dining room and outside to the back.

A dozen tables are set up on the veranda, hemmed in by a low wall of stacked fieldstone. Votive candles light the crisp white linens on the tables. A line of blazing torches beyond the wall throw streams of light onto a field. I hear the sound of rushing water.

In the middle distance, there's a magnificent waterfall pouring down the mountainside and into a small lake. The moonlight on the water looks like ruffles of white lace on black taffeta. 'If the food is anything like the view, we've got a winner,' I tell him.

Gianluca pulls my chair from the table. He seats me facing the waterfall. Then he turns his chair toward me, sits, and crosses his long legs. The last time I saw a man sit in this fashion, it was Roman, at Gram's counter after he made me dinner.

The waiter comes over and they converse in rapid Italian and in a Tuscan dialect that is beginning to sound familiar to me. The waiter opens a bottle of wine and places it on the table. He is balding, wears glasses, and looks me up and down, like he's buying stew meat, before he returns to the kitchen.

I close the menu. 'You know what? Order for me.'

'What do you like?' he asks.

'Everything.'

He laughs. 'Everything?'

'Sad but true. I'm in that lonely category of

woman called *Actual* Eater. I have no aversions, allergies, or dislikes.'

'You're the only woman in the world like this.'

'Oh, I'm one of a kind, Gianluca.'

The waiter brings a plate of crisp Italian toast topped with thin slices of Italian prosciutto drizzled with blackberry honey. I taste it.

'You like it?'

'*Love* it. Told you. I love all food. Get me a jar of that honey.'

As the meal is prepared, we talk about our day at the mill, and the fine art of embossing leather. Eventually, the waiter brings a large serving bowl of pasta, drizzled in olive oil. Then from his vest pocket, the waiter takes a small jar. He opens the lid and removes a truffle (which looks like a lumpy beige turnip) from a small, white cotton cloth. Then, with a sleek silver knife, he makes long, smooth strokes on the truffle, which falls onto the pasta in filmy slices, until the hot pasta is covered.

'Do you like truffles?'

'Yes,' I say through a mouth full of buttery pasta and woodsy, sweet truffle. I feel odd having the truffles, like I'm cheating on Roman.

'You love to eat. Women always say they love to eat, but then they pick at their meal like birds.'

'Not me,' I tell him. 'Eating is in my top three.'

'What are the other two?'

'A four-speed bicycle on a hot summer day and a John Galliano ball gown on a cold winter night.' I sip my wine. 'What are your top three?'

Gianluca takes a moment to think. 'Sex, wine, and a good night's sleep.'

The good-night's-sleep category highlights our eighteen-year age difference. My *parents* spend lots of time talking about sleep. However, I won't point this out to Gianluca nor will I mention that the only older men I have ever spent time with were my grandfather and my dad. May-December romances have never been for me. When it comes to love, I like my four seasons, individually savored and spread out. I certainly don't want to skip summer through fall and go right to winter, but spending time with Gianluca has helped me see the value of a friendship with an older man. They have a lot to offer, especially when romance is safely out of the equation. I learned a lot from him today – his advice on sewing repeat patterns alone was worth the trip. He also listens, as though whatever I have to say matters. Young men often pretend to listen, their minds on where the evening is going, and not where it actually *is*.

The waiter offers to bring us espresso. Gianluca tells him to wait.

'I want to show you something. Come with me.'

There is a series of stone steps off the portico that leads down to the vast field in front of the waterfall. He skips down the stairs, making it clear he's been here many times before. I follow him.

The grass is already wet with night dew, so I slip off my sandals to walk barefoot. Gianluca reaches out and takes my sandals from me, holding them in one hand while taking my hand with the other. I find this more than slightly intimate, but I can't figure out how to let go without being rude. Plus, there's the wine factor. I had two glasses. I hardly ate today, so I'm floating on that wonderful cloud called double-cocktail buzz while we cross the field.

We arrive at a deep pool of water, the color of blue ink, at the base of the waterfall. He turns to me. The rush of the water is so loud, we can't talk. I slip my hand from his and put it in my pocket. He might be older, but he's still a man, and if I'm going to be holding on to anything, it's going to be to Roman Falconi back home.

I hold my hand out for my shoes. He gives them to me. I skip ahead and back to our table where the waiter has left a caffe latte for me, an espresso for him, and a bowl of ripe peaches.

I climb into bed and open my cell phone. I dial Gabriel.

'How's Italy?'

'It's dangerous,' I tell him.

'What happened?'

'Gram has a lover.'

'Oh, *that* kind of danger. Let me get this straight. *Gram* has a lover and I'm single? Go figure.'

'Hey, I don't like how that sounds.'

'You know what I mean. She's eighty! Evidently a spry eighty,' Gabriel admits.

'It gets worse. Her boyfriend's son put the moves on me.'

'Go for it.'

'I will not! I would never cheat on Roman.'

'Then why are you telling me this? Hey, *no ring no thing*.' Gabriel's philosophy: there is no such thing as cheating unless there's an engagement ring. 'How old is Marmaduke?'

'Gianluca. He's fifty-two.'

'Good fifty-two or bad fifty-two?'

'Good fifty-two.' At least I'm honest. 'He's gray though.'

'Who isn't?'

'Forget I said a word. I'm in love with Roman.'

'I'm glad, because that's the only way I can get a table at Ca' d'Oro. And I want a table at Ca' d'Oro as often as I can get it. Your boyfriend is the bomb.'

'He treated you well?'

'Roman pulled out all the stops. You would have thought I was the food critic for the *New York Times* when I barely know a pork shoulder from a lamb shank.'

'Good for you. Hey, did you check out Roman's sous-chef?'

'Yes, I did. Her name is Caitlin Granzella. I met her on my tour of the kitchen.'

'And?'

'You're far from home. You don't need a mental image.'

'Gabriel!'

'All right, all right. I have to be honest. Think Nigella Lawson. Face *and* body. Trim *but* curvy. She's built like a bottle of Prell.'

371

I don't say a word. I can't. My boyfriend has a gorgeous sous-chef and I've been gone for *weeks*.

'Valentine? Breathe. And don't worry. I think Mr Falconi has permanent plans for you.'

'You think so?'

'All he could talk about was Capri, and how he was going to show you everything, and how for the first time in his life he was going to take a real vacation because there was only one girl in the world he wanted to be stranded on an Italian island with – and that's *you*. So don't worry about Miss Slice and Dice in the Ca' d'Oro kitchen. He doesn't dream about her. He's crazy about you.'

As we say good night, I lean back on the pillows and dream of Roman Falconi. I imagine him, the blue sea, the pink clouds, and the hot sun over Capri. As I sink into a deep and satisfying sleep, I imagine my lover's arms around me in warm sand.

CHAPTER 12

THE ISLE OF CAPRI

Gram, Dominic, Gianluca, and I did the cobbler's tour of Italy in the week before our last day in Arezzo. We drove up to Milan and went through the Mondiale factory, buying enough buckles, clips, and fasteners to supply our shop for another ten thousand pairs of shoes.

While we were in Milan, we met with Bret's international business connection, a group of Italian financiers who work with designers who coventure in Italy and America. They reinforced Bret's idea that we develop a line secondary to our custom shoes. I explained to them that we were in development on that front. I mentioned the possibility of the Bergdorf windows, which was an exciting notion to them, as they have done a lot of business with the venerable Neiman Marcus Company that now owns Bergdorf Goodman.

We also went to Naples to meet with Elisabetta and Carolina D'Amico, the embellishment experts. I got lost in their shop, a playground for any designer, rooms of jeweled straps and laces, beaded links, clips and bows. The women have a sense of humor, so their work can be whimsical, shell ornaments on a sea of dyed rice, glued to look like grains of sand on a beach; or miniature jeweled crowns on cameo faces; or my favorite, the Wedding Cake, cushion-cut rhinestones in the shape of a cake across the vamp, with gold charms of a bride and groom at the top of the ankle, affixed with matching straps. Brilliant.

It's our last morning in Arezzo, and while I'll miss Signora Guarasci's soup and my bed with the open windows to let in the night air, I'm anxious to drive to the airport to drop off Gram and to pick up Roman. I try not to show my anticipation because, as happy as I am to go, Gram is equally sad.

She waits for me in the hallway outside our rooms. 'I'm ready,' she says quietly.

'I'll get your luggage.' I go into her room for the suitcase. I've already loaded my bags into the car, along with a new duffel filled with fabric swatches. The leather and fabric I ordered are being shipped and should be at the shop by the time I get home.

Signora Guarasci is waiting for us at the bottom of the stairs. She's made us box lunches for the trip, prosciutto and cheese panini, with two cold bottles of Orangina to wash them down. She gives us each a hug and a kiss and thanks us for our patronage.

Gram goes out the front door, takes the banister, and goes down the stairs. Dominic waits for her on the last step. I quickly skip around Gram to give them a private moment.

I go to the car, which is parked at the side of the

inn, load her suitcase into the trunk, and wait. Through the thick boxwood hedge, I can see the two of them embrace. Then he dips her, gives her a kiss, backbend style, the likes of which I have not seen since Clark Gable kissed Vivien Leigh, in the commemorative DVD of *Gone With the Wind*.

'Papa is very sad,' Gianluca says from behind me.

I'm embarrassed to be caught spying. 'So is Gram.' I turn to him. 'Thank you for everything you did for us on this trip.'

'I enjoyed our talks,' he says.

'Me, too.'

'I hope you visit again sometime.'

'I will.' I look at Gianluca who, after weeks of traveling around with us, has become a friend. When I first met him, I was judgmental, all I could see was the gray hair, the big car, and a daughter nearly my age. Now, I can appreciate his maturity. He is elegant without being vain, and he has excellent manners without being grand. Gianluca is also generous, he put Gram and me first throughout our stay. 'I'll bet you're happy to see us go.'

'Why would you say that?'

'We've taken up so much of your time.'

'I enjoyed it.' He gives me a slip of paper. 'This is my friend Costanzo's number in Capri. Please stop and see him. He's the finest shoemaker I know. Besides you of course,' Gianluca says and grins. 'You must watch him work.'

'I will,' I lie. I don't plan to look at shoes much less wear them while I'm in Capri. I want to make love, eat spaghetti, and sit by the pool, in that order.

'Well, thank you.' I extend my hand. Gianluca takes my hand and kisses it. Then, he leans forward and kisses me on both cheeks. When his lips brush against my face, his skin smells like cedar and lemon, very cool and clean, reminding me of the first time I climbed in his car, the day we went to Prato. I check my watch. 'We'd better be going.'

Gianluca and I walk to the foot of the stairs below the entrance of the Spolti Inn. Gram and Dominic are laughing, doing their best to make their good-bye a happy one. I touch Gram's arm, but they keep talking as they walk to our car. Dominic helps Gram into the car, while Gianluca holds my door open. I climb in, and he closes the door, checking the handle just as he did when we went to Prato.

Gram sinks into the front seat as I start the car. She's moving in slow motion, when all I want to do is blow this Tuscan pop stand (my father's words) and get to the airport, drop off Gram, and pick up Roman, and at long last, let the fun begin.

I peel down the hill to the main street of Arezzo, check the signs, and head for the edge of town to take us to the autostrada.

I look over at Gram, who seemed like a peppy teenager during our stay and now shows every day of her eighty years. The white roots peek through her brown hair, while her hands, folded over her lap, seem frail. 'I'm sorry,' I say, trying not to sound too chipper while she is so sad.

'It's all right,' she says.

I pick up speed on the autostrada and we sail along at a good clip. The highway is ours today, and I take full advantage. When Gram nods off to sleep, I think that it's better this way. The more she naps, the less she'll miss Dominic.

My phone buzzes in my pocket. I fish it out and open it.

'Honey?' Roman says.

'You landed?'

'No, I'm in New York.'

'They canceled your flight?' My heart sinks. I hate the airlines!

'No, I didn't make the flight. And I didn't want to call you in the middle of the night to tell you.'

'What happened?' I raise my voice.

Gram wakes up. 'What's wrong?'

'We got a tip that the *New York Times* is coming to review us this week, probably Tuesday night, so I'm going to fly out Wednesday and meet you in Capri. I hope you understand, honey.'

'I don't understand.'

'A review in the *Times* could make or break me.'

'A vacation in Capri could make or break *us*.' I've never threatened a man in my life. So much for being adorable; what does Katharine Hepburn know about men anyway? She never dated Roman Falconi.

'This is just a delay. I'll be there as soon as I can.'

'Save it. I'm tired of waiting for you to show up when you say you will. I'm tired of waiting for us to begin. I want you to go on vacation like you promised.'

He raises his voice. 'This review is really important to my business. I have to be here. I can't help it.'

'No you can't, can you? It shows me what's important to you. I'm a close second to your osso buco. Or am I even in second place?'

'You're number one, okay? Please, try and understand. I'll be there before you know it. You can relax until I get there.'

'I can't talk to you. I'm about to drive into a tunnel. Good-bye.' I look straight ahead; there is nothing but a clear ribbon of autostrada and blue Italian sky. I snap the phone shut and throw it into my bag.

'What happened?' Gram asks.

'He's not coming. He's going to be reviewed by the *Times* and he has to be there. He said he'd fly over Wednesday, but that hardly gives us any time once he lands, gets to Capri, and gets over the jet lag.' I begin to cry. 'And I'm going to turn thirty-four years old alone.'

'On top of everything else – your birthday.' Gram shakes her head.

'I am done with that man. This is it.'

'Don't be hasty,' Gram says gently. 'I'm sure he'd rather be with you than at the restaurant with a critic.'

'He's unreliable!'

'You know he has a difficult professional life.' Gram keeps her tone even.

378

'So do I! I'm trying to hold it all together myself. But I *needed* Capri. I *needed* a break. I haven't had a vacation in four years. I could almost face the nightmare back home if I could just rest before I had to deal with Alfred again.'

'I know there's a lot of pressure on you.'

'A lot? There's too much pressure. And you aren't helping.'

'Me?'

'You. Your ambivalence. I half-think you'd like to stay in Arezzo and just forget about Perry Street.'

'You've read my mind.'

'Well, guess what? We're both going home today. I am not going to lose everything because of Roman. At least let me keep my job.'

I fish for my BlackBerry to e-mail our travel agent Dea Marie Kaseta. I pull over on the side of the road. I text her:

Need Second Ticket On Alitalia 16 Today 4 pm to NYC. Urgent.

I pull back onto the road.

'I've never seen you this angry,' Gram says quietly.

'Well, get used to it. I'm going to stew all the way home to New York.'

The woman behind the counter at Alitalia looks at me with a lot of understanding, but very little hope. There isn't an extra seat available on flight

16 from Rome to New York. The best Dea Marie could do was get me a hotel room and a ticket to fly out the following morning.

I put my head down on the stainless-steel desk and weep. Gram pulls me off the line so the impatient passengers behind me can pick up their boarding passes. 'I'll go with you to Capri.'

'Gram, please don't take this the wrong way, but I don't want to go to Capri with you.'

'I understand.'

'Why don't you go with Dominic? The hotel is all set. And I'll take your ticket and fly home.'

'But you should have a vacation. And Roman said he's coming on Wednesday.'

'I don't want him to come at all.'

'You say that now, but Roman will be here soon and you'll make up.'

Gram opens her phone and calls Dominic. I survey the long line of passengers. Not one look of understanding or sympathy comes my way. I cry some more. My face begins to itch from the tears. I wipe my face with my sleeve. I remember my father's words to me: *Nothing ever seems to go right for you. You have to work for everything.* Well, now I have a new revelation – not only do I have to work for everything, but the work may go totally unrewarded. What is the point?

'We're all set.'

'Gram, what are you talking about?'

'I'm going to Capri with you now. Dominic will join me there. I will stay with him at his cousin's home, and you can have the hotel room all to yourself.' Gram takes my arm. 'Listen to me. Roman didn't do this on purpose. He'll be here on Wednesday, and this way, you can have a little alone time before he gets here.'

'Yeah, yeah, yeah,' I mutter as she leads me away from the hellish whirlpool of Alitalia check-in and out into the airport. I follow Gram, who now walks ramrod straight, with a spring in her step as she anticipates her reunion with Dominic. I push our enormous luggage cart forward with the full weight of my body through the Leonardo da Vinci-Fiumicino International Airport. I arrange for another rental car and pile all the luggage *back* into the trunk of the new rental while Gram straps into the passenger seat in the front. I e-mail Dea Marie for a credit on Gram's missed flight, asking her to rebook it for the day of Roman's and my return. I climb into the car and fasten my seat belt.

'See there? There's a solution to every problem.' Gram throws my cheap inspirational phrase right back in my face like a slap. 'On to Capri!'

When we arrive in Naples, I drop the rental car at a location by the docks. I look around for help with the bags, but there doesn't seem to be the Italian version of red caps working the pier.

I load up another luggage cart with the bags and push them, like a sherpa, to the pier. Our baggage seems to multiply every time I move it, or maybe the carts are getting smaller, I don't know, but it's overwhelming. I'm sweating like a prize fighter, my hair is wet by the time I reach the dock.

Gram stands guard next to the cart while I go and buy the tickets for the boat to Capri. We stand in the line as the boat backs into the harbor. When the attendant lets down the gate, a stampede of anxious tourists beats us up the ramp and onto the boat. I send Gram up the ramp and I follow her, pushing the cart.

Just when I think I may collapse, then be crushed under the wheels of my own cart, the ticket taker takes notice of my dilemma and hollers at a kid working on the deck. Finally, someone comes to my aid! He's tall, with black hair like Roman, and I can't help but think I wouldn't need him if my boyfriend had arrived on time. Inside the ferry, I take a seat next to Gram. As the ferry leaves the harbor, I exhale and look out over the sea. A few minutes go by, and then I see the island.

Capri is jammed into the rolling turquoise waters of the Tyrrhenian Sea, like a party hat. The jagged cliffs, born of volcanic eruptions thousands of years ago, are draped in vivid jewel tones. Fuchsia flowers cascade over the rocks, bursts of purple bougainvillea spill off the cliffs, while the emerald waves along the water's edge reveal glossy red coral, like the drips of red candle wax on a wine bottle.

The bustle on the pier in Capri with bellboys from the hotels grabbing bags and loading them onto carts in a frenzy puts me smack in the middle of a Rossellini film where a small village is evacuated during wartime. Porters are shouting in Italian, tourists scramble to flag down drivers, and tour guides wave small flags to herd their groups together. Gram and I stand in the center of it poised out of need, not choice.

I can't imagine how our luggage will make it to the correct hotel until I recognize the logo of the Quisisana on one of the bellboy's lapels. I show him our mountain of luggage. His eyes widen and he laughs. 'All yours?' he says.

'What's it going to take?' I shout over the din.

'Just a tip, *signorina*. Just a tip.' He laughs but he's getting a big tip based solely on calling me *signorina*. The i-n-a makes all the difference to a woman turning thirty-four in a matter of days. It's the difference between miss and ma'am, and I'm grabbing the miss like a winning ticket.

I take Gram's arm as we climb into an open dune buggy/taxi with a cloth canopy as a roof. The driver speeds up the mountain on hairpin curves, past opulent gates surrounding private villas. The stone walls of ancient palazzos are covered in waxy green vines bursting with white gardenias. The high-rises on the Bay of Naples, from whence we came, look smoky and industrial from here, like a stack of gray shoe boxes in a warehouse.

When we reach the top of the cliffs, the driver drops us off in a piazza. Tourists mill about, corralled into the town square like circus animals in a ring. Elegant shops line the piazza, their entrance doors propped open to encourage customers. The driver points to the street that will take us to our hotel.

Gram and I weave through the tourists. Free of the luggage, I begin to feel like I'm really on vacation. We walk down a narrow street lined with shops that sell coral and turquoise, Prada, Gucci, and Ferragamo. I make note of a small stand where you can buy a fresh coconut ice. The shoppers are shaded by the leafy green pompadours of old cypress trees as they walk the strip.

The Quisisana hotel is tucked into a row of grand stucco fortresses on the top of the cliffs. The hotel looks like the dream set in a lavish Preston Sturges comedy where a runaway heiress, wearing an evening gown of peacock feathers, winds up in Dutch on a jet-set Italian island. It's spectacular. I look at Gram, whose eyes widen at the sight of it. Her reaction is priceless, but I sure wish it was Roman's face I was looking at in this moment. She knows what I'm thinking and squeezes my hand.

Inside the hotel, the guests seem to move in slow motion under the Renaissance murals in the grand lobby. The diagonal black-and-white-patterned marble floor is splashed with thick white rugs. Statuary of Roman goddesses on pedestals peeks out of corners, while opulent crystal chandeliers twinkle over soft white silk sofas and chairs covered in gold damask. Glass walls in the back of the hotel reveal a wide staircase to the gardens, with circular sidewalks that wind lazily through patches of green shaded by palm trees.

The visitors on this Italian Brigadoon dress with lavish simplicity, swaths of white silk and cobalt blue cashmere flit by, offset by lots of gold everywhere you look, chains, hoops, drops, and links. Women drip in platinum and diamonds, splashes of glitz against their tawny skin.

I stand near the reception desk, manned by some of the best-looking people I have ever seen. The women have the high cheekbones and straight jaw lines of a Giacomo Manzù marble sculpture. The bellhops, lean and tan, wear white tuxedos with gold epaulets, all of them versions of Prince Charming, saying very little, but eager to please.

I explain my situation. The attendant smiles and gives me a plastic key that looks like a credit card. 'Mr Falconi has taken care of everything.'

This announcement reminds me that Roman really meant to be here today, that he made excellent plans and had a dreamy vacation arranged for us from start to finish even if he isn't here to share it on day one. It's not enough to make me forgive him, but at least I'm beginning to look forward to Wednesday in a whole new way.

Gram follows me into a tiny elevator to the top floor, called the attico. When we step off the elevator, there is an alcove with a pale blue tufted love seat and an oil painting of pastel Mondrian-style squares. The wood floors glisten.

Gram and I enter an enormous suite filled with light and beautifully appointed in serene blues and eggshell white. We stop to drink it in, half-expecting to catch Cary Grant and Grace Kelly on the love seat toasting each other with champagne.

I put my purse down on a secretary of cherrywood with gold-leafed accents on a black-leather-inlaid writing surface. A long, white Louis XIV sofa is staggered with pillows covered in blue silk.

Gram whistles, 'Wow-ee.'

I walk into the bedroom where a king-size bed is covered by a bright white coverlet, a row of pastel blue buttons up the seam. Beyond the bed is a bathroom with a deep white tub and matching marble double sinks on legs of braided brass. The floor is a kicky sky-blue-and-white-tile pattern. I catch my face in the mirror, drinking in the details of this romantic suite, where everything is outfitted in two's. My expression says, *What a waste without a man!*

The French doors off the bedroom open onto a large balcony with a small white wrought-iron table and two chairs in the corner. There's a chaise longue facing the sun. There's another chair with a matching ottoman on the other side of the chaise.

I hold the railing and look out beyond the gardens to a stunning oval swimming pool, set in the ground like an agate. Crisp navy-blue-and-white-striped umbrellas are open around the pool, looking like spools of hard candy.

The restaurant where Roman spent a summer working lies beyond the pool. There is an open veranda that leads to stairs and an elegant indoor dining room. The veranda is dressed for dinner, with small tables covered in pristine white tablecloths.

Beyond the restaurant and down the jagged stone cliffs is a view of the *faraglione*, a trio of large rock formations that rise out of the sea, inside which is the famous Blue Grotto.

Summer is almost here, as evidenced by a bunch of small, waxy lemons dangling from a tree in a terra-cotta pot on the terrace. Amateur but serious gardener that I am, I check the black earth in the pot to see if the plant needs water. It doesn't. Somebody tends lovingly to this little tree. I pull a leaf off the branch and rub it between my hands, releasing the scent of sweet citrus.

The anxiety of the past few hours leaves me as I watch a white yacht cross the horizon leaving a trail of foam on the blue water. The breezes of Capri have the scent of a scooped-out blood orange filled with honey.

'Oh, Valentine. The ocean.' Gram stands beside me on the balcony.

'I've never seen anything like this, Gram. You sit. I'm going to get you something to drink.' I go into the room to the refrigerator and pull out two bottles of pomegranate juice. I find glasses on a tray on the secretary.

'Now aren't you glad I made you come here?' Gram puts on her sunglasses.

'I guess.' I unsnap the bottle opening and pour the juice into the glass. I give it to Gram, and then fill my own glass. 'You seem relieved. You really weren't ready to go home, were you? Why?' I take a sip.

'You know why,' she says quietly.

'Mom is gonna be very hurt that you haven't told her about Dominic. You might want to call her.'

Gram waves her hand. 'Oh, I couldn't. How would I explain it? It doesn't make any sense. I'm an eighty-year-old widow with bad knees. On a good day, I feel seventy and on a bad one, I feel ninety-nine.' She sips her drink. 'I didn't count on falling in love at my age.'

'Well, we never do, do we? It's all fine until you actually submit to the call. Then, overnight, it's a relationship, all compromise and negotiation. Once he loves you, and you love him, you have to figure out where it's going and what it means, where to live and what to do. Really, if you boil it all down, love is one giant headache.'

Gram laughs. 'You just feel that way today. When Roman takes you in his arms on this balcony, you'll forgive him. You will if you're my granddaughter. In our family, we're built to overlook things that make us unhappy.'

'Gram, that's the single most unhealthy thing a woman can do. I'm not going to overlook what makes me unhappy! I'm going to seek my own happiness. Why would I settle for less?'

The phone in the room rings. Gram closes her eyes and turns her face to the sun as I go to answer it. She is not about to argue with me.

'Gram, it's your *inamorato*. He's downstairs. He's got your bags. He's ready to sweep you away to his cousin's villa.'

Gram gets up out of her chair and smooths her skirt. 'Come with us.' She looks at me tenderly.

'No.'

Gram laughs. 'Are you sure?'

'God, Gram, I'm a lot of things, but a third wheel ain't one of 'em.'

Gram takes her purse and goes to the door. I follow her into the hallway and press the elevator button. The brass doors open and Gram gets on. 'Have fun,' I tell her as the doors close. The last thing I remember is her face, shining, bright with anticipation of her reunion with Dominic.

I wake from a nap on the balcony. The sun is low in the sky. I check my watch. It's four o'clock in the afternoon. Great, I slept three solid hours. I stand up and look down to the pool. The navy-and-white umbrellas are still up. I see a woman doing laps.

My luggage rests by the closet in the bedroom. I lift out stacks of clothing, new outfits I saved for my week with Roman. I find the red Macy's bag that Mom sneaked into my suitcase. I open the bag. It's a new bathing suit. I take the black Lycra suit out of the bag. 'No way,' I say aloud as I hold it up in front of myself before the mirror.

Mom bought me a black one-piece bathing suit (so far so good), with a plunging V-neck in the front. Forget plunge, this is a nose-dive. The straps are shirred and wide and create a matching deep V in the back. That would be fine, except for the wide rhinestone belt that anchors the waist across the front. It has an enormous buckle with two interlocking C's. Faux Chanel when people around here are wearing the real thing. I check the seams on the side of the belt. It's sewn on. Even if I could remove the belt (and who could since they don't allow travel scissors through security), it would leave a gaping hole in the fabric and what this suit *doesn't* need is more peekaboo.

As I pull the straps of the suit up over my shoulders, I can't believe my *mother* bought me this suit. I'm selling something in this getup and it isn't full coverage. I'm Gypsy Rose Lee on the Italian Riviera, dressed by a determined stage mother whose goal is an engagement ring.

To be fair to Mom, this was probably the only bathing suit in captivity that had a rhinestone belt, and everyone knows that my mother never saw a Swarovski crystal she didn't like. And it *is* a one-piece bathing suit, which can be flattering, but this one is so revealing it needs a turtleneck under it.

I look at my reflection in the full-length mirror. The V in the front is so deep it exposes parts of my body that have never experienced direct sunlight. I turn around and look over my shoulder. The back looks okay, but that has more to do with the construction of the suit than my body.

There's a tag on the suit that says *slimsuit*, so the rear end of the thing is double backed, which means extra coverage à la the old Spanx. I pose like John Wayne and hang my thumbs on the belt buckle like it holds the directions to the cattle drive. How can I possibly leave this room? I look like the girl who was kicked out of the chorus line for showing too much skin back in the days when they showed *a lot*. After about ten seconds of internal fashion debate, the blue pool calls to me. *What the hell*, I tell myself, *nobody knows me here, and there surely has been more cleavage on display at the Quisisana*. I pull on my black capri pants and hoodie over the suit. I put on my sunglasses, take my key and wallet, and head down to the pool.

A young Italian boy runs over with a towel when he sees me standing at the side of the pool. '*Grazie*,' I say as I tip him.

The water is the same shade of turquoise as the ocean, made more deeply blue against the contrast of white trim and white statuary in the shallow end. Beyond the low walls, the waiters set the tables for dinner, unleashing a series of dark blue awnings overhead. I look around. There's no one in the water, and only one woman on a chaise reading David Baldacci's *Simple Genius*. I have the pool to myself. Heaven.

I unzip my hoodie and slip off my capris. I wade into the warm water until it's up to my neck. I shuffle the water on the surface with my hands. I lift my feet off the bottom and float in the silkiness. I extend my feet in front of me, until I'm floating on my back. I close my eyes and let the gentle rolls of the water envelop me.

The late-afternoon sky is powder blue, and a breeze from the grove beyond the hotel carries the scent of ripe peaches. After a while, I swim over to the lion statuary in the shallow end. I catch the water in crystal bursts as it flows through my hands. The warm water and soft breeze comfort me as the sun sets. What will I do for dinner? I have no plans, so I swim.

Back and forth I go, from the shallow to the deep end, doing a slow Capri version of laps, owning the pool. My arms hit the water in rhythmic strokes, and soon I'm panting. I float on my back again. I imagine, years from now, I'll remember this, me in a tacky bathing suit, alone at a glamorous resort. I think about Gram's advice to overlook what makes me unhappy. Hilarious, as she seeks her own happiness this minute at a villa with Dominic.

The pool boy snaps the umbrellas down, signaling that the pool is closing. The umbrellas look like blue pins sticking into the purple sky. He straightens the chaise longues into a wide circle, then rolls a hamper of towels behind a rattan screen.

'Valentina?' I hear someone call my name. I pirouette in the water and look toward the voice.

'Gianluca?' I shade my eyes from the setting sun. Gianluca kneels by the pool, holding my towel. The lady with the thriller, and the pool boy, are gone, it's just Gianluca and me. 'What are you doing here?'

'I couldn't let Papa drive to Naples alone.'

I climb up the steps and out of the pool. Gianluca holds the towel, and like everything else in Italy, he moves slowly as he hands it to me. I extend my hand, dripping water on his arm. I pat his arm where the water goes. Then I open the towel and wrap it around me like a cape.

'Coco Chanel?' He points to the belt.

'Chuck Cohen.'

'Chuck Cohen?' he says, confused.

'It's a knockoff.'

'*Si, si,*' he laughs. 'Outlet?'

'Yeah, yeah.' I hold up my hand. 'My mother is an outlet queen. Long story.'

'*Mi piace.*' Original or not, he likes the suit.

'Gianluca, I'm in no mood to flirt. Let me warn you. I'm basically a blowfish filled with so much angst, that if I hit a wall, I'd explode. I'm supposed to be with my boyfriend on this romantic island; instead I'm alone and just north of miserable. *Capisce?*' I pull the towel tightly around me, like a bandage. I am the walking wounded in a towel embossed with a giant Q.

'*Capisce.* What are you doing for dinner?'

'To tell you the truth, I was going to order up and watch a movie.'

'Why?'

'That's what I do when I'm alone.'

'But you're not alone. I'm here.'

Gianluca, like all men of a certain age, looks best in fading sun. The gray in his hair turns silver, his height is magnified, and his strong features throw just the right amount of shadow on his bone structure, giving the impression of youthful invincibility or wise old warrior. Take your pick. I size him up as a night breeze happens through. I could do worse for a dinner companion, plus, the idea of eating alone in the attico suite without Roman borders on self-punishment. So I say, 'Let me get dressed.'

I check my BlackBerry while Gianluca waits in the lobby. Roman has sent a total of eleven text messages, all of them dripping with apology when they're not loaded with promises of great sex and endless sampling of regional wine. I scroll through the texts like they're a Chinese take-out menu and I'm trying to get to the noodles. I have decided to stay mad at him for the time being, and I believe I am entitled. Instead of texting Roman, I dial my mother.

'Ma, how are you?'

'Forget me. How are *you*?'

'I'm on Capri. You don't have to pick Gram up at the airport.'

'I heard all about it. She called. How nice she has a good friend to show her around. She must have made wonderful alliances on her travels.'

'Are you watching Jane Austen?' My mother's turns of phrase are a dead giveaway that she's on a British bender.

'*Sense and Sensibility* was on last night. How did

you know?' she says. 'Listen, honey, she told me about Roman. I'm sorry. What can I say? The man has an all-consuming career. This is the price of success. You'll just have to be patient.'

'I'm trying. But Ma – the bathing suit?'

'To die for?' she squeals.

'If you're Pussy Galore in a James Bond movie.'

'I know! It's so retro and chic. Very Lauren Hutton *Vogue* 1972.'

'The belt?'

'I love the belt! They're good rhinestones.'

I *knew* she'd defend the paste. 'Ma, it's too much.'

'On Capri? Never. Liz Taylor and Jackie O vacationed there. Believe me, they dazzled at the pool and why shouldn't my daughter?'

'*That's* how you justify this suit?'

I hang up the phone and slip off the hotel robe. I take a bath with the Quisisana shower gel that's loaded with shea butter, vanilla, peach, and some woodsy pine. I smell so good, *I* could fall in love with me tonight.

I pick out a cute black skirt and a white blouse with billowing poetry sleeves. Somewhere in my mother's old magazines, there was a dog-eared page with a picture of Claudia Cardinale on a Roman holiday, and she wore a similar getup. I pull out silver sandals with a simple pearl closure on the ankle. I spritz on my Burberry and head for the elevator.

I walk the long hallway to the main entrance.

All sorts of couples of different ages are dressed for dinner and milling around the lobby. I walk through them and go outside. Gianluca is waiting for me at the outdoor bar. I wave to him. He stands as I approach.

'I ordered you a drink,' he says. My drink rests on the table with his. He pulls out my chair. I sit, and then he does. He picks up his drink and toasts me. 'I'm sorry your trip didn't work out the way you had hoped, Valentina.'

'Roman will be here on Wednesday.'

'*Bene.*'

'However, I won't be nice to him until Friday.'

'Why do you let him treat you this way?'

'He's running a business. Sometimes things are out of his hands.' I can't believe I'm defending Roman, but the tone in Gianluca's voice makes me defensive. 'You don't know him. All you know is that he was supposed to come to Capri, and he had to cancel, but he'll be here as soon as he can. It's not the end of the world.'

'But this is your first visit.'

'Right.'

'You should see it with someone you love.'

'I will see it with someone I love. Just not today.'

We finish our drinks and join the throngs of visitors on the small cobblestone street that weaves through town. We walk for a while and then Gianluca steers me off the busy street and through a wooden gate. He closes the door behind us.

'This way,' he says, leading me through a garden

and under a portico to the back of the building. Carved into the side of the mountain is a small restaurant, built on the incline. Every seat is taken with people who look more like locals than the fancy guests of the Quisisana. No Bulgari jewels, Neapolitan gold, Prada purses, or cashmere here. Just lots of clean, pressed cotton with embroidered details and fine leather sandals. I fit right in. These are my people, the working class, relaxing after a hard day's work.

The maître d' smiles at Gianluca when he sees him. He shows us to a table overlooking the bluffs to the sea below. The tables remind me of Ca' d'Oro, intimate and beautifully set. I must remember to bring Roman here. 'What's this restaurant called?' I ask.

'Il Merlo. It means blackbird,' Gianluca replies.

We sit at our table. The waiter doesn't bring a menu, just a bottle of wine. He opens the bottle and pours.

'*La sua moglia, bianco e rosso*?' the waiter asks.

'*Rosso,*' Gianluca tells him.

'Excuse me. But did the waiter just call me your wife?'

'*Si.*' He grins.

'Oh, okay. Either you look young, or I look old. Which is it?'

Gianluca laughs.

'Not funny. In my family *old* is something to avoid and deny until death, when it doesn't matter anymore.'

'Why?'

'Well, for one thing, it's a downer.'

'What does that mean?'

'A downer is the opposite of hope. *La speranza. Non la speranza.*'

'Ah, so . . . I'm too old for you.'

'I don't mean to insult you,' I say. 'But your daughter is almost my age. Well, not almost. I could be her sister.'

'I see.'

'So, it's really Mother Nature talking, not me. I don't think you're old, in fact, in many circles a fifty-two-year-old is young. Just not for a thirty-three-year-old woman.'

The waiter brings us tiny shrimp in olive oil and a basket of small rolls. Gianluca scoops up the shrimp with the bread. I do the same.

'How old is Roman?' Gianluca asks.

'Forty-one.'

'So, he could be *my* brother.'

'Technically, yes.' I scoop up some more shrimp. 'I guess.'

'But he is not too old for you.'

'Oh, God, no.'

Gianluca nods his head slowly and looks out to sea. Between the coconut-and-rum cocktail at the hotel, and the wine I'm sipping now, I'm feeling chatty. 'Look, Gianluca, even if you were thirty-five, I could never go out with you.'

'Why not?'

'Because your father is dating my grandmother.

Now, if that isn't a Jerry Springer episode waiting to be Tivoed, I don't know what is. If your father married Gram, you would be my uncle. Are you beginning to see the picture here?'

He laughs. 'I understand.'

'Look, you're a handsome man. And you're smart. And you're a good son. These are all wonderful attributes.' I scan Gianluca for more positives. 'You have your hair. In America, that would send you to the top tier of Match.com. I just don't think of you *that* way.'

Gianluca reaches across the table and dabs my chin with his napkin.

'I cannot argue with that,' he says.

I lean on the railing of the balcony outside my room as a full moon pulls up over the *faraglione*, throwing silver streamers of light on the midnight blue water. I feel full and happy after that delicious dinner. Gianluca can be a lot of fun for an older man. I like how Italian men take care of things. He reminds me of my father and my grandfather, and even my brother, all of whom swoop in, like the Red Cross, during a crisis. That's why I'm so impatient with Roman. I know what he's capable of, so when he can't fix something, I assume it's because he doesn't want to.

I hear muffled voices, followed by soft laughter as two lovers make their way back into the hotel from the garden below. I watch as they weave through the cypress trees on the twirling path, stopping only to kiss. If you can't be happy on the isle of Capri, I doubt there's anyplace on earth you could be.

I go inside to my bedroom and pull the sheer draperies to the side, leaving the terrace doors open. I climb into bed and lie back on the pillows. The gauzy moonlight cuts a white path across my bed, like a bridal veil.

I put my hand on the pillow next to me and imagine Roman there. I can't stay mad at him, and I don't want to. Maybe I had too much to drink and the island alcohol triggered my forgiveness. Maybe I want romance more than acrimony. Whatever it is, I'll call him in the morning and tell him about the cobblestone streets, the pink stars, and this bed, which seems to float over the ocean when the doors are open and the night breeze happens through. The anticipation of sharing all of this and more with Roman sends me into a deep sleep.

CHAPTER 13

DA COSTANZO

When I wake the next morning, I roll over and reach for my phone. I open it and text:

The hotel phone rings. I go to the desk and pick it up.

'Valentine, it's me,' Roman says softly.

'I was just about to text you,' I say.

'I'm so sorry,' he says.

'It's okay, honey. I got all your messages and I know how sorry you are. I totally understand. When you see this room and the view, you won't even remember what it took to get here.'

'No, I'm *really* sorry,' he says.

I sit down on the couch. 'About what?'

'I can't come at all now.'

I don't know what to say, so I say nothing.

He continues, 'There's a problem with my backers. It's serious.'

I still say nothing. I can't.

'Valentine?'

Finally, I say, 'I'm here.' But I'm not. I'm numb.

'I'm as upset about this as you are,' he goes on.

'I want to be there with you. I still do,' he says. 'I wish . . .'

Someday I know I will look back on this as the moment I stopped pretending I was actually in a real relationship with Roman. Who allows this sort of thing? I forgive and forget his cancelled dates and missed opportunities with such regularity, I believe that it's part of working at our relationship. It's our *normal.* Roman's first obligation is to his restaurant. I knew that when we began dating, and I know it now, stranded here on Capri without him. I'm not surprised; I'm resigned. But that doesn't make it hurt any less.

I crawl back into bed and pull the covers up to my chin. I am a failure at love. Roman's excuses seem real, I believe them every single time. The excuses can be grand: threats of imminent financial ruin, or silly: the sink flooded in the restaurant kitchen. The scale of disaster doesn't matter, I take it in and accept whatever he throws at me. I pretend I can handle it while I seethe inside.

I feel terrible, so why not surrender to the worst of it? I search my heart and list all the ways in which I am a failure. I make a mental list. I'm almost thirty-four (*old!*), and I have no money saved (*poor!*), and I live with my grandmother (*needy!*). I wear Spanx. I want a dog but won't get one because I'd have to walk it, and there's no time in my life to walk a dog! My boyfriend is a part-time lover who spends more time at work than he does with me, and I accept it because

402

that's what I believe I deserve. I'm a lousy girl-friend. In fact, I'm as bad at relationships as he is! I don't want to sacrifice my work for him either.

Roman Falconi makes promises and I let him wiggle out of them because I understand how hard it is to live a creative life, whether it's making shoes or tagliatelle for hungry people. The phone rings. I catch my breath and sit up before reaching for it. Roman must have come to his senses and changed his mind. He's going to make the trip! I know it! I pick up the phone. I tell myself not to blow it. *Be patient*, I tell myself as I breathe.

'Valentina?'

It's not Roman. It's Gianluca. 'Yes?'

'I want to take you to meet my friend Costanzo.'

I don't answer.

'Are you all right?' Gianluca asks. 'I told him that you are waiting for your boyfriend to arrive and so he made time for you this afternoon.'

'This afternoon is fine,' I say, hanging up the phone after we agree upon a time to meet.

I pull my notebook off the nightstand and pick up the list of things I wanted to do with Roman on Capri. There it is, in plain English, a list of fabulous, romantic side trips and excursions, places to eat, foods to try, the hours the pool is open! I even wrote *that* schedule down.

Suddenly, I am overcome with sadness that I have to do these things alone. I begin to cry, the disappointment almost too much to bear. This place is so romantic and I'm miserable. Rejection is the worst, whether you're fourteen or forty. It stings, it's humiliating, and it's irreversible. I take the box of tissues and go out on the balcony. The sun blazes hot orange in the deep blue sky. Boats, with their sails bleached white, bob in the harbor below. I watch them for a long time.

I think about calling Gram, but I don't want her to waste this week worried about me, or worse, trying to include me in her plans with Dominic.

I see a family, two children and a mother and a father, on their way to the pool. The children skip along the winding path through the garden as their parents follow closely behind. I watch as they reach the pool. The children pull off their cover-ups and jump in, while the mother chooses chairs and arranges the towels. The husband puts his arms around his wife, surprising her from behind. She laughs and turns to him. They kiss. How effortless happiness looks from here. People, everyone else that is, find happiness by falling in love and making their own families. It will never happen for me. I know it.

I take a shower and dress. I load a tote bag with my phone, wallet, and sketchbook. I head out the door. I can't stay in this room another minute; it's just a reminder of who is not here. The thought of this makes me burst into tears, so I stuff the box of tissues into my tote bag.

The lobby is quiet since it's early yet. I go to the front desk. I open my purse and pull out my wallet.

'Checking out?' the young man asks.

'No, no. I'll be here for the week, as scheduled. I'd like to take Mr Falconi's name off my room. I want to put the room on my credit card instead, please.'

'*Si, si*,' he says. He swipes my room key and finds my information. He takes my credit card and makes the change on the bill.

'Thank you. Oh, and I'd also like to take a tour boat around the island.'

'Absolutely.' He checks the schedule. 'There is one leaving in twenty minutes, from the pier.'

'Would you call me a taxi?'

'Of course,' he says.

The tour boat is not really a boat at all, but a skiff, with several rows of wooden benches painted bright yellow, upon which tourists, including me, sit four across. There are about eighteen of us, mostly Japanese, a few Greeks, a couple of other Americans, an Ecuadorian, and me.

The captain is an old Neapolitan sea dog with a white beard, a straw hat, and a beat-up megaphone that looks like it's taken its share of dips in the Tyrrhenian Sea. As the boat pulls away from the pier, the thrust of the motor plows us to the surface of the water.

Captain Pio explains that he will show us the natural wonders of Capri as the woman next to me shoves her elbow in my face getting a picture of Pio with her cell phone camera. Soon, all the tourists are snapping Pio with their phones. He pauses and smiles for them. I think of Gianluca, who said that he hated all this technology. In this moment, I do, too.

I miss big, bulky old-fashioned cameras that you wear around your neck on a strap. Most of all I miss the fact that you used to have to save the film for the best moments because it was too expensive to squander. Now, we take pictures of everything, including pictures of people taking pictures. Maybe Gianluca is right, technology doesn't lead to better living and art, it's madness.

I love watching the boats on the Hudson River, but it is a very different thing to be *on* one pitching and bouncing over the waves. I am surprised at how rocky the ride actually is because from the docks, the boats appear to move smoothly over the water. Isn't this the way it is in love? It looks so easy and effortless from the distance – but when you're in it, it's a different experience. You feel every bump and wonder which wave will overtake you, will you survive or drown on the treacherous water, will you make it or capsize?

Our skiff is unwieldy as we are tossed in the surf like an old plank. Big waves come out of nowhere, tossing us a foot in the air, to land us with a thud on the water. The bouncing begins anew when a new wave rolls under us. My teeth begin to hurt from the pounding of the surf against the sides of the boat. I feel the weight of every human body on this boat. We sit so closely together that when a rogue wave hits the side, it's like the group is body-slammed with a lead pipe.

Pio guides the boat into a calm inlet (thank God) and points to a natural rock formation that resembles a statue of the Blessed Mother as she appeared in the grotto at Lourdes. Pio says the Blessed Mother is a miracle of wind, rain, volcanic rock, and faith. At that point, even I pull out my phone and take a picture.

Pio backs us out of the inlet, showing us the indigenous coral growing beneath the water's edge along the sea wall. As the waves lap against the rocks, we catch glimpses of the glassy red tentacles of coral. I begin to cry when I remember the branch of coral that Roman gave me when he promised me this trip. The Asian woman next to me says, 'You okay? Seasick?'

I shake my head no, I'm not seasick, I want to scream! I'm *heartsick!* Instead, I smile and nod and look away at the ocean. It's not *her* fault that Roman Falconi didn't show up! The stranger is just being polite, that, and she doesn't want me throwing up on her faux Gucci purse.

As Pio guides the boat back onto the sea, and we are tossed to and fro anew, I see lots of other boats like ours stuffed with shoulder-to-shoulder tourists making the rounds. When we pull out of one inlet, another boat pulls in to take our place.

'When are we going to see the Blue Grotto?' the American husband of the American wife asks.

'Soon, soon,' Pio replies with a weary smile that

says he answers this question a thousand times a day.

We hear the sound of accordion music drift across the water. All heads turn toward the playful tune. A sleek catamaran, with a black-and-white-striped canopy, sails into view from around the rocks. A man plays the accordion as his companion reclines on a pile of pillows on the carpeted deck, a wide-brimmed sun hat shielding her face. It's a romantic sight, one that makes every person crammed on this dinghy sorry that they didn't splurge and hire the private boat.

The music grows louder as the catamaran sails into view.

'Isn't that wonderful?' the American woman says. 'Senior love.'

I take a closer look at the catamaran. Dear God. It's my grandmother under that hat, like a Botticelli courtesan in repose, except she's not eating grapes, she's being serenaded by Dominic. I'd put my face in my hands to hide, but there's not enough room to bend my elbows.

Captain Pio calls out to the skipper of the cata-maran, 'Giuseppe! Yo, Giuseppe!' The skipper salutes in return. Given the way our loaded skiff is being pummeled by the waves, I'm surprised the skipper didn't read Pio's greeting as a distress signal. The tourists on our boat wave at the lovers, and then commence snapping *their* pictures of *them*. How odd to be on vacation and take photos of other people having fun. Gram and Dominic have their own paparazzi. I could scream, so I do.

'Gram?' I holler. My grandmother sits up, pushes back her sun hat, and peers across the water toward our boat.

'You know them?' the American woman asks from behind me. Too tight a squeeze to turn to face her, I shout, 'Yes,' while facing forward.

'Valentine!' Gram waves to me. She pokes Dominic, who waves with his accordion.

'Enjoy!' I shout as we sail by. Gram settles back on the pillows and Dominic plays on.

How do you like that? My eighty-year-old grand-mother is being seduced on the Tyrrhenian Sea and I'm crammed on this boat like a tuna haul for the local fish market – as if I need another reason to weep on the isle of Capri, I just got it.

'How did you like the Blue Grotto?' Gianluca asks as we walk to Costanzo Ruocco's shoe shop.

'We couldn't get in. The tide was too high.'

'That's too bad,' he says, as he smiles.

'Is that funny?'

'No, no. Just typical.'

'I know all about how the locals put up a sign to keep the tourists out.'

'Now, don't give our secrets away.'

'Too late. I know all about you Italians and your secrets. You keep the best extra-virgin olive oil over here instead of shipping it to us, you keep the best wine, and now I find out it's true, you close down a national landmark whenever you want a private swim. Nice.'

I follow Gianluca down the narrow sidewalk along the piazza and down the hill. The front door of Da Costanzo is propped open, between two large picture windows that anchor the door. They are filled with open, jeweled sandals for ladies, and men's loafers in every color from lime green to hot pink.

We enter the shop, which is one small room filled from floor to ceiling with dozens of shoes on slanting wooden display shelves. The leathers range in color from hearty earth tones to jelly-bean brights. The basic sandal is a flat with a T-strap. The embellishments, bold geometrics, are what makes them special: interlocking circles of gold leather, open squares of moonstones attached to small circles of aquamarine, jeweled ruby clusters, or a large emerald triangle attached to thin green leather straps.

Costanzo Ruocco seems to be about seventy years old and wears his white hair brushed back off his face. He leans over a small cobbler's bench in the back of the shop. He looks down at his work, squinting at the job at hand. He holds *il trincetto*, his small work knife, and trims the straps on a sandal. Then, he trades the knife for *il scalpello*, a tool with a sharp point. He plunges a small hole in the sole of the sandal and threads a braid of soft leather through it. Then he takes *il martello* and hammers the strap to the base. His hands move with dexterity, speed, and accuracy, the signs of a master at work.

'Costanzo?' Gianluca interrupts him gently.

Costanzo looks up. He has a broad, warm smile and the unlined skin of a person without regrets.

'I'm Valentine Roncalli.' I extend my hand to him. He puts down the sandal and squeezes my hand.

'Italian?' he says to me.

I nod. 'Both sides. Italian American.'

A young man in his thirties, with wavy dark hair, pushes open a mirrored door that leads to a storage area behind Costanzo and enters the shop. He places a box of nails, *le semenze* on Costanzo's worktable.

Costanzo says, 'This is my son, Antonio.'

'Ciao, Antonio.'

Gianluca places his hand on my shoulder. 'I will leave you with Costanzo.'

'She is not safe,' Costanzo jokes.

'Good,' I tell him.

He laughs heartily.

'I'm taking Papa and your grandmother up to Anacapri today,' Gianluca says as he goes out the door. Antonio waits on a customer as I pull the work stool close to Costanzo. He doesn't seem to mind. I wasn't entirely prepared to spend my afternoon with the shoemaker, but what else do I have to do? The thought of another solo tourist outing like the boat ride this morning is enough to make me seasick. So, I do what all Roncalli women before me have done – I make the best of it.

'How long have you been a cobbler?' I ask Costanzo.

'I was five years old. I have four brothers and we needed to learn a trade. I'm the third generation of shoemakers in my family.'

'Me, too,' I tell him.

He puts down his *scalpello*. 'Do you make sandals?'

'Wedding shoes. In New York City.'

'*Brava.*' He smiles.

The walls behind Costanzo's work space are cluttered with a collage of photographs. There are plenty of pictures of people I've never seen before wedged between Italian icons like Sophia Loren, on holiday and wearing flat gold leather sandals, and Silvio Berlusconi, wearing Costanzo's loafers in navy blue. I point to a picture of Clark Gable.

'My favorite actor,' I tell him.

'Not me. I like John Wayne.'

We laugh.

'I made Clark Gable's shoes for *It Started in Naples*,' he says as he picks up *il martello* and hammers the edge of the strap.

'What was he like?'

'Tall. Nice. Very nice.' He shrugs.

'Do you mind if I stay and watch you work?'

He smiles. 'Maybe you can teach me something.'

'I don't think so.'

'Do you design your wedding shoes or do you build other people's designs?'

'Both. My grandfather designed six basic patterns, and now I hope to create new ones.'

'*Va bene*,' he says. He picks up *il tricetto* and takes the blade of the knife along a calfskin sole, trimming it like he's peeling an apple. A ribbon of leather falls to the floor. He hands the sole to me, and indicates his tools on the bench. 'Show me how you sew,' he says.

I take the sole, mark the points around it to place the stitching with *la lesina o puntervolo*. Then I pick up *la bucatrice* and punch a series of holes where I made the markings. I pull a thick needle from his pincushion (a velvet tomato, just like Gram's!) and thread it with a sturdy but thin skein of beige hemp. I knot the end cleanly and pull it through the hole at the heel first, working along the side to the toes, and then down the other side. The process takes me about three minutes. 'Fast. Good.' Costanzo nods.

I spend the rest of the afternoon at Costanzo's side. I hammer and sew. I cut and scrape. I buff and polish. I do whatever he asks me to do. I appreciate the work; it keeps my mind off what was supposed to be my vacation.

I lose track of the time until I look up and see the pale blue of twilight settling over the cliffs. 'You come for dinner,' Costanzo invites me. 'I have to thank you.'

'No, I appreciate that you're letting me work with you. Here's how you can thank me.'

Costanzo looks at me and smiles.

'May I please come back tomorrow?' I ask him.

'No. You go to the beach. You rest. You're on holiday.'

'I don't want to go to the beach. I'd rather come back and work with you.' I'm surprised to hear myself say it, but the minute I do, I know the words are true.

'I must pay you.'

'No. You can make me a pair of sandals.'

'*Perfetto!*'

'What time do you open?'

'I'm here at five A.M.'

'I'll be here at five.' I sling my tote bag over my arm and go out into the piazza.

'Valentine!' Antonio calls after me. 'Thank you.'

'Oh, are you kidding? *Mille grazie.* Your dad is amazing.'

'He never lets anyone sit with him. He likes you. Papa doesn't like anyone,' Antonio laughs. 'He's besotted.'

'I have that effect on men. See you tomorrow,' I tell him. Yes, some effect I have on men, except the one who counts, Roman Falconi.

As I walk past the tourists who climb onto their buses, talking too loudly and laughing too much, I feel more alone than ever. Maybe I've figured out a way to turn this disaster into something wonderful after all; I spent the day learning from a master, and I actually enjoyed myself. And, if my instincts are right, or at least better at work than they are at love, I have a feeling I have just begun to learn what I need to know from Costanzo Ruocco.

★   ★   ★

'Valentine? *Andiamo,*' Costanzo calls to me from the back of the shop. Costanzo was surprised when I actually showed up for work as I'd said I would. Little does he know he's actually doing me a favor by salvaging this vacation.

I put down my work and follow the sound of his voice through the supply room and outside to a patio garden where there is a small table and four chairs. A white cotton tablecloth covers the table, anchored from blowing away in the Capri breezes by a pot of fragrant red geraniums.

Costanzo motions for me to sit next to him. He opens a plain tin lunch bucket and unloads the contents. He unwraps a loaf of bread from a sleeve of wax paper. Next to the bread, he places a container of fresh figs. Then he lifts out a tin of what looks like white fish covered in black olives. He pulls out two napkins. From under the table, he lifts a jug of homemade wine. He pours me a glass and then himself.

He cuts into the bread, which isn't bread at all, but pizza *alige,* soft dough filled with chopped onions and anchovies. He slices the hearty pizza in thin, long slices, then places two on a plate for me. I bite into the crisp crust, which gives way to the salty anchovy, softened by the sweet onions and butter in the folds of the dough.

'Good?' he asks.

I nod emphatically that it is.

'Why did you come to Capri?' he asks me.

'It was supposed to be a vacation. But my

boyfriend had problems at work and couldn't make it at the last minute.'

'He canceled?'

'Yes.'

'When you go home, you end it, right?'

'Costanzo!'

'Well, he likes his work more than you.'

'It's not like that.'

'I think so.'

'You know, I'm actually glad he couldn't come here because if he had, I wouldn't be spending time with you.'

He smiles. 'I'm too old for you,' he laughs.

'That seems to be the case with most of the men I'm meeting in Italy.'

'But if I were young . . .' He fans his hand.

'Yeah, yeah, yeah, Costanzo.' We laugh heartily. I'm feeling genuinely happy for the first time in days.

Italian men put women first. Roman's priorities are more American than Italian, as he puts the restaurant first. To be fair, I can't say that I have my priorities straight, or that I've mastered the art of living. I live for my work, I don't work to live. Roman and I have lost our Italian natures. We're typical overextended, overworked Americans with the worst kind of tunnel vision. We waste the present for some perfect future we believe will be waiting for us when we get there. But how will we get there if we don't build the connection now?

The way I live from day to day in New York City suddenly seems ridiculous to me. I've mortgaged

416

my happiness for a time that may never come. I think of my brother, and the building, the Bergdorf windows, and Bret's investors. I love making shoes. Why does it have to be more complicated than that? Costanzo walks to work, builds shoes, and goes home. There's a rhythm to his life that makes sense. The small shop sustains Costanzo and his sons beautifully. I sip the wine. It's rich and intense, like every color, mood, and feeling on this island.

Costanzo offers me a cigarette, which I decline. He lights up his cigarette and puffs.

'What do you do in the winter, when the tourists are gone?' I ask him.

'I cut leather. I make the soles. I rest. I fill up the hours,' he says. Costanzo looks off in the distance. 'I fill up the days and wait.'

'For the tourists to return?' I ask him.

He doesn't answer. The look on his face tells me not to pry. He puts out his cigarette. 'Now, we work.'

I follow Costanzo back into the shop. He takes his seat behind the workbench as I sit down behind my table. Costanzo lifts a new pattern out of his bin and studies it. I pick up *il trincetto* and a sole from the stack Antonio has left for me. I follow the pattern and peel the outside edge of the sole like an apple, just as I saw Costanzo do on the first day. He looks over at me approvingly and smiles.

'Go and get your sketchbook,' Costanzo commands as we finish a cappuccino in the afternoon. 'I want to see your work.'

I get up from the table and go back inside the shop. I pull my sketchbook out of my tote.

'Everything all right?' Antonio says to me.

'Your father wants to see my sketches. I'm scared to death. I'm a self-taught artist, and I don't know if my drawings are as good as they might be.'

Antonio smiles. 'He'll be honest.'

Great, I think as I go back through the storage room to the portico. Costanzo peels a fig as I sit down next to him. I tell him about the contest for the Bergdorf windows, then I open the sketchbook and show him the shoe. He looks at it. Then he narrows his eyes and squints at it.

'High fashion,' he says. '*Molto bene.*'

'You like it?'

'It's ornate.'

'Is that a good thing?'

'This I like.' He points to the vamp of the shoe, where the braiding meets the strap. 'Original.'

'My great-grandfather named his six basic dress shoes for brides after characters in the opera. They're dramatic. They can also be simple. They're classics, and we know this for sure because a hundred years later, we're still making his designs and selling them.'

'What shoe do you make for the working girls?'

'We don't make everyday shoes,' I tell him.

'You should start,' he says.

This is not the advice I expected to get from an Italian master craftsman, but I go with it because Costanzo knows so much more than me. 'You sound like my friend Bret. He wants me to come up with a shoe to sell to the masses. He said that I could finance my custom shoes with a shoe made to be sold in large quantities.'

'He's right. There should be no difference between making shoes for one woman and making shoes for many. All of your customers deserve your best. So, sketch a shoe that can serve them all.'

'I don't really know how.'

'Of course you do. You drew that shoe for the window; you can draw another shoe for every day. I am giving you an assignment. Take your pad and go out on the piazza. Sketch as many shoes as you can.'

'Just general shoes?'

'Anything that you see that you like. Watch how the woman moves in her shoes.'

'The tourists wear tennis shoes.'

'Forget them. Look at the Capri shopgirls. You'll see what to draw.' He smiles. 'Now go.'

I take my pad and pencils and go out into the piazza.

I pick a spot in the shade, on the far stone wall, and sit. I put down my sketchbook and watch, just as Costanzo instructed me.

My eye sifts through the clumps of tourists wearing Reeboks, Adidas, and Nikes to find the locals, the women who work in the shops, restaurants, and hotels. I look down at their feet as they move through the crowd with purpose. These working women wear flats, practical yet beautiful shoes, smooth leather

419

slip-ons in navy blue or black, beige lace-ups with a slight stacked heel, sandals in plain leather with a functional T-strap, and one daring shopgirl wears sensible mules made of bright pink calfskin. My eye typically goes to the color, but I notice it's only the occasional woman who wears a vivid shade on her feet. For the most part, the women choose a classic neutral.

After a while, I pull my legs up and cross them under me. I begin to sketch. I draw a simple leather flat with a low upper that covers the toes but does not come too high on the vamp. I sketch it over and over, until I get a shape that pleases my eye and that would best flatter a woman's foot regardless of size, length, or width.

I see a mother and daughter talking outside the jewelry store on the corner of the piazza. The mother, in her forties, wears a slim navy blue skirt with a white blouse. On her arm, thick bangles of shiny silver click together as she talks. She wears navy blue leather flats with a simple bow on the upper. Her daughter wears a black tissue paper T-shirt with a cropped bolero of brown linen. Her slim-legged jeans ride low and tight. She wears brown flats with a matching grosgrain ribbon edge. The flats on the mother are classic, and she stands tall, with an ease that comes from wearing a comfortable shoe. The shoe is soft, but not slouchy. The daughter bounces on the balls of her feet as she talks excitedly with her mother. The brown flat fits her foot without gapping at the heel, and the leather moves with her in a smooth, full bend of the arch when she's on her toes. The leather does not crease or buckle.

An older woman, around Gram's age, moves toward the wall and sits down a few feet from me. She is round and squat, and has thick gray hair pulled back from her face with a red ribbon. She wears a black cotton A-line sundress with cap sleeves. Her shoes are plain, black suede slip-ons. She leans against the wall and opens a brown paper bag. She reaches in, pulls out a ripe cherry, and takes a bite. She throws the pit over the wall and down the cliffs. The sun hits something sparkly by her collar. A brooch. I lean over to get a closer look.

The brooch is in the shape of a wing. It's inlaid with small beads of turquoise and coral, hemmed by what have to be genuine diamond chips. I can tell they're real from the way they throw light. I work with the faux jewels, and they give bright shine, but a real diamond ingests the light and sparkles from the facets within.

I get gutsy and move close to her. I smile. 'Your brooch is beautiful.'

'Mia Mama's.' She smiles and points to the jewelry store. 'My family shop.'

'Oh, how nice.'

'My father made this pin for my mother.'

'It looks like an angel wing,' I tell her. My mother has a Christmas ornament of a cherub with beaded wings that reminds me of the wing shape on the brooch.

'*Si. Si.* My mother's name was Angela.'

The woman folds down the edge of her paper bag, closing it. She stands up and waves to me as she goes. I open my sketchbook and draw the pin, an angel wing dense with stones and outlined in diamonds. I take my time drawing the shapes. Slowly, I begin to fall in love with this shape. I draw it over and over until the page is full of wings. The piazza empties as the tourists get on the bus for the last haul down the mountain to the piers.

I draw one last wing, connecting the curve to the line to the point of the wing. Simple, but I've never seen a shape like this before, not on a shoe. I write:

Angel Shoes

Then I close the notebook and return to Costanzo to show him my sketch.

By the time I return, Costanzo is closing up the shop. He checks his watch and makes a tsk-tsk sound, faux guilt from my pretend padrone. He's joking that I'm late, and he's getting a kick out of himself. I let him. Then I show him my assignment. I hand him the sketch. He looks at it and points to the embellishment. 'Wings?'

'Angel wings.'

'I like it,' he says. 'Why angels?'

'Our shop is called the Angelini Shoe Company. But the sign is very old where the rain hits it, so now it says, "Angel Shoes." So when I saw the old lady's brooch in the piazza, it got me thinking. The great designers have a simple logo, instantly identifiable. So, I thought, what if my design incorporated an angel wing?'

'And when you put the shoes together, two wings.'

'Symmetry! And I can make the wings out of jewels, or leather, or brass. Even embroidery.'

'Anything,' Antonio says and shrugs.

'Right. Exactly!' I beam. 'Thank you for sending me out there. I would never have seen the brooch.'

'Every idea I ever had for a shoe came from observing women,' Costanzo says. 'You see my shop? There are thousands of combinations to be made. Just like women, no two alike. Remember this when you draw.'

I pack up my tote and go. When I return to the piazza, it is completely empty. I make my way down the hill to the hotel. When I arrive at the entrance, Gianluca is sitting outside reading the newspaper by the fading light.

'Reading in the dark is bad for your eyes,' I tell him.

He looks up at me and smiles, takes his reading glasses off, and puts them in his pocket. He pulls out the chair next to him. I sit down. 'Are you going to work there every day? You're going to spoil Costanzo.'

'I wish I could stay for a year.'

'You came here to rest.'

'I don't want to. I don't know if I'll ever have

the chance to come back here. Or if Costanzo will be here when I return.'

'He'll be here. We will all be here. Except your Roman.'

'Who told you?' I lean back in my chair. Italy is getting to be an awful lot like America, where my family is hot-wired to move private information at the speed of sound.

'Your grandmother. Your mother called her.'

'My relationship is an international scandal.' I look around for the waiter. Now, I need a drink.

'He's a fool,' Gianluca says, flagging down the waiter.

'I'm allowed to be angry at Roman, but you are not allowed to call him names. He's still my boyfriend.' Sometimes Gianluca sounds more like my father than he knows.

'Why not?'

'I'm not breaking up with him. And even if I were, I wouldn't do it over the phone or on one of those godforsaken text messages.'

'Good point.' Gianluca places our drink orders with the waiter.

'And by the way, it just makes it all worse when you point out what an idiot I've been. I do have a little pride.'

'There is nothing wrong with you,' Gianluca assures me.

'Really? I think there's something completely wrong with a woman who won't ask for what she needs, and then when she does, she apologizes.'

'There is a difference between trying to make a relationship work and forgiving things you should not forgive,' Gianluca says. 'Your grandmother wants you to come and stay with us.'

'Thanks, but I like it here at the hotel.'

'There are some things I'd like to show you on Capri,' he says.

'Sure.' I would agree to anything, because the truth is, nothing matters now that the old vacation I dreamed of is not to be. 'I'd like to show you something,' I tell him.

Gianluca raises an eyebrow in a way that borders on sexy. I will not go *there*.

'Relax. It's a sketch.' I pull the pad out of the tote bag, opening it to my new shoe. Gianluca pulls his reading glasses out of his pocket and studies the drawing.

'Lovely,' he says. 'Orsola would wear it.'

'Good. It's a shoe that Gram could wear, or my mother would buy, or I would wear. I'm aiming to hit a nerve. I even have a name for them. Angel Shoes. What do you think?'

'You have so many ideas,' he says.

'Well, I'm going to need them. When this little dream of Italy is over, I'm going home to a war zone.'

'It can't be as bad as that.'

'You know, Gianluca, this is the difference between you native Italians and those of us called Italian Americans. You live a balanced life. You work, you eat, you rest. We don't. We can't. We live as though we have something to prove. There's

425

never enough time, we eat on the run, and we sleep as little as possible. We believe the one who works the hardest wins.' The drinks arrive. We toast each other and take a sip.

'What makes *you* happy?' he asks.

The question catches me off guard. Roman has never asked me that question. I don't remember Bret ever asking me either. In fact, I don't even ask myself that question. After I think for a moment, I answer him, 'I don't know.'

'You can never be happy if you don't know what you want.'

'Oh, okay, oracle of Capri, man-with-the-answers to life's major questions. What makes *you* happy?'

'The love of a good woman.'

'Good answer. That wouldn't have been my answer a week ago. I had the love of a good man, and I didn't put him first.'

'Why?'

'If I'd put him first, maybe he'd be here.'

'If he were smart, he would put *you* first. Why do you blame yourself for the man's terrible manners?'

'I'm pretty sure I had something to do with it.'

'That's ridiculous. If you have love, you honor it. You take care of things you love. Yes?' Gianluca has raised his voice a bit. I remember the first day in Arezzo when Gram and I went to the tannery and he and Dominic were having a screaming match.

'Hold on there, Gianluca, don't get all geared up like you do back at the tannery. This is a peaceful island. No yelling.'

Gianluca smiles. 'Come and stay with us.'

After a month in Italy, I'm an expert on the Vechiarellis. Gianluca is all about family. He likes to herd everyone together, whether it's around a dinner table at home, or in a car, or at a factory, and watch protectively over the lot of us, like a shepherd. He prepares the food, gets the drinks, shows the way; in general, he takes care of everyone around him. My need to be separate must seem weird to him. Why wouldn't I stay with them in their cousin's villa? The idea that Teodora's granddaughter is off in a hotel when she could be in the next room, safe, rested, and well fed is anathema to him. 'No thank you. I really love my room here.'

'But we have a room for you.'

'It's not the attico suite.'

'The room at our cousin's is very nice.'

'I'm sure it is. But trust me, it's not *this* room. Do you want to see it?'

'Sure,' he says.

Gianluca follows me through the lobby of the Quisisana and down the hallway to the elevator. It's crowded in the elevator, and we laugh at the tight squeeze. Gianluca puts his hand over the open door and guides me out of the elevator as the doors open on my floor. He follows me into my room. The cool breeze of early evening fills the suite, blowing the sheer draperies gently. The maid has placed fresh white orchid blossoms in the vase in the sitting room.

'You have to see the view,' I tell him. I point to the doors that lead to the bedroom, and open onto the balcony. 'I'll be there in a second.' Gianluca goes out on the balcony as I set my tote down and check my phone messages, one from my mother, one from Tess, and three from Roman. My mother wants me to find her an alligator bag. I don't think she reads the paper; alligator skins are illegal. Tess leaves a message that Dad is doing great, and could I bring coral bracelets home for the girls?

I listen to messages from Roman, who tells me he loves me and wishes he were here. Three in a row with the same level of pleading passion. It's interesting that when I let go of my anger, it brought Roman close. Maybe it's the cocktail, but I text him:

Found a job on Capri. Loving it. May never come home. You may have to come here after all. Love, V.

I join Gianluca on the balcony. 'What do you think?' I point to the gardens of Quisisana and the sea beyond.

'*Bella.*'

'Now you see why I want to stay.'

Nightfall over Capri looks like a blue net veil has settled over the glittering island. I put my hands on the railing and arch my back, looking up, to drink in as much of the endless sky as I can.

Suddenly, I feel hands around my waist. Gianluca pulls me close and kisses me. As his lips linger on mine, softly and sweetly, a ticker tape of information runs through my head. Of course he's *kissing* you, what did you think he was going to do, you invited him up to your *room*, at *night*, you showed him the romantic *balcony*, with a jillion *stars* overhead, you asked him what he *thought*, and his thoughts went to *sex* and now you're in a *pickle*. Gabriel's words ring in my ears: *no ring, no thing*. This kiss was lovely and I want more. I've never bounced back from a failing love affair in the arms of someone new, so why start now?

I put my arms around him, and slide my hands up to his neck. He kisses me again. *What am I doing?* I'm giving in, that's what. I'm also initiating, that's worse. Everything on this island encourages making love, while every scent, texture, and tone creates an irresistible backdrop for one thing, and one thing only. It starts in the cafés at intimate tables and chairs where knees and thighs brush person against person; the sweet sips of coconut ice after a long walk in the hot sun; the decadent scent of soft leather in Costanzo's shop; the fresh food, ripe figs plucked right off the tree; the delicious salty sea air and the moon like a prim pearl button on a silky sky longing to be unfastened. Even the shoes, especially the sandals, filmy straps of gold on brown skin, ready to be slipped off and undone, say *sex*.

The Italians lead sensual lives, *everybody* knows that, *I* know that, and that's why I'm not resisting these kisses.

Somehow it would feel like an insult to life itself

to resist what seems so natural. These kisses are as much a part of an Italian summer day as pulling a fig off a tree and eating it. Whatever romance is left in the world, the best of it can be found in Italy. Gianluca holds me like a prize as the touch of his lips surrounds me like the warm waves in the pool. I find myself going under as Gianluca kisses my neck tenderly. When I open my eyes, all I see are stars, poking through the blue like chips of glass.

Then I remember Roman, and how it was supposed to be *us* on this balcony, under *these* stars, making our way to *that* bed by the light of *this* moon, and I begin to pull away. But I'm not sure I have the strength to resist. I'm the girl who always has the second cannoli! Don't I deserve this? Doesn't everybody?

'I'm sorry,' I tell him.

'Why?' Gianluca says quietly. Then he persists, kissing me again. This is not like me. I never so much as look at another man when I'm involved with someone. I'm very faithful, in fact, I'm often faithful when it hasn't been agreed upon in advance. I can be true after one date. I'm *that* faithful. My natural inclination is old-fashioned devotion. Spontaneity and variety are not for me. I think things through, so I've never had to tiptoe around my past with regret. I skip through, unencumbered, free! I'm a clean-slate woman. I need to tell Gianluca that I don't do this sort of thing before we go any further. I take his hands and step back. Even worse. I like his hands around mine. The touch of his fingers, those strong working-man tanner hands, sends small shivers up my arms and down my back, like cold raindrops hitting my skin on a hot day. I've got some kind of malaria going on here.

'What am I doing?' I let go of his hands and turn away from him.

'I understand,' he says.

'No, you don't.' I bury my face in my hands. Nothing like taking cover in a moment of shame, only I wish I had a hood and a pashmina shawl and a lonely cell to crawl into.

But before I can explain what I'm feeling, or take the blame for my impulsive behavior he is gone. I hear the door from my room to the hotel hallway snap shut. I put my hand on my mouth. Underneath my hand my lips are not pursed in indignation. No, instead, much to my surprise . . . I'm smiling.

As I pack up my tools on my last day at Costanzo's shop, I try not to cry. I can't explain what this time has meant to me. I feel foolish that I ever wanted to come here as a tourist and lie around the pool and sleep all day, when what I gained in the exchange cannot be quantified. Under Costanzo's direction and subtle encouragement, I became an artist.

Sure, Gram taught me how to make shoes, but there was never time to teach me how to walk in the world as an artist. There was never time to encourage me on that path, because it wasn't something my grandmother knew. The dreamers were my great-grandfather and grandfather. Gram is a technician, a practical cobbler. She designed a shoe once, but it was only out of necessity. She drew the ballet flat and built it only after she lost customer after customer to Capezio. She did not sketch it out of a desire to create, but rather, a need. She needed to make money. Shoemaking was never a form of self-expression for Teodora Angelini, rather, it was food on the table, clothes for my mother, and money for the collection plate at Our Lady of Pompeii Church. There is nothing wrong with that, but now I know I want more. I want to *say* more.

New York City is everything to me, but I know now, in the frenzy and the noise, amidst the urgency and rush, that the voice of the artist can be drowned out in the pursuit of making a living. I understand the lure of security, the need to make money to pay our bills and meet payroll, but an artist needs time to think and to dream. Time, unstructured and free, nurtures the imagination. Afternoon siesta may appear to be restful, but for artists like Costanzo, it's time to review the work of the day and reflect on new colors and combinations. Costanzo also taught me that ordinary life is artful. He taught me to look at everyday things and find the beauty in them. I'm not just a cobbler, I am creating a particular shoe for a customer who is trying to express something about herself to the world. My job is to deliver that message, to find the meaning in the ordinary.

I don't see a pesky seagull looking for crumbs anymore. I see a palette of clean white, dressed in black feathers with bold white spots. Shoes. I don't see a stone wall where the sun hits it full on at noon, I see a particular shade of gray with a gloss of gold. Leather. I don't see a gnarl of vines on a black fence. I see forest green velvet and black leather laces. Boots. I don't see a blue sky with clouds, I see a bolt of embroidered silk. I don't see a bunch of pink peonies being carried through the piazza by a new husband on the way home to his bride, I see a jeweled tassel on the vamp of a party shoe. Embellishments.

And when I look at a woman now, I don't see fashion, I don't see age, I don't see size. I see *her*. I see *my customer*, who needs me to give her the very thing that says who she is, as I express who I am through the work I do. Simple. But this knowledge has transformed me. I wasn't the woman I was when I landed in Rome a month ago, and I won't be the same when I return home. I will see *home* with these new eyes. Now, this frightens me a little: what if I've changed so that I don't have the same goals I was focused upon when I left? What if I return home and Roman isn't the man for me, and fighting with Alfred isn't worth saving the shop and the building? What if the eyes of this artist have changed the very soul of who I am? What if I don't want what I once dreamed of?

Costanzo told me over lunch one day that he was a widower, and his eyes filled with tears, so I didn't pursue it. But I don't want to leave Capri without knowing about his wife. As much as he has taught me about art, I feel there is much to know about other things, the guts of life, the pursuit of true love.

I join Costanzo on the veranda, where he has our lunch laid out on the table, as he does every day. I see buffalo mozzarella and luscious ripe tomatoes sliced thin. He's drizzling olive oil on them as I join him.

'Our last lunch.'

'The Last Supper,' he laughs.

'I don't want to leave you.'

'No woman wants to leave Costanzo Ruocco,' he laughs again.

I sit down and place a napkin on my lap. Costanzo fills my plate with the fruit of his garden. A quiet breeze moves through the garden rustling the tablecloth. 'Before I go, I wish you would tell me about your wife.'

Costanzo reaches into his shirt and pulls out a gold neck chain with a wedding ring attached to it.

'What was her name?' I ask gently.

'Rosa,' he says. 'She was born Rosa de Rosa.' Costanzo holds up his hand. He gets up and goes into the shop. When he returns he hands me a manila envelope. I open it. Inside are many pictures, some black and white, some small colored snaps, in the vivid blue Ektachrome from the 1960s, some from an instamatic camera in the 1970s, when their sons were born, and more still with a Polaroid instant camera, the kind of pictures that we used to take, develop on the table, and adhere to cardboard squares.

Gently, I place the stack of photographs on the table. The largest, a black-and-white picture of Costanzo and Rosa on their wedding day, was taken by a professional. She is a petite brunette, with gorgeous, wide-set brown eyes. She reminds me of my sister Jaclyn. Rosa wears a small whimsy in her hair, with a circle of net, and a white satin ballerina-length gown with a neck and a fitted waist that gives way to a full circle skirt. On her tiny feet are elegant kid pumps. Costanzo stands behind her, his hands on her waist.

'I married her on September 23, 1963. The happiest day of my life.'

'*Bella*,' I tell him.

'I called her Bella Rosa. And sometimes, just Bella.' Costanzo's voice breaks.

'And you are very handsome.' I make the hand-fanning movement just like Costanzo. He laughs. After all, I remember, and will never forget, he is Italian. The male ego arrives intact with the birth certificate. 'You miss her terribly.'

'I can't speak of her because, in my life, with all the words I have ever heard, there have never been any to describe what she meant to me.

435

I try, but even the word *love* is not enough. She was my world. I have never, for one moment, since she died, stopped loving her or thinking of her. Even now, if she could walk through that door, I would give up my own life for just a moment with her.'

I reach across the bench and take Costanzo's hand. 'Every woman should be loved the way you loved Rosa.'

'It's hard for me to live without her. Almost impossible. I welcome death when it comes because I will see her again. I only hope she wants this old man.'

'Oh, she will. There's a lot to be said for older men.' It hasn't been just art I've learned about in my time on Capri.

'She died in 1987. Nothing is the same. The figs don't taste the same, or the wine, or the tomatoes. She took everything good with her. I learned everything about life from her. About love, of course.' Costanzo stands and looks at me. 'You wait. I have something for you,' he says as he goes back into the shop.

I spent the week in Da Costanzo learning things I needed to know. I learned about *gropponi*, the best cowhide for making soles; *capretto*, the softest lamb leather, is wonderful for straps; and *vitello*, the firmer hide, works well on a full shoe. And I learned that the world outside this island is encroaching on the craftsmanship that was born here, gobbling up Costanzo's techniques and designs without his permission, only to mass-produce its version for the resort crowd.

Shifty entrepreneurial Americans come through, buy Costanzo's sandals, take them home, copy them, and steal the designs outright, and actually have the crust to go to the same suppliers as Costanzo and try to buy the elements he uses to build his signature sandals. The suppliers, wise to the thieves, refuse to sell supplies to the upstarts. Loyalty is still the best Italian trait.

Costanzo also taught me little things, tips that add up to the work habits that eventually become an artist's technique. When shaping a heel, I now take my knife and peel the edge like the skin of an apple until it's winnowed down to the exact size of the customer's foot. Costanzo taught me to sew flat seams inside a shoe, which make them more comfortable for the customer. He taught me to embrace color, to never fear it. If the prime minister of Italy can wear melon-colored leather loafers, anyone can.

I learned things on my own, too. I learned that tourists on Capri are very loud because they are so enthralled by the view, they raise their voices in excitement. I learned that travel is still the best way to shake up your life, shift your point of view, and embrace inspiration, but you must be wide awake and eager to take it in, or it's a waste. And I learned that my grandmother doesn't need me to care for her, or worry about her, she is self-sufficient. She does just fine on her own.

Costanzo returns to the table carrying a shoe box.

'Costanzo, I can never thank you enough for this week.'

'You're a good cobbler.' He nods his head slowly. 'Like me when I was young.'

'That means everything to me. That's all I want.'

'You work hard, and when you're as old as me, you will know what it feels like to have spent your life making something beautiful for someone else. This is what we really give in the world. Now, I have a gift for you,' he says.

'You don't have to do that.'

Costanzo gives me the shoe box. Before I remove the lid, I remember his promise to me on the first day of work. 'You made me sandals!'

'Not for you. Your feet are too big for these shoes.'

I shoot Costanzo a look. *'Mille grazie,'* I say in a tone that makes him laugh.

I open the box and look inside. I lift the felt liner away. I catch my breath and lift out the shoe, a revelation in shape, detail, and form.

Costanzo has built my design for the Bergdorf's competition. I place in on the palm of my hand, like a crown, and examine it.

My sketch has come to life, the upper of calfskin, the gold-and-white-braiding embellishment; the stacked heel, carved and sleek; the vamp with embossed leather, every detail is there, done to scale and tone as drawn and measured in my sketchbook.

438

The materials are luxe, the execution masterful, each stitch so tiny, they're practically invisible. The overall effect of the shoe is opulent with restraint, and the execution of the details is immaculate. The shoe says *new* bride, *new* life, *new* steps to carry her there! Size six. The sample size! The shoe that has lived for so long in my imagination is now in my hands, a glorious one-of-a-kind creation that calls back to my grandmother's youth and yet is completely in the moment.

My eyes fill with tears. 'I don't know what to say.'

'It's your design,' he says. 'I was just the cobbler.'

'But it's your craftsmanship that brought it to life.'

'That would be impossible without the vision,' he says. Then he lifts the shoe about a foot above the table and drops it. The shoe lands, in perfect pitch, and it rocks from side to side on the table until it stops. 'Do you know this test?'

I shake my head that I don't.

'When you build a heel, test it. If it rocks evenly and stops, like this' – he drops the other shoe onto the table; it sways and stops in the same fashion as the first shoe – 'you have built the shoe properly. If it falls over, you must rework the heel to achieve proper balance.'

'I will,' I promise him. 'Costanzo, we name our shoes at Angelini's. The truth is, I'm not an opera buff. But I am a woman who loves a good story. So, if you don't mind, I'd like to call this shoe the

439

Bella Rosa in honor of your wife. That is, if you don't mind.'

Costanzo gets tears in his eyes; they cloud over the blue, just like the mist on the sea at nightfall. He nods that I may name this shoe after his wife. I have his permission. It's so simple really. True love is without whim. It's hardware. Durable. Everlasting. This world is where Costanzo and Rosa's love happened, but eternity is where it lives. Love stays as long as someone remembers. I know their story and now I will tell it. I will think of Costanzo and Rosa every time I go to sketch, or cut a pattern, or sew a seam. He changed my point of view, so I will never forget him. I couldn't.

I hold the shoes in my hands and remember the story of the shoemaker and the elves. The shoemaker and his wife were so poor, so beaten down by circumstance, that they left their last bit of leather out on their worktable, and so weary, they went to bed. The next morning, they found a perfect pair of shoes made from the leather. They put the shoes in the window and a customer bought them immediately. With that money, the shoemaker and his wife bought more leather, and night after night, they left out the supplies. And every morning, they returned to new shoes, made by the elves, more magnificent than before. It's a story about when you're most defeated, someone will come along and help, maybe even save you. This is what Costanzo did for me. And tomorrow,

I must go home and do the same for the Angelini Shoe Company – the artist's way.

The sun, the color of a ripe apricot, burns high in the sky over the pool of the Quisisana Hotel on my last day in Capri. The veranda and garden are filled with guests, sunning and swimming. I get out of the water and lie down on a chaise, and let the sun warm me through to my bones. This isn't a bad way to turn thirty-four. It's not what I had in mind, but I'm in the mood to embrace whatever life sends me. For example, instead of fighting the bathing suit my mother sent, I accessorized. I bought a pair of enormous silver hoop earrings studded with tiny white sapphires to wear with the suit. Now, the ensemble looks like it's part of a plan. A gaudy, sparkling plan.

'Happy birthday,' Gianluca says as he sits on the chaise next to me.

I sit up. 'Gram told you.'

'No, no, I looked at your passport when we stopped at security at the silk mill.'

'Why would you do that?'

'I wondered how old you were. I was happy you were thirty-three.'

'So was I. It just took turning thirty-four to appreciate thirty-three, if you know what I mean.'

'I do.' He gives me a look that says he's been thinking about those kisses on my balcony as much as I have. The thrill and shame of it turn my cheeks red. He'll think it's the sun.

'What are your plans today?' he asks.

'You're looking at them.'

'I'd like to celebrate your birthday with you,' he says.

I lean back on the chaise and pull my hat down over my eyes. 'I've done enough celebrating with you.'

'You didn't enjoy it?'

I push the brim of my hat off of my eyes. 'Oh, I enjoyed it. But I shouldn't have. I made it to my thirties without ever cheating on a boyfriend. Then you broke my streak.'

'How can you worry about a few kisses when he didn't keep his word and join you here?'

An American woman on the next chaise, with a spray tan and wearing an orchid print swim dress, puts down her Jackie Collins paperback and commences to eavesdrop on our conversation.

'I know you Italians invented the vendetta, but I don't believe in it. I won't hurt Roman just because he disappointed me. I kissed you because I wanted to . . . and now,' I say loudly enough for the lady to hear, 'I will have to kill you.'

Gianluca laughs.

I lean toward the nosy woman. 'I'm a take-charge type,' I say to her.

'Let's go,' he says.

I'm not big on surprises, so when Gianluca hustles me into a taxi in the piazza to go down to the pier, I'm pretty sure we're going somewhere on Capri by boat. When I went on my tour of the

442

island, I wasn't observant about the politics of the dock. All I noticed were the lines of tourists waiting their turn to board the skiffs and experience the natural wonders of Capri. This time, we pass the hordes and I follow Gianluca around the pier to the end, where the local fishermen and families keep their boats. We get onboard a small white motorboat with a red leather interior.

'This is the exact color scheme of my dad's 1965 Mustang,' I tell Gianluca. 'He still has it.'

'This belongs to my cousin's family.'

'You mean I didn't have to cram in with the tourists to see the points of interest? I could have been on this little number?'

Gianluca starts the boat and maneuvers it out onto the open sea, past the tourists. As fast as he drives on land, he goes twice as fast on the ocean. He steers the boat out to where the water is smooth. We bounce over the waves effortlessly. *This is the way to go*, I think as we skip over the turquoise waves, drenched by a saltwater mist that cools us in the hot sun. Gianluca handles the boat with skill, but I keep my eyes on the water, and off him. There is much to admire about Gianluca Vechiarelli, but the last thing I need is another Italian man in my life.

We speed around the island until the back of the Quisisana comes into view. The entrance to the Blue Grotto is open. Satisfied that there is no one inside, Gianluca idles the boat near the entrance. He climbs out onto a ledge, and retrieves

443

a sign that says *NON ENTRATA IL GROTTO*. He hangs the sign on an old nail over the entrance, then pulls a small rowboat from an alcove behind the ledge. He drops the rowboat into the water and reaches up for me.

'You have got to be kidding.' I point to the sign. 'You mean it's true?'

I step down into his arms and he lifts me into the rowboat.

'Stay low,' Gianluca instructs me. I duck my head as we enter the grotto. At first, all that I see is a gray cavern, the stone entrance, and then, as Gianluca rows, we enter the blue.

When I was a girl, I was obsessed with panorama Easter eggs, the kind made of white sugar shells decorated with swirls of colored icing. There was a window at the end of the candy egg, and when you held it up to look inside, a scene would be depicted. With one eye, I would study a field of swirly green icing for grass, a miniature princess in a tulle skirt sitting on a tiny mushroom flecked with sugar, a green candy frog resting near her feet, and bright blue jelly beans, placed around the scene like stones in a garden. I would look inside the egg for hours, imagining what it would be like to be inside. This is the same feeling I have inside the Blue Grotto.

It's a wonderland of slick gray stones, walls worn away by the seawater, leading to a smooth lake of sapphire blue. Light pours in through holes in the rocks overhead, making silver funnels of light on the water. At the end of this cove, and deeper into the cavern, there's a tunnel that leads beyond this lake, and through it, I see more light piercing between the rocks and reflecting on the water, creating a dimension of depth and a deeper blue.

'You can swim,' he says.

'Seriously?'

Gianluca smiles. I take off my beach cover-up and slip into the water. It's cold, but I don't mind. I swim over to where the light comes through the *faraglione*. I place my hand in the silver beam, which makes my skin glisten. I swim around the edge of the lake. I touch the coral that grows on the seawall. The waxy red reeds hold to the wall tightly, beautiful veins that lead deeper into the water. I imagine how deep the coral must go, the vines rooted in the bottom of the ocean in some magical place where colors are born. I hear Gianluca enter the water. He swims toward me.

'Now I understand the sign,' I tell him. 'Why would you want to share this with anyone?'

'It's meant for sharing.'

'You know what I mean.'

'I do,' he says. 'Is it all you dreamed it would be?'

'Yes.'

'There are so few things in life you can say that about,' he says.

'Ain't that the truth?'

'Follow me,' he says. I swim with Gianluca through the tunnel and deeper into the grotto to another cove, this one filled with light. When I look up it's as if the cap on the stone mountain is gone, and this is the place the moon goes when the sun is out.

'We should go now,' Gianluca says.

I swim over to the boat and reach up for him. He pulls me in. He hands me a towel. 'Nice earrings,' he says.

'They go with the suit.'

'I can see that.' He smiles.

'You know, sometimes there's no point in fighting the inevitable,' I tell him. Of course, I'm talking earrings, not Italian isle hookups.

Once Gianluca returns the boat to its hiding place, and the sign back to the ledge, he helps me into the motorboat and we speed past the beaches of Capri and around the far side of the island where the villas of Anacapri are visible from the shore. Massive palazzos, built into the side of the mountain in layers, connected by breezy porticos, show how the rich live, and so much better than the rest of us. 'We should have that view,' I tell Gianluca.

'Why?' he asks.

'Because we'd appreciate it.'

Gianluca nods at the mention of 'we.' Above and beyond my bad behavior, he's been a good friend on this trip. We have a lot in common. This is such a small thing, it seems, to have mutual interest in work and the same kinds of family issues, but we do, and it's been nice to talk to someone who understands where I come from. I have that with Roman to some degree, but the truth is, he spends his days and nights in a very different way than Gianluca and I do. I have appreciated Gianluca's view of the world. I suppose a tanner and a shoe-maker have a marriage of true minds, we rely on each other to sustain our crafts, at least in the workshop.

Gianluca stops the boat in a calm inlet. He pulls out a picnic basket of the food I love most: fresh, crusty bread; pale green buttery olive oil; cheese; tomatoes, so ripe their skin is caramelized by the sun; and homemade wine that tastes of hearty oak, cherries, and sweet grapes. We sit in the sun and eat.

I try and make him laugh, which is easy. Gianluca has a good sense of humor, not that he's funny himself, but he appreciates it in others. I do a drop-dead impersonation of an American tourist who tried to talk Costanzo's prices down until finally he said to the woman, 'You're terrible. Get out.' She left in a huff. Gianluca loves that story.

We sit in the late-afternoon sun until the breeze turns cool. 'It's time to get back,' he says.

Gianluca revs up the boat, and invites me to steer. I've never driven a boat before, but I like to think that I'm open to trying new things, so I take the wheel of the boat with confidence and a dab of chutzpah. You would think that after driving a stick shift from Rome to Naples, commandeering this little boat would be easy. But I'm amazed by how much brute strength it takes to turn the wheel. After a few moments, I begin to feel my way on the water, and gripping the wheel just so, I use my entire body to guide the boat.

When we get close to the docks, I slow down and give Gianluca the wheel. When I let go and surrender my grip, I almost fall, but he catches me with one arm and takes the wheel with the other.

As we reach the pier, he throws a line to a boy working on the dock, who places the rope around a piling, securing the boat. Gianluca climbs out first and then lifts me up to the pier. We walk to the cab stand, and he helps me into a car. We don't talk as the driver takes the twists and turns of the road at a clip up to the piazza and back to the Quisisana.

There's a long night rolling out ahead of us, and I wonder where this ride will take us. One time, back in the shop, June told me a story about a married man she had an affair with, and she said, once she kissed him, she was already guilty, so why not just go the distance? I look over at Gianluca, who looks out over the hills of Capri to the blue sea below. He has a look of contentment on his face. When we reach the top, Gianluca climbs out of the taxi with me.

'I leave you now,' he says, taking my hand.

'It's so early.' I sound disappointed. I *am*.

'I know. But you should have your last night to

yourself. Happy birthday.' He smiles and leans down. Then he kisses me on the cheek. I must look confused, because he raises both eyebrows with a look that says, *We're not going there again.* He places a small package tied with raffia into my hand. I look up to thank him, and he's gone.

I walk back to the hotel alone. I stop in the lobby of the Quisisana and look around, imagining how much I will miss this grand entrance when I go. I decide to redo our dingy entrance on Perry Street as soon as we get home. We need a paint job, new lighting, and a rug. There's another thing I learned in Italy – entrances matter.

When I get off the elevator in the attico, I look at the painting over the love seat for the last time. For every day I have come and gone from the hotel, I have waited here for the elevator, and looked at this painting. For days, it has been a mystery to me. Now, I understand what all those Mondrian checks represent – they're windows, hundreds of windows. For me, this trip was all about seeing out of them, and for sure, I did. I sit down on the love seat underneath the painting I have come to love and open the package from Gianluca.

As I loosen the ribbon and unfold the paper, my hand shakes a little. I open the lid on the box and lift out a shoemaker's tool, a new hammer, *il trincetto.* Gianluca has engraved my initials on the handle.

I open the door to my room and there's a large

antique urn on the coffee table bursting with blood red roses and branches of bright yellow baby lemons. The air is filled with fragrant sweet roses, tart lemons, and rich earth. I close my eyes and inhale slowly.

Then I pick up the card on the table. *That Gianluca*, I'm thinking as I open the card. That's why he rushed off. He wanted to surprise me with the flowers. I open the envelope and lift out a single card.

Happy birthday, honey, I love you. Come home to me. Roman

Of all the great lessons I learned in Italy, the most important is: travel light. Pushing our mountain of luggage through three regions of Italian countryside has turned me into a minimalist. I'm *this close* to becoming a nun and rejecting all worldly possessions. Gram, however, is not. She clings to these suitcases, fills them carefully, and knows the contents of each Ziploc bag and bundle. Old people need stuff. It makes them feel secure, or so Gram says.

Gram holds on to the handle of the cart as I push the bags through customs at John F. Kennedy Airport. We're back in the United States, which means I must begin to live a real life again and face my responsibilities. I begin with a commitment to Gram's health and general well-being. I will call and make an appointment for

450

her with Dr Sculco at the Hospital for Special Surgery. Gram needs new knees, and she's going to get them if it's the last thing I do.

I survey the line at pickup. Families, friends, and chauffeurs wait for us, looking us over from head to toe as we search for familiar faces from our side.

Roman waits with my parents. Mom is wearing a red sundress with matching sunglasses and waves a small Italian flag. Nice touch. Dad stands next to her, waving plainly with his human hand.

Roman stands tall over them, in jeans and a blue Brooks Brothers button-down shirt. He looks handsome. He always does, which makes hellos and good-byes sweet. When our eyes meet for the first time in a month, my heart races. I really missed him, and as angry as I was with him, I love him. My nose stings as though I might cry.

I kiss my father and mother, and then Roman. He takes me into his arms, and my parents and Gram vamp about the trip, as if they don't notice that he can't let go of me. This ought to be an interesting car ride. Roman takes the luggage cart from me and pushes. Mom and Dad and Gram follow. I fill him in on Costanzo and what he missed on Capri. We go through the doors to the parking garage.

'Honey, we'll take the bags. You go with Roman,' Mom says.

'I drove, too,' Roman says.

'Oh, two cars. Great. Okay. You can take my bags. I never want to see them again.'

451

Dad helps Roman load up the back of his Olds Cutlass Supreme with the bags I lugged through Tuscany and farther south. I lift my carry-on out of the car and hold it in my arms. 'Precious cargo,' I tell Gram. 'The shoes. I want to keep them with me.'

'Of course,' she says.

They climb into Dad's car, while Roman opens the front door of the passenger side of his car for me. I get into his car, and shiver, even though it's almost June. I remember the first winter night I sat in this car, and how happy we were. He climbs in and pulls the door shut. He turns to me. 'I missed you.'

'I missed you, too.'

'You're beautiful,' he says and kisses me.

'It's the Capri sun.' I shrug, deflecting his compliment that sounds sincere. I don't know what to believe. When it comes to Roman, all I know for sure is that things are constantly changing. 'You want to stay over?' he asks quietly.

'Sure,' I tell him.

With my quick answer, Roman, like all men, is satisfied that all is forgiven. He believes what I tell him, and why shouldn't he? I don't want to over-think our reunion and turn it into a monster discussion of our future and our relationship. We've got years for that, or do we? When it comes to love, this is where I'm weak. I don't fight for myself or what I want. I'm perfectly happy to pretend that we've moved past my hurt, Italy, and all the unpleasantness. Now I'm home and all will be well. We can pick up where we left off.

Roman talks about the restaurant-review night, and how the pressure was on. When he tells me Frank Bruni of the *Times* gave him three stars, I throw my arms around him. I act excited for him, giddy even, and I'm all the things he needs me to be: supportive, interested, and utterly *on his side*. When he asks me about Italy, I give him the broad strokes, but I don't explain how I think I've changed, and how the people I met had such an impact on me. I begin to tell him about the old lady's brooch, but it sounds silly, so I change the subject and switch the conversation back to him.

I look at his face, and his glorious neck, his hands and his long legs, and I get stirred up. But it isn't stirred up of the deep variety; it's a fashionable fake of the real thing. This is the part of me that loves being in a relationship. I like the stability and being part of a couple. Never mind our problems, we're *together*, and that's enough. More than enough. Roman Falconi might be the Chuck Cohen of love, the knockoff, whereas I'm looking for a couture label, but he's mine.

I'm going to his apartment and I'm probably going to make love to him, but it's not going to mean what it would have meant a month ago, or even a week ago. Then, we were building on a solid foundation. Now, doubt has seeped in and I've got to find what I saw in the beginning. I only hope that my feelings will all come rushing back just as they were the first time he kissed me. Maybe then our relationship can begin anew, and I can figure out how to be in a relationship with Roman *and* his restaurant.

'Someday, we'll go back to Capri together,' he promises. Gratefully, the traffic on the LIE gets thick and he has to keep his eyes on the road. In this moment, I try to believe him. But somehow I know he's just saying it because he thinks that will keep me focused on the future, and out of the present, where our problems with each other are alive and well.

'That would be great,' I tell him. It's not a lie. It would be great.

The next morning, I wake up in Roman's bed, buried deep in the warm comforter. I slept soundly, exhausted from the drive to Rome and the flight back to New York. I look over and see my overnight bag by the door, and my carry-on with the Bella Rosa inside.

I get up and go into Roman's kitchen. There's a pot of coffee and a bagel on the counter with a note: 'Went to work. So happy you're home.'

I pour the coffee. I sit down in his kitchen and look across the bright, sunlit loft, and instead of seeming masculine and romantic, as it did before Italy, in full daylight it appears to be unfinished, bare, in need of things. Temporary.

CHAPTER 14

58TH AND FIFTH

Today is the deadline for the delivery of the shoes for the competition for the Bergdorf windows. I get off the subway at Columbus Circle, holding the shoe box containing the Bella Rosa in the crook of my arm, like a newborn baby. Let's face it, this is my version of precious cargo. Some people give birth to babies, I give birth to shoes.

In my backpack is the sketch of the Rag & Bone gown. For fun, I photographed the shoes, reduced them to scale, and put them on the feet of the model in the sketch of the wedding gown Rhedd Lewis sent to us. I also included my original ink-and-watercolor sketch of the shoes, the photograph of my inspiration – Gram at her wedding – and a photograph of Costanzo and me under the Capri sun, giving him credit as the cobbler who built my design.

I push my way through the revolving door at the side entrance and walk past the specialty handbag section to the elevator. I look around at the customers, wanting to shout, *Pray for me*, but I imagine the only soul connection these ladies experience is the Zen that comes during a micro-dermabrasion facial. I don't believe they light candles to Saint Crispin for spiritual guidance.

When I get off the elevator on the eighth floor, it's not the serene waiting area I remember from our appointment months ago. It's packed, full of people and loud, like the subway platform at Forty-second Street, except no one's waiting for a train. They wait for Rhedd Lewis. It seems that all the major shoe labels are represented in flashy, attention-getting ways. Donald Pliner has wedding shoes dangling off a tabletop palm tree; a delivery boy from Christian Louboutin carries a tray of cookies, upon which is a wedding shoe filled with candy; an actual six-foot-tall Amazon model, dressed as a bride, wears what look like Prada shoes. A publicist carries an enormous blow-up of a Giuseppe Zanotti wedding shoe with a phrase in French staggered across the poster. Alicia Flynn Cotter's signature patent leather pumps are hanging artfully in a small-scale hot-dog stand turned wedding wagon. It's a madhouse. I work my way through my competitors to the receptionist.

'Rhedd Lewis please,' I tell her.

'You here with a shoe?' she asks as she types.

'May I speak with her assistant please?'

Without taking her eyes off the screen, she says, 'She's on her way out for Craig Fisse. And I'm just a temp. You can leave your submission on the pile.'

My heart sinks as I look at a pile of submissions: shoe boxes, some FedExed, others hand-delivered, dropped in the corner like rejects on their way to the garbage. I cannot leave the Bella Rosa there, I won't.

Rhedd's assistant appears in the doorway. She smiles tensely and looks over the crowd. I push to the front. Suddenly, I feel like the kid at Holy Agony who will never get chosen for Red Rover during recess. But I've come too far to be shy now.

'Remember me?' I say to her.

She doesn't.

'I'm Valentine Roncalli of the Angelini Shoe Company. This is our submission.' I place the box in front of her. I don't move until she instinctively reaches for it. She tucks the shoe box and the envelope of extras under her arm like yesterday's newspaper.

'Great. Thanks,' she says, looking past me to the model with the gown.

'Well, thank you for the opportunity . . . ,' I begin, but the din escalates in the room when the deliverymen and the sideshow attractions realize that the woman I am speaking with is Rhedd's assistant. This, clearly, is the moment they've been waiting for, and they press forward in a heap and commence shouting to get her attention. I push through them and back to the elevator.

Once I'm outside on Fifty-seventh Street, I lean against the building. I imagined this moment so differently. I thought I would give the shoes to

Rhedd herself, and she'd open the box and swoon; or I imagined her staff in a conference room where some lowly but gifted assistant stands up and says, 'We have to give the underdog a chance,' bringing Rhedd Lewis to tears, and finally her senses, when she chooses Angelini Shoes over the fancy-pants designers. I played so many scenes through my mind, and now, I imagine our shoes in a heap on the floor among all the other submissions. I imagine them getting lost. I imagine them losing. Us. Losing.

I walk at a rapid clip back to the subway. My face burns hot with embarrassment. Let me tell you, you cannot feel smaller than you do when dwarfed by the skyscrapers of Midtown Manhattan after you've just been dismissed like an old shoe at Bergdorf Goodman. What will they think of Gram's photograph in the fussy wedding gown or that silly snap of Costanzo and me in front of the shoe shop? I didn't dramatize fine Italian crafts-manship in my presentation, I went homey and heartfelt, and above Fourteenth Street in Manhattan, that means *hokey*. Why would they care that I am part of a tradition that extends back a hundred years? So do Nathan's hot dogs and Durcon zippers. I deserve to lose.

But the shoes? They deserve a chance. For a moment, I consider running back to the store, going up in the elevator, bypassing the crowd, the receptionist, and the assistant, and marching right into Rhedd Lewis's office and telling her exactly, in a rousing speech, why the little guy should win. Instead, I fish my MetroCard out of my backpack and go down the stairs to home, to the Angelini Shoe Company.

June attempts to cheer me up about the Bergdorf competition by telling us a long story about her uncle who used to buy lottery tickets, convinced he'd win. Week after week, he'd buy them, and when he was dying, he sent his son out to buy a ticket. He died, and the ticket brought in five thousand bucks. The moral of her story: I must die in order for our shoes to be in Bergdorf's windows, though I don't believe that was June's intention when she told it.

'Here it is.' I hold up a black flat embellished with a silver-pavé angel wing. This is my first pair of everyday shoes for the every-woman, the first sample for the secondary-line launch from the Angelini Shoe Company. I'm calling the line Angel Shoes, inspired by our sign, and by the wings I drew on Capri. Also, in any new venture, particularly one as precarious as this, it doesn't hurt to call on all the powers of heaven to tilt things our way. I have no problem relying on angels or calling upon my saints, on this plane or elsewhere.

I place the finished shoe on the worktable. Gram and June examine it. June whistles. Gram picks it up. 'It's whimsical.'

'Functional,' June adds.

'Now I just have to figure out how to mass-produce it.'

'You will,' Gram says gaily.

Since we returned from Italy, it's as though Gram has been on a high. She flits around the apartment, does her work cheerfully, and has even tackled some projects that she swore she'd never do – like clean out the closet in my mother's old bedroom. We even visited Dr Sculco, who will give Gram new knees on December first, with plenty of time to rehab before the new year.

While she's been busy reorganizing, I've been busy researching how to get my new line of shoes made. I am determined to manufacture the shoes in America so that I might oversee the production. Of course, I have to keep an open mind because, after all, this is a new arena for me, and there's no master to show me the ropes. All I bought in my business agreement with Alfred was time. He's my full partner, and he has a say, to the tune of 50 percent. I have a year to establish a profit margin in the shop, which would prevent him from selling the building out from under me. I try not to think of the six million dollars that would free me from this partnership forever, but rather, take this venture one shoe at a time. We hear the buzzer sound in the vestibule.

'I'm ready for the unveiling,' Bret says from the entrance. Then he pushes through the workshop door. 'How are we doing?' he asks.

'Say hello to the first pair of Angel Shoes.' I hold up the sample. While Bret examines it, I place my business plan on the table. 'Here's the breakdown of costs for the shoes. I found some innovative materials in Italy. This is actually a fabric that mimics leather. We'll market it as a fabric, not a leather look, which should appeal to the customer and keep the cost down. In leather, the same shoe goes up in base price by thirty-three cents on the dollar. I found the new materials in Milan. What do you think?'

'Val, you really pulled this off. I'll be happy to take your plan to the investors. Any news on the Bergdorf windows?'

'I just dropped off the prototype. I wouldn't count on winning that contest, Bret. The competition is fierce *and* French, two elements that are unbeatable in the world of fashion.'

'I'm going to tell the investors that you were handpicked by Rhedd Lewis to compete, and hopefully, I'll have them sign on the dotted line before Rhedd makes her announcement.'

'Sounds like a great plan.' I smile gratefully at Bret as my cell phone rings. I pick it up.

'Val, it's Mom. Meet us at New York Hospital. Jaclyn is having the baby! Bring Mom!' My mother hangs up on me in an obvious panic.

'Jaclyn is having the baby at New York Hospital.'

'Get my purse,' Gram says calmly.

The entry to New York Hospital is a lot like an old-time bank; there's a lot of glass, an enormous atrium, multiple swinging doors, and people, lots of them, waiting in lines. I have Mom on the cell, which she is using as a tracking device in order to

461

describe every twist and turn that will lead us up to the maternity floor. 'Yeah, yeah, I know – no cell phones. I'll be off in a minute. I just gotta get my people up here,' I hear her say to a muffled voice in the background. Gram and I manage to find the maternity ward on the sixth floor, where Mom is waiting for us when the elevator doors open.

'How is she?' I ask her.

'The baby will be here soon. That's all we know. I told everyone the doctor miscalculated! Jaclyn got so big so fast. Somebody didn't do the math.'

We follow Mom back to the waiting area. Dad is reading a beat-up copy of *Forbes*, while Tess corrals Charisma and Chiara away from people in the room we are not related to. Gram sits down on the couch, while I take the chair next to my father.

'We came too soon,' Gram whispers to me after an hour passes. 'This could take hours.'

'Remember when Jaclyn was born?' Tess says, sitting down next to me.

'You named her after your favorite Charlie's Angel, Jaclyn Smith. I still can't believe Mom went for that.' I put my arm around Tess.

Mrs McAdoo shows up with her sister; they wait patiently for an hour and then go. To be fair, this is Mrs McAdoo's fourteenth grandchild, so the thrill is essentially gone.

Finally, Tess, too, gives up and takes Charisma and Chiara home. Dad falls asleep on the couch and snores so loudly, the nurse asks us to have him removed. And then, after six hours, two rounds of Starbucks coffee and an hour and a half of Anderson Cooper on mute on the TV in the waiting area, finally, at ten minutes after midnight on June 15, 2008, Tom comes out of the labor room.

'It's a girl,' he says. 'Teodora Angelini McAdoo.'

My mother cries, Gram clasps her hands together, honored and stunned. My father embraces Tom, slapping him on the back. Mom gets on the cell and calls Tess, and then Alfred, to tell them of the arrival of the newest member of our family. Gram, Mom, and I go into the recovery room to see Jaclyn. She lies back in the bed holding her daughter. She's exhausted and puffy, her usually large and limpid eyes buried in her face like raisins in the top of a bran muffin. She looks up at us. 'Isn't she beautiful?' Jaclyn whispers.

We gather around her and coo.

'Never again.' Her expression changes from bliss to resolve. 'Never again.'

In the cab ride home, I check my phone. I listen to the messages. There are three from Roman, the last one downright terse. I call him. He picks up. I don't even say hello. 'Honey, I'm so sorry. Jaclyn had the baby. We've been at the hospital all night.'

'That's great news,' he says. 'Why didn't you call?'

'I just told you, I was at the hospital.'

'I left you messages everywhere.'

'Roman, I don't know what to say. I was all

caught up in it. I had my phone off. I'm sorry. Do you want me to come over now?'

'You know what? Let's rain-check. We can do this another night,' he says, sounding exhausted, and truthfully, more annoyed than tired.

I snap the phone shut. Gram looks out the window pretending not to have heard the conversation.

'You'd think I left him stranded for a week alone on Capri. It was only dinner,' I tell her. 'Men.'

Gram and I are weary the next morning after our long day at the hospital. Gram has called all of her friends to tell them that her new great-granddaughter is also her namesake. Never let it be said that it doesn't matter who a baby is named for, in my family, it's the highest honor. I've never seen Gram so happy.

I bring the mail into the workshop, sorting through it until I find an envelope from Italy. I hand it to Gram. 'You got something from Dominic.'

She puts down the pattern she is working on and takes the letter from me. She opens it carefully with the blade of her work scissors. I pick up a brush and polish the kid leather on the Ines. When she's done reading the letter, Gram hands me some pictures that came with the letter.

'Orsola got married,' she says.

In a vivid color photograph, Orsola is a stunning bride in a simple, square-necked white silk slip dress, with ornate trim made of white silk roses along the bottom. The hem of her dress stands away from her feet, like the edge of a bell. She carries a small bouquet of white edelweiss.

On Orsola's other side is her groom, a match for her beauty, his blond hair slicked back for the big day. Next to the groom are his parents, a nice-looking couple. Holding Orsola's hand on her other side is a woman I've never seen before, she must be Gianluca's ex-wife, and Orsola's mother. She is the same height as her daughter, with short hair, and the same delicate features. I can see that she's tough, and she's definitely got the number elevens going between the eyes. Gianluca described her well.

My heart races when I see Gianluca in the photograph next to his ex-wife. Maybe I'm embarrassed about kissing him, or maybe seeing his ex-wife, a woman around his own age, reminds me of *our* age difference. Gianluca wears a stately gray morning coat. He looks handsome and refined, not like the working-class tanner he is in life. His smile is full of joy for his daughter. Dominic, the Duke of Arezzo, wears a gray morning coat and a black-and-white-striped ascot, and stands proudly next to his son.

'Dominic writes that Gianluca asked about you.'

'That's nice.' I change the subject quickly. 'How's Dominic?'

'He misses me,' she says. 'You know, he's in love with me.'

Gram says this as casually as she might when she places a lunch order. I put down my work brush. 'Are you in love with him?'

She places the letter off to the side carefully. 'I think so.'

'Don't worry, Gram, soon a year will go by and we'll need more leather and you'll be with him again.'

She looks at me. 'I don't think I can wait a year.'

'You can visit anytime you want.'

'I don't think a visit is enough anymore.'

I'm stunned. My grandmother is eighty years old; would she actually uproot her life to go and live in Italy? It doesn't seem possible, and it certainly doesn't seem like her.

She continues, 'I've had a struggle within myself all my life. I'm always torn between doing what I *want* to do and what I *should* do.'

'Gram, when you're eighty, I think you get a pass. I think it's time to do what you want to do.'

'You would think so, wouldn't you?' She looks off and then continues, 'But it's not easy to change what is fundamental and basic about yourself, even if you wish you could. I've been working in this shop for over fifty years, and I imagine that I always will.'

'But you fell in love . . . ,' I remind her. 'That's a game changer,' I say aloud, as though it's something I actually know to be true.

'Love only works when two lives come together without sacrifice. No one should give up who they

466

are for someone else. People do it, but it doesn't make them happy, not in the long run.'

The phone rings, interrupting our conversation. 'Angelini Shoe Company,' I say into the phone.

'Rhedd Lewis calling for Teodora Angelini,' the assistant says.

I cover the receiver. 'Gram, it's Rhedd Lewis.'

Gram takes the phone from me. It seems like it takes twenty years for her to say, 'Hello?' She listens carefully, then says, 'Rhedd, if you don't mind, I'd like Valentine to take the call. It's her design. One moment please.' Gram hands the phone back to me.

'Valentine, I've sifted through every shoe submitted for the windows. I was wowed, disappointed, shocked, and appalled. There was real junk, and genuine genius . . .'

Why is she telling me this? I don't need a critique on top of a rejection. Get to the point, lady.

Rhedd continues, 'But nowhere in all the submissions was there such élan, such energy, such a new view but with a respect for the past. You rose to the occasion splendidly, and in creating the Bella Rosa, you married tradition with the pulse of the moment in an artful and seamless way. In fact, I'm in awe. We are going to feature Angelini Shoes in the Christmas windows at Bergdorf's. Congratulations.'

I hang up the phone and scream so loudly, the pigeons on Charles Street take flight. 'We won! We won!' Gram and I embrace. June comes in from lunch.

'What the hell is going on?' she says.

'We won, June! We're doing the windows at Bergdorf's!'

'Dear God, I thought somebody hit the lottery,' June says.

'We did!'

I put on one of my mom's vintage Diane Von Furstenberg wrap dresses. This one is black and white, in a paint-splattered-style print. My hair is long and cascades down like DVF's own mane back when these dresses were in style the first time around. I want to look good to celebrate our wonderful news with Roman. He doesn't know it yet, as I'm going to surprise him at the restaurant. He has workmen fixing the electrical on this, his night off, so I'm going to whisk him off for a great celebration meal in Chinatown. I pull on my coat.

'Gram, what are you having for dinner?'

'I heated up the manicotti you made.'

'How is it?'

'Just as good the second time around.' Gram has her feet up, watching television in her easy chair.

'What are you gonna do tonight?' I ask her, as I always do.

'I'm going to watch the news and then I'm going to bed.'

'Don't wait up.'

'I never do.' She winks.

The cab drops me on Mott Street. Before I push the security code to enter Ca' d'Oro, I check my lipstick in a compact mirror. The balloon curtains are down in the front windows. I punch in the security code and enter the restaurant. I'm greeted by votive candles flickering on the ledge of the mural, as well as on the tables. Roman must already know my news. He probably called Gram and Gram told him and he prepared a celebration feast for me. God, life is good.

I hear Roman's voice in the kitchen, so I tiptoe back to surprise him. I sneak up to the doorway. I look inside.

Roman is hovering over a skillet on the stove, while a woman, with long blond hair the color of flat champagne, and wearing a cook's apron, sits on the island, her legs dangling as she sips a glass of wine. She takes her foot and taps him on the ass with her toes. He looks around and grins at her. Then he sees me. And then *she* turns and sees me.

'Hon, what are you doing here?' he asks.

I look away from him, and place my gaze on her. She's ashamed. She looks away.

'We won the Bergdorf windows.' Then I turn and go back out into the restaurant. I'm not good at these kinds of scenes, they are way too dramatic for me. I head for the door at a rapid clip. I can't say I'm upset. I'm numb. But of course, as Tess is eager to point out, if there's ever a crisis, go and stand by Valentine, because she remains flatly in denial for a full twenty-four hours after something horrible happens. I put my hand on the door to go out. I push it open. Roman is right behind me.

'Wait,' he says.

I'm outside on the sidewalk. I am not waiting. 'Good night, Roman.'

'Stop. You owe it to me.'

Now, I'm angry. Every word he utters is an excuse for me to be mean right back at him. 'What exactly do I owe you?'

'Let me explain.'

The idea that he'd actually come up with an excuse for what I saw unnerves me. I'd like to scream at him, but I'm so furious, I can't form the words.

'She's a maître d' I was going to hire, but now I won't.'

'You know what, Roman? I'm not buying it.' I turn to go.

He stops me again. 'Look, there's nothing going on here. She had some wine, that's why she was flirting.'

'I love a liquor defense.' I turn away, but this time, it's because there are tears in my eyes. So much for Tess's twenty-four-hour rule, I broke it tonight in thirty seconds flat. Let him see that I'm crying. I don't care. 'Roman, your idea of a relationship is seeing me when you can. I'm like spackle. You fit me in between the important stuff.'

'You're just as busy as I am.' His expression softens. 'I think you like the idea of being with me, but I don't think I'm the one.'

If I were younger and he were a different person, I'd think this was some sort of a rap, designed to distract me from the sexy indiscretion in the kitchen. But it's not a rap, he's right. I like him to be there when I want him, but I'm not really present in this relationship either.

'I'm sorry.' It's almost impossible for me to say I'm sorry, but I did. And then I say the one thing that is hardest of all, because I truly believe it. 'I do love you.'

Roman looks at me. Then he shakes his head, as if he can't take this in. 'I think there's someone else.'

'You're kidding. I'm the one who just caught you in the kitchen with a woman.'

'You didn't catch me. It was innocent. Since you came back from Italy, you've been distant, and I can't get in. I've begged your forgiveness for missing our vacation. I've been trying to make it up to you. Other people have busy careers and make it work. I think our schedules are just excuses. We don't have what it takes. We just don't.'

'I think we do.' The thought of losing him makes me feel desperate. I feel a rush of panic, wanting to promise him anything just to have him give me another chance. I want an opportunity to get it right, to prove my feelings, to surrender, to commit, and to *show* him how much I love him. My mind fills with images of him, on the roof last Christmas roasting marsh-mallows with the kids, playing basketball with my nephews, taking Gram's arm in the street for no reason. I'm not ready to say good-bye to this good man. But I don't know how to help him understand who I am and what I'm capable of, because I haven't given him one indication of the real person I am inside. I hold him at arm's length, and most of the time, even *farther*, and I don't know why.

'Valentine, if that's true, then we should try.'

'I need to think about you, Roman. I don't want to turn this into a big Band-Aid that ends up with us in bed and we smooth it over, and then everything's fine for a few weeks, and then this . . . this happens again. There's something wrong, and I need to figure out what. You deserve better.'

'Do you mean it?' There's an expression on his face that I haven't seen in a while: hope.

'Besides, I kissed a man in Capri. There. I've said it. It's been bothering me and I'm sorry. I'm so sorry. The truth is, I have no right to march into Ca' d'Oro and judge you with Blondie-blonde when I did a stupid thing.'

'Why?' he asks.

'I was mad at you. That's all it was.'

'I'm relieved.'

'What?' I can't believe this is his reaction. Where's the rage? The jealousy.

'I knew something was wrong, and now you've told me.'

'I still want to be with you,' I tell him.

'And I want to make it work,' he admits.

'So, go in there and tell that maître d' that the position is filled.'

He doesn't let go of my hand. 'You want to come with me?'

'I don't think so.' I kiss him. 'Come over tonight.'

'What about Teodora?'

'I'll close her door and put on Cousin Brucie and she'll never hear a thing.'

'I'll see you later,' he says.

'Here.' I fish in my purse and give him the extra set of keys, the keys that I've been meaning to give him for months. They dangle from a Quisisana Hotel keychain.

Roman looks at the key chain. 'You're serious.'

'Yes I am.'

I turn and walk down the street, and when I get to the corner, I look back. He's standing there, watching me. I wave to him. He does love me. That's not something I'm ready to lose.

'Gram, I'm home!' I holler from the stairwell. I'm anxious to take off this dress and put on my pajamas and finish our discussion about Dominic. I want to get her tucked in and comfortable before Roman comes over. Tonight, I want to confide in her about Roman, and kissing Gianluca, and find out what she'd do if she were me. I think she'd choose Roman, just like me. 'Gram, I'm home!' I shout again as I enter the kitchen. The TV is on, but she's not in her chair. Strange, she usually turns off the set before she goes upstairs. I place my purse on the table and start to take off my coat, then I see Gram's foot on the floor behind the counter. I run over to the counter. Gram is lying on the floor. I kneel next to her. She's breathing, but she doesn't respond when I call her name. I grab the phone and dial 911.

The ambulance took Gram to Saint Vincent's hospital. She revived at home, but was confused, and wasn't sure when she fell. My mother and father arrived at the hospital quickly, as there's barely any traffic from Queens into the city this time of night. Tess, Jaclyn, and Alfred push through the doors, their faces full of dread. It's almost ten o'clock, but Gram asked Mom to call her lawyer, her old friend Ray Rinaldi who lives on Charles Street. My mother did exactly as she was told, and Ray is inside the ICU with her now.

Roman pushes through the glass doors and runs to me. 'How is she?'

'She's weak. We don't know what happened,' Mom says. Gram has never been sick, or sustained any kind of serious injury. Mom is not used to this, and she's frightened. My father puts his arms around her. She cries. 'I don't want to lose her.'

'She's in good hands. It's going to be all right,' Roman reassures Mom. 'Don't worry.'

A nurse steps out of the ICU and surveys the crowd. 'Is there a Clementine here?'

'Valentine,' I say and wave.

'Follow me,' she says.

The ICU is full, and Gram lies in the farthest corner with two flowing blue curtains separating her from an old man whose chest heaves as he sleeps. As I approach Gram's bed, Ray Rinaldi closes a large paper folder. Ray's a grandfather now, with a thick thatch of gray hair and a briefcase that has seen better days.

'I'll see you outside,' he says to me. Then he gives me a pat on the back. 'Teodora, everything will be done just as you wish.'

'Thank you, Ray,' Gram whispers and manages a smile. She closes her eyes.

I go to the side of the bed and hold her hand. Her eyes barely flutter open, looking like two black commas, certainly not the wide, almond-shaped Italian eyes she has when she's in good health. Her glasses rest on her chest on a chain, just as they were when she fell. A blue-and-purple bruise has formed over her brow, where her face hit the counter. I place my hand gently on the bruise. It feels warm. She looks at me then closes her eyes. 'I don't know what happened.'

'They'll figure it out.'

'I wasn't feeling right. I got up for a glass of water, and that's the last I remember until the ambulance came.' Gram looks off, as though she's searching for a road sign in the distance.

'You're not seeing the Blessed Lady, are you?' I joke. 'Let's not start having mystical visions.' I look in the direction of her gaze, and all I see is a wall with an eraser board filled with names of patients and numbers of medications written by the nurses.

'Is this it?' she says to me.

'What do you mean?'

'Is this how it ends?'

'No way! You're not going anywhere. Buck up. You have a new great-granddaughter named after you. Mom wants to take you on a cruise. Scratch that. You'd hate it. Here, this is better: You still have to teach me how to cut embossed leather. I have lots more to learn and you're the only person who can teach me. And Dominic. Dominic loves you!'

'All I want to do is make shoes and play cards.'

'And you will!'

'. . . and grow tomatoes.'

'Absolutely. Grow tomatoes.'

'. . . and I want to go home to Italy.'

Gram looks off, and in her way, she has defined the boundaries of her life for me. Could anything be simpler? All anyone needs to be happy is something to do, friends who gather to talk and play cards, a good meal made with the tomatoes from your own garden, and every once in a while, a trip to Italy, where she finds peace and comfort in the arms of an old friend.

I look around Saint Vincent's ICU. It's clean and functional. Not a frill in sight. What a place to contemplate getting well, never mind your salvation. The nurses no longer wear crisp white uniforms with little hats like they did in old movies. They wear Hawaiian shirts and green scrub pants. I have a hard time taking in a medical prognosis delivered by someone in a luau costume.

'I had your mother call Ray,' Gram says softly. 'I put you and Alfred in charge of the Angelini Shoe Company and on the deed of the building. I trust the two of you to figure things out.'

I hear Gram's words in my head, admonishing me for fighting with my brother: *More than anything I want my family to get along.* Alfred and I are an unlikely match under the best of circumstances. Running the business together will never work, I can only pray that Gram will get better quickly so she can have the life she dreams of, and while she's living it, I might run her company, on my own terms. 'Okay, Gram,' I say. 'We'll take care of everything, I promise. And you'll be back on Perry Street with me in no time.'

'Valentine?' My mom wakes me gently. I am sleeping in the chair in Gram's room at Saint Vincent's hospital.

'Is she okay?' I sit up and look at the empty bed. Gram is gone.

'They just took her for tests.'

'What time is it?' I lift my sleeve and check my watch. It's almost noon.

'She's been out of the room since eight,' Mom says and I can hear the worry in her voice.

'Do they know what happened to her?'

Dad, Jaclyn, Tess, and Alfred come into the room.

'Did she have a stroke?' Tess asks.

'We don't know yet,' Mom tells her.

Alfred takes a deep breath and clears his throat.

'I don't want to be right. But this time you have to listen to me. Gram can't do what she used to.' He looks directly at me. 'You have to stop pushing her,' he says quietly.

Armand Rigaux, Gram's doctor, a slim, dashing man with salt-and-pepper hair, comes into the room carrying his clipboard. We gather around him in a circle.

'I have some good news,' Dr Rigaux begins. 'Teodora didn't have a stroke, and her heart is not compromised in any way.'

'Thank God!' My mother puts her hand over her heart in relief.

'But she has severe arthritis in her knees. They lock and she falls. When she took the spill the other night, it was a doozy. She hit her head pretty badly, and we want to make certain there wasn't any neurological damage. So we're going to keep her here and run some more tests.'

'How about knee replacement?' I ask.

'We're looking into that now. She looks to be a good candidate. And the recuperation period would be a snap with all of you pitching in.'

'I'd do anything for my mother,' Mom says.

'The truth is,' Dr Rigaux says, looking at us, 'surgery is the only way to ensure that this won't happen again.'

Gram's third day in the hospital is spent doing more tests, with Mom and my sisters and brother and I staying in shifts to keep her company. I left for a couple of hours to check in with June at the shop, take a shower, and change clothes. I changed the sheets in Gram's room for Mom and Dad to stay over, as well as the ones in Mom's room so Jaclyn can stay here if she wants to.

Gram is craving some decent food. She can't face another day of pressed turkey with yellow gravy and a cup of Jell-O. I load a bag with Tupperware containers of penne, hot rolls, artichoke salad, and a wedge of pumpkin pie.

Back at Saint Vincent's, I push through the doors and make my way up to the third floor. As I turn the corner down the hallway, I see a group gathered outside Gram's room. I panic and break into a run.

When I get there, Tess, Jaclyn, and my mother are standing together outside Gram's room. In the garish green hospital lights, the women in my family look like peasants in an Antonioni film with their bleak expressions, dark hair, black eyes, and the matching circles under them.

'What's wrong?'

'It's a little crowded in there,' Jaclyn says.

'Why?' She doesn't answer, so I go in. Mom follows me.

Sitting on the bed, next to Gram, holding her hand, is Dominic Vechiarelli. I must look like I've seen a ghost, because I gasp and all eyes land on me. But it's true, there's proof, Dominic's suitcases are propped next to the visitor's chair.

My father stands at the foot of the bed. He motions

for Mom to join him. Dad puts his arm around her. Roman stands next to him, wearing jeans and his work clogs. I only look down at them because as he sways from foot to foot, I hear the squish of the plastic.

As my eyes drink in the roster of visitors, I see Gianluca. I try not to have a reaction. He looks more handsome in America than I ever remember him in Italy, and younger, wearing a leather jacket, a sweater, and faded jeans. My throat closes at the sight of him, but for now, I will blame the dry hospital air. Pamela and Alfred stand away from the bed, by the window.

'What, what is going on?' I say softly. I grip the bag of food I'm holding because, in this room, it's beginning to feel like the only thing that's real.

Mom puts her arm around my shoulders. 'Dominic flew over when he heard Mom was in the hospital. Evidently, Ray Rinaldi is instructed to call him anytime Gram is ill or in need of . . . something.' Mom looks at me, confused. She doesn't know about Dominic, and now, suddenly, she finds out that Dominic Vechiarelli is the first name on Gram's emergency contact list.

'And, um, you're here . . . ,' I stammer when I look at Gianluca.

'I flew with my father. I don't think it's wise for him to travel alone,' Gianluca says, keeping his eyes on Roman.

Roman's eyes narrow as he looks back at Gianluca. He's got a hunch this is the man I kissed.

But he's above his suspicions when he says, 'And I brought Gram panna cotta, because she likes the way I make it.' He buries his hands in his pockets and looks at me.

'Now that Valentine is here, I can ask Teodora something I have longed to ask her since the summer. Please, everyone, come in,' Dominic announces.

'There's no room,' Tess chirps from the doorway.

'Please, everyone, squeeze,' Mom says. 'We're a big Italian family, togetherness is our thing,' she announces, as if to apologize for the cubicle-size rooms in this city hospital. The group shifts to accommodate my sisters and their spouses.

Dominic takes Gram's hands and looks into her eyes. 'Will you marry me?'

The room is completely quiet save for the beep of Gram's heart monitor.

Then, my mother blurts out, 'Dear God, Ma, I didn't even know you were dating.'

'For ten years. Since your father died,' Gram says softly.

'You mean I could have been happy for you for ten years and you didn't tell me?' Mom wails. 'Honestly, Ma!'

'Mike, for God's sake, be happy for her *now*,' my father says. 'Look at her. Her head was cracked open like a coconut and she can't stop smiling. This is a good thing.'

'Let her answer,' I interrupt. I hold my breath. A yes from Gram means the life I cherish will be over.

481

I'll lose her to Dominic, the hills of Arezzo, and the isle of Capri faster than I can say *Gianluca*. But the truth is, I love her so much, I want her happiness more than my own. I cross my fingers for a yes.

'Yes, Dominic, I will marry you,' Gram says to him. Dominic kisses Gram tenderly.

My family, including my mother, sort of freeze upon hearing the word *yes*, as if they're watching a pot of oil pretzels explode on the stove. It's up to me to soften the shock of it all. After all, I *knew*.

'Congratulations!' I go to her and put my arms around Gram, careful to avoid the IVs in her arm. 'I'm so happy for you.' Tears fill my eyes, but I am truly filled with joy for my brave Gram who is showing me, even in this moment, how to take a risk, how to *live*.

I feel my sisters and brother gather around me.

Jaclyn begins to cry. 'I didn't know you had a boyfriend either! I wish everyone would stop protecting me. I can handle it.'

Mom mouths *postpartum* to Gianluca as she takes Jaclyn in her arms. Tess embraces Alfred as Dad reaches out to Dominic to shake his hand. Dominic leaps to his feet and embraces Dad instead.

'Pop?' Dad says to Dominic, then looks at us and shrugs. 'Everybody say hello to . . . Pop.' My sisters and I laugh. Soon, everyone is laughing. The whole family.

I believe it's fair to say that when things fall apart in my life, they do so in every way, so fate is assured that I have learned my lesson. There is only one place I could go to collect my thoughts and make sense of what Gram's new life will mean for all of us, and I'm here, high above the fray, on our roof.

I slipped out of the hospital, leaving Gram to celebrate her engagement with the family. I walked Roman out, who had to return to the restaurant, but was honored that he was present for Dominic's proposal. He kissed me on the street, inspired by the love he'd seen in room 317.

There's a traffic jam on the West Side Highway, a clutter of cars at the intersection, flashing lights, horns, some barely audible angry shouts, and instead of wishing the city noise would be quelled, I wish there was more to drown out the thoughts in my head.

The sight of my newly betrothed Gram in her hospital bed signaled the end of an era. Forget the fact that I'm now the only unmarried woman in my family, it appears I'm also the only sensible one, who knows what all this change means, for now and for the future. Here's the truth of it all. Gram will marry and go. My sisters will raise their families. My mother will make certain that my father eats soy cheese on whole-wheat pasta because that's her guarantee that he will live and avoid a recurrence of his prostate cancer. My brother, as soon as the champagne toast is cheered at Gram's wedding, will put a for sale sign on 166 Perry Street, leaving the Angelini Shoe Company, and me, homeless. It would appear all will be well for everyone in my family, except of course, for me.

The sun sets deep into the haze over New Jersey, making a lilac stripe on the horizon. The wind snaps the roof door behind me. I don't turn to see that it's just the wind, rather, I keep my eyes on the Hudson River that has the smooth swirls and purple hues of carnival glass as the sun sets.

'Valentina?' a voice says from behind me.

'Unless you're Salvatore Ferragamo with a job or Carl Icahn with a check to save this shoe company – go away.'

Soon there's six foot plus of pure Italian man standing next to me. If I close my eyes, I would know for certain it was Gianluca Vechiarelli from the clean scent of cedar and lemon and leather. If I were my mother, or one of my sisters, I would throw myself into his arms. In despair, they like to lean on a man. But I don't. I cross my arms over my chest and take a step away from him, leaving plenty of room for him to view the expanse of lower Manhattan from our roof. 'You can stay in the purple bedroom. Your dad can stay in Gram's. The bathroom is at the end of the hall, but you know that because you had to pass it to get to the steps to the roof.'

'Thank you. But we are staying at a hotel. The Maritime,' he says.

'That's unnecessary. You're family.'

'You're not pleased about the engagement?' he asks quietly.

'For her. For Gram. Yes. And for Dominic. Sure I'm pleased.'

'*Va bene.*'

'And you? Are you *va bene* for them?'

Gianluca shrugs and, pursing his lips, his mouth is a straight line. These are his noncommittal lips. I remember this expression from the Prato silk mill when I held up a perfectly lovely but evidently lame selection of duchess satin. 'Yeah, well, you'd better get on the love bus, Gianluca, because they're going to be living with you.'

'I know.' He smiles.

'I guess love finds willing victims no matter where, no matter when. It's like anything in life, really, including disease. We're all fair game.'

'Why are you—'

'Sarcastic? It's a hard shell covering another hard shell.'

'Why do you push love away, as if you can find it every day?'

'I thought we were talking about my grand-mother.'

'Talk to me. You're afraid of me. I'm not what you dreamed of.'

'How do you know what I dream of?'

'It's very simple. You make no time for the cook even though you love him. Or perhaps you believed you loved him, so now you're obligated. The woman you are, the woman of passion, comes through when you're working. Then, you're at peace. With men? No. With leather? Very much so.'

'You're wrong. I would welcome a man who welcomes me as a woman *and* a shoemaker. But a man, at least the ones I know, might say it's fine for a woman to be devoted to her career, but what they mean is: not so devoted as to take time away from him. I can have my big life, but it must fit into his big life, as the perfect handkerchief in the most tailored breast pocket. Sacrifice – to use a Catholic word, and to be exact – is what it takes. Men want total surrender. They need it.'

Gianluca laughs. '*You* know what men require?'

'Don't make fun of me.'

'If you know what a man requires, why not give it to him in order to provide you with your own happiness?'

I look out at the river. And then, my moment of personal transformation comes toward me like the deck lights on the night run of the Hudson River Water Taxi. The illumination happens slowly and surely. First, in the far distance, the lights are dim and flicker in the murky waves, then, as it moves closer to shore on the Manhattan side, the beams turn into searchlights, guiding the boat into the harbor in bright, unrelenting light. The kind of light that cannot help but reveal the truth in all its detail. Suddenly, I see myself, clear and plain. 'Dear, dear Gianluca . . . ,' I begin.

He seems surprised that I address him tenderly.

'Roman Falconi needs a wife at the cash register of Ca' d'Oro, just like his mother was there for his father in their restaurant. You need a friend. You

486

need a woman who can drop everything and go sit by a lake . . . that one with the cranes . . .'

'Lago Argento.'

'Right, right. A woman who can sit with you at this stage of your life and be there. You want peace and quiet and nature. You want to coast.'

'Now, you analyze me.'

'Gianluca, it's true. Listen to me. I am completely attracted to you. I was blindsided by that attraction. I had a boyfriend when I met you, and frankly, you are not my type. You are, however, handsome, and you have beautiful hands, and the sexiest thing of all, you're a good father. But I'm not for you. I'm not for any man right now. In fact, in this moment, I choose art. I choose the bliss that comes from creating something from the labor of my own hands.'

'You don't have to choose one or the other. You can have love and work together.'

'But I can't! I tried. I spent the last year trying to be there for Roman. I can't spend the next one trying to be there for you. Everybody winds up disappointed and sad and unfulfilled . . .'

'This is what you believe?' He shakes his head.

'This is what I *know*.'

Gianluca looks out across the Hudson River, as I've done so many times. He sees a dull gray waterway, whereas I see a river that connects to a wider ocean, a universe of possibility. He doesn't like my river at all, I can tell.

After a while, he says, 'Your city . . . is very noisy.'

He goes to the door and I hear the door snap shut as he goes back down the stairs into the house. I turn to my river that has never let me down. It's my constant, my muse. I lean over the railing and look up and down the West Side Highway, which in sunset looks like an unfurled bolt of violet Indian silk punctured with tiny mirrors. This is the river I love and the city that is my home. Yes, it's noisy, but it's mine – just how I like it.

Gram's Thanksgiving table has a flock of construction-paper geese down the center, made by her great-grandchildren. I light bright orange candles in the candelabra underneath the chandelier. Gabriel helps my sisters bring the platters from the kitchen to the table. I give Gabriel a quick hug. 'Thank you for coming.'

'My pleasure. I needed a reason to pound my own cranberries, and your invitation gave me the perfect excuse.'

'Is Roman coming?' Mom asks me.

'He sent a cobbler.' I always thought it was funny that he made his girlfriend, the shoemaker, *a cobbler*. 'He had to work,' I lie. Instead of making this holiday about my breakup with Roman, I decide to be as vague about it as my mother has been about her age all these years. Roman and I tried to make time for each other after Gram got out of the hospital, but between filling orders in the shop and taking care of her, I didn't take care of him. We decided to take a break.

'Nobody works harder than Roman,' Mom sighs.

Tess hands me a pitcher of ice water to fill the glasses on the table. She follows me with the gravy boats.

'You're not going to tell Mom about Roman?' she asks quietly.

'Nope.'

'She was curious about Gianluca, you know.'

'There's nothing to tell.' I avoid looking at Tess, who knows the whole story: the moon over Capri, the kisses, the grotto. In her mind, that's *a lot* of nothing.

'There's plenty to tell! You fell in love with Roman, and then you were hit by lightning again in Italy with Gianluca. Two fabulous men in one year! That's a fairy tale. You're Cinderella with two, count them, *two* princes.' Tess straightens the cloth napkins next to the plates.

'Oh yeah, except when I tried on the slippers they were sample-size six. And I'm a nine.'

'So *cram*,' Tess says.

'I *tried*! But let's face it: this is one Cinderella who's going to make her own slippers.'

We gather the family around the table. Dad sits down at the head of the table, and Gram at the other end. He raises his glass.

'Let us first give thanks for the good health of our family, especially Ma's recovery from her spill. And then, while we're at it, let's thank God for the new Teodora, baby T.'

Jaclyn rocks her new baby in her arms.

He continues, 'And as per usual, Lord, we give thanks for the surprises life holds. Ma's engagement springs to mind, and why wouldn't it? That was a shocker. Gabriel, it's good to see you—'

As with most of my father's prayers, they don't have actual endings, so we look at one another and gamely make the sign of the cross around the table so we might serve the food.

'I just want everybody to see this.' Tess holds up *In Style* magazine. 'I am so proud of you.' Tess passes around a glossy picture of Anna Christina, the star of *Lucia, Lucia*, wearing a pair of Angel Shoes, in coral calfskin with gold angel-wing embellishments. I sent Debra McGuire a pair in California and she asked for five additional pairs, one of which wound up on the feet of a rising movie star.

Mom looks at the photograph proudly. 'I love them. They're very Valentine.'

'The orders will pour in. I just know it,' Tess says supportively.

When the magazine reaches Alfred, he looks at it and passes it along to Pamela, who, for the first time since she met my brother, seems duly impressed with his family.

'Have you set the wedding date, Gram?' Jaclyn asks.

'Valentine's Day in 2009 in Arezzo,' Gram says, smiling at me. 'I adore that holiday and my granddaughter's name, so there it is.'

As my family discusses their travel plans to the

wedding, what airport, which rental car company, how many hotel rooms we'll book at the Spolti Inn, my sisters imagine what they'll wear, how their husbands will take time off from work, and my mother, perplexed, wonders how she'll find a good caterer and wedding florist in the hilltop Tuscan town, we eat our Thanksgiving dinner.

Alfred hands the magazine to me. 'A lucky reprieve,' he says quietly.

'As long as I make the payments on this place, you cannot close me down,' I say pleasantly and firmly. I don't engage in the petty anger anymore. I don't have the energy to fight with my brother and take over the operation of the shoe company. Alfred, of course, does not respond. He knows that the woman I was a year ago has been replaced by an eight-hundred-pound gorilla with a business plan. We're not done wrangling, but at least he knows where I stand. For now.

My sisters help me do the dishes and clean up the kitchen while the men watch football. This is the last family Thanksgiving on Perry Street. This time next year, Gram will be living with her new husband in his home over the tannery.

I pack up leftovers for everyone to take home. Gabriel takes the last of Roman's cobbler, knowing it's the last time he'll ever get it without ordering it at Ca' d'Oro. I send Gram up to bed to talk with Dominic on the phone. I'm thrilled to be alone at the end of a long day. I hear the key in the lock downstairs. My mother must have forgotten something. Then I hear a voice call softly to me from the stairwell, 'Valentine?'

Roman enters the living room. I stand by the kitchen counter and look at him.

'How was the cobbler?' he asks.

'Delicious. I have your pan.' I hold it up.

'That's why I came over here. The pan.' He smiles.

I look at him, drinking in the details of him, from the layers of his long hair down to his Wigwam socks. I look down at his feet, even in the mood to embrace his yellow plastic clogs, but tonight, he's wearing real shoes, and they are (at long last!) a pair of Tod's fine suede loafers. From this vantage point and at this moment in our history, I can't believe we broke up. Isn't that weird, how I want what I can't have, and when I have it, I don't understand it. 'Do you always check up on girlfriends when you break up with them?'

'Only you.'

He comes to me, takes me in his arms, and kisses me on the cheek and then the neck. 'I'm not over you,' he says.

'Roman, heat was never our problem.'

'I know.' He's been thinking about us, too. And evidently, he's come to some of the same conclusions I did. 'There's a lot of passion, Valentine.'

'Maybe we'll stay friends, and then when we're old, we'll reconnect like Gram and Dominic and rent a Silverstream and travel around the country.'

'What a terrible idea,' Roman says. The way he

492

says it makes me laugh. 'You know, I think about the first time I saw you on the roof. And how I shouldn't have looked, but I couldn't help it. I didn't want to help it. Sometimes I think back to that night when I didn't know you, and how I imagined what you would be like if I was ever lucky enough to get to know you. And then I got to know you and you were so much better than the woman I imagined you to be. That's when I fell in love with you. You exceeded my expectations, and even still, you surprise me like no other woman ever has. It's strange. I know it's over, but it can't be for me.'

I hold Roman close. 'I'm not going anywhere, but right now, I can't be with you because you don't deserve to be second, you should be first. I don't want you to wait for me, but if, down the line, when things settle down, and you think of me,' I say, taking his face in my hands, 'use the key.'

'It's a deal,' he says.

Roman knows and I know that he will probably never use the key, that it will wind up in the bottom of his drawer, and someday, when he's looking for something, he'll find the key and remember what we meant to each other. But for now, he'll keep it in his pocket, and when he needs to believe that there's a possibility, he'll take it out, look at it, and consider the trip across town to the West Village.

I remember the cobbler pan, and I tuck it under his arm. I watch as he goes. Then, as his footsteps fall on the stairs, I remember that I never made him a pair of boots as I promised. So many things I meant to do, so many things that went undone.

The sun glows behind the skyscrapers, like a tiger's eye on this early December morning. The sky holds the light like it's buried inside a gray wool coat. Gram and I stand on the corner of Fifth Avenue and Fifty-eighth Street, holding our paper cups of hot coffee, hers black, mine with cream and no sugar. Her emerald-cut diamond engagement ring sparkles against the blue columns on the Greek-diner coffee cup. Nice color composition.

Like two architects in ancient Rome, we squint before our masterpiece with cold, clinical eyes and take in every detail. I shift my weight from foot to foot as I study it. Gram takes a few steps back and tilts her head, slightly adjusting her point of view. We haven't built a duomo, a cathedral, or even garden statuary, we've made wedding shoes, and here they are in Bergdorf's holiday windows. Our entire line is represented. To see one hundred years of our shoes in the windows takes our breath away.

Delivery trucks rumble by, but we don't pay them any mind. Jackhammers punctuate the din, reminding us that no matter what time of day or night in New York City, somebody somewhere on this island is making something. We stand for what seems to be a long time. 'So. What do you think?' I finally ask.

'You know, for the longest time, your grandfather and I would argue about which was the better movie, *Dr Zhivago* or *The Way We Were*. I voted for *The Way We Were* because it was about my group . . . but now' – she sips her coffee and then continues – 'now, that I see these windows, and the drama in the details of the Russian style, I have to say I'm going to go with *Dr Zhivago*.'

'Me, too,' I say, putting my arm around her shoulder.

These holiday windows are for grown-ups. A few blocks south, you can stand in line behind a red velvet rope at Saks Fifth Avenue or Lord & Taylor to view miniatures of enchanting Christmas villages for children. You'll see snow-covered mountains trimmed in glitter, ice skaters pirouetting on mirrored lakes, and toy trains carrying tiny foil presents chuffing through the scenes.

Here at Bergdorf's, though, you get none of the kitsch, and all of the cream. Here's a sophisticated holiday tale of true love Russian style as dramatized by glamorous American brides. Rhedd Lewis's wedding feast for the eyes begins in the side windows of West Fifty-seventh Street, wraps around the front of the store on Fifth Avenue, and concludes in the side windows on West Fifty-eighth Street.

As our eyes follow the action from the first window, we see full-size, gilded wooden horses pulling magnificently costumed brides standing on enameled chariots and baroque sleds, festooned

495

with jewels. Upon closer inspection, you see that the modes of transportation are decorated with actual jewelry – cabochon-laden earrings, gold necklaces that drip with chunky gemstones, gleaming cuff bracelets, and enormous dome rings, the effect of which makes a resplendent mosaic.

Fabergé eggs are cracked open in the foreground, spilling forth loose diamonds and pearls on a bed of wedding rice. Antique books are strewn on the ground, while loose pages float through the air. Window to window the pages and words change – there's *Dr Zhivago* (of course), *Anna Karenina, The Three Sisters, The Brothers Karamazov*, and *War and Peace*, appropriate for a wedding(!).

The backdrops are hand-painted murals of the Russian countryside, flat, squarish hills behind fields of white snow. These windows, sophisticated tableaux, actually tell a story, as the brides are surrounded by mannequins depicting working-class Russians – dressed in dull green factory jumpers, burlap aprons, and work boots over hand-knit woolen stockings. Dramatized as artists in service to the brides are seamstresses, orchid farmers, dressers, drivers, and yes, even a cobbler, who kneels and places a shoe (our Lola!) on a bride swathed in white velvet with an ermine headpiece.

The juxtaposition of the sophisticated brides portraying the very rich in love countered by the workers who facilitate their dreams is not lost on me. It takes many hands to create beauty. The brides wear elaborate gowns by great designers, including Rodarte, Marc Jacobs, Zac Posen, Marchesa, John Galliano, and Karl Lagerfeld. Their signatures appear in the corner of each window in gold.

The first bride, in a mélange of tulle over a satin sheath, wears the Ines, which peeks out from the hem of her skirt, lifted by the cobbler; the next window has a bride in white silk pants and a flowing blouse paired with the Gilda, whose mule shape and embroidered vamp are a sleek fit with the wide-leg pants.

She is followed by a bride with her back turned to the street. The bride wears a theatrical, fringed column gown with the Mimi ankle boot. Rhedd replaced our white satin laces with indigo-dyed hemp for a stunning contrast in texture.

The next window shows a bride in a minidress made of bugle beads and marabou feathers, standing en pointe in the Flora, with gold chains instead of ribbons crisscrossing up her calves. In the corner window, a bride wears a medieval gown with a square neckline and an elaborate bodice of enameled squares offset by long, sheer trumpet sleeves. The mannequin carries her shoes, the white linen Osmina with plain straps as she looks down at her bare feet in the snow.

But it's the final window that means the most to me. The Bella Rosa is worn by a bride in a white wool traveling suit by Giorgio Armani. She holds a ticket in one hand, and a tiara in the other as she flees an unhappy romantic scenario on the streets of Saint Petersburg. The substantial shoe works fluidly with the tailored suit, as though it was made to anchor the ensemble.

I wish Costanzo Ruocco were here to see the Bella Rosa, but for now, I will hold this moment in my memory, and when I return to Capri, will relive it for him the best I can. In the corner of the final window, it says,

All Shoes Created by the Angelini Shoe Company
Greenwich Village
Since 1903

'Oh my God! Oh my God!' Gram and I turn to see my mother hanging out of a livery-cab window. She leaps out of the car before it comes to a complete stop and joins us on the sidewalk.

I wondered what my mother might wear to view the windows for the first time. She does not disappoint. Mom wears a gray wool pantsuit with a fake gray leopard shrug slung over her shoulders. Her high-heeled pumps are dull silver, with large square leather buckles on the toe. I don't know how she does it, but my mother manages to match the weather. She also wears a pair of large, black, oval sunglasses, an homage to *Breakfast at Bergdorf's* no doubt. She holds a sack of bagels from Eisenberg's in one hand and peels off her sunglasses with the other. She hands the bag to me and then runs down the block to take in the windows.

Mom raises her arms high in the air in triumph as she surveys the windows. She looks for our shoes, and when she finds them in the tableaux, she shrieks with joy. I've never seen her this proud, including at the culmination of Alfred's astonishing college career, when he graduated summa cum laude from Cornell. This is another big moment for her. She runs to Gram and throws her arms around her. 'Daddy would be so proud!' Mom wipes away a tear.

'He would be.' Gram straightens Mom's fur shrug on her shoulders, which shifted when she ran.

'And you!' Mom turns to me. 'You made this happen! You picked up the mantle of the Angelini family and you wore it . . . do you wear a mantle or do you carry it? Anyway, it doesn't matter – you kept up our tradition' – she makes a fist – 'and you persisted and you apprenticed yourself to the master and now look – you took all that hard work and you brought our little family business into the new century in a very public way. Bergdorf freakin' Goodman!' Mom can't resist being a *home girl* from Queens, even for just a moment. Then she continues, 'Angelini shoes, side by side with Prada and Verdura and Pucci! Viva Valentine! I marvel at you. And I'm so proud of you!'

Sometimes when my mother fawns, I taste metal in my mouth, but not this morning. She is genuinely moved and full of love. Every mother should have this moment of glory, when her hard work is brought to fruition and the investment she has made in her children on a daily basis comes full circle, the results on display for the whole world to see.

This moment isn't about branding, or profits, or marketing. It's about our family and the tradition of our craft. It's about what we *do*. These windows are about our commitment to beauty and quality – every stitch, seam, lace, and binding made by hand and perfected with the skill that can only come from practice, technique, experience, and *time*. We have been recognized and rewarded in a world where the concept of *built by hand* is fading fast. Imagine that.

The sun, as white and pure as a full moon, pulls up and parts the gray clouds over the glass buildings on the east side of Fifth Avenue, creating a glare on the store windows that turns them into mirrors. In an instant, the images behind the glass are gone. We can't see the brides in the snow, or the jewels and the eggs, or our shoes made of leather and suede and satin and silk. All that remains is our reflection, mother, daughter, and granddaughter, this morning an unbroken chain of the finest Italian gold. I wish I could hold on to this moment forever, the three of us, here on Fifth Avenue. But, I can't. So I do the very best I can and take my grandmother's hand in mine and slip my other arm around my mother, and wait for the pale winter sun to move so we might revel in our good fortune once more.

ACKNOWLEDGMENTS

My mother, Ida Bonicelli Trigiani and her sister, Irma Bonicelli Godfrey, have vivid and wonderful memories of their father, Carlo, to whom this novel is dedicated. I used the terrain of their childhood freely in this novel, bringing me close to the man, my grandfather, whom I never met. My deepest gratitude to them!

Jane Friedman is a visionary and a superb leader who brought me to Harper, put me in the hands of the great Jonathan Burnham, Brian Murray, and Michael Morrison, and into a family of folks I am crazy about: my beloved and brilliant editor, Lee Boudreaux, her capable/fabulous right arm, Abigail Holstein, and the talented team of: Kathy Schneider, Christine Boyd, Kevin Callahan, Tina Andreadis, Leslie Cohen, Mary Bolton, Archie Ferguson, Christine Van Bree (oh the cover art!), Sarah Maya Gubkin, Lydia Weaver, Emily Taff, Nina Olmsted, Jeff Rogart, Stephanie Linder, Kathryn Pereira, Jeanette Zwart, Andrea Rosen, Virginia Stanley, Josh Marwell, Brian Grogan, Carl Lennertz, James Tyler, Cindy Achar, Roni Axelrod, Kyle Hansen, Carrie Kania, and David Roth-Ey.

501

I had the adventure of a lifetime researching the craft of shoe-making in Italy. Gina Casella coordinated the fun, the learning and the translating (!), along with the talents of Patrizia Curiale, Confartigianato MODA; Andrea Benassi, Secretary General, UEAPME (European Association of Craft, Small and Medium-sized Enterprises); Emanuela Picozzi, Public Affairs, U.S. Embassy, Rome; and Elio Chiarotti, our Roman guide. As we traveled and studied, Gina's daughter Isabella Padasak was a perfect sidekick for our Lucia.

My heartfelt thanks to the master craftsman, shoemaker Costanzo Ruocco and his son Antonio of da Costanzo on the Isle of Capri. Costanzo was generous with his time, technique, and family stories, which I treasure beyond the pages herein. In Rome, Carmelo and Pina Palmisano of Il Calzolaio, shared their knowledge of shoemaking and insights into the family business, which were invaluable.

Suzanne Gluck, my dear friend and agent, is a font of pep, knowledge, and wisdom (not to mention good taste!). Thank you also to the William Morris team: Sarah Ceglarski, Liz Tingue; Cara Stein, Alicia Gordon, Philip Grenz, Erin Malone, Tracy Fisher, Eugenie Furniss, Cathryn Summerhayes, Theresa Peters, David Lonner, and Raffaella de Angelis.

At Endeavor, thank you to my longtime friend and agent, Nancy Josephson, to Graham Taylor, and the adorable Michelle Bohan.

In Movieland my love and appreciation to: Susan Cartsonis, Roz Weisberg, Julie Durk, Lou Pitt, Raquel Carreras, Mark Lindsay, and Nancy Klopper.

Michael Patrick King, I treasure your advice, counsel, and support beyond all telling.

Thank you to the world's best assistant: Kelly Meehan. More thanks to our interns Megan Stokes and Kasey Tympanick. For your eagle eyes, my thanks to: Suzanne Baboneau, Emily Lavelle, Lauren Lavelle, Jean Morrissey, Rachel Desario, and Brenda Browne. My thanks to Antonia Trigiani for her marketing savvy and vision.

Ann Godoff, thank you for opening the door to my literary career.

Thank you and love to: Larry Sanitsky, Ian Chapman, Caroline Rhea, Nancy Bolmeier Fisher, Catherine Brennan, Craig Fisse, Todd Doughty, John Searles, Jill Gillet, Kim Hovey, Libby McGuire, Jane Von Mehren, Laura Ford, Nigel Stoneman, Debbie Aroff, Meryl Poster, Gayle Perkins Atkins, Joanna Patton, Bill Persky, Mario Cantone, Jerry Dixon, Debra McGuire, Gail Berman, Tom Dyja, Jake Morrissey, Carmen Elena Carrion, Cynthia Rutledge Olson, Brownie and Connie Polly, Susan Fales-Hill, Connie Marks, Wendy Luck, Mary Testa, Dolores and Emil Pascarelli, Elena Nachmanoff, Sharon Watroba Burns, Jim and Mary Hampton, Dee Emmerson, Diane Festa, Joanne Curley Kerner, Jack Hodgins, Ruth Pomerance, Donna Gigliotti,

Sally Davies, Sister Karol Jackowski, Allison Roche, Karen Fink, and Max and Robyn Westler.

Thank you Tim and Lucia, for everything else under the sun, and including the sun!

And finally, I am grateful for the photograph of my grandfather Carlo Bonicelli that appears on the dedication page. It was taken around 1930 in his workroom at The Progressive Shoe Shop at 5 West Lake Street in Chisholm, Minnesota. It brought me comfort, strength, and inspiration throughout the process of writing this novel, and it always will.